FEELING A COP . . .

I was watching the detective's blue eyes and his hands alternately. We were talking about me, about the crimes, but I kept thinking of how he looked, how he smelled, how he would feel. Finally I spoke my persistent thoughts. I always do sooner or later. It gets me in a lot of trouble. On the other hand, very little is left unsaid.

"I wish this wasn't happening," I interrupted.

"Well, that's understandable," he said, but he looked at me with a question.

"No, I mean, I wish I would have met you another way." There. It was out.

He looked at me with a mysterious smile. "You do present a challenge to the working detective."

"What does that mean?" I asked

"It means I find you almost unbearably attractive, but you are still a murder suspect. I'd take myself off the case but I don't think anyone else would find you less attractive." He said it lightly.

I was watching his mouth as he spoke. And it was saying something else.

"But I wouldn't have to do this to them," I said and I crawled toward him, got up on my knees, leaned in, and kissed him

Loaded

SHARI SHATTUCK

POCKET BOOKS
New York London Toronto Sydney Singapore

An *Original* Publication of POCKET BOOKS

 POCKET BOOKS, a division of Simon & Schuster, Inc.
1230 Avenue of the Americas, New York, NY 10020

Copyright © 2003 by Shari Shattuck

ISBN: 0-7434-6384-6

First Pocket Books printing August 2003

10 9 8 7 6 5 4 3 2 1

POCKET and colophon are registered trademarks of Simon & Schuster, Inc.

Designed by Melissa Isriprashad

For information regarding special discounts for bulk purchases, please contact Simon & Schuster Special Sales at 1-800-456-6798 or business@simonandschuster.com

Cover design by Christine Van Bree

Printed in the U.S.A.

For Emily,
who said, "I do."
For Paul,
who said, "I can."
And for Amy,
who said, "I will."

1

I was staring down the vocal end of a forty-four magnum. Any second now, it would scream at me, shout, blow my fucking head off. I was scared, pinned down, trapped. In spite of being overcome with terror, I noticed how the night wind felt on my face; it made me feel alive and I wanted to stay that way.

I moved the fingers of my right hand lightly against my thumb, to see if I could move at all. The fear only seemed to be immobilizing; I willed myself to do something, to think.

Behind the gun there was a desperate young man and behind him were two more men, exactly like the first, except they didn't have the gun.

Think Cally, I screamed to myself, *don't die because you're afraid.*

It occurred to me to be annoyed that this little shit with soulless eyes was going to kill me. It deeply bothered me that this dark-faced punk was experiencing a sense of power over me. I became angry, intoxicatingly pissed. Still terrified but something else, too, I was furious.

So he thinks I'm helpless, fine, good, just maybe that

could save me. A cold, honest drip of fear-sweat hit my right eye as my indignation took control. I let loose a frightened cry and pulled my hands to my mouth. Cowering in true terror but using the move as a cover, I turned away from the gaping mouth of the weapon. My hands moved across my chest, down to my stomach, toward my bag hanging against my right hip. He was screaming at me not to move. From the corner of my adrenaline-pumped vision I saw him think about firing. Even as I crouched and twisted instinctively away from his weapon, the edge of my reason used the motion to hide my hand reaching for my own pistol. The weapon I carried but had never imagined I would have to use. His cracked-out eyes darted to my waist; my right hand found the hilt of my gun. The weapon in his hand was shaking, jerking as the drugs coursed through his veins, yanking his nervous system out of focus, out of control. His eyes followed my hand back up as it extended out toward him and he turned his head slightly to protect his face from his own bullet's explosion. Through the sights of my gun I saw his eyes closing as his fingers began to squeeze. I forced my eyes to stay open, to aim, giving me my only chance. Accuracy. I heard two sharp cracks. His first, I think, but I had drawn, aimed and fired all in one sweeping motion. He had thought about it. Fired blind. Bad choice. He fired his second shot as my first round hit him. I was five feet away, maybe. Point-blank, but he'd missed me. Can't close your eyes and aim.

I fired again, tracking his body in my sights on his way down to the pavement. I broke my tunnel vision away from him to quickly check his friends who had been standing behind him, but they were already turning, running, back into the darkness like cockroaches escaping the light.

Melting ice was running down my face and body. I couldn't hear anything except the smashing of my heartbeat against my eardrums. Turning back to my assailant, I saw he was looking at me with absolute surprise. It had never occurred to him that he was mortal. Not until this instant had he realized he would die. In his final moment, something real flickered back into those inanimate eyes.

It made me sad. What he could have been, the choices he might have made, the brilliant endless possibilities of life. But this was the choice he had made and those possibilities were ending here. For the first time he seemed human to me and I wanted to take it all back, to give him another chance.

He still had the gun in his hand, it still had a voice, but it seemed to whisper at me now as he shakily tried to point it at me. I decided not to listen.

"I'm sorry," I whispered to whatever spirit was left in him.

Blam. I watched myself shoot him in the head.

The eyes went dead again. I was alone. Isolated in an unreal world, time seemed to be elongated and distorted, my senses weren't responding the way they were supposed to. My eyes saw a picture that my brain would not accept.

It was oddly quiet. Then slowly, I noticed my right arm felt very heavy, so I let it fall to my side. Because it seemed so obvious, I walked over and kicked the gun from the dead boy's grasp. Alarmingly, I heard nothing as I watched the metal scrape across the cement. The gun explosions on my unprotected ears had deafened me, just as the explosions of fear and horror had numbed me. I backed up to the storefront on Ventura Boulevard, where death had come, and leaned my cheek against the cold, hard window, needing to feel something. My lips, slightly parted, rested hard against it.

The bitter taste of the glass made me roll away. I leaned back against the building for support but it couldn't hold me up and I slid down hard to the cement.

I looked again at the still twitching body in the unnatural position between myself and the curb. There was no way I could grasp that he was dead. That this man/boy would never speak or breathe again, that the life would not return to his eyes. I hadn't intended that. It had been this barbaric contest to see who could make it into the next few minutes, and sitting there on the sidewalk, I couldn't process what that meant or how it felt to have been responsible for ending his life. I was bludgeoned with the overwhelming blow of it, it was just too much to absorb. Leaning my head back, I shut my eyes. *Ah, there's the breeze.*

What was I doing here? I never came to the valley. It was ugly, stark. It seemed a fitting epitaph that this boy would die here, and nothing would change, except me. I would be changed forever.

Dinner with a business associate at a mediocre Italian restaurant had bought me this. I had spent the evening telling him how to do the job I paid him to do, avoided his predictable, not-so-subtle attempts to hit on me, *I even picked up the fucking tab*. I looked down again at the dark stain of blood coming from a dark stain of a human.

"Shit," I said.

That helped a little, so I tried it again.

"Shit. I'm fucked."

Talking out loud seemed to bring the surreal moments into sharper focus.

"Okay, now what? Run? Where? If they find me, I am double fucked. Stay and try to explain." My turn to take responsibility.

I was offering alternatives, but I'd already made my choice; Daddy raised a law-fearing girl. That thought made me grimace. How law fearing was it to carry a concealed, loaded nine-millimeter? Well, there's fear of the law and there's fear of the lawless. Daddy didn't raise no victim either.

I pulled out my cell phone and pressed 911 with a shaking finger. My brain was so rattled that it took a minute to remember those three digits. I sat back to wait and watched as cars started to slow down and the faces inside them stared blankly. Nobody stopped though. I started to laugh to stop myself from crying. No matter how cynical I become about people's bad behavior, it's never cynical enough.

A rising scream choked off the laugh as my eyes fell on the body again, and in shocked silence, my mouth still hanging open gasping silently for air, I thought, somewhere in East L.A. tonight, a mother who could never teach her son respect will cry, and blame me. Tomorrow his friends will tag his name all over the city, to honor him. Because they are in pain, they will hate more, be more violent, cause more pain. The jagged cycle will continue.

"Are you alright?"

Startled, I looked up into the handsome brown eyes

of one of L.A.'s finest. *The police here are so buff.* Even as the thought crossed my mind, I knew it was a strange thing to notice at that moment.

"I don't know yet," I said. "I'm not physically hurt. I don't think." I was too disconnected to be sure. I was watching myself from another place, a mercifully numb and ignorant place just outside my body, but a glance at the blood seeping into the cement thrust me back into my body with a slap that smacked. The feeling came back, and the onslaught was too much. My head reeled and my heart pounded.

I had put my gun down on the scratchy stone surface in front of me. I waved a hand at it; the movement was smaller and weaker than I intended. "That's mine, it's loaded, less three rounds. You'll find them in him." It was all I could think to say.

"You want to tell me what happened?" he asked, snapping on a rubber glove and carefully picking up my gun with two fingers. He let it hang, suspended but out of reach until another officer produced a plastic bag, marked "evidence," and then he dropped it in.

"Well, he pulled that gun on me and told me he wanted my bag. He looked cracked out of his mind and well, I shot him." It was the truth, but even to me it sounded like a thin explanation for the most horrific moments of my life.

"Did he fire?"

"Yeah, twice. He missed." My smile felt even more anorexic than my story sounded.

"But you didn't." He looked at me with a combination of suspicion and something that inspired my trust. "Three shots."

"I took pistol training classes with a friend, you

know, self-defense? I got to be a pretty good shot. They tell you, two to the body, one to the head." It was the dogma they teach you in the classes. But I remembered what else they taught me, the reason you were supposed to give if you ever did shoot somebody, so I added, "He was going to kill me."

"Probably. It's a good thing you were ready, huh?" That suspicion again.

"Is it?"

"Well, it was lucky." He was a bit of a smart-ass. I narrowed my eyes and looked straight back at him.

"Yeah, it's my lucky day." I said.

2

I was sitting in the back seat of the black and white when the detective arrived. I watched him walk the scene and speak to the officers before he turned his attention to the shooter in the back of the car: me. I waited nervously as he approached the window; a well-shaped silhouette in a nice suit, he had a strong confident walk that any other time I would have enjoyed. At that moment it only made me more nervous.

He opened the car door and leaned down into the light to look at me. To my infinite relief he extended his hand to me.

"Detective Paley, Homicide." He shook my hand firmly with a strong, steady grasp. I felt a little better but still razor-wire edgy. "And you would be . . . ?"

"Your suspect?" I tried. He didn't laugh but he didn't look disgusted either, that was something. I mean, damn, it's hard to keep a sense of humor when there's a dead man on the sidewalk wearing your bullets. I tried again, "Your prisoner?"

He smiled now, just a little bit of a curve, but my shot-to-hell nerves leaped on it like a ray of hope. "We'll see about that. How about we start with your name?"

So I told him my name, and everything else I could think of, such as it was. He put me in his car and we took a little ride. I expected to be questioned, maybe charged, and to wait in some kind of cell until I found a good lawyer to get me out. Detective Paley explained that I *was* being charged with a misdemeanor, carrying a concealed weapon. But, he also told me killing someone in defense of my life was not illegal. I sorted out slowly that I was guilty as charged of carrying a gun, but not necessarily of killing someone with it.

I mentioned to the detective that if I had beaten my assailant's head in with a crowbar, I wouldn't have been guilty of anything. I added that a tool designed for prying versus one manufactured for killing didn't seem like a fair fight.

I could have sworn he was mildly impressed.

The precinct was perfect for the valley, an ugly, stark, harshly lit building on Van Nuys Boulevard. We went in and they booked me for murder. Detective Paley told me that was standard procedure, but the district attorney would have the final say whether or not I would be formally charged with homicide.

They didn't give me my gun back. But they didn't throw my ass in jail, either. Not even for a night. They let me walk out.

Now I felt lucky.

I guess I got the right cops. I guess they'd just seen one too many citizens minding their own business get blown away. Used to be armed robbery meant you lost your wallet. Now for no reason, you lose your wallet *and* they kill you. I guess these cops were glad they hadn't had to take my body away in a bag and have to explain it to my family. Sadly, they would still have to visit a family with the mortifying news. But perhaps, because it was the attacker's family and not the victim's, they felt there was some kind of justice in it.

Detective Paley gave me his card and told me to call if I needed anything.

He advised me not to be alone; it was good advice, I was still shaking. I called my friend Ginny, and she came and picked me up. She was the one who helped me buy my gun and went to pistol classes with me, but she never knew I carried it with me. I'm sure she never thought I'd actually use it. Hell, I never thought I'd actually have to.

Her gold-flecked brown eyes were worried as she hugged me awkwardly. The quiet of her watchfulness in the car was out of character for her. She was usually so vibrant and vocal.

"You okay?" she finally managed.

"I've said yes to that about fifty times tonight. But I don't think I'll know for a while," I answered, starting to shake again. Biting my jaw down hard, I tried to keep my teeth from chattering. "Can I have a cigarette?"

For the first time she looked at me straight on. Usually, I was a walking no-smoking sign. But she said nothing as she pulled out a pack of Camel Lights and passed them over. I twisted off the filter and fumbled with the lighter.

"Jesus, I feel like I've done a quarter ounce of blow." I hadn't done that in ten years either, but the molar-grinding edginess isn't something you ever forget.

"You come sleep at my house. And that's it, Cally, no arguments." With long, strong brown arms she gripped the steering wheel tightly, willing the car home more quickly.

I could hear the concern climbing into her voice. It was scary for me to lean on anyone, unfamiliar, I wasn't used to doing it. She instinctively understood this about me and said nothing more, that's why she was my best friend.

Tightness gripped my throat and moisture came to my eyes, as I turned my head to look out the window and exhaled gratefully. Santa Monica was blurry through my tears. I didn't feel sorry for myself, not one bit, not sorry for what I'd done, either. I was alive because of it. I had had no choice. The adrenaline was still dancing throughout my body and now in the first quiet moments when I was neither defending my life nor my actions, the full intensity of the last few hours hit me like a fucking mud slide. Ginny's long-fingered hand reached out and landed firmly on my thigh, just above the knee. She just squeezed, an even constant pressure of support and strength, something no one had given me for so long. I was suffocated by the need for it. I had been alone for so long that I hadn't realized how desperately sad that made me. My whole body was sucked into the wet sticky thick emotion of it and I gasped once for air, for the surface, and then started to sob. I cried the whole way to her house, and she never took her hand away. If she would have let go of me I would have been lost, and she seemed to know it. I cried until the murky pain grew thinner, more watery, until it could flow around me. It didn't leave, but I managed to get my head above it, to breathe again.

Ginny drove into the underground parking of her condo and I pulled myself together enough to walk inside. A tall glass of scotch and a long nuzzle from Ginny's terrier Dudney blunted the rest of the pain enough for me to speak. I told Ginny as much of what had happened as I could land my brain on and after I was done, she hugged me and put me to rest in the sofa bed. Dudney never left my side. He curled his small wiry-haired body up next to me and went to sleep. His breathing calmed me.

Until I closed my eyes.

Tonight was the second time in my life I had watched someone die. I rolled on my side and tried to block the faces. But they were seared onto my brain, leaving their images blistered and still smoking. Scarred portraits that wouldn't leave me.

My father had died quietly, in the end. The cancer had gone to his brain and that was the most horribly unfair thing in the whole long unjust illness. He, who had always been so smart, such a bright conversational-ist and so aware of everything, was not able to string a sentence together, to hold a thought in his head. He would cry and not know why.

I had tried to help him, but there was very little I could do. We moved a hospital bed into his bedroom in the house and hired hospice nurses. When he couldn't function at all anymore I had sat beside him and held his hand, cried with him and busied myself trying to make him more comfortable. By then, I don't think he knew me. I'll never know.

I had already said good-bye. I had already thanked him, forgiven him, and encouraged him to go. In the last weeks of his life I'd done all those things they tell you to do. That last day, his breathing slowed down and I knew it was almost over. I sat beside him, holding his hand. At noon, he just stopped breathing, nothing else seemed to change, not the feeling in the room, not the silence. The nurse felt for his pulse and then said quietly, "That's it." Like I didn't already know. He had still been so handsome when she closed his eyes. She had rubbed my arm and smiled at me bravely with infinite pity and then left me alone with him.

I just sat there. I squeezed his hand a last time and let it go. I kissed his cheek and felt his still firm skin. I had whispered in his ear, "Good-bye Daddy, thank you."

Then I went and sat in the armchair in the corner and watched his face and listened to nothing. He was all I had and he had left me. My best friend and protector had left me alone and I had no choice but to let him go.

It was odd that I didn't cry. I'd just lost my father, the only person in the world that really knew me but all I had felt was an overwhelming sense of quiet. I had stayed with him until the funeral home came for him. Standing only when the dark-suited men intruded into that sacred place. They had waited with practiced reverence while I'd walked away from him, from the only thing that had ever mattered.

When I walked out of that room, I moved into a life alone. From his last breath forward I was my own provider, protector, friend. Nobody else, not even Ginny, had ever been that close to me, I didn't think they ever would be. I would never, ever forget my last view of his face. He looked so beautiful, so peaceful.

I scratched Dudney's ears to bring me back from that permanent pain. The thought of my father's face still hurt me like a freshly opened wound. I wondered if anyone felt that way about the man I'd shot tonight, if anyone was sitting with him.

The image of that second face of death, thrust on me in an ungodly moment of stress and fear, ugly in its panic and its hate, ripped through me with a high-voltage jolt. I'd had no time to make my peace with that one. Two men, one I killed, one I would have traded anything to keep alive. I would never forget either of those final faces.

I rolled onto my back again trying to exhale the evil shakiness. Death is permanent for the living, too; the sight of it never leaves you.

3

I felt like a cliché the next day as I made my way to meet my lawyer for a drink. Out of the frying pan into the fire. The night before was a bad dream. A bad dream that makes you sweat and wake up violently, but a dream nonetheless.

Walking into the lobby of the Four Seasons Hotel, I followed a wide marble stairway down into a plushly carpeted paneled room and I found the bar. It always made me feel comfortable to be in ritzy places with sparkly chandeliers. Nothing bad could happen here.

My estate lawyer, Hervé, was sitting at a high stool in front of the bar. He was in his late thirties, pudgy, Latino and as always he seemed too shiny in a greasy sweaty way. He looked as though his skin was made of oily earth, a mud puddle with a thin layer of Quaker State scumming up the surface.

"Hello, Cally, you look beautiful, as usual," he said.

"I feel like shit," I replied, in no mood for niceties, especially from an attorney.

"What's up? Rough night?"

"You could say that. Somebody tried to rob me."

"You got robbed?"

"No." My mouth and not my eyes smiled and I changed the subject. "So who wants Daddy's money today?" I asked.

"Seems he had a third cousin in Georgia." Hervé couldn't quite muster the sympathetic tone he was going for. More delay meant more money for him, and lawyers love legalities.

I sighed. "How many more trematodes?"

"What?" He looked up, afraid that I had come up with a legal term he'd never heard of.

"Trematode. It's a parasite, actually a flatworm with external suckers. Fitting, don't you think?" I looked at him pointedly. He missed it.

"It shouldn't be too much longer, the will is fairly clear, it's just that . . ."

"They happen to have a letter." I'd heard this game before.

"Listen, doll, why don't you just settle? I think they'd take a couple of hundred thousand and walk away." He picked up his drink and watched for my reaction over the rim of his sweating glass. I heard the glass click against his teeth.

"Because it's bullshit. It's Daddy's money, he wanted me to have it, and it's bullshit." I looked at him and realized suddenly he smelled badly to me. He exuded cheap cigars and bad ethics. A walking miasma.

"Look Hervé, just finish it. I'll fight if I have to. Drag this out anymore and I'll get a new lawyer."

"Ah, Cally. Now you know you can't do that." He smiled smugly; the son of a bitch's firm was named in the will.

It was ironic that I had inherited Hervé along with my fortunes. Because our fathers had worked together and respected each other and Hervé and I had both continued with the family businesses. In Hervé's case he had embraced some risky ventures and I had heard too many rumors of questionable practices for it to be all smoke and no fire, nothing I could prove, but he wasn't as smart or as reputable as his father, that much was plain. I hoped I gave my father reason to be proud of how I had carried on with his interests. Ethics had meant something to both our fathers, and they still meant a great deal to me. I was pretty sure they didn't mean a damn thing to the man sitting in front of me.

I turned to look out at the well-lit restaurant, cursing every greedy relative and lawyer who had contested this will. It had been more than two years and tens of thousands in legal fees. But it was my money, all I had left of my father, and I'd spend it all before I gave a dime of it to a bunch of parasitic bloodsuckers.

"Just fix it, Hervé." I got up and walked back toward the stairs. I couldn't help it; I kept flashing on Hervé's eyes down the barrel of my gun, the shiny, greasy lids blinking dumbly as I squeezed the trigger.

It amazed me that even now I could still feel like I was coked out. It was a too familiar sensation that I hated so much, vibrating and exhausted, unable to think clearly or calm down. For two years I'd been an addict, six months of that I'd barely been human. I was thin now, and I'd weighed thirty pounds less then. I wouldn't sleep for days at a time. I moved in with a loser boyfriend, who valued me for sex alone. Things got weird, so weird that I still sometimes flashed on memories of things that I had blacked out. My father would call and leave messages but I couldn't face even returning the call. I didn't speak to him or see him for months at a time.

That's when I'd met Ginny. She was a cocaine user, too, but not as far gone as I was. A few days with me convinced her we'd both be dead soon. She'd helped yank me back with the help of my dad. Now I knew my limitations; they were many.

I exited the lobby and walked out into the sunshine. I made myself stop, take a deep breath and focus on who I was now. *You are not that person anymore, you don't have to feel guilty about it, not anymore.*

I took long slow breaths of the balmy day, got in my sedan and drove. *Get me to the pool,* I thought. *Sex would be good,* I added.

"Dial Thumper," I purred at my voice-activated car phone. The electronic connection hummed dully until a voice picked up. A richly timbered male voice answered.

"Hello?"

"Hi. Boy, am I glad you're home," I mused.

"Me, too," he hummed back.

"Want to go swimming?" What the hell, I was already all wet; some voices do that to me.

"I've got a meeting at five." He sounded a tiny bit resistant. I would have to put a stop to that.

"I've got a hairdryer. Joe, I'll see you in twenty minutes, I'll be the one wearing only pleasant-smelling suntan oil and the hot sun. My eyes will be closed. Be kind."

The phone beeped when I pressed "end." I settled back into the leather, breathed deeply of the sultry wind and blew kisses to the vibrant life I still owned.

The phone interrupted my communing with Mother Nature and I glanced at the readout to see the word "office."

"Yes, Kelley?" I greeted my capable assistant. Her voice, when she answered, was as cute as she was.

"Ms. Wilde, sorry to bother you on your cell but I have a Detective Paley on the line and he says it's important that he speak with you."

My brain suffered another minor emotional stroke and it was only with great effort that I retained an audible level of nonchalance. "Thanks Kell, patch him through."

As I waited for the click I cleared my throat, forcing my voice and my heart back down into my chest.

"Good morning Detective, how can I help you?"

"Good morning." There was a pause that was thick with assessment, he was trying to sum up my attitude. I hate that. "I need to meet with you today," he said, and I noted that it was a statement not a request.

Exhaling, I tried to force the tension out in a breath, to unclench the muscles around my larynx, to match his professional coolness. "Fine, of course." It sounded okay.

"I can come by your house about, say, two o'clock, if you would like."

No, I thought, I would *not* like—what I *would* like is for you and this whole fucking nightmare to go away. I would like to rewind, erase, and retape that worst night of my life. But, "That would be fine," was all I said.

He confirmed the address and signed off, adding, "Have a nice day," out of rote.

I said good-bye, thinking, *Yeah right, fucker*, and punched the "end" button savagely. But I knew it wasn't his fault that my neck had fused my head to my shoulders in a solid lump of knotty, petrified wood.

4

An hour later, I was stretched out facedown on a deck chair next to my pool. The pool itself was as large as the one I had left behind at the Four Seasons Hotel, and my pool cabana doubled as a small spa and guest house. As I had come around the line of cypress trees that separated the massive back lawn and gardens from the pool area I had voiced the word, "fabulous," just as I always did when the view hit me. Which was, of course, the favorite adjective of my exterior designer. Everything was done in white, marine blue and tan. The whole look was long and lean and reeked of class and coolness.

I had collapsed onto my favorite chaise and tried to relax. The sun had melted some of the tension in the back of my neck. I could feel a hot spot between my shoulder blades that I couldn't reach to put oil onto, and I was thinking that it was going to sting there when I put my shirt back on. Other than that, my brain was cruising somewhere between the multicolored prisms of a drop of sweat a quarter inch from my nose on my forearm and the insistent flashback of blood on the cement. Just as my consciousness dissolved, that ugly image would snap me awake enough to make me focus on something else.

My breasts were pressing down comfortably into the lounge cushion and I let my arms fall over the side, turning my head in time to see Joe, a South American deity, walking quietly toward me, taking off his shirt. Good boy, I thought. I loved his stomach, all the right cuts and nice, not large but plenty meaty, arms. Arms I needed around me, though I was loathe to admit it.

I closed my eyes so he could surprise me and arched my back just enough to invite him to do so. His hands found the oil, and the last dry spot was quenched. He kneaded and I rose, then I kneaded and he rose, finding the spot and working out all the kinks. We rolled over that frothy crest sitting up in a chair with me facing him, my legs planted firmly on the decking with my toes splayed out for traction. His hands were so firm on my ass that I couldn't move until he was finished with me. It was a big finale.

He opened his handsome dark-lashed eyes and whipped me with that look, the one I always dreaded: time to share.

"All right, what happened?" he asked.

"What?" I asked, admiring his chiseled jaw and sinking my fingers into his lush, wavy hair.

A sigh came from his full mouth. Ah, Brazil, to shape such a man, you must be a lovely country.

"You haven't returned my calls," he said simply. "I hear *on the news* that you've been involved in a fatal shooting, and . . ." I sighed and looked away, not wanting to go through explaining the hell ride again. "Callaway," he took my face in his hands and made me look at him, "I was really worried about you. I needed to hear from you, to know that you were okay."

I felt myself sinking, I needed him to be a sanctuary, someone fun and comforting, not another need to be filled. "I know, I know, I should have called, I'm sorry. I thought about you though." I had, once or twice.

He shook his head and tried to connect, looking meaningfully into my eyes, desperately wanting me to need him. "What am I going to do with you?"

"You are going to enjoy me, and I'm going to enjoy you." I hoped it didn't sound too much like a dismissal, but though I did enjoy him, and his company, I had no interest in sobbing on his shoulder. I did need him, but not for that.

"I have to go, I have a meeting."

"So you said." I nodded stupidly and smiled, we had come undone and I felt awkward. "Can you join me for a swim first?"

He sighed and I watched him release me, his eyes dimming as he resigned himself to giving me up. It was sad. "You go ahead."

Walking deliberately, slowly to the water, I dove with relief into the chilly blue. I loved the silence and the dancing web of sunlight that met me below. Turning in the water I looked up at the surface, my blond hair floating around me. I could see the outline of Joe standing at the edge, handsome, distorted and distant. A pang of reluctance pierced me, *don't lose him*, but the truth was, I didn't have the strength to give him what he wanted.

Instead, I swam upward and my face broke through the surface of the water. Joe was dressing.

He took one sock in his hand and sat down in a

chair near the edge of the pool, the edge of our intimacy. "I keep saying this to myself so I guess I should say it to you." He wasn't looking at me.

"You're not going to tell me you're in love with me are you?" I tried to joke.

He looked up at me, surprised, but the look turned quickly to irony. "How could I be in love with you? You won't even let me get to know you."

The simplicity of his sentiment shocked me a little. I hadn't expected him to be so objective about me.

"The fact is," he continued, "you're so hard to get close to, and I don't know if I have that kind of patience." He smiled just a little.

"Oh." This was a first; usually I just faded out of a relationship, saw the men less and less until they found someone who paid them more attention. "Look, I'm sorry, I'm selfish about my time and my privacy; I know I ask a lot," I said in way of agreement.

"No, you don't ask enough." He was fully suited now, except for the jacket and tie, which he picked up as he stood. "And that would be okay, because the sex is terrific, except that I have more to give than sex, and I think pretty soon, if you don't let me give more, it's going to start to hurt. I get a little selfish myself about that."

He laid his jacket and tie over the back of the chair and reached down into the water, pulling me out in one steady, easy motion. He put his arms around me and pulled me against him. The hug felt so good, and so final. "I'm not saying I never want to hear from you," he said in a very soft voice in my ear. He let me go and we both looked distractedly at the front of his shirt, which was all wet. "It'll dry." He smiled again.

I was so surprised by the presence of tears in my eyes that all I could do was nod and try to laugh a little. His face softened at my tears, looking hopeful again, and I had to let him off easily.

"Don't worry, they'll dry." I said.

He turned to go. Halfway across the deck he turned back, "I'm not saying this wasn't great, you understand."

"I'll keep you on direct dial," I promised.

And he was gone, his V-shaped back disappearing behind the cypresses that lined the walk to the driveway.

It was odd to let a man that good walk out of my life without so much as a bolt of lightning. At least this one had lasted a couple of months before he needed more than I could give. I only kept one lover at a time, but I never kept them for long. I comforted myself by making it his fault. "Greedy son of a bitch," I muttered.

Turning toward the pool house to get a robe I saw my reflection in the glass doors, and frankly I admired it. I turned a little left and then right, and watched the water run down my full breasts, across my flat stomach, watched the way my long legs flowed gracefully into my well-shaped ass. I tilted my face up to catch more sun and see a brighter reflection. Almond eyes, high cheekbones, nice mouth. I liked my body, it brought me lots of pleasure, and there was so much power in it. Never met a man I couldn't have. The trick was finding one I wanted enough to keep.

But a second look showed me something different. In the polarized picture of me with the huge pool and house reflected behind me, I seemed very small and alone.

A memory of my father flashed on me again. I must have been less than seven years old, standing on the screened-in porch of our old house when we were still in middle suburbia and my mom and dad were still married. The memory was so sharp that I could recall the way the rain smelled and how the gray slate felt pressed smooth and cold against the bottom of my bare feet. Mostly, I remembered exactly the feeling of being alone, of feeling small. Then my father was next to me; I leaned against his strong leg, and we stood together, feeling the moistness from the drizzle, being alone together. I was overwhelmed by the memory of how it felt to just stand there, looking out through the screen at the rain, the melancholy that morphed into contentment. I closed my eyes and tried to trap that morsel of belonging, to keep it inside me.

I took a deep breath, but the smell of rain wasn't in it. Instead my nostrils filled with dry warm air. I leaned a little to my right and met nothing but more air. No father's solid strength to hold me up. Sighing, I opened my eyes and looked again at my reflection. I was young, pretty and worth several hundred million dollars. Who the hell's heart would bleed for me? I shared a look with my likeness and kept it to myself. I could be the loneliest, most unhappy person in the world, but I wasn't likely to find a sympathetic ear. Besides, I hated feeling sorry for myself. Hated weakness.

Wrapping myself in a light robe, I padded across the neat lawn through the French doors into the library. My house was far too big for one person to live in, but I loved it. Especially this room. Twenty-foot ceiling with books all the way up. Huge, comfortable cream-colored sofas for reading, and the marble fireplace, all of it overlooking the gardens. I really only used a small part of the house, but I always had this image of one day having enough family or at least friends to fill it up. Ginny, however, had declined to move into one of the rooms and live with me, since she knew it would probably end our friendship. I pushed the little button on the desk and "rang" for the butler.

Moments later, a soft cough announced the unobtrusive presence of the woman Ginny teasingly likes to call my wife.

"Deirdre, come in."

"Of course." She came into the library and closed the door silently behind her the way only butlers in literature and Deirdre can do.

Deirdre was the perfect butler, quiet, reserved, British, and female. She was about thirty-seven years old. Her face was attentive and eager to please, yet distant and removed at the same time. She radiated intelligence and refined humor. If she hadn't worked for me, she would have been someone I would like to be friends with. As it stood, she worked for me and we were friendly, with that unspoken gap between us. It was comfortable for both of us. She was worth a king's ransom, which I paid to her, happily. Right now, I was just relieved to be able to count on her.

"I'm expecting some company later. A police officer, actually. I'll see him in here, and would you ask Sophie to make some sandwiches?"

"What kind of sandwiches would you like?" I detected only the slightest raise of an eyebrow at the mention of police.

"The usual," I said, meaning Sophie's yummy finger sandwiches. "And how is your day?"

She straightened her stylish yet refined black suit as she answered. "Satisfactory, thank you. I do need to ask you to write an additional check for the household account."

"Did you spend all last month's allowance, Deedee?" I was teasing her. She disliked being called Deedee.

"Yes, ma'am, I did." She inclined her head and then resumed her perfect posture, smiling at me because, of course, it was my bills and payroll she spent the money on. She ran the whole shebang, hiring and scheduling staff, buying and paying for groceries, utilities, repairs, everything. I gave her whatever she needed to do it. God knows I didn't want that full-time job.

"I'll do it now, but try to lighten up on the champagne and caviar for the staff teas, will ya?"

"I will ask them not to use the soup spoons for the beluga." She turned her tall slim body and left to the sound of my laughter. I sat down and wrote out a check for thirty thousand to my name and left it on the silver tray for her to deposit to the household account.

I followed her out a few moments later and crossed the entrance hall to the huge, open stairway. Up I went, down the hall, into the master bedroom.

When the water splashed over my head in the shower I found myself reminiscing again about the worst times in my life, lost in the oblivion of narcotics, and I wondered what the hell was dredging all those shitty memories up out of the muck.

I could have used a little blunting right now. Just a little cocaine and a few cocktails might suit the bill.

I pushed the temptation away and braided my frayed nerves into something resembling a sturdy rope. *I am not that person anymore*, I told myself again, but I

couldn't help feeling that the addict was still imbed-
ded deeply inside me. There was no denying the fact
that with anxiety came the physical urge, the taste for
oblivion.

I dried off and dressed in a white silk top and draw-
string pants. Not the most modest of outfits for meeting with a Los Angeles detective perhaps, but I wanted
the comfort of cozy clothes. I stroked on some mascara
and was combing back my wet hair when I heard the
door chimes.

With a last encouraging look at my reflection I
headed out of the bedroom, hitting the top landing of
the staircase in the entrance hall just as Deirdre reached
the front door.

"Detective Paley, I presume." I greeted him as I
crossed the mosaic marble floor and shook his hand,
hoping I was hiding my bitterness adequately. "Thanks
Deirdre. Come right this way, Detective."

"Wow," he said as his eyes spanned the room and
then came to rest on me, "Nice."

"Hungry?" I asked, ignoring the compliment. We
crossed back into the library, where Deirdre was finishing laying out the tray of snacks on a table in front of
the fireplace. She had lit a small fire and I gave her a
sideways glance; she thought fires were romantic.

"A bit warm for a fire isn't it, Deirdre?" I asked,
annoyed; this was not a social visit. The food and
drink gave me the comforting illusion of being in control by playing hostess, but I wanted him gone as soon
as possible.

"Your hair is wet, madame, and I didn't want you to
catch a cold." She paused by the thermostat and turned
it down.

I narrowed my eyes and she countered with an approving glance to the detective. Then with a graceful swoosh, she was gone.

"Please, sit down." I gestured to a deep, overstuffed leather armchair as I settled myself in its mate across from him. "Coffee?" I asked, already pouring.

"Yes, thank you. Well, I'm a little overwhelmed. I'm used to a noisy station."

"I think I had enough of that last night." I was sincere about that at least.

"Uhm . . ." He was trying not to look at my body through the white silk.

"And speaking of last night . . ." I said pointedly, nailing him for taking the liberty, and he looked up at my face. Damn, his eyes were shockingly blue for a man with such black hair.

"Yes." He took the cue and found his professional voice. "I know we went over most of this, but I thought you would like to know the coroner's report confirmed your story."

My cool was shaken once again. "I wasn't aware 'my story' was in question."

"A shooting death is always technically a homicide until it's been investigated," he said as though he were repeating himself. I wondered if he had told me that the night before and I hadn't retained it. I set my mind on paying much closer attention today.

"I'm sorry. I understood that I *wasn't* being charged with homicide." I was suddenly very afraid again.

"You haven't been charged, that will be determined by the investigation." He continued. "And the angle of the first bullet shows that he was standing with his right arm raised toward you." He pointed at his torso just below his outstretched arm. "It entered here and came out the back. If his arm had been down, the trajectory of the bullet would have been quite different."

I nodded, dumbly. What he was telling me made sense and I was so relieved that I didn't trust my voice to stay steady.

"Also, there were traces on his right hand that showed he had fired his weapon, and we found the two rounds." He smiled wryly, "And that wasn't easy. He wasn't a very good shot."

"He closed his eyes," I said, the seared image of his face flashing through my brain.

"He what?"

"He closed his eyes, when he fired." I reiterated, forcing the picture out of my head.

"Most amateurs do." He seemed to be insinuating that I was not one. That lingering feeling of being assessed returned. I did not like it.

"Am I in a lot of trouble?" I needed a direct answer and my voice sounded small to me.

He answered more softly than before. "I can't really say. That's not up to me. To be blunt, it doesn't matter what I think."

"I shot that man because he was going to kill me," I said plainly. "I might be in trouble, but I'm not dead."

"What I think would go something along that line though." He smiled. It seemed that Detective Paley, at least, thought I was the good guy. I felt heartened by that. "I'm sure you must have a good lawyer." He gestured to the opulence around us. "Don't you want him or her here now?"

"No. I'm not going to say anything different from

last night. If you *charge* me, I'll get one. But, I've had enough of lawyers lately."

"You find yourself needing lawyers often?" He was fishing.

I had to laugh. "You mean, have I shot anybody else? No. Before yesterday I would have said that there are a few people I'd like to shoot, but now that I know what that really feels like, I don't think I'll be using that expression lightly again."

"Then why do you need lawyers?" he pressed.

I paused and composed myself to get through the hard part, deeply resenting that I had to share my private tragedy with a snooping stranger. "Actually, my father died two years ago," I said as I fought the tightness in my throat, willing it to relax and leave my voice steady, "and left me all this." I swung my hand in a generous circle. In my head I added to myself, "And only this."

"And everybody else wants it?" he asked.

I nodded, wishing he would go away, stop prying, it was none of his business. "A piece. They want at least a piece."

"Who wouldn't?" His eyes were on me again. I had to wonder if he was talking about a piece of my wealth, or of me. I thought I'd test him, it would please me to watch him fail.

Letting a hint of suggestion into my voice, I said, "Some pieces are sweeter than others."

"And some people are just plain greedy," he stated flatly, dismissing the subject.

He passed. Oh well.

"And speaking of pieces, I know you said last night that your gun was registered. Can you tell me where you bought it?"

"Pony Express."

"Yep, that checks out." He took a beat to flip back and forth in his little pad. I knew he wasn't reading anything. "You seem pretty well adjusted today."

"You said that last night."

"Most people are in shock for the first day or so after a shooting."

"Is that being shot at? Or actually shooting?" I asked.

He looked at me for a minute thoughtfully and then said, "Being shot at actually."

"Not that it matters in my case, I've got both ends covered." As I said it I heard all too realistically the sound of my assailant's gun going off as it was pointed at me and I knew I would hear that explosion for years to come. I smiled a little sadly. "I don't really have any choice but to accept my situation. Whatever that might be. Maybe that's why I seem 'well adjusted.' "

"So you've put it all behind you?"

"Not at all." I watched his eyes intently to see if he believed the truth. "I have accepted that this will be something I have to get through, and it will take a certain amount of time and pain to get through it." A small shudder went through me in spite of my fledgling attempts at a Zen acceptance of my predicaments. Truly wanting to believe that my tribulations were part of a bigger plan gave me some way of justifying my losses. But my reasoning that we are all sent difficulties as an opportunity to grow wasn't much to hold onto: I couldn't even pretend to find a spiritual meaning in this new nightmare.

I took a hot sip of coffee and swallowed the inclination to tear up along with the searing liquid.

"Sounds like a healthy approach." I could see that he

was doubtful of the outcome. Can't say I blamed him. "I feel I should tell you, however, it might help if you showed some remorse. If there is a hearing."

"Ever shoot anybody?" I asked impulsively.

He looked up sharply. "Yes."

"How did you feel after?" I asked.

"It's really not relevant. I'm a detective." Dropping the personal note that had entered his voice, he looked down into his cup and I watched him go somewhere distant for a few seconds, somewhere far in the past.

"Did you feel remorse? Did you show remorse at your hearing?" My voice sounded dangerous. Inside of me, anger, like a large dog was growling viciously.

"I'm just stating a fact," he said, but the message he was sending me was, Stay calm.

"I don't feel guilty, which is, of course, another definition of remorse. I don't think that criminal I killed would have felt guilty about killing me, but I bet he would have pretended to have 'remorse' at a hearing." My rage was straining at the end of its chain, barking and snarling.

"How do you feel?" Detective Paley asked quietly.

"Angry. I'm really angry. He pulled a gun on me, wanted to rob me, would have killed me, and now I'm going to be treated like a criminal." And, I realized, with a snapping yank, that in the eyes of the law, I was a criminal.

I stood up and took a deep breath, turning away to hide my emotion. The tears came now, not of pity or fear but of anger, the hardest ones to hold. Detective Paley waited, sipping coffee. I was grateful that he didn't patronize me by asking if I was all right. It took a minute to soothe the angry beast inside myself.

"Okay, I'm back," I said. "I'm sorry. That didn't help you in any way." I sat down, forcing my body to relax. "What else can I do for you?"

"Tell me why you carry a gun." His eyes locked on mine.

"I live in L.A. I watch the news."

"And the news told you it was okay to carry a gun?"

"It told me everyone else does. It made me aware of my odds."

"So, it wasn't something personal, like maybe you've been robbed before?" I wasn't sure if he was asking or suggesting.

"Why? Would I be more sympathetic if I'd been a victim before?" If I had been a cat, I would have hissed at him.

"Unfortunately, yes." He sighed deeply, and I understood that he felt the same as I did—the system was ruled by people who always thought it would happen to someone else.

"At the risk of sounding redundant," I said more quietly, "I have not been a victim before. It was my first, and I pray last, experience with that kind of violence. And while it might make me more sympathetic to have been victimized previously it might also make me dead. I suppose if I had been maimed or killed last night it might make the jury more compassionate toward me, too, you think?"

He narrowed his eyes warningly at my sarcasm, but he didn't bite. Instead he nodded thoughtfully. "You never met the boy before?"

"Funny, he didn't look like a 'boy' down the barrel of a forty-five." I answered tersely, and watched his jaw sharpen as he bit down. "No, I never met him." It was becoming more and more of a confrontation and we were bristling at each other. I braced myself to launch into him, ready to take somebody on, to fight. I welcomed it at this point. *You have no idea how I feel*, I thought.

He watched me warily, but when he spoke he wasn't challenging or insulting, just curious and polite. "Why do you think he picked you? May I?" He gestured to a sandwich. In view of my dramatic outburst, the casualness of the request disarmed me.

He was changing tack and offering me a way out of my impotent fury. With a sense of relief I let go of the offensive tactic. "Of course." I smiled at him.

He picked out a salmon sandwich and took a big bite. I answered his question while he ate the sandwich. "I don't know why he would pick me. Single white girl? Looked defenseless? He didn't want what was behind curtain number three?"

He held up a finger to show that he wasn't finished chewing and then he asked, "You seem like an upper west-side kind of person; why were you up in the valley?"

"I told you last night, I was having a business dinner with the CEO of one of my companies. He recommended a restaurant near him. He thought it was good."

"Was it?" He seemed legitimately curious.

"No."

"Oh, too bad. Why didn't he walk you to your car? Not very gentlemanly."

"Under the circumstances I thought it best we parted in the company of strangers."

"What circumstances?" he pressed.

"He wasn't very gentlemanly." I raised an eyebrow and went on. "He was hoping to make it a social evening as well."

Detective Paley nodded, looking amused. "Not very professional either, this Mr. Salton." He consulted his notebook, "I spoke with him this morning, he confirms the business dinner as well. Strange though, he didn't mention the licentious part."

"Maybe because he was driving without one," I commented.

"Driving is a privilege, not a right." He smiled at me wryly.

I liked his sense of humor, and the way his wide chest tapered slightly down to his waist.

He washed the sandwich down with a generous swig of coffee. "This is delicious, thanks." He wiped his mouth on a soft linen napkin. It was a nice mouth, full and turned up enough to imply a mature sense of humor, strong enough to deliver the truth. "May I say something? Off the record?"

"I'm not recording anything," I answered. It was dusk outside now, and the room was soft gray, with a saffron infusion from the fire.

"You appear to be a very strong woman." He stopped and considered his wording. "Shit, woman nothing, you're a strong person. And a sense of humor can help you through a lot. I know that. But . . ." he paused and got up, walking around to the wall of books, ". . . it's not in your favor to be indignantly righteous in this matter. A human life has been taken, and whether or not he would have taken yours, and, aside from the fact that you may have saved countless other lives by ending his, people will want to see that you did not do this lightly." He was facing the books, tracing the embossed titles with a long strong finger. "All this is, as I said, off the record. It's not my place to advise you."

"Then why are you?" I asked. "Off the record," I added.

He opened his mouth to speak, then shut it quickly. He turned and looked at me, shrugged his shoulders and asked, "Is there anything else you'd like to tell me?"

"No." I could think of a thousand things in another situation.

"Well, I'll see you when the D.A. decides, then." He picked up his pad and stood for a moment by the fire. It might have been me projecting, but he seemed reluctant to leave.

"Can I ask you something?" I said quietly, my eyes fixed on the flames.

"Of course." He turned to look at me again, his face lit softly by the bluish twilight outside the windows.

"Do you think I was wrong?" Suddenly I wanted his approval, I wanted someone to be on my side.

"It doesn't matter what I think. I don't make the laws. I just try to help enforce them." He responded gently but I could have kicked myself. Why did I bother asking? Feeling stupid I smiled bitterly to myself. *So what? I can take care of myself.*

"Good night, Detective," I said and offered my hand. He took it and I was surprised to find that his hand was very warm because it meant that mine felt as cold as my heart.

5

I had put it off as long as I could. Today, despite what I had happened the other night, I had to have lunch with my mother. I use the label "mother" loosely. Often as not I call her Rudy. We hadn't lived together since I was a child, and there was very little illusion between us.

As I got ready I kept repeating the words my father used to say to me when I was facing something new or scary, *you can do it, nothing to it.*

Rudy had called when she saw my picture on TV and the story about the shooting. It made a good sound bite to lead into the commercials, flashing a glamorous photo of me taken at a charity affair a couple of years before and the headline "Heiress shoots assailant." Even as she was asking if I was all right, Rudy seemed more concerned about the gossip value than about me. Something else to enthrall her friends with at her next ladies' luncheon. As far as my involvement went, she took it in stride that that was just the sort of thing I would get myself into, and out of. One more cross she would have to bear in her long, trying association with me, her only daughter. I was glad to have gotten through the formalities of her concern on the phone. I knew this lunch would be about what she wanted next.

I chose a cream Valentino suit because it was expensive and I knew that would piss her off. I was never above a bit of petty competition. Long ago, we battled for my father's attention. Now we fought for his money.

The day my father died she surprised me by coming to the house. We weren't close by any standards but I let her comfort me, because I needed solace so desperately. We sat in the kitchen and she made me tea while they took his body away; she even closed the door so that I wouldn't have to see them bring the body down the stairs.

Crying, I had babbled like a child about how much I would miss him and I had talked about some of the more horrible moments of his illness. Him taking baby steps to get to the bathroom and not making it. Me finding him naked in a dry bathtub where he had sat for hours unable to get up, unaware that he hadn't even had a bath. Trying to eat his own fingers in between bites of soup that I was feeding him. I needed to tell someone, anyone.

She had listened, nodding sympathetically and saying how hard it must have been for me. But it hadn't even been half an hour before her true motive for coming reared its ugly head.

"Have you seen the will? Did I get anything?" she asked.

I had told her to get out. And then I cried for how stupid I'd been to trust my own mother with my feelings.

As I walked into the restaurant I steeled myself, hardening on the outside so that whatever she fired at me would glance off. She was seated at the bar, drinking what appeared to be a club soda, which surprised me. Bourbon was more like her. The second I got a good look at her, my shell softened. It didn't fall away, but I felt it melt from calcium to sponge. She looked old. It scared me a little, made me feel even more mortal than facing the loaded gun. Looking down the barrel of the revolver at a killer's eyes I thought I *might* die. Looking at the weight of age on my mother's face, I knew it. Rudy's famous beauty was just on the edge of gone, for all her scrupulous efforts to lure it back. The tucks to tighten her skin were well hidden in the line of her hair which was skillfully dyed a light blond to cover the gray. Her cheekbones were still articulate, though perhaps too well pronounced now since the facelifts. She was thin and perfectly made up, as always; her gray eyes swept the bar with their usual abrasive critique. I approached her and kissed her on the cheek.

"Hello Rudy." I smiled at her and felt some genuine feeling, compassion more than love.

"Hello Callaway." Her first glance held something new, a bit of fear. I had surprised her, I guess. "How are you?"

"Not bad." I wasn't, considering. I ordered an iced tea and relaxed onto the bar stool. This wasn't going to be our usual bloodletting session, maybe.

"How's Bill? I've got to get over there, maybe I'll stop by after lunch." I liked my stepfather, he was okay.

"He's the same. He'll always be the same."

"That's not so bad, he's a nice guy," I said encouragingly. I knew the fact that he was not as successful as my father ate at her every day.

"I just can't understand him." She sighed and little

creases of tension and disappointment radiated from her mouth. "He had such potential."

"Is there a reason we are speaking of him in the past tense?" I asked. "Don't tell me you're thinking about leaving him." I squeezed the lemon into the tall tea before me and licked the sour juice from one finger.

She smiled at me sadly and asked, "Where would I go?"

I nodded. She'd backed herself into a corner years ago. Leaving Bill would mean admitting she'd made a mistake divorcing my father for his partner. She was always hungry for better. The irony, of course, was that my father had gone on to amass a fortune, while Bill had been happy with half ownership in the bottling plant. Now, though she lived a very comfortable upper-class lifestyle, I lived in the "palace," as she referred to it bitterly.

"And how is baby brother Biff?" I inquired of my half sibling, who held little fondness for me. It was not his fault, of course. Rudy had worked on him for years. I'd deprived her of everything that was her right. That's the way she saw it. Convenient to forget that she was the one who walked.

"Don't call him Biff. You know he hates that," she reprimanded. "You have everything, you can afford to be more generous."

"Fair enough. How is Binford?" I amended.

"Fine. I imagine you'll see him later at the plant." She was alerting me that he was in town. Maybe she thought I wouldn't go there if I knew I'd run into him.

"I'll look forward to it," I lied. Thousands of times I had wished that this loosely connected "family" could just relax and accept and get along, but it was a wishing-well wish and the coin was still falling, the water deep and dark and cold.

"Ladies?" The maître d' was behind us, most of his body hidden by huge menus. "Your table is ready."

He helped my mother into her chair and her mouth tightened again as she sat. I was already settled in by the time he crossed quickly to make the gesture of seating me.

"Are you all right?" I asked, when he had finished placing our napkins in our laps, setting down our drinks and hovering solicitously.

"I'm fine." She presented that tight, thin-lipped smile again. "How are *you*?" she asked me. She leaned forward and put her hand over mine; I felt myself tense. It was so unfamiliar to receive physical attention from her. I desperately wanted to trust her, to submit to the sweetness of a mother's love, but I had given up on that long ago. I would find no empathy in her.

Instead it was time to get to the point. "Oh, you know me," I answered with a flippancy I certainly did not feel. "Was there a reason you wanted to have lunch?"

"Besides seeing my only daughter?" she jabbed, and I was furious with myself for letting her sarcasm burn me again, in spite of my resolve. "Yes, in fact there is," she said.

Of course. "Hit me," I said.

"I know you object to my claim on your father's will."

"You left him before he made this money, you got a fair settlement at the time." I said it again as I had said it a hundred times before, stating a fact clearly.

"But," she persisted, "what about Binford? Don't you think he's entitled to some of that?"

I tried to be patient. "Binford is Bill's son. He's entitled to whatever you and Bill think he's entitled to."

"Is he?" She raised her well-penciled eyebrow and pointed it at me.

"What?" I didn't even want to know what she was scheming up now.

"There is something I never told you."

"There's a lot you never told me, but I've got a vivid imagination and excellent powers of deduction, so I know most of it," I said sarcastically, but I meant it.

"You don't know this." She paused dramatically.

"Oh, for God's sakes, Rudy, you are not going to claim that Binford is Dad's son." It was clear from her face that she was. I couldn't stop myself from rolling my eyes and I half snorted, more amused than disbelieving. "Binford was born two years after you were married to Bill. Dad wouldn't have anything to do with you and besides, he looks exactly like Bill."

"I've always thought he had your father's eyes, and you should know your father and I did have an affair after I was married to Bill."

"Bullshit." I was too amazed at her stupidity to be angry.

"It's true," she nodded knowingly.

"Well, I guess we're going to have a hard time asking Daddy's side of it, aren't we? And a swab test might be a little tricky, seeing how Dad's spit's all dried up now he's been cremated." It stabbed at my heart to make the acerbic remark but it was time to drive my point home, with hurtful words or a blunt instrument if necessary. "Please, Rudy, what do you want from me? Another legal battle? I won't 'settle' and give Biff money, it won't work. Dad wanted me to have it. That's that. I'm sorry to say this, but you won't win. If you fight me, it will only cost you a fortune. Even if Biff was Daddy's, Daddy didn't leave him, or you, the money. It's mine, Mom. Accept it. You want for nothing in your life, you have a great house, jewelry, cars, a son and a terrific husband who loves you more than I can fathom considering the nasty way you talk about him. What more do you want?"

She was staring at me. She hadn't expected this. But years of dealing with her had finally brought me to a simple acceptance of her manipulations. I was neither surprised nor threatened. I held all the cards, and now, finally, I was showing my hand.

"How could you do this to your brother?" was all she could muster.

"Mom, listen to me carefully." I looked at her and softened my face. Remember, I told myself, *if she acts crazy, treat her like a crazy person.* "I'm not doing anything to him. I'm not doing anything to you; you need to let go of this. Just be grateful for all the wonderful things you have."

"Well, that's very easy for you to say, you have it all." She spoke from a feeling of genuine loss.

With an odd sense of déjà vu, I flashed on Joe's outline standing at the edge of the pool while I looked up at him through the undulating silence of the water. It seemed that my mother, sitting right beside me was also in a totally different element. She was breathing air and I, water. From that vast distance, I smiled back.

"Everything's a trade-off, Rudy." I turned my attention to the menu, "One thing costs you something else."

"You can afford anything you want," she answered wistfully.

I smiled sympathetically. She didn't understand. I could afford almost anything, except peace of mind that my money wasn't the most attractive thing about me. Men who weren't threatened by my money were in love with it. I was married to my wealth as sure as a nun is to the church. It was intertwined in my personal self like a physical trait, blond hair, blue eyes and big bucks. That was me. I was jealous of my own money. Not that I didn't want to share it with anyone else, I would have gladly done that. I just couldn't stand the competition. I wanted my mate to love only me, not have my money for his mistress.

And there was one more thing I couldn't afford; all my assets couldn't buy my father back.

I guess Rudy had given up because she ordered lunch and didn't say anything else about the will. I watched her while she was lording it over the waiter, complaining about anything she could think up. Mostly, I felt sorry for her. I didn't know when she'd become this kind of person, desperate to be the queen. Maybe it was my fault. I would never love her like a daughter should love a mother. I hoped Binford loved her the way a son should.

When she was picking at the beautifully presented entrée I remembered loving her, long ago. I remembered one day when I was in the first grade, she had come to the door of the classroom and motioned to the teacher. Mrs. Chisom had called me up and told me to get my things, I was going home early. In the hall, my mom took my hand and smiled at my bewilderment.

"I have a surprise for you," she said in a secret voice and squeezed my hand. She took me out to the car and I remember the sky, the kind you seldom see in smoggy

L.A., clear and drenched in blue. We drove to the beach, listening to Vivaldi and talking the whole way. When we got there, she took a picnic basket out of the trunk and we sat on a blanket and ate, and took our shoes off and ran through the edge of the freezing surf, my short gray uniform skirt getting splashed and salty. I remembered looking up at her, as she rested her hand on my hair and smiled at me with love in her eyes. Just for a moment, she had been as clear as the sky, and focused only on me.

I looked at her hands now, pushing the gourmet meal away as though it was rotting garbage and I felt the loss again. Pretending to cough, I wiped my mouth to cover the welling of tears until I could force them back to where they started, many years ago, when I was still a little girl.

When the divorce proceedings had begun, I became a casualty of war. I was no longer something to love, I was something to fight over. Of course, when there's a winner there's a loser and that had been me.

We finished the rest of our meal in silence which Rudy broke only to complain about the coffee not being hot enough as the host rushed to help her with her coat. I mouthed an apology behind her back and paid the check, overtipping considerably to compensate for Rudy, my own walking, talking maternal weakness.

6

The glass bottling factory sat next to the railroad tracks like a hobo waiting on a ride that would never come. I drove across the hot asphalt and parked in a reserved space with my name on it. The plaque read, "Ms. Wilde." The paint on the letters "ms" was shinier than the rest of it; it used to read, "Mr. Wilde."

My cell phone rang just as I shut off the car; checking the caller ID I saw that it was Ginny.

"Hey girl, what's up?" I answered.

"Oh, not much, I'm just spending a few hours waiting to fall down for some actress who might bruise her pretty face, you know the routine." She sounded like she was yawning.

"Well, don't bruise your pretty face either," I said. Her stunt work worried me sometimes; though I knew how good she was at it, there was always that element of risk.

"Not likely. She trips over a root and hurts her ankle so the star of the series can save her from the bad guy. Typical," she laughed. "What's up with you?"

"Oh, I'm having *such* a good day," I enthused sarcastically. "I had a *really* relaxing, *fun* lunch with my mom." I heard Ginny's heartfelt groan for me but I continued on, "And I'm about to go say 'hello' to my beloved half brother."

I paused for a reaction, and heard nothing but static. I pushed the phone harder against my ear only to yank it away a second later. "What are you, a fucking masochist?!" she screamed so loudly I could hear her perfectly though my hand was stretched away from my body.

Listening cautiously from a distance to see if there was more, I could only make out vague cursing. By the time I put the speaker back to my ear she was on a steady but nonviolent rant.

"I mean, what the hell, Cally? Your mother? You know how hard it is on you to deal with her, I mean, don't you? I do! Here I sit in my little trailer worrying about, oh, you getting shot at and thinking you're probably an emotional wreck. But hey, I'm comforting myself with the thought that at least you're home taking care of yourself, but do you? No, not Callaway Wilde, she's got to go out and have lunch with Atilla the Mum, are you listening to me?"

"Yes, but I have to go in now, it's getting really hot in my car."

"I'm not done with you . . ."

"What do you want me to do? Life goes on," I said lamely.

"What do I want you to *do*? Take a hot bath, a break, a pill. Drink a glass of wine, get a massage, a therapist, an acupuncture treatment. I don't fucking *know*. Take care of yourself!" she raved. God love her.

"I will, I promise."

"Yeah, when?" She sounded extremely doubtful. In fact, I don't think she believed me at all.

"Bye, love you. Gotta go." I hung up.

I went through the glass door to the carpeted offices and smiled at the girl at the desk. "Hi there." I couldn't remember her name. Maybe I didn't come in often enough. The truth was, nobody needed me to run the place. Bill did that perfectly. I just sat on the board and shared in the profits.

I went down the hall and peeked into a small windowless office on my left.

"Hi Elena."

My half brother's wife looked up and her pleasant face broke into a wide grin. She wasn't classically beautiful but she was so nice that it made her seem much more attractive. Her hair was plain brown, her face a little long, her lips thin, but when she smiled at me in her overtly friendly way I couldn't help thinking how pretty she was. We'd gone to the same college and both been on the basketball team when she was a freshman and I was a senior.

She had a curious way of talking about our past as though she had been my closest friend in college. The way she told it, you would think we were inseparable, although I hardly remembered seeing her other than at practice. I supposed it was her way of connecting to me.

She'd first met my brother briefly during that one year we were both at college, but because he was four years her junior, it had taken him a few years to grow into her, in more ways than one. As she got up now from the desk to come and hug me, I had to look up. She was tall. Tall enough to have been the center on our team, have trouble getting a date, and tall enough to be laughed at by some of the other girls. Elena apparently dated our friendship back to the day she had overheard me telling off a couple of snotty sorority girls who had been making fun of her height. Knocking some bitches down a notch or two sounded like something I would do, not out of friendship for Elena, necessarily, but because petty cruelty galled me to the core. Personally, I couldn't recall the episode. I had always assumed that was because for me it hadn't been a big deal, but for her, having someone take her side *was* a big deal, so she always remembered it.

"Cally, hi!" Her super long legs took two strides to cover the whole room and she folded me into an embrace. "I heard about what happened to you, I'm so sorry. I cannot believe you didn't call me, I would have been there in a minute." She leaned in conspiratorially, "You know I'd do anything for you, don't you?"

"Yes, thank you, Elena."

"And I know you'd do the same for me." She nodded knowingly, "It must have been absolutely frightening."

"It wasn't fun," I agreed.

"What are you doing here?"

"I came to talk business with Bill," I said, and then added quickly, "and Binford." I didn't want to slight her husband.

"Oh." She nodded as though we were sharing a great secret. She always did that, made little things seem like a big deal.

"You keeping everything straight here?" I asked. She had sort of moved herself into a position of book-keeper, even though there were accountants for the company. It was an unofficial position that kept her busy and occasionally caught a mistake or two.

She rolled her eyes to the popcorn ceiling. "You have no idea what a mess things are. I don't know how they managed before." She sighed. "But you know I was always an organizer, even in college. I mean you remember my dorm room, for goodness sake, I kept my shampoos and lotions in alphabetical order." She laughed.

I nodded, though I couldn't remember ever having seen her dorm room.

"Don't let anything slip by. I've got to go." I smiled.

"Call me if you need to talk or anything, or let's go for a walk or have lunch. I miss seeing you," she said.

"Okay, things are a little crazy right now, but maybe in a couple of weeks. I tell you what, you call me, end of next week and we'll find a time, okay?" I said, being deliberately vague.

"Okay!" She seemed pleased.

I made a mental note to surrender a couple of hours to Elena. It wouldn't kill me to spend time with someone who was genuinely happy to see me for a change. Then I moved on to my stepfather's office. "Hi Nina," I said to his secretary, a hard-looking redhead packaged in a skirt two sizes too small. "Is Bill in?"

"He's in the factory. I'll page him." She picked up the phone.

"No, that's okay, I'll take the tour." I turned back and went through the heavy door down a short hall and entered the belly of Signa Glass and Bottling.

The noise greeted me with a familiar onslaught. Too loud, I thought, but you got used to it quickly, and all the workers wore earplugs. I started along the floor and passed one of the huge machines pressing out the hot glass.

Halfway across the factory, the blue oscillating neon light gave way to actual daylight and I looked to my left at the huge loading-dock doors that were standing wide open. I saw the foreman Musso and headed that way to say hello. He'd been with the company for a couple of decades, and my father had always respected him. I did, too. He had a way of greeting me with a big smile that made me feel genuinely liked. That was mutual, too.

I was just a few paces away from him, extending my hand with a smile, when behind him, in the harsh light of day, a worker's face turned toward me, and midstep I stopped, all my attention focused on the youth on the loading dock.

It was him. It was the kid I had shot. Like taking a punch to the stomach, the wind was knocked out of me in a sharp exhale and I couldn't take any air in again. My chest was paralyzed.

His face kept turning toward me and my eyes kept adjusting to the bright daylight streaming around him from behind. He was looking right at me when the background faded as my pupils closed down to shut out the painful brilliance and the shadows of his face balanced into distinguishable features.

It wasn't him. I breathed in, finally, and put my half-raised hand flat on my chest. *Deep breath*, I told myself, *and keep breathing*.

"You okay, Cal?" Musso laid his heavy, work roughened hand on my shoulder. I whipped up a smile.

"Yeah. I'm fine, I just . . . the sight of manual labor, well, it makes my palms sweat." I was still trying to get a good look at the dockworker, just to make sure. It wasn't him, of course. He looked just like the kid. Maybe a year older, Hispanic, sharp eyes. He saw me staring at him and his body language dared me to keep doing it, with a perfectly eloquent sentence of arrogance. I looked away and collected myself. *Please, God, don't let this happen to me. Let me forget him.*

"I remember when you used to work on the line in the summer," Musso said, smiling.

"Well, I needed the money." I smiled back. "If my relatives have anything to say about it, I might be back here hosing off those hot bottles."

He laughed. "I doubt that." He said, "You're not afraid to work, but you're too smart to have to now."

"Speaking of relatives, where's Bill?"

"In the plant manager's office." Musso pointed to a corner of the massive room, where a one-way mirror lay flat and tarnished against the white wall.

"Thanks, Musso. Tell Fay 'hello' for me, would you?" I moved off through the rasping, ragged noise of a dragon's breath, to the metal door.

Inside the manager's office, Bill was leaning over a blueprint on the desk. The cheerful shine of his balding head greeted me first before he looked up and smiled. The door closed behind me, sealing out the decibels, delivering an audible sensation of relief.

"Hey Cally." Bill always reminded me of a piston, compact, strong, consistent and happiest when working steadily. He maneuvered around the desk without uprooting his planted right hand, his quickness in pivoting toward me emphasizing his enthusiastic greeting. I thought again what a great guy he was.

"Hi Bill!" I gave him a strong, heartfelt hug. I wished I could spend more time with him, but that would have meant seeing more of my mother and I couldn't take much more of that.

"Ready to take over that office I'm saving you?" he kidded.

"If only you needed me," I answered with a familiar, sweeping sense of relief that he didn't. "Actually, I wanted to tell you something."

The door on the other side from the plant opened and a younger, also balding, version of Bill stood in it. He stopped when he saw me and tried to adjust quickly. Boy, he hated working for me.

"Well if it isn't my handsome little brother." I beamed at him. I really did like him, and I wasn't too proud to beg for a little sibling affection.

"Hello Callaway. I didn't mean to interrupt," Binford answered politely enough. I sometimes sensed he might have liked permission to like me, too. But it was never granted. We never had a chance.

"Come on in, Binford," Bill welcomed. Binford's rounded shoulders and thinning hair gave a first impression of meekness that was dispelled by the look in his eyes. He glowered at me and slouched in reluctantly. I had the brilliant initiative to sit, and everyone followed my lead. Now I'd have to think of something to say.

"I saw Elena down the hall, she seems to be holding down the fort." I knew Binford was proud of his wife, although I secretly suspected the true love of his life was a golden retriever that I was rather fond of myself.

"She seems to think so."

"How's married life?" I hadn't seen him much since his wedding more than a year before, which I'd begrudgingly attended, knowing our mutual mother would take the opportunity to stab at me as often as possible.

"It's great. Maybe you ought to try having a relationship with someone besides yourself sometime." He couldn't resist the dig. Not his fault and I was in a non-condemning mood.

"And ruin a lifelong romance? Don't be ridiculous! Maybe one day I'll try it, not today, of course," I quipped. "Today, I'd like to let you know that if and when this will is ever finished being contested, I'd be very interested in knowing if you would like to buy me out of the company."

I had addressed myself to Bill, because technically he was my partner, but I had glanced at Binford to acknowledge him as well. He spoke first.

"Need the money?" he asked. It was sarcastic but, call me gullible, I think he meant it as a shared joke.

"I'd like you to have the company free and clear. It seems to be doing well enough and I'm sure we could agree on a fair price." I meant that. My next statement, however, was a lie.

"I'm awfully busy with my other companies, and handling my father's affairs has made me realize that I'd like things simplified." I smiled. The truth was, I wanted to give Binford something, and I wanted to be done with my mother.

Bill hadn't spoken but I could see that a glint had sparked to life in his eye. It's something to be *the* boss.

"Why don't you just sign it over?" Binford asked with his usual, coarse directness. "I mean, you could. It's not like you get that much from it, comparatively." He finished, referring to my many other, more profitable holdings.

"Binford," snapped his father, "if we do this, a fair price will be paid."

"Fair? Her father screwed my mother out of everything, and now we should pay a 'fair' price to her?" He snapped his head in my direction.

I sat uncomfortably while Bill closed his eyes and breathed a lifelong, tortured sigh.

"Binford," he said at last with a voice of exhausted but valiant patience, "you cannot believe everything your mother tells you. Frank was a fair man, a good man. I've told you that before and I'll have to tell you this again. I love your mother, but Frank did not 'screw' her."

It was interesting; in that statement and its expression I saw Bill's life. He had married his partner's wife, and felt guilty. He had not done as well in business as his partner, and felt small. He had lived his life with Rudy, and felt spent. Through it all he had tried hard to be as good a man as he could be, and in that he had succeeded.

"And I won't screw you, either," I said as gently as I could. Just in time, I stopped myself from adding, "Daddy wouldn't like it." I rose and smiled at them both.

"Let us know, Cal. Thank you," Bill said, rising. Binford rose, too, a little deliberately late, but I think he felt badly.

"Sure. Nice to see you Bill. You, too, Binford."

He nodded at me and I crossed between them, through the door, and back into the hot, noisy breath of the dragon.

7

Home again, home again. I threw open my living room doors, which led to the front gardens, and breathed deeply. From the recesses of the house I dimly heard the door chimes. Two minutes later Deirdre's polite knock preceded her entrance.

"Miss Ginny," Deirdre announced, but her propriety was shot down by the sudden blast of motion and noise that often accompanied the appearance of Ginny.

"Ms. Wilde, can we get over these pretentious formalities?" Ginny was wearing an oversize man's shirt, leggings and cowboy boots made of the hide of something she probably shot herself, with a toothbrush sticking out of her pocket. She carried a small overnight bag.

I saw Deirdre tense at the unflattering reference to her professional acumen. Can't say I blamed her, nobody *likes* to have their job called a pretentious formality.

Ginny noticed it, too. "I'm sorry Deirdre, you know I'm just jealous, especially of your posture, it's not your fault." She turned on me, "But for God's sake, woman, I come here, what, three times a week? And every time

Deirdre walks me to you and says my name. Don't you think the ritual is becoming ostentatious?"

"Ostentatious?" I registered shock. "I don't know, can I look that up and get back to you?"

I appealed to Deirdre who was hiding her chagrin with admirable calm. "She's awfully cute though, isn't she?" apologizing in my way for Ginny's overtly American behavior.

Deirdre returned my query with a look of infinite patience.

"Well, much as I love her, I hope she's not going to do that all night, because I am sleeping over!" Ginny whipped out her toothbrush and struck a pose: the toothbrush raised aloft in her right hand, her toes pointing in, ducklike, and her free hand saluting the exalted dental tool. She looked like a demented tribute to good oral hygiene, sculpted by a disturbed dentist.

"You are out of your mind," I said, meaning of course that was exactly the sort of lightheartedness I desperately needed right now.

"Will there be two for dinner?" asked Deirdre, unimpressed as usual.

"So far, Deirdre. One can never be certain when Miss Ginny checks in." I smiled and beckoned to my friend. "Last one in the pool's a rotten lay!"

She can run really fast.

After that brief spurt of furious competitiveness we slowed down considerably, and spent a leisurely hour chatting and watching the light fade. It was pleasant doing nothing; I told Ginny I should put more nothing into my schedule. She responded by saying doing nothing made her hungry; it was time for dinner.

I have always had a penchant for things Greek and

Roman, so my formal dining room is intensely indulgent. Instead of a traditional table and chairs, I have a huge low table with lounges all around. More often than not, people sat up and ate and then lay back for a cognac or a cigar. But Ginny and I positively lolled.

I was eating pasta out of a huge bowl with my fingers. Ginny was alternately taking bites of roast chicken and filling me in on why her latest paramour had not been paramount.

"His dick went off to the right," she said simply.

"His lover ran off with Rush Limbaugh?" I asked. "I always suspected as much." I was nodding sagely.

"No, I mean it bent to the right. Curved."

"And you don't," I said.

"Well, it just wasn't very comfortable, unless I was like this." She rolled on her side and raised one crooked leg in the air, in an embarrassingly profane position.

"Oh, that looks comfy," I remarked.

"It's not. I did like him though. Too bad." She sighed dramatically.

I laughed a little, adding, "Oh well, once I dated a guy whose dick was too big."

"I remember him," she nodded thoughtfully.

"Yeah, what's-his-name. Anyway, I kept getting cystitis. He had to go."

"Didn't you meet him in Atlanta?" Ginny asked, fixing her eyes on a not-too-distant place in the air before her. She zoned out and then moaned orgasmically.

"What?" I was almost afraid to ask.

"Donuts. Hot Krispy Kremes."

"Oh my God, that was my favorite thing in Atlanta." I salivated at the thought of the hot, sugary orbs that melted in your mouth.

"We were stoned. I wish I could still get stoned," Ginny said nostalgically.

"Can I tell you something?" I set up my confession.

"What?"

"Lately I've been thinking about drugs again." I grimaced in my gut as I said it, but I needed to tell her, to get it out.

She looked at me, frightened. "You wouldn't do that, would you?"

"I don't think so," I said as honestly as I could. "But I think it's all this uncontrollable shit in my life, it's like a programmed response in me."

"But you know it's not worth it," she pleaded.

"Oh, I *know* that, what's logical and smart doesn't have anything to do with the, uh . . ." I searched for the word.

"Craving?" she suggested.

"Yeah, kind of, it feels more like I'm fighting a basic need. I guess the addict in me isn't ever going to go away." I felt better telling her about it.

"I know what you mean. There are definitely certain situations that make me wish I could just get fucked up and forget for a while." She understood, I knew she would. "And I was never as deep in as you were."

"I was pretty far gone." I twitched uncomfortably, recalling the addiction. "It was ugly."

She smiled at me. "You've come a long way baby."

"Well, it was quit or die," I summed up. "Thank God I didn't have to give up the donuts."

She froze her gold-flecked eyes on me, one hand floated a pointed finger in a circular motion at my face.

"We are going and don't even say we're not." She was

already headed down the hall when I shouted after her, "There are no Krispy Kremes in L.A.!"

She froze, turned and stared at me, mouth agape. "Where have you been? Get with it! They opened a Krispy Kreme in Van Nuys months ago. I sent you an E-mail!" Then she spun around again, muttering something that sounded suspiciously like a reference to the correlation between my hair color and my intelligence.

My mouth started to water. "No way!" I shouted back and took off after her.

So that's how I found myself driving down Ventura Boulevard just before midnight on a Thursday night, the breeze whipping our hair and me watching everyone in sight nervously. Ginny had wanted the top down and I hadn't. She won by insisting that there was no point in having a convertible car if you were never going to put the top down. Call me crazy but I felt a little exposed driving a Jaguar convertible on the streets of L.A. after what had happened to me. Especially since we were passing the site of the shooting. She knew that, of course, but I think it was her way of making me face my fears and I always felt better when she was with me.

As we drove by I kept my eyes straight ahead but I couldn't stop myself from seeing his face, the surprise in his eyes, and his blood on the pavement. I shook my head and took a deep breath. A couple more blocks brought us to the precinct where I'd been booked and Ginny had picked me up.

Ginny stayed mercifully quiet but when she noticed the precinct she said, "The valley twice in a week, what's the world coming to?" I wondered if she had planned this, maybe on the spur of the moment, to get me back on my horse, so to speak.

I smiled at her, grateful for her humor, her under-standing, for her.

She was watching me, "You okay?" she asked more seriously. I nodded. I wondered if Detective Paley was there, working on some new case.

We pulled into the parking lot, and I parked in the light from the store windows. Ginny jumped out.

"Let's go, and I want them hot," she called.

"We can always nuke 'em at home," I said helpfully as I opened the door to the stark sugary store.

There was a man at the counter paying for his two dozen assorted. Ginny poked me. She leaned in to my ear.

"Nice ass," she said and smiled innocently.

"Thank you. I work really hard at it," I answered. She punched me. "Oh, you mean him."

So I looked. It was a nice ass, nice shoulders and hair, too. We were both curious now, but he had yet to turn toward us. Ginny was looking off through the win-dow to where the donuts were made.

"Oh, no, she did not!" she exclaimed.

"What?" I spun my head to see what had caught her attention.

"That cook just put two donuts in a box with her bare hands, licked her fingers, and then went on load-ing more donuts."

"Get out of here," I said, begging her to be kidding.

She nailed me with her eyes. "Girl, I swear on Dudney's life." Dudney was her terrier-cum-child. "Do I have to say anything more?" She really loved her dog.

For some reason it struck me as the funniest thing I've ever heard. I grabbed Ginny's hand and doubled over, holding my stomach, helpless with laughter. The last days' tension was leaking from me in a kind of insane hysterical reflex, like too much pressure on the valve of a helium tank.

My outburst caused the man at the counter to turn around. I looked up, still laughing so hard I had to wipe my mouth with the side of my hand to stop from drooling, which of course, sent Ginny into spasms.

Through the haze of girlish silliness, I saw the gorgeous blue eyes of Detective Paley.

He raised one eyebrow at my behavior, but I could tell he was glad to see me. With an effort I straightened up and took a deep breath.

"Hello," he offered while he was waiting.

"Hi, Detective Paley, uhm, this is my friend Ginny." I gestured helplessly. "Ginny, Detective Paley."

"Uh-oh. Hi, uh, Detective." Ginny always froze up a little around authority. There's a little history there. She once bought some drugs from an undercover detective. She didn't mind being popped for the crime. She figured, she was bad, she got spanked. Fine. What pissed her off was the fact that he let her give him a blow job first.

"Nice to meet you." He didn't shake hands. He was holding those two boxes of assorted.

"Going to work?" I asked, motioning to the donuts.

"Yeah, I've got the night shift."

"I know," I said wryly. "Remember? We met at your office."

"Well, more like in the field," he contributed.

"More like, in the dark." I hadn't noticed how defined his jaw was until I saw him smile at me the way he did now. "And then we carpooled to your office."

Ginny had not been included in eye contact past the

hello stage. She took it as an exit cue. "I'll get the donuts," she said as she left.

"Try the chocolate frosted," Paley advised, still without looking at Ginny, as she walked away. Then more intimately to me, he said, "You seem to be in good spirits."

"She's a good friend." That seemed to sum it all up for him, and he nodded.

"I'm glad." The only thing thicker than the attraction was the inappropriateness. I tried hard to pretend I wasn't interested.

"Nice to see you." There didn't seem to be anything else to say. How do you mention to the man who booked you for murder that you'd like to see him sometime?

"I'd like to give you your gun back," he said.

That would do. Okay, my turn.

"Do I need to stop up and see you sometime, or could you bring it by?"

"I wish I could. You'll have to come and get it. There'll be paperwork, of course." He sighed.

"I could come by tomorrow or Saturday," I offered. "Unless you have weekends off." I started to sweat a little. Too far?

"Come by tomorrow. I have Saturday off." Nope, just far enough.

"Well, I'll see you tomorrow," I said letting the availability of his weekend hang there for the moment.

"Evening," he added.

"Right, tomorrow evening." I nodded and looked away.

He waved the boxes a little. "I'd better get these to the precinct, you know what they say about to starting the day with a nutritious breakfast."

"And I thought the cop-donut thing was just a cliché."

"It is. But, fortunately, very few of us speak French. Good night, be careful." He turned to where Ginny was watching us from the counter. "Nice to meet you."

"Oh, yeah, sure. You, too." She waxes a bit sarcastic at times.

"Au revoir," I said as he passed me.

"Bon soir," He pronounced perfectly and went out. I crossed to Ginny with a twinkle in my eye. She watched me with a crooked eyebrow and a squint.

"The arresting officer?" she asked.

"Yeah," was all I could think of to say.

"Did he cuff you?" she deadpanned.

"As a matter of fact, yes."

She nodded slowly, knowingly. "And you liked it, didn't you?"

We burst into laughter again, and for a few moments at least, the whole ugly saga of the past two days seemed mercifully unreal.

8

Sitting in the waiting room of the precinct the following evening made the past two days undeniably concrete. I was there alone; Ginny had left that morning to blow up in the desert. She'd made that drive several times since I'd known her. Apparently the fire marshal is jumpy about giving permission for large-scale explosions in heavily populated areas, so they build a set on a nice arid stretch of cactus-infested scrubland, then they incinerate it, while highly trained professionals, like Ginny, fly through the air, or fall off the ledge or whatever. I missed her; I felt like I might explode soon myself, and I was definitely feeling that this was not something you should try at home.

The officer sitting at the front desk had a look on her face that managed to be vapid and hard at the same time, a look that usually takes years of Department of Motor Vehicles work to perfect. How many blatant lies can you listen to before you come to expect them?

My musing was cut short by Detective Paley standing in the doorway holding a file.

"Ms. Wilde. Could you come with me please?" He sounded formal, but he could barely meet my eyes.

We walked along a hallway lit by nasty green fluorescent lights until we came to a larger room separated into those sectional offices. The ones that give the illusion of privacy up to about six square feet.

He gestured for me to sit down in a chair wedged between the desk and the gray fabric facade. He took the chair across and opened the file.

"Thanks for coming. You'll need to sign these." He looked really tired. A stack of files on his desk was so high it was enough to make you give up hope of a better world.

"Tough job you've got," I commented by way of commiseration.

"I picked it." He didn't have any excuses. How rare.

"Does this mean I'm not going to be charged?" I asked, a little afraid.

"Yes. I'm glad to say the D.A. decided it was clearly self-defense. You will have to pay a fine to get the gun back." He smiled. "I guess that probably won't sting too much." He looked directly at me now.

"I keep a gallon jug of Bactine at home." I smiled back. "I seem to be getting stung a lot lately."

"Sorry to hear that. Stock market down?" he chided.

"Inheritance taxes are up." I grimaced in spite of myself. "Way up."

"So I've heard," he said, like he really had, and then he slid the files across the table to me. As he did I noticed the watch he was wearing. A stainless-steel Breitling. Expensive.

"Nice watch," I commented.

"Thanks, I like it."

I wondered if it was a gift from a wealthy girlfriend. Now that I was relatively sure I wasn't doing eight to ten without the possibility of parole, I could relax a little. I turned my attention to him. He certainly was handsome enough to inspire such a generous gift. Or, was it possible he was skimming a little graft to make the paperwork more palatable? It happens. I tried to imagine what kind of man he was and had some flowing images of him sweaty and naked.

I stayed with the visual while he showed me where to sign and by the time we actually set off to retrieve my gun, I was speculating on how a handsome cop on the take would be in bed. It was definitely more interesting speculating on that than it was to look at the scenery we were passing.

When we got on a crowded elevator I was into the really good part of my personal porn. The elevator made two stops, taking on more people and taking away the space between Paley and me each time. He stood against the back wall and I was just in front of him. Everyone instinctively backed away from two uniformed officers and a dangerous-looking man, his hands ratcheted behind his back with plastic restraints, as they squeezed on last, pushing me right up against my escort. I had to resist the overwhelming urge to press my weight back against him, the proximity and the private screening in my head were making me sweat. *This is business*, I started telling myself.

I was trying to ignore the heat between our bodies and focus on the floor numbers, when I felt him take a deep breath and exhale slowly. It was the scent of me he was summoning, I could tell.

When we stopped at our floor and the doors slid open, I thought I was very well mannered not to look at the front of his pants. I did know what a hard-on felt like, after all. So apparently I wasn't the only one playing a special feature. He gestured me ahead of him anyway.

A short walk brought us to the evidence locker. More signatures brought me my gun with an empty clip, I noticed. I'd brought a lockbox so I could take the firearm home legally.

He walked me down to the front again and out past the solid clay face in uniform and into the night. We stopped on the steps; neither of us said anything.

"Thanks," I mustered finally.

He nodded.

"Well, if you need anything, you know where to find me." I tried to keep it light not to pressure him.

"Same here." He offered his hand and we shook, real straight and proper, but he smiled softly and his eyes danced a little. "Do me a favor, huh?"

"Sure." Whoops, a little too eager.

"Don't shoot anybody else."

He turned and went back into the building, leaving me slightly dazed and wondering what the hell just happened. Okay, he wasn't interested in me; that was fine, I could accept that, fucker. But, what about the rest of my life, would it go back to the way it had been before? I doubted it.

One thing I knew for sure, I would never feel totally safe again. That illusion was as dead as the body in the morgue.

I tried to shake off the fear as I crossed to my car, but I was scared. Paley's warning not to shoot anyone else might have been in jest, but driving home alone in the dark, I didn't think it was funny.

9

I walked into the house through the garage door and called out, "I'm home," to anyone who might care, before I remembered it was Friday, and nobody did. I flipped on a few lights to vanquish the gloom and a bit of my own trepidation. It was a big house.

I passed through the entrance hall and walked toward the library. As I reached for the handle of the door, I heard glass shatter.

It was a distinct noise. Like someone had put a fist through one of the windowpanes on the French doors in the library. Exactly like that. I backed away and ran, fast and silent, for the kitchen.

The lockbox was on the table where I had left it, and I dove for it like a lifeline rope on a steep rock face. My fingers fumbled through the combination, my thumbs snapped the clasps, then my left hand searched desperately for the clip I knew was in the drawer under the phone, while my right snatched the weight of the gun into its grasp. I found the clip and almost dropped it trying to figure out which side was the front. I jammed the clip in with my palm and yanked the action back with that same hand, landing a round in the chamber, I hoped. It took seconds. It felt like forever.

"Slow down," I breathed. Trying to calm myself. Paley's parting words rang in my ears. "Damn him." My attention had been on loading the gun, away from the hall outside, and now I forced myself to be still, to focus. The pounding of my heart was back in my ears. I couldn't hear anything else. I shook my head and swallowed, trying to clear it. I heard nothing. I picked up the phone and dialed 911.

An operator answered crisply, if somewhat bored: "911 Emergency."

"There's someone in my house." My raspy whisper sounded stentorian in the big marble kitchen.

"Are they armed?"

"I don't know, I didn't stop to ask them." It seemed like a reasonable answer from my point of view.

"Police are on their way, please stay on the line."

She was efficient, I'll say that.

"Are you in a safe place now?" she asked.

"I'm in my kitchen behind my gun. That's the safest place I can think of," I answered. It was also the most casual way I could think of to let the cops know not to shoot the blonde with the pistol.

"You have a firearm?" she asked.

I was about to answer, when I heard footsteps across the marble foyer.

"Gotta go," I whispered. "Someone's coming." I had to hide and it would be a dead giveaway to leave a phone off the hook on the counter with a voice saying, "Are you there? Don't hang up," repeatedly.

"Don't hang up." I barely heard her as I placed the phone as quietly as I could in the receiver and willed myself to shrink into the little cubbyhole between the phone and the stove.

The door to the kitchen swung open. I could hear it creak and then freeze. Someone was holding it open, looking in. Then it squeaked closed again. Silence. Finally I heard footsteps moving back through the hall. Moving like a sloth on barbiturates, I leaned around the corner. The kitchen was empty. I tip-toed carefully to the door and got down on my hands and knees, looking through the half-inch crack underneath it. Just floor, no feet. I stood up again, and with my gun in front of me, I pushed open the door. Nothing. Empty shadowy entrance hall.

I was stunned. Part of me wanted to go hide in the laundry room until the police got there, the intelligent part of me. But there was something else in me, too. Anger. Rage at having my home violated. Furious indignation at the prospect of being a victim. Again! *Get out of my house!* The gall burned hotter and grew nastier inside of me, until it took over, shoving the timid, smart part of me roughly aside. Shoring me up with bravado and recklessness.

The library door was standing open now. I crossed carefully over to the edge of the jamb and peered in. Sure enough, the French door was open and the pane smashed out. Even in the limited watery light from the grounds outside, I could see that. The drawers of my desk had been gone through and some books pulled off the shelves.

Behind me, a noise on the stairs made me spin around and back defensively into the violated room. Someone was on the landing. I leaned my head against the doorway, straining to see around it.

Dammit, where are the police?

Whoever it was was now coming down the stairs. I was hoping they'd pick another room, praying they wouldn't be armed. The only light in the library was that eerie, undulating dim blue from the submerged pool lights outside. I pressed myself against the wall. They were definitely coming back through the office. They got to the doorway and stopped.

What is he doing?

I waited, pressing my mouth closed so that I would breathe silently through my nose. Then I heard it. Sirens. The police were coming up the street. I realized that the heavy iron gate across the driveway in the front would keep them at bay.

I've got to open the gate!

The intruder picked that moment to move. He ran forward, just inches to my left, heading for the open door. I could have tripped him easily if I had expected the move. But instead I pulled back, instinctively recoiling from the onrush. Oblivious to my presence, he moved intently across the room toward the desk and the open door beyond it. My anger frothed again. I steeled myself and dropped to one knee, shouting, "Freeze, right there."

What the fuck am I doing?

Too many episodic cop shows, I guess.

To my surprise, he did stop. It was a he. Definitely a male build, middle height, looked like dark hair in the dim light. He not only stopped, he stooped down on one side of my desk, which was just inside the French doors.

Great, he's taken cover, now what do I do?

I crouched down myself, wondering if I could get away with shouting "freeze, police."

And then he fired. Three quick, sharp cracks. I crawled to the doorway and got behind it. Either he was a really bad shot or he just meant to scare me. He didn't even seem to be aiming at me, but he was scaring me just fine. I leaned around the doorjamb, gun in front of me, just in time to see him rise up from behind the desk and bolt, straight out the door, then through the cypress trees.

I kept my sights trained on him and tightened my squeeze on the trigger, but I just couldn't shoot somebody in the back. Funny, the guy looked stockier crossing the lawn than he had when he came down the stairs. Less graceful. Panic will do that to some people, I guess.

Crossing quickly to the desk phone, I punched the gate button and then started around the desk to the light switches on the wall. Midstride my right foot hit something solid and I pitched forward, hitting my cheek on a side table. Even lying on the Persian carpet of my office in the semidarkness, I knew what was underneath my shins. I scrambled up and hit the lights, then stood for a long ten seconds facing the wall, reluctant to turn, to see what I knew was there.

10

I didn't touch it. It lay there until the cops came in, and I told them my story. They took my gun again. I sat anxiously in the kitchen, as more and more people arrived and took photos and sprinkled dust and ruined my Persian carpet even more thoroughly than the bloodstains would. I was slumped over with my head in my hands, trying not to wonder "why me?" when somebody spoke to me.

"Now, what did I tell you?" Detective Paley, of course.

"I didn't shoot him," I said, my hands muffling my words, and then I looked up.

"I'm inclined to believe you, since last time you told me you did." He was quiet for a minute, thinking. Then he stood up. "Mind if I make a pot of coffee?"

"Be my guest," I said sarcastically. "I'm afraid you'll have to find things by yourself. I don't come in here much."

"Ah yes. The staff." He started opening cupboard doors, and on his third try he struck Colombian gold. "Speaking of," he stood in one place and pivoted, seeking the coffeemaker, "where is that woman who works for you, your valet?"

"Butler. Deirdre. She's off Fridays; they're all off Friday. Night that is. They do work Friday day. It seems to be the most desirable night to go out. They are all off Sundays, too."

"Always?"

"Unless I'm entertaining, but I'm pretty lenient about that sort of thing. And it's nice not to trip over people in my underwear at least one day a week, if you know what I mean."

"I do. Help makes more work. No alarm was set?" he asked. Having located the coffeepot, he was filling it with tap water. I winced.

"There's filtered water from the little spigot on the right. No, I had just come in and I turned off the alarm inside the kitchen entrance. I hadn't reset it yet."

"But who could have known that?"

"I don't know. They must have seen me drive up, known I would have had to cut it off to get in."

"So they wanted you to be here?" he asked.

This hadn't occurred to me. "I guess that's why you get paid for this, huh?" This new thought disturbed me. "I just figured they wanted to rob me."

"Did you know the victim?" he asked.

"I haven't seen him yet, he was facedown and I was hesitant to flip him around, you know, scene of the crime, general distaste for nightmarish visuals, blood on my hands. The usual." God knows I didn't want to look. I'd seen one dead man. That was enough.

"Was anything taken?"

"I don't know. I've kind of been preoccupied. I haven't really taken inventory." I thought about it. "He wasn't carrying anything that I could see."

"Well, we've got two things to do: inventory and

identification." Paley turned back to the coffee, which was sputtering out its last bit of super-heated water, filling the air with a vitalizing aroma.

"Can we take our coffee?" I was hoping he'd say no, and we could put it off for a while, but I forgot he was a cop, used to bodies.

"Sure. You take milk?" My stomach reeled, and I had to put my head down again.

I refused the coffee but we went on a quick tour of the rooms I guessed the robber had been in and didn't turn up anything obviously missing. My jewelry seemed intact. Most of it was locked up anyway. The safe was untouched. The drawers by my bed had been gone through, as had my dresser. We went to the library last.

It was brightly lit now and a forensics team was finishing up. A woman in a white jacket was pulling rug fibers out of my ruined carpet. I felt like telling her to just take the whole bloody thing. But in view of the sanguine pun, I resisted. The body had been rolled onto its back, but the face was still turned away from me. I tightened my stomach muscles and bit my lip as we crossed toward it.

Paley and I walked around the desk, and when I saw the face, I sucked in a shocked hiss between my teeth.

"You know him," said Paley, watching me.

"Not exactly," I said. "But look at him, who does he look like?"

The detective turned and studied the face again. Meanwhile I couldn't stop glancing at the three dark holes in the man's chest. When Paley looked back to me, I knew he knew, but he wanted me to say.

"Give me a clue," he said steadily.

"Name a seventies sitcom about Archie and Edith," I said shakily, and then I had to turn away.

He nodded and muttered. "All in the Family."

Paley took one of the uniforms into the hall and spoke to him for a few moments. The marble of the entry hall amplified their soft voices to an insistent but indistinguishable muttering. Meanwhile, I tried not to listen to the sounds of lifting a heavy object, the crinkle of plastic and the grating sound of a zipper.

I was deeply absorbed in the gilded font of a book title, or I was trying to be, when Paley called me. I stumbled gratefully to the door and back to the kitchen. Now I accepted the coffee, with milk, folding myself protectively into the sofa in the seating area as I took a tentative sip from the hot mug. Paley sat, more self-assuredly, next to me. He sipped his coffee like an afterthought and concentrated on me.

"What's going on here?" he asked, his voice hard and direct.

"I saw him, this one, once. I think I did. At my stepfather's plant. On the loading dock. I thought I was just being paranoid, thinking they looked so much alike, that, I don't know, the man I killed was haunting me. Or . . . something, I don't know." My head was swirling like cheap spin art, the thoughts kept dribbling outward, all the clear colors turning to muddy brown. I took a couple of big gulps of hot coffee. The burn in my throat and the caffeine helped a little.

"Are you sure the man you saw on the loading dock was the man you saw in there tonight?"

"No, not absolutely, but it shouldn't be too hard to find out." I rubbed my fingers roughly over the skin around my eyes and slapped my cheeks a little. That helped, too. "Anyway, what would he be doing at the plant? The man I saw there seemed to be one of the dockworkers."

"Maybe he is, was," said Paley, in a still pitiless voice. "Why don't you tell me."

"Look," I said, getting my anger back, "I don't expect you to feel sorry for me. I don't know what's going on. I've got more interest than anybody in finding out. So if you could maybe drop the accusatory cop shit, I'll try to be as helpful I can." I wasn't sure I was making sense, but I had to lash out somehow.

"Just doing my accusatory cop job," he said.

I could have sworn he was amused.

"If you don't know him, maybe he knows you," he added in a more human tone.

At this point, the uniform Paley had talked to in the hall appeared at the door.

"Yeah?" Paley snapped.

"The prints match. The name is Luis Herado. Brother of Oswaldo Herado."

"Thanks J.D."

The uniform left. Paley sighed.

"That's the name of the guy I shot? Oswaldo?" Hearing the name chilled my gut. A name. A person. Somebody's baby.

"Long juvenile rap sheet. Gang member. Do you recognize either of those names?" he asked.

"No." I'm not good with names, but I'd never seen Oswaldo's face before. "Who would kill his brother, and in my house?"

He ignored my question, asking his own instead, "Do you go to the factory often?"

"Almost never, I haven't been there for six months."

"Well then, my first guess would be that the brother figured out who you were, probably after you put in your appearance at the plant and wanted revenge, but you got him first."

"I did not shoot that man," I interrupted angrily.

Paley's hand shot up to quiet me. "But, if there was a second man here and he shot his buddy, then either the second intruder, or somebody who hired him, had an interest in making it look like you finished their partner off." He sipped his coffee without seeming to notice. "Who?"

"I have no idea." My brain felt heavy and slow.

"Who would want you dead?"

"What? Nobody," I sputtered. "At least I hope not. There are a lot of people who'd like to get their hands on my father's money, which is now my money, but getting it is not as simple as killing me." Although that sounded about as complicated and final an action as I could contemplate.

"Who's in line to inherit after you?" Paley asked with the focus of a bird dog that has located the rustle in the reeds.

"Well, that's tricky. The government would get most of it. The relatives would fight over what was left, but it would take years." I flashed on Hervé's sebaceous face again. "Unless someone had legal paperwork, a will or letter postdating the current one."

"Do they?" He leaned in a little.

I sighed. Here was the other source of my exhaustion. "A few have claimed to. But nothing has stood up. They would need my father's legal signature and clear wording. All anyone has come up with are vague letters mentioning visits or job possibilities. It's dismal, how people behave. You wouldn't even believe it."

"Oh, I might," he said simply.

"Your family fight over the hidden millions?" I asked

meanly and regretted it immediately, but he didn't seem to notice my misplaced venom. Maybe he understood why I would lash out right about now and he was kind enough to ignore it. I hoped so, anyway.

"Oh no, we get along quite nicely, thanks for asking."

"No offense, but I don't think it's quite the same. I'm telling you people behave atrociously when there's money involved."

I had forgotten for a minute who I was talking to. He smiled at me with those eyes that have seen things that most people don't even want to think about and he said, "I've seen one man kill another over a pack of cigarettes, never mind millions."

"I'm talking about family," I said.

"So am I. They were brothers." He could easily have slotted in the word "animals." "Anyway, this is a little more than a pack of Parliaments," he said, gesturing to the trappings around him.

The uniform was back, standing in the doorway. "We're finished up here. We'll be going now."

"Right," said Paley. "Okay, I'll be a little while longer. Check to see that things are locked up, will you J.D?"

"Sure thing." J.D. disappeared again, his dark blue uniform blending perfectly into the hallway shadows.

"You have to go now, too?" I asked, suddenly aware of how empty the house was going to be.

"When will your people be back?" he asked.

"Tomorrow morning," I said. "Deirdre will, anyway. Most of them work on Saturdays, I think. They alternate, or something; Deirdre does the schedule."

He stood up and crossed over to the coffee. Then he turned and looked at me. From the hallway we heard a door close and then cars pulling out of the drive, taking the clutter and confusion with them. I could feel the sudden solitude like cool air in an open space. Paley still stood looking at me, thinking or feeling, I couldn't tell.

"I'll stay for a little while longer," he offered. Then he turned away a little too casually, "Unless there's someone else you'd like to call, someone besides me." He glanced back at me hopefully and I understood why he had asked. To hear me say I wanted him to stay instead of someone else.

"No. Nobody." I answered quickly, thinking that Ginny wasn't due back from her shoot until tomorrow. Suddenly, the kitchen felt cold and dark. "C'mon then." I stood up and had to stop myself from taking his hand. "I need something stronger than even your coffee."

The library being out of commission and the living room too large, we went upstairs and I made a fire in the sitting room of my bedroom suite. I poured myself a glass of cognac.

"Cognac?" I offered.

"I'm working here." He smiled.

"Why don't you just hold it so I don't feel like I'm drinking alone?" I splashed the gorgeous tawny liquid into a huge snifter and handed it to him.

He took it, passed it under his nose and savored the aroma. "Louis the Fourteenth. Nice." He set it down on the ledge in front of the fireplace, settling himself next to it. It surprised me that he was familiar with the brand, it was way out of a detective's price range yet he was cultured enough to know it and not be threatened or overly impressed. It pleased me.

I sat down on the floor a few feet from him with my back against a chaise, not wanting to be far from his protection, his calm and his presence.

"Aren't you going to ask me something?" I said, taking the first tentative sip of the very old cognac and loving the warm burn as it passed through me.

"Okay." He hadn't taken his eyes off me and he tilted his head to one side in a way that made his gaze more intent, more personal. "Why do you live alone?"

"Because my father died." I said and looked down into the liquid.

"Yes, so you've said. But that still doesn't explain why you live alone."

I looked at him. What the hell was he asking me? "Do you mean, why aren't I married, or have a boyfriend, or something?" I sounded bitter. I was disappointed in him.

"I mean, why don't you have anybody?" he asked simply, his eyes still on me.

I felt it come, the drowning uncontainable wave of loneliness. It swept up from inside me and choked me down. I hadn't realized it was so present, a lurking threat, until it leaped out at me, leaped out from me. I cried for a moment before I could push it back down, compose myself.

He made no move to comfort, or patronize me. He just waited, calmly, understanding. That had never happened before.

It was wonderful.

"I just miss him so much," I said finally, wiping my face. "I don't think I'll go into the whole pathetic story. I can't stand self-pity, anyway."

He smiled and it made me feel safe, not physically safe, but something more. "It's not self-pity to feel sad, even desperate, because we've lost someone."

"No, it isn't." It was a relief to say it, to know I was alone and to give myself permission to feel lonely.

"And it's not for anyone else to tell you that you

have no right to feel that way," he added softly.

I melted. The feeling of my cognac burning my throat was nothing compared to the warmth I felt from his simple statement.

"People see what they want to see," I said.

"I know," he answered. "I have a little bit of first-hand experience there." He picked up his glass and took a tiny sip; it was a peace offering.

I couldn't even imagine the side of humanity he must deal with everyday. But I nodded as though I could.

"This is delicious." He swirled his glass again and held it up to the fire. The light raced through the old wine and gilded his face. He turned his eyes back to mine and they were warmer than before.

"So, no more men in your life?" His eyes flicked away.

I smiled. He had let me back on top. How thoughtful. "Oh sure, lots, and none at all." I raised my glass to him and drank.

Then, as if to avoid embarrassment we started talking again about the shooting, about possibilities and suspects. It was all very businesslike, and yet there was a feeling in the room, like a humming from the floor and the walls. It was making me squirm.

I was watching the detective's blue eyes and his hands alternately. We were talking about me, about the crimes, but I kept thinking of how he looked, how he smelled, how he would feel. Finally I spoke my persistent thoughts. I always do sooner or later. It gets me in a lot of trouble.

"I wish this wasn't happening," I interrupted.

"Well, that's understandable," he said, but he looked at me with a question.

"No, I mean, I wish I would have met you another way." There. It was out.

He looked at me with a mysterious smile. "You do present a challenge to the working detective."

"What does that mean?" I asked.

"It means I find you almost unbearably attractive, but you are still technically a murder suspect. I'd take myself off the case but I don't think anyone else would find you less attractive," he said lightly.

I was watching his mouth as he spoke. And it was saying something else.

"But I wouldn't have to do this to them," I said and I crawled toward him, got up on my knees, leaned in and kissed him. The first touch was sure and enthusiastically met. It was a wonderful kiss, full, and felt much lower. He wrapped his arms around me and I had both hands in his hair. I let myself fall backward and he came with me, putting his gorgeous solid weight on top of me, and I felt again what I had felt in the elevator but now without restraint. I pressed up against him and he moved firmly down on me. We kissed a long time and our bodies moved easily against each other. Finally, he pulled his face away and looked down at me.

"I'd better go," he said.

"I'm glad we had this little chat," I added.

"Will you be okay?" he asked, sincerely concerned.

"Well, 'okay' is a relative term in my life these days." I was a little afraid. I didn't even have my gun. "But, I'll put the alarm on and have the security company put a car out front. I pay extra for that."

"Good, that makes me feel better." He kissed my mouth once more, firmly and quickly, and then he stood up. "I'll wait while you make that call."

I did that and brushed my teeth while he checked the house and all the locks. When he came back in, I was sitting on the end of the bed, dead tired. "Thanks," I said.

He stood in the doorway, watching me intensely. I wanted him to stay. I wanted it badly. He crossed slowly to me, leaned down and put his hand flat on my chest above my breasts. He just left it there for two long, full breaths and then he unbuttoned my blouse and took it off. Ever so gently he pushed me back on the bed and unfastened my jeans. I lifted my hips enough for him to pull them off. He did the same with my panties, sliding them slowly down over my legs. He stood up again and looked down at me, lying back with nothing but the firelight on my body. I waited for him to undress, to see him naked but instead he reached down and lifted me effortlessly. Moving me to the side of the bed, he threw back the sheets and laid me down again.

He stood up and looked at me for a long, slow, sexual moment. Then he came down on one knee next to the bed, kissed the nape of my neck, and moved down my body, never taking his lips from my skin. He breathed down to my left breast, kissed it firmly and then across to my right breast, another kiss, softer, more teasing. His hands joined his lips now, and they ran down my body, circling my waist and lifting me slightly to mold around my ass. His lips paused and pressed lingeringly on the inside of each thigh, just below my curly blond hair. His hands and his lips went all the way down the inside of my left leg and back up my right, pausing again for a kiss at each point that I most needed, most wanted. But only for a kiss before he covered me with the cotton sheets and the coverlet. Then he leaned in again, breathed "good night" in my ear and disappeared with the soft footfall of a thoughtful lover.

11

Your coffee, ma'am." She'd opened the drapes and I could see from the intensity of the sunlight that I had slept through the morning. It had to be late because Deirdre never woke me.

"What time is it?" I asked, sitting up.

"Noon. I hope I'm not wrong in thinking you would want to know that."

She crossed the room without looking at me and took my blue silk robe off the hanger in the closet. She was dying to know what had happened; she was stalling, waiting for me to fill her in.

"Everything okay downstairs?" I asked.

It was amazing how nonchalant she could be about taped-off police lines and blood on the Persian.

"Everything is under control, if that is what you mean. Detective Paley was inquiring, but he seemed intent that you not be disturbed." She looked at me for the first time, quickly, with one eyebrow slightly raised, and then she went on. "Mr. Hervé Tesauro deigned to wait."

"Yuck, lawyers in the foyer, it's enough to put me off my breakfast." I flopped back on the pillows and sighed.

"Did the good detective deign to leave?" I glanced at her with a smile.

"Apparently he needed sleep." She swished that eyebrow past me again but would never ask. "He and another detective spent some time looking over the grounds in the daylight."

"Did they find anything?" I sat up.

"Yes." She was picking up the clothes that Paley had littered the floor with last night and then, straightening up, she added, "Would you like breakfast in your room?"

"Deirdre." I was a little put out; I mean professionalism is one thing, but passive aggression is quite another. "What the hell did they find?"

"A gun." She stood looking at me, waiting for me to explain.

"I'll have two eggs over light, some turkey bacon and wheat toast, thanks."

She turned and left the room in a beeline of efficiency.

"Great, now she won't talk to me," I said to nobody and put on my robe as I went for my coffee.

I took it into the shower and put in on the little tile ledge. I washed my hair with my knees bent so that the shampoo wouldn't splash in my cappuccino. I do love that frothy foamy lift in the morning. Especially this morning. Afternoon. Whatever.

I dressed quickly, brushed my wet hair away from my face and went down the back stairs as the perfume of sautéing butter was floating up to meet me. My cook, Sophie, was sliding the perfectly cooked eggs onto a plate on a tray. Deirdre was putting a rose in a vase. Carmine, my housekeeper and Joseph, a handsome young apprentice butler of sorts, the other housekeeper, Toni, and the groundskeeper, David, were all having coffee after lunch. They started to get up when they saw me.

"Oh, sit down," I said with an exaggerated wave. "You're allowed to eat, for God's sake and I approve of massive caffeine consumption. You'll all work faster." I crossed over to the coffeemaker and got myself a clean mug. "Good morning, by the way."

A chorus of good mornings answered me.

I filled my cup, and Deirdre handed me the creamer. I turned and took a sip, leaning against the counter. I regarded all these people who took care of me and mine.

"I guess you're all wondering why I called you here today," I began. I hadn't, of course, but it seemed as good a start as any. "Sophie, I'll eat that down here, but first, I want to explain to you what's going on."

So I did. As best I could, anyway. I couldn't make a lot of sense out of it. I started with the attempted robbery-shooting a few days ago and the events of last night. I used the theory that Detective Paley had presented—that it was a brother who wanted revenge. I didn't want them to feel they were in danger any more than they needed to protect themselves. That was plenty. I stressed that I didn't shoot this brother, and I said that there would be a lot of inquiries, and that they, too, would be questioned.

"What should we say?" Toni asked.

"Just tell them the truth; they are far more likely to believe you," I said, remembering how that had helped me, so far. "If you can think of anything to help them, let them know. But I don't think any of you will be involved past that."

I turned to take the tray off the counter, then had an afterthought and faced them again.

"I'm sorry about all this. If any of you want to leave, I would understand." I really hoped they wouldn't.

They were quiet. These were really good jobs, benefits and everything. They didn't want to leave, but I got the feeling that the term grievous bodily harm was rolling around in their minds, and they were not eager to amend it into their job descriptions. Their faces looked gray, as though they'd been through the wash too many times, but nobody said anything.

"Well, you'll let me know later."

I tried to be flip, but I had to turn away too quickly to pull it off. Taking the tray, I went out into the dining room and sat at the huge table to eat alone. When Deirdre came in, I was almost finished.

"What's the scuttlebutt downstairs?" I asked.

"No one seems inclined to terminate their employment. More coffee?" She was pleased that I had filled them all in, and her voice was kinder now.

"No thanks. I've got to go deal with ol' sweaty face. You might have a glass of water and couple of Alka Seltzer ready for me, though."

I was only half kidding. I've known a couple of nice, decent lawyers in my day, but Hervé definitely was not one of that rarefied species. He was the kind with a voracious appetite for legal turmoil, a taste I didn't share. My stomach went sour on that particular diet.

I walked into the sitting room. It was empty. That snooping son of a bitch. I went straight to the library, where I knew I'd find him. Sure enough, there he was, having pulled the "Do not cross, Police" neon yellow tape off the door to go in. I just shook my head and watched him snoop. I picked up one tendril of the tape that was now loosely swinging and called to him.

"I guess you didn't see this Day-Glo police order here. Too subtle?" I watched as his head snapped up on his fat neck. "I do the same thing with those 'Danger, bridge out' signs and the pylons in the road. Sometimes I drive right through 'em."

"I'm so sorry." He oozed insincerity. "But I was curious. I almost became a criminal lawyer."

It physically hurt me not to say, "Instead of a criminal?" but I endured. "Hervé, get out of there."

He hurried over like the guilty dog he was and followed me back into the sitting room. When I had thrown myself on the settee and crossed my arms, he sat in an armchair and tried to look sympathetic.

"You want to tell me about it?" he gurgled.

I swear, I could see a trail of slime across the floor he'd just passed.

"No. Why are you here?"

He sighed, ever the wounded martyr. "As your father's attorney I wish you would trust me more . . ."

I cut him off. "Your *father* was my father's attorney, not you." I had wanted to say this for a long time, and I was finally frayed enough to do it and not care. "It's only by some freak of law that your father died first, giving you his law firm, and my father died before he got a chance to pick a new firm. I'm stuck with you. I didn't choose you, and neither did my father. Now say what you came to say."

"You have a sibling." His eyes grew even meaner.

"His name is Binford, and he really dislikes me," I said coldly, "and I'm sorry for that." I meant it.

That smarmy, pseudo-apologetic smile appeared as though suddenly smeared across his face. "Not Binford."

In spite of my confidence, a little pit of fear opened

darkly before me, and I stepped across it. "Not Binford. Who?"

"A girl. She lives in Alabama. Nineteen, name of Sabrina Valley. Her lawyers contacted me this morning. They have documentation."

"Even if it were true, it has nothing to do with me. The will clearly states that I get the estate, all of it; she's legally an adult, she has no claim!" I was trying to keep my hysteria from rising.

He opened his briefcase like the pettifogging lawyer he was. He pulled out a single sheet of paper and handed it to me.

The pit appeared again between us, and I had to reach across it to take the document.

It was a letter, or a Xerox of one, to a person named Sabrina Valley. I was stunned to see Hervé's firm listed on the letterhead. It seemed to imply that his father or one of the other legal partners had drawn it up. It stated in a few lines that if anything happened to him, my father wanted her to have twenty million dollars. Cash. It postdated the will and at the bottom of the page, underneath a typed version of the same, was my father's unique signature.

"Is there an original version?" I asked, shaken.

"I saw it this morning. They are reluctant to give it up." He could barely veil his excitement. This would really draw things out and up my bill.

"If your firm drafted this, wouldn't there be a copy in your files?"

"I'm having that checked now." He tried to appear concerned.

"And?" I was impatient.

"Nothing yet."

"Well, isn't that interesting?" I dripped. "The original will have to be analyzed by a third party before I'll even consider fighting it." I was getting my indignation back. "This would appear to be a conflict of interest on your part Hervé, since it seems your firm drew up the letter."

"I only have your best interests at heart, Cally." He tried for a wounded look, opening his eyes and letting his jaw hang slack a little, but it just made him look more amphibious.

"Nonetheless, I think it's a good idea that I get someone else who has no one *else's* best interests at heart, too." I smiled my glacial smile now.

"You can't fire me, Cally." He looked a little more nervous than usual.

"Technically, no. I'll still have to pay you a retainer. But I *can* hire someone else." I stood up, eager to be rid of his physical presence.

"Fine." He was truly insulted. Aw, too bad. He took the Xerox from my hand and put it in his briefcase. "You'll be hearing from me."

"And you'll be hearing from my new lawyers. No hard feelings, huh, Hervé?" I extended my hand. He shook it, confused that I should be so nice.

"Good-bye," he said, tight-lipped, his feelings hurt. And they talk about a woman scorned.

"Oh, one more thing," I said sweetly. He stopped and turned back. "If this thing is a fake, which I think it is, and I find out you had anything to do with it," I let it hang while I spotted an imaginary snag in my fingernail, then I looked up at him and stabbed, "I'll ruin you."

He drew himself up and said in his best legal parlance, "Be careful, or you'll be liable for defamation of character."

I laughed; that was rich. "You can't sue me for slander if it's true. Good-bye."

He turned and slunk out. I left the room after him and walked boldly into the library. I was afraid to face that room, but sometimes if you behave bravely, your emotions will follow. Maybe there isn't a difference between feeling brave and acting bravely. It was worth a try anyway.

I managed to be heroic until I saw the bloodstains. They made me look away quickly and mutter to myself aloud, "you can do it, nothing to it." I stepped around the other way and rummaged in a drawer until I came up with the card Detective Paley had given me that first enchanted evening. I studied it, an office number, and bingo, a pager.

I left the office to find another phone. It was a lovely day outside and I needed the air, so I headed to the pool cabana. I dialed and then punched in my private line number. While I was waiting for the phone to ring I changed into a bikini and let my body collapse on a terry cloth-covered deck chair. When the intercom buzzed I turned my head to the phone but didn't sit up.

"Yes Deirdre?"

"Would you like anything?"

"I'd like a large bottle of scotch and a couple hundred milligrams of methaqualone."

There was no response, just polite static silence punctuated by well-mannered patience.

"Please?" I added.

Still, hissed silence.

"Okay," I said. "I'll take a couple of Advil and a Perrier."

"Very good," she said. I think she'd been watching BBC again.

Two seconds later, the private line buzzed.

"Hi there," I said nonchalantly after leaping out of my deck chair, afraid it wouldn't buzz twice.

"This is Detective Paley, returning a page," he said, unsure.

"This is your favorite murder suspect," I said, then added, "at least, I hope I'm your favorite."

"Hello. Get some sleep?" He asked, dropping his voice to a delightfully gruff level that I thought had a note of nostalgia in it.

"Oh, yeah. I heard you found a gun."

There was a slight pause and then he spoke, "Would it be all right if I dropped by?"

"Detective, on your day off?" I teased.

"You remembered, how sweet," he parried beautifully.

"Saturday is my day off, too. Oh, so is the rest of the week."

"Convenient. I'll stop by in a few hours, if that's okay."

"And do plan to stay for dinner." I tried to sound friendly, but it came out rather seductive.

There was another pause. "I don't mean to be presumptuous, but we need to clear some things up before we get social. I mean, if we were going to get social, which is, of course, up to you." He was not actually stuttering, but he came charmingly close enough to make the last part of his statement true.

"If it's up to me, then I say, you've gotta eat." I chuckled and he said nothing. "See you soon."

"Bye."

I hung up and buzzed Deirdre.

"Yes, ma'am?"

"Make that a sangria and three Advil, Deirdre. Thanks." I tapped the intercom off and immersed my tingling ganglia of a body into the pool.

12

His blue eyes looked even better with jeans and a linen jacket. I asked him if he wanted to take the jacket off, but he smiled and declined. I guess it's best not to be sporting a gun in an oxford button-up.

"How about a beer? Don't say you're working," I warned as we sat down in the shade of the cabana. Deirdre was still hovering, waiting for just such a request.

"Okay, I will, and I won't." He turned and smiled at Deirdre. "A beer please. I'm not working."

She allowed herself a polite smile and a nod. "Ale, red, stout or hefeweizen?" she asked, one-upping as usual.

"What's on tap?" he asked dryly. God, I liked him.

"Unfortunately, none of them."

She liked him, too. I could tell.

"Okay, make it a hefeweizen. Thanks." He turned to me, bemused as she shimmered off into the bright sunshine toward the house. "How do you like living this way?" It was straightforward.

"It doesn't suck," I said. We both smiled, and then I added, "It'd be pretty ungrateful of me to complain about it."

"But sometimes you do?" he asked.

"Well, everything has its price, even money. Why, just this morning I added another person to the list of those who no longer, shall we say, wish me well."

I put my feet up on the ottoman so they'd be a little closer to him. He looked at them and then followed the trail of my body up to my eyes.

"Is it a long list?" That pesky, professional note crept into his voice.

"It's a long list of people who've tried to get my money and have lost." I waved a hand and relaxed deeper into my chair. "So few people lose gracefully."

"Someone did not emerge victorious this morning?"

A shadow fell across my mood, and, I'm sure, my face. "This race is still on. I fired my lawyer. Which reminds me, know any really good inheritance lawyers?" Sarcastic maybe, but I said it with a laugh.

"As a matter of fact, smart-ass, I do." He pulled his jacket away from his breast, giving me just a glimpse of that leather shoulder harness, and took a small address book from his breast pocket.

"Really? Detective Paley, are you a closet heir apparent?"

His turn to laugh sarcastically. "Here's the number."

He picked up a little pad by the phone and jotted down the name of a firm, an individual and a number.

"Why do you recommend them?" I asked, a bit wary of a lawyer recommended by someone making a detective's salary. I'm not a snob, just a realist.

"Her. Recommend her. She's the only lawyer I've ever heard say a case was taking too much time."

"She's hired."

We smiled again, and Deirdre returned with the beer in a frosted glass on the rim of which a slice of lemon dribbled a tarty trail. Whoever said good help is hard to find has never been to my house. I watched Paley take an appreciative sip, and waited a polite few seconds for him to settle back in the oversize wicker armchair.

"And I believe you have some news for me," I said, inviting him to get through the business.

"Yeah." He sat up and leaned toward me a little, but he didn't look at me. "We found a gun, as you've already told me. It was just inside the wall by the street. Someone either dropped it climbing over, or threw it there to get rid of it, or wanted us to find it. They're running tests now. It looks like the gun that killed Luis Herado." He picked up his beer and took another drink.

"So you know I didn't kill him," I said because he hadn't, and I really felt this was a sticky point.

"You mean, was it your gun?"

"Well, it wasn't. You've got my gun. There are no other guns registered to me." I knew I sounded sophomoric, but my understanding on this was shaky.

"No, it wasn't registered to you." He looked at me now. "But it was registered."

"To whom?" I asked.

"To your father," he said and looked at me steadily.

I, on the other hand, was anything but steady. In fact, the view of the pool before me fluttered like a mirage in a bad movie. My comprehension was hanging by a thread, and that fragile, single strand was fraying.

"I had all my father's guns, most of them were antiques, they were all catalogued and the applicable registrations transferred to me. I sold them to a collector." I didn't know what else to say.

"Nope, you missed one. It's a very old registration."

"So, it's logical that I never even had it. I mean; I

reregistered everything to my name, two years ago. It just makes sense that I didn't even know about that gun."

He sighed deeply and reached for the beer again. "I have to allow for the possibility that you did. It's my job. But I do believe what you told me, about a second intruder, *and* knowing the gang history of both of the deceased it makes sense that the brother would try to take you out. Eye for an eye is pretty much the standard street mentality. So, even if you did shoot him," I opened my mouth but he held up a hand and went on quickly, "which I don't think you did, he broke into your house, and you legally had every right to defend yourself. So, it's really a moot point."

He leaned back again and took a longer drink of beer, watching me with more pleasure now, "Unless of course, you knew him."

"I didn't," I said coldly.

"Okay then," he said quickly and affably, "I didn't really think you swam in the same circles." His finger reached out and followed a drip of condensation as it crept down his frosty glass. "There is one other interesting point."

"Oh God, what now?" My stomach was churning already.

"The coroner thinks something was taken out of his hand after he was dead."

"Really?" I wondered how they knew these things. "Like what, a gun?"

"No, something smaller, we don't know what, but there was ink all over the inside of his fingers. The second intruder, the one who got away, either wanted it badly enough to stop and get it from a dead man. Or . . ."

"Or what?" I leaned in.

"Or, the second intruder was already crouched behind the desk and when intruder one met up with him, he shot him."

"Who shot whom?" I asked, relieved it wasn't me.

"Intruder one did the stealing, and intruder two shot one and took the . . . whatever it was. Then two made a dash for it while you were doing your Charlie's Angels impression."

"I resent that."

He didn't even try to hide his amusement. "You told me you yelled 'freeze.' "

"I never flipped my hair!" I said, using my finger to accentuate my point. "Maybe his pen leaked."

"Nope, wasn't on his fingertips; it was in here." He pointed at the inside crease of his cupped fingers. He looked away for a minute, thinking. "Whatever it is, Ms. Wilde, somebody wanted it, and they want the whole scenario to look bad for you."

"First of all my name is Callaway, friends call me Cally."

"What should I call you?" He smiled.

"Anything but guilty." I smiled back. "I wish I could think of something to help you, Detective Paley." I exaggerated the name.

"Evan. My friends call me Evan."

"What should I call you?" I smiled.

"Eager to finish this case." He raised the glass to his mouth and finished off the beer.

We talked of this and that, nothing and everything until dinner was announced. Deirdre had bypassed the dining room and set a lovely table for two in the breakfast room. That room was one of my favorites and over soup we had a chance to really enjoy the light illuminating the stained-glass windows. By the time the mousse and cognac arrived we had mellowed with the sun into a warm, glowing mass.

We'd exhausted the subject of the shootings, and it had exhausted us, so we gave it up before the fish course. I noted with satisfaction that he had used all the right silverware and hadn't been intimidated by the two-butler service. Someone had trained him well.

"Tell me about yourself," I said.

"What do you want to know?" he asked.

"Where'd you learn your table manners?" I teased him.

"My father was a sort of ambassador. I traveled a lot as a kid."

"Ambassador to what?" I asked.

He smiled and reached across to take my hand. "Many things."

I let him take my hand in both of his and trail his fingers lightly across the inside of my wrist. Then he sighed deeply and released it.

"Still holding to that noble notion of not getting involved?" I asked.

"I don't know how noble I've been."

"Tell me *something* about yourself. Did you always want to be a detective?" I asked, sipping cognac.

He sat back and sighed again. "Yes."

"Why?" I asked. "No wait, don't tell me. Let's change rooms." I arched my eyebrows playfully, he looked at me reproachfully, but he rose and, taking his glass, he followed.

"I usually like to go to the library and read by a fire this time of night, but it's in a bit of disarray," I said pointedly.

"I think you can go ahead and rearray it." He smiled

and we went up the stairs, through my bedroom onto the veranda.

We leaned forward against the balcony with our cognac in our hands and looked out over the glistening city. I wrapped my arms around myself and Paley looked at me. He took our crystal snifters and balanced them precariously on the balustrade. Then he took off his jacket, revealing his gun in a shoulder harness. In a deeply female place it flipped a switch; it turned me on, this strong man with a lethal weapon. Of course, at this point if he had been packing a water pistol, I probably would have gotten wet. He draped his jacket over my shoulders. I snuggled into it.

He didn't move away from me. And he didn't touch me, either. Just stood close. I waited.

He was behind me and I felt his fingers touch my waist. Not holding, just touching lightly. Ever so slowly, he ran his hands up the outline of my body. When he got to my shoulders he turned me around. Then, sinking both his hands in my hair at the nape of my neck, he kissed me hard. I hadn't yet touched him, and before I could dislodge my arms from the jacket, he turned me and dropped down to his knees. Leaning me back against the stone, he unfastened the top metal fastener of my jeans and loosening them, he pushed them down my legs to the ground. I stepped out of them and kicked them away as he slid his fingers inside my panties and grasping my ass firmly in the palms of his hands, pulled me against his face. His mouth kissed the front of my silk underwear but his warm breath passed through and heated my skin.

In a quick hungry movement he twisted one hand in the fragile fabric and ripped it away. His mouth explored the soft smoothness of my inner thighs while his tongue grew more insistent. My fingers sank into his thick hair and I pulled his face harder up against me, moving my hips in a slow circular motion. I threw my head back and, through my half-closed eyes, the flickering lights of L.A. blurred ecstatically out of focus and then steadied again. My legs were shaking when his face came back up to mine.

He put his arms around me and pressed hard against me. His hardness was getting to be a familiar feeling. I tried to move my hands to him, but he took both my wrists and pulled them around behind my back, pinning me up against him. We swayed and kissed for a moment.

"I have to go," he said.

"Why?!" I was aching now, and I was angry that he could walk away from me.

"Because otherwise, I'll stay," he said. He turned me around again. Using both hands to push my hair up, he kissed the back of my neck. "Good night, Cally."

I leaned against him, and then he walked away. He was in the doorway when I stopped him.

"Evan," I said in a quiet tone. It sounded strange. Evan.

"Yes?" He turned, blue eyes burning.

"Don't stay away too long." I wanted him to know I wouldn't wait, that I wasn't to be toyed with.

An expression flashed across his face that dared me to test him, that called my bluff. "Too long?" He met my challenge and upped the ante. "How long would that be?" Arching an unruffled eyebrow he left me, standing alone, unsure of who had the upper hand.

Goddamn, he was good.

13

The lawyer Evan had recommended was good, too. Dana Scheiner, of Scheiner, Myers and Alexander, was so busy that she had to shut off her phone to pay attention to me. She was pretty with shiny black hair stylishly cut, aggressive, feminine and multifaceted. She focused hard and bright on what I told her, asked smart questions and didn't waste one minute of her valuable, and expensive, time. I loved her.

"Now, what about your will?" she asked me when we were through discussing my father's.

"I don't have one." It was uncomfortable to have to think about it. "Why? Are you telling me I'm not immortal? Honestly, I don't think I can deal with that right at the moment." I had put this off before; I was going to live for a long time yet, wasn't I?

"It's a good idea to get things in order." She smiled ruefully, "I'll draw up a basic and we can meet again when you're ready to fill in all the details. There are lots of options."

I was relieved. My immediate demise was something I was trying not to think about these days. But before I left there was one thing I needed to know.

"How do you know Evan Paley?" I asked and was surprised to feel a little twinge of jealousy as I watched her cross her slim, stockinged legs under her Armani skirt.

"He's a client." She smiled at me, a nice smile, very intelligent. I guessed that was all she could say.

"Ongoing?" I pushed.

"Many of our estate-planning clients are lifetime clients. We often are involved in management of the trusts, etceteras, after the client is deceased."

"What kind of estate does a detective have?" I tried to sound casual, not really that interested, but she was, as I said, sharp.

One eyebrow went up about as high as I imagine her IQ must be. And the question in her eyes lasted as long as it took her to figure the answer, about a nanosecond: I was more than casually interested in him.

"I'm afraid, of course, that I can't say anything about another client's situation. I would call that an indiscretion." She didn't patronize. I really liked her now.

"Well, I wouldn't want you saying anything about mine to anyone else, so I'll call it a virtue." I couldn't stop there though, could I? "So, do you know him socially, as well?" I'm not positive, but I don't think I could have been any more transparent.

She smiled and made it perfectly clear. "Not anymore." I stood to cover the freeze I felt on my face. There didn't seem to be anything else to do, businesswise, until I got files over to her. "Thank you so much for taking me on." I held out my hand and as she extended hers I noticed her watch, a Breitling, the smaller gold version of the one Evan wore. We shook, her hand was firm and sure. I thought about that hand on Evan, I didn't like it one bit.

"I'm pleased to be working with you. We'll get these matters settled as quickly as possible." She referred to a yellow legal pad on which she'd been taking notes. "I'll need to get a copy of Sabrina Valley's claim as soon as possible."

"I was going to send for the files, but since I'm downtown I may go over and pick them up myself." I grimaced at the thought of facing Hervé again, but maybe I could just sneak in and out. "In that case I'll get them to you by tomorrow morning."

"That would be great. Nice meeting you." She moved to the door and opened it, and when someone says it was nice to meet you and they're standing at the door, it's time to leave.

I decided against moving my car from one subterranean parking lot to another two blocks away. I was hoping the walk would clear my head; my thoughts were dark and my mood darker.

As I walked my worries tripped over each other in an effort to get my attention. I tried giving them a good airing but it was like cleaning out a basement by moving everything into your living room. Try as I might, I couldn't seem to find the bright side.

Not caring if it was babyish or irrational, I was pissed to think that my new lawyer had gotten more intimate with Evan than I had. *I'll bet he fucked her right away.* I geared myself up to hold it against him that he thought she was irresistible and I, obviously, wasn't. That done, I moved on to the next depressing feeling: holding up the world alone.

Working with my father, I had had a mentor I could trust, an ally. I had spent the last two years learning to run his businesses, no small task even for someone with a magna cum laude degree in business like myself. The day he died the sharks had started to circle, and I had turned to fight them off without his encouraging smile, his knowing proud look that told me I was making the right decision. I had had to prove myself to every board member at every company, and every single one of them, with the exception of Bill, had tried to benefit from my inexperience. Bad behavior and dirty tricks were part of the game and my father had showed me how to play it, but what was depressing was that there didn't seem to be *anyone* left in the game who was trustworthy or decent. The reason for that was simple, everyone was out for themselves. *Fuckers.*

And speaking of ugly relationships, it seemed that every person who could claim a drop of my blood was after my money to the point that my life was bogged down with lawyers and semantics and the parties of the second part; even my own mother was trying to rip a hole in every well-crafted legal document. *Piranha.*

It was hard enough facing the struggle by myself, but the idea of struggling through to victories with no one to share them left a bitter, sooty taste in my mouth.

Scowling, I neared the end of my self-pitying stroll. As I approached the door of my destination I passed a gathering of homeless men sharing a bottle on the sidewalk. One of them cheerfully rushed to open the glass door for me, smiling toothlessly as he said, "Have a nice day, pretty lady."

The perspective check was much needed. I smiled back at him gratefully. "Thank you so much, sir." And I meant it, more than he knew.

Twenty-two floors above, the offices of Tesauro, Erikson and Nash were climate controlled and aesthetically pleasing to the eye with cream carpet, bleached wood accents, and tan leather sectional sofas in the waiting area. Beyond the attractive receptionist was a glassed-in conference room with a twenty-foot table and a view of the mountains to the north. It was all designed to make you beg them to take your four hundred and fifty bucks an hour.

I asked to speak to someone in records, explaining in a quiet voice that the atmosphere of reverence dictated, that I needed my files. The office manager, a serious-looking woman with a deep attachment to lip liner, introduced herself and inquired nervously why that could possibly be necessary. I briefly confirmed her worst fear; I was changing law firms, which she seemed to take personally by sniffing at me as though I wasn't worthy of them anyway. She testily proclaimed that it would take several hours to make all the necessary copies.

"Fine," I said. "Just make sure I get the originals."

I told her I'd send a messenger for them later and she said I'd have to settle up on my bill. I said I'd expected as much, and if she'd take a look at the obscene amount I paid them on a monthly retainer, added up the hours of work that had actually been done, and figured out what they owed me, she could write me a check at her earliest convenience. That shut her up.

Down the hall something snagged my eye. Something familiar. I turned and looked full on at my mother. When she laid eyes on me, she actually froze midstride and then continued the step as though it had never been interrupted. It was almost as if she was caught for a split second in the ray of a stun gun, and the effect was comical. I almost laughed out loud, but Rudy never found jokes about herself amusing.

She walked toward me, and I leaned against the counter and watched her approach.

"Hello Callaway." She smiled tightly at me.

"Hello Rudy, what are you doing here?"

"Going over some business with Hervé." She dared me to ask what business, and since I didn't, she added, "He doesn't just handle your estate, you know."

"You mean he doesn't *even* handle my estate," I said. Her eyebrows went up but I continued. "C'mon, I'll ride down in the elevator with you."

We waited for the elevator in silence. I couldn't remember if it had always been this uncomfortable with her. I hoped not.

"So, how you doing?" I said as we moved into the elevator.

"I've been better." Rudy sighed as she reached into her purse for a compact. She opened it, rotated her head in a small circle to see all of her face, and then snapped the lid shut with a resigned bitterness.

"That kind of sums it all up, doesn't it?" I muttered, turning to watch the numbers light up.

"What do you mean by that?"

"Just a life philosophy. I'm sorry, I don't want to get into it."

"I heard you saw Bill," she said after a minute.

"And Binford. My, he's a strapping lad." I smiled at her, my attempt at a joke. She didn't get it.

"He's a grown man," she said simply.

"I know, Mom." She was sapping my strength.

"By the way, we're having a birthday party for him at the house Saturday. Why don't you come?" She turned and smiled at me.

"Excuse me?" I was truly taken aback. Where the hell

did this come from? I usually got the perfunctory embossed invitation to major family functions, but a note and a gift usually made up for my absence at the more intimate gatherings.

"He's your brother. Surely you could come. After all, we are family."

"Are you going to slip me a mickey and get me to sign something?" I joked, and to my shock and surprise, she burst into tears.

We reached the lobby and the doors slid open. Since there was no one waiting to get on, I pushed the penthouse button and they closed again. When they had sealed I turned to her.

"What's going on?"

She had taken a linen handkerchief out of her purse and was dabbing her eyes, taking deep breaths trying to calm herself. She rolled her eyes to the ceiling to carefully cleanse any mascara that might have misplaced itself before she spoke.

"I'm tired of this. I'm tired of fighting with you. I'm tired of fighting for everyone else, I just want a little peace," she said, as though it were all my fault.

"Rudy . . . Mom, there isn't anything to fight about. I've been telling you that for years."

The elevator door opened again, and two numb-faced men in suits looked at the directional arrows. Up, not down. They didn't move. The doors closed.

"I don't expect you to understand, Cally. You've got everything." She blotted again and then put her handkerchief away. She was finished crying.

I felt badly. I had never meant to be mean, but so often the hurt I felt backlashed through my smart-ass mouth.

I softened, "All right. I'll come. I told you before, I like Binford; I just don't think he likes me very much."

"Don't be ridiculous," she said with finality. I bit my lip; maybe it wasn't as obvious as I thought. Did she really think he cared for me? I doubted it, but though I didn't say so, I knew I might sometimes, possibly, maybe, be a little jaded. Probably not though. I might be cynical but I wasn't stupid.

When we reached the top floor, the doors slid open and she punched the lobby button angrily with a click of her acrylic nail. A few floors down, we picked up the suits and rode to the lobby in silence. Once we were in the lobby she turned toward the parking elevators as I turned to the street doors. Rudy looked at me in surprise.

"Aren't you parked downstairs?" she asked.

"No, actually I walked over from another building." I knew that would throw her. "Well, I guess I'll see you Saturday. You might want to warn Binford that I'm coming." I winked.

She nodded. "I'm sure he'll be delighted to see you," and then whispered conspiratorially, "especially if you buy him something really nice." Then she smiled and went regally on her way.

Just when I think she can't get any worse.

14

The next morning, Deirdre woke me up again—this time with a phone call from Dana, the gorgeous, brilliant, successful lawyer who was probably Evan's ex. Hopefully his ex. Taking the phone, I thought, if I really use my imagination maybe I could come up with something about her that would make me feel better, like, she snorted when she laughed, or *something*.

"Good morning," she said in her crisp, efficient way. "I wanted to let you know they sent over your files. You seem to have received a plague's share of contentions. I also got an analysis of the Sabrina Valley letter. Everything looks authentic, with one little tick."

"And that would be?" I was hopeful.

"The signature is a stamp. Your father would have had a legal stamp for documents and checks, of course. He couldn't possibly have signed everything personally. But it seems curious."

"It seems suspicious to me," I responded. "Why the hell would he write such an important and personal letter, and then let someone else stamp his name?"

"Who had access to the stamp?" she was asking before I finished musing.

"Evan was right, you don't dick around," I said, "no pun intended." I wasn't as microscopically focused as she was, so I thought, charge me for the time. "His personal secretary, a woman by the name of Fiona Laasko."

"Yes, I saw her name in the will, your father bequeathed her an annual stipend."

"Enough to retire on; she earned it," I told her.

"We'd better look her up. Interesting name, Laasko. Swedish?"

"Finnish. When she closed up his personal office, the stamp came to me."

"So you have it now?" she asked. When it came to directness she was a legal wormhole through the time-jargon continuum.

"Yes. I don't know exactly where. There were so many things to do when . . . at that time." I didn't want to think about it. "I threw it in a drawer somewhere. I figured it wasn't effective after his death."

"And dead men don't sign documents," she said.

I felt the mixture I always feel when I deal with my father's loss and his business at the same time, a combination of indignation at having to speak so casually of the death of my father and a resignation that sometimes it couldn't be avoided.

I drew a deep breath before I answered. "No, they don't."

"In this case though, I think you'd better hope he did." She rustled some papers. "We can always find out if they'll settle without a fight."

"Would you?" I asked.

"Ask, or settle?"

"Settle."

"No," she said, "not if this is as fake as it looks."

"Then fight, fight, fight," I said.

"We need to get you in to fill in the details of your will. I've drawn up the rough draft, but you've got to give me a good amount of information to finish it."

"Oh, well, it's going to be a couple of weeks before I get to that." I said good-bye and hung up, then made a mental note to find that damn stamp and burn it.

I got dressed and decided it was time to pay Fiona a little visit and find out what she knew about the stamp and the impending sibling. She lived in a condo in Westwood, and I thought I'd drop by to chat about old times. Needing some moral support, I waited until Ginny was back from her shoot, and bribed her with a gourmet lunch if she'd go with me. I could have just told her that I was feeling bruised inside and needed help and of course she would have come. The lunch was a cover that made it easier for me to accept her support; we both knew that.

I gave my name to the doorman and he sent us right up to the tenth floor. Fiona opened the door, looking as if she were expecting visitors but surprised that it was us. She was an attractive older woman. Great cheekbones, those Finns. Short blond hair with streaks of silver showing through. She covered her surprise with a bright smile and expressive volume in her greeting.

"Cally, how wonderful to see you. And you, too, Virginia, it's been a long time. You look terrific!" Ginny returned the compliment, which was honest enough, and then Fiona put her hand on my arm and dropped her tone to one of concern. "How are you, are you doing all right? I know you still miss your father. Of course, we all miss him. But it will get easier, in time."

She had a real catch in her voice. I knew she felt the loss, too. We crossed the foyer into the living room and I was not surprised that it was furnished in the sparse style preferred by so many of her Finnish countrymen. I sat on a red sofa beneath a textile print.

"How are you, Fiona?" I asked sincerely. She had been at my father's side for as long as I could remember.

"I'm doing fine, thank you. I just returned from a trip to visit my family."

"Oh, I didn't know you'd gone to Finland."

She smiled vaguely and didn't seem to want to pursue the subject because she moved on. "Can I get you anything?"

I looked to Ginny who shrugged her shoulders, letting me take the lead. "No, thank you, we're on our way out to lunch," I explained.

"She's taking me to Pink's for a hot dog," Ginny threw in.

"You better be nice, or I will," I scolded.

"You better be nice, or I'll order chili." She folded her arms and sat back on the sofa.

Appealing to Fiona I asked, "Do you see how mean she is to me?" Fiona smiled indulgently; she remembered my "friends" before I met Ginny, a nasty lot.

"I'm glad to see both of you," Fiona said, including Ginny in her smile. "I'm a little surprised though, is there something I can do for you?"

"I wanted to stop by to ask you a few questions. I hope that's okay," I opened.

She seemed to tense a little. "What questions?" she asked. "Is something wrong?"

"Well, it could be." I tried to look casual. "Do you remember my father ever mentioning another daughter?"

Ginny smacked the sofa with one of her hands and touched my leg with the other in a compassionate gesture. I ignored her because I was watching Fiona, who blanched visibly.

"I know it sounds crazy, but there is a girl, woman, from Alabama claiming to have a letter from my father legitimizing her and an inheritance, and it's going to cause me a lot of headache, or a lot of money." I considered. "Or both."

She was fiddling, avoiding my eyes. It was making me nervous. "Cally," she said at last, "I can't really discuss any of your father's business with you. He didn't ever involve me in his personal affairs anyway. There were quite a few dealings in which I was not included, or needed." She looked at Ginny nervously. So did I, needing support. But Ginny's eyes were riveted on Fiona; like myself, she was sensing a threat.

"Are you saying, 'yes'?" I asked Fiona, incredulous.

"No, I'm not. I'm saying I can't get involved in anything. It was seen to legally, years ago, that I could never disclose any details of transactions or business dealings, *ever*. I'm sorry." She looked at me and then added, "I'm sorry for any problems that causes you. I don't mean to hurt you, Cally."

"No. I know you don't. But maybe you could answer one question for me," I said, and she regarded me steadily.

"I'll try."

"Did anyone except you have access to Dad's signature stamp?"

"Your father did. And occasionally someone in the lawyer's office, if there was a backup of paperwork. But everything had to be final-approved by me or your father."

"Are you sure?" I asked.

"Well, that was the rule." She wrinkled her brow, thinking back. "There was a period of several months when I took a sabbatical to visit my family, but other than that, to my knowledge, that's the way it always worked." She looked at me directly with almost a challenge.

I didn't want to question her integrity or the value of her loyalty and her work, so I let it drop for now and I stood to go.

"Thank you, Fiona. I hope I didn't make you uncomfortable, but you are the only one who I thought might know about the signature stamp at least."

"Of course. It's always nice to see you. You, too, Virginia, how's your work?" she asked as we moved to the door.

"Oh, you know, same old nine to five."

Fiona laughed and opened the door for us and then spontaneously she hugged me. She had always had a mothering hug for me when I needed it and it was nice, getting one now. It had been a long time.

"Good-bye, Fiona, take care of yourself," I said, and Ginny and I turned toward the hall.

"Cally . . ."

I turned back. "Yes?"

She opened her mouth and then closed it again. "You be careful."

"I always am."

"I know, but I worry about you not having people in your life you can trust." She looked genuinely sad, and then she smiled. "Except Ginny, of course."

Fiona and I had known each other since I was small, and she understood more than anyone about my relationship with my father and the emptiness his death had left in my life.

"I can trust you, too," I said with a smile.

"That's not what I mean," she said quickly.

"I know." I stopped her. I knew she was talking about Rudy, but she would never criticize her directly.

We smiled at each other again and then she closed the door.

As we started down the hall Ginny said, "I wonder who the hell she was talking about?" And it hit me that it might have been someone besides my mother. I had so many options.

Ginny stayed quiet as we slipped into the elevator and contained herself until the second the doors had sealed.

Then, "Why didn't you tell me you had a fucking sister!" she asked, her voice filled with concerned sympathy.

"I don't!" I responded defensively but she was rolling on, gathering some indignance.

"Here I am, supposed to be your best friend, thinking you're an only child except for that evil step-thing . . ."

"I don't have a sister and he's not my *step*brother, he's my *half* brother."

"Whatever. And now you go and drop on me, in a highly uncomfortable social situation, that someone is claiming to be your 'sister.' And then you expect me to sit there and act natural?"

"She's not my sister," I repeated, louder. "It's just another phony claim." But I was thinking about Fiona's fidgeting and it was making me twitch a bit myself.

"It's really important to you, so it's important to me!

I'm your friend." She was pretending to use her hands like sign language. "You can share these things with me." She enunciated very clearly as she flashed her hands in front of my face.

I raised my hand and showed it to her, "I'm going to smack you. There's some ASL you'll understand."

"So anything else? Like, you're pregnant or gay or engaged?"

"No, not engaged," I teased, thinking about my interlude on the balcony.

"No." So she laughed, "You fucked the arresting officer?"

"You think you're so smart, you don't know everything," I said and I meant it to sting.

"You didn't?" She looked honestly surprised.

The elevator rudely interrupted us by exposing us to the lobby. We crossed through, waving our thanks and good-byes to the security guy, and picked up the conversation outside.

"No, I didn't, I mean, he didn't." Frankly I found his resistance to me a little embarrassing; that had never happened to me before and I didn't want to feel like I was losing my touch. "I mean, I would have, but . . ."

"You had oral sex." She finished for me.

"Well, yeah. He went down on me, I wasn't allowed to reciprocate," I said.

"Well." She actually seemed confused. "That's certainly novel."

"He says he won't have sex with me until the D.A. closes the case, it's not 'ethical' I guess," I summarized.

"So let me get this straight: He's not going to have intercourse with you until the D.A. says so, *but* he can make you orgasm?" She looked at me questioningly.

"Um, yeah, I guess that's right," I agreed.

"But, you can't make him orgasm?"

"At this point, I'm going to say, no, he won't do that."

"Okay." She moved on toward the car thoughtfully. "How was it?"

"Great. That part was really great," I said begrudgingly.

"Which part wasn't great?" She stopped at the sedan and leaned against the door, in no hurry to get in.

"Well, I mean, no pun intended but not getting it all kind of sucks doesn't it?" I sat on the hood.

"How do you feel about him?" she asked.

"I'm pissed. I mean, I want to have sex with him, but he's playing some kind of stupid game, and I'm not going to go there, I don't need that. It's bullshit. What does he think? There are no other guys out there?"

"So you like him." She nodded as though I had stated simply that. "And it's making you insecure that you can't control him, like you usually do with your men."

It pissed me off to be nailed so definitively to the ground. "I don't care one way or the other about him." I defended myself. "And anyway, how would it make you feel, if someone would only give you oral sex and not do anything else?"

"I would have to ask myself one question," Ginny admitted seriously and then she asked it. "How long can I possibly drag this thing out?" She hooted with laughter and I stood next to her hanging onto my pout. Then she put her arm over my shoulders and locked me next to her with an iron grip. "Listen up. *This* one, he's smart, he's not going to run through your fingers like the putty you usually work with, and he's got you wanting more. When is the last time that happened to you?"

I had to admit it'd been a long time. "Well, I'm not afraid to say that I don't like it that he won't sleep with me."

"No, you're not afraid to say that. What you *are* afraid to say is that he might be good for something *other* than sleeping with you." Ginny gripped me even more tightly to counter my flight response, then she leaned in until her mouth was almost against my ear, "Callaway Wilde?" she whispered, "You're scared."

That's why I have so few friends, you show them your soft spot and they know where to thrust the knife.

15

Bill and my mother lived on the eighteenth hole of a prestigious golf course. They had an expensive house, meticulously designed and landscaped to make sure that anyone looking would notice that it was meticulously designed and landscaped. It was brick with huge custom arched windows put there not so much to enjoy the view from within as to allow a glimpse at the coveted trappings from without. As I drove into the circular driveway, I could already see people framed by the billowing silk draperies, like a curtain on a stage, milling around in the regal living room. I wondered for the bizillionth time what my mother felt so deprived of.

I parked and took a deep breath. I gathered up my gift and headed for the door. One of the staff hired for the birthday party answered the door and took my wrap.

I picked a glass of champagne off a silver tray and wandered into the midst of the festivities. I spotted my mother across the room speaking to some of her guests and she made a big show of coming straight to me and giving me a generous hug. I smelled liquor on her breath and assumed she'd started early.

"Hello Mom," I said for her guests' benefit. She ushered me over quickly.

"Cally, darling, you simply must come and meet the Uncers. They've recently moved into that glorious house on the corner."

We had reached the attractive older couple, both of whom I already knew.

"Hello Ileanna, hello Bernard, you look great, as always." I embraced them both warmly. They were wonderful people and I was glad to see them there.

Rudy on the other hand, looked like I had told her punch line.

"I didn't realize you knew my daughter." Her face held the doting expression she had chosen.

"Of course we know Callaway," Bernard said graciously. "How could we not? I don't think she's missed a fundraising meeting in the whole time we've been involved with City of Hope." I had been on the hospital's board of pediatric fund-raising for six years, helping out with strategies, corporate connections and, sometimes even, a much needed personal wish.

Ileanna took my hand in hers and held it. "Thank you for the car, I can't tell you how much easier it's made Adel's life."

Most recently I had purchased a car, anonymously, for a family with a six-year-old daughter who was going through bone marrow treatment. With no transportation it had taken them three buses and over an hour each way to get her to the hospital for her treatments, not the best way for a child to travel when she is violently nauseous and in pain.

"How's she doing?" I asked, afraid as always; sometimes it was good news, but so often, it wasn't.

"Not too well, I'm afraid." Ileanna had the look of wisdom and compassion on her face that only someone who had been on that journey, and lost a child, could have.

"Oh no," I said. "We need to think about doing something for them, something fun, if it's still possible."

They both nodded. "I'll speak to her social worker about it, see what she would like to do," Ileanna said.

We often sponsored wishes of trips or outings, not just for the child, but so that the families would have special, good memories with their children at the end, instead of only the pain and the struggle. Of course, the child had to get strong enough to leave the hospital, but I was always amazed at how they could rally, for a short time, if they had something to look forward to.

"Let me know," I said, wishing there was more I could do.

My mother was looking back and forth from one of us to the other. Ileanna turned to her. "I'm so sorry Rudy, this is a birthday party and from now on we are only going to talk about happy things!"

Ileanna Uncer's heart was bigger than my house. Fortunately before the situation could become uncomfortable, Bill came and rescued me.

"Callaway, I'm so glad you made it tonight. It really means a lot to your mother, to us all," he said when we were on our own.

"Of course I'm here, Bill, and very glad to see you. I didn't know the Uncers were friends of Binford's?"

"No, quite a few of the guests are friends of ours. I guess because your mother threw the party." He smiled at me. I could see he was as relieved to see me as I was to see him. "But speaking of our guest of honor." I followed his eyes across the room.

Binford came in and started a round of hellos. When he got to me I was surprised to be given yet another hug. He seemed unusually glad to see me. I wondered if he'd begun "celebrating" early as well.

"Cally, I'm really glad you came. I wasn't sure you would."

"Well, I was a little surprised to be invited, quite frankly, but now I'm very glad I came." I meant it. "Oh, yeah, this is for you, happy birthday." I handed over the telltale blue box with the white ribbon.

"Tiffany's. Whoo." He smiled again and looked genuinely pleased and excited.

"Go ahead, open it," I said. I was thinking my gift would look nice with his tux.

He untied the ribbon and slid off the lid with Bill and me looking on. I was looking for a big effect and I got it. For a minute I thought he was going to cry. It was an eighteen-carat Bulgari watch with a black face. It was definitely what Rudy would have termed "something really nice."

"Wow. I don't know what to say." He looked up at me, a little confused. I guess he was expecting a silver key chain or something. "Thank you, Cally."

"I didn't know if you already had a dress watch, but you can always trade it in if you want something different, like a house or something."

It was a sarcastic reference to how much it cost, but he looked up at me as though it was more.

"What?" I queried. "Does Elena want a new house?" I laughed and drank some of my champagne.

"Don't go giving her any ideas," he said good-naturedly. The quartet in the corner started to play, and he bowed in a mock manner, handing the box off to Bill. "May I have this dance with my sister?"

"Delighted, I'm sure," I replied.

Bill accepted my champagne flute as well, and Binford led me out to the small rented dance floor under Rudy's approving eyes.

It was a little strange dancing with my brother, but I felt like maybe we were making a tentative peace. It was a good thought, and I liked the feeling, so I waltzed with it.

"Where *is* your lovely wife this evening?" I asked.

Binford looked around as we turned and seemed surprised not to see her. "Uhm, she must be in the other room, or possibly fixing her lipstick again."

"Don't sound sour, this kind of thing is very important to us girls. Just be glad she's keeping herself up for you," I said coyly.

"I'm sure she'll be glad to see you," he said. I just couldn't get hold of his attitude. What was going on? I hoped that when Elena did see me she didn't hug me too hard. I was already feeling like a favorite stuffed toy.

Bill was dancing near us with Rudy, and at the end of the song we switched.

Bill was making fun of the other guests through his clenched smiling teeth to me while tossing off greetings and compliments to them. He had me laughing into his shoulder, wiping away tears of amusement.

He went on charmingly entertaining me until the end of the tune, at which point I protested sore feet and made my way to the dining room.

The buffet was lavish and I was touched that Rudy had gone to such pains. I remembered she took me to lunch on my birthday. I remembered I picked up the tab.

I surveyed the dance floor and saw Elena dancing with Binford. They were an interesting couple. He always seemed to keep to himself and she was *so* gregarious. Watching them, I wondered what attracted such different people to each other? Elena spotted me and made a beeline.

"Callaway! I'm so glad you came," she gushed.

"Hello Elena." I smiled up at her.

"Isn't this sweet of your mother?" Elena gestured around the room.

"Cloying," I said, and I hoped she didn't think it was too sarcastic.

"I'm sure it's not too fancy for you, but it's quite the shindig for us," she said, looking proud. Then she took my arm and led me a few feet away.

"How are you?" she asked intently, leaking concern like a bad valve.

"I'm fine," I answered, because I was. Considering.

Binford appeared next to us. "Sorry to interrupt," he said and turned to Elena. "Honey, my mom said the caterer is running out of something called flutes and . . ."

"I'll handle this." Elena's face went hard and professional. "Excuse me, Callaway, duty calls." She hustled off in a down-court press just as Binford was attacked by new arrivals with open arms.

I nabbed another champagne and wandered out onto the porch. It had a lovely view of the lake on the fairway, where I noticed a spraying water fountain had been added recently.

"Looks like Disneyland, doesn't it?" came Rudy's

voice behind me. "If only they'd dye the water a really fake aqua, the effect would be complete."

I regarded the effect. "I rather like it. In fact, I like your whole house. I think it's wonderful."

"Wanna trade?" she asked.

I turned and looked at her. "No," I said honestly. "But it would be great to have someone like Bill around. That I do envy."

Rudy sighed and sat down on a wrought-iron bench. I sat across from her. "He's a good man," she said with such surrender that it sounded like more of a life sentence than a gift.

"I always wondered why Dad never remarried," I said and I was instantly sorry I had. I should have known Rudy would have an opinion about that.

"He didn't need to. He got the bread without paying the baker."

"He never dated anyone seriously that I know of," I responded.

"There's a lot you don't 'know of.' " She raised her drink to her painted mouth and took a swallow. "Your father had a mistress for years."

"While he was married to you?" I asked, genuinely surprised that Rudy wouldn't have played this card before now, or at least let everyone know how she'd been wronged.

"No. I don't think so, anyway. It was later. But she knew he'd never marry her, so she finally broke it off."

"Why wouldn't he marry her?"

Rudy snorted. "Why should he?" Her eyes swept over the gentle greens and blacks of the fairway at night. "And she was too proud to keep seeing him when she knew she would never be anything more than his mistress," my mother said. "Good for her," she added, barely audibly.

"Who was it?" I asked. "Do I know her?"

Rudy laughed and shook her head. "I don't suppose it matters now. Yes, you know her."

"Rudy. Are you going to tell me or not?" I was impatient. No reason my father shouldn't have a girlfriend or "mistress" as my mother called her, but if it was someone I knew, I felt stupid being left in the dark.

"It was Fiona, darling. Dear, loyal Fiona."

That I had never heard or even suspected and it pleased Rudy to have shocked me. *If it was true.* I had too often listened to my mother's version of the truth to accept her word as gospel; it was seldom more than her opinion that she was stating as fact. I let that thought sink in while I quickly tried to decipher what she had to gain by telling me this. There was always that aspect as well.

"Come on. You're telling me that Dad and Fiona had an affair up until he died."

"Oh no. It was over years ago. She left him for a little while when she realized it wasn't going to get her anywhere and then came back in her former capacity of executive secretary, with a little agreement that recently came to fruition. Nice little annuity she got in the will."

"Rudy. She worked for him for twenty-five years. I think she was entitled to something." I was putting less and less weight on Rudy's deductions.

"Oh, yes. She was definitely entitled to something." Rudy tried to drink again but only ice met her lips. She rose to remedy that and left me there, thinking.

I was sitting in the shadow of a large potted ficus tree, absolutely motionless. In a moment, I saw someone come out the doorway and glance around. It was Binford, but he missed seeing me. Something in his furtive nature stopped me from greeting him. He moved across the slate and down a few steps onto the lawn, crossing to the trees on the right side of the property. On the other side of those trees was a short path to the clubhouse.

When he got to the edge of the grass, he stopped and looked back at the house. Still having no idea that anyone was watching him, he seemed to call out, but I couldn't hear from that distance. In a moment he got a response.

Just into the edge of the light stepped a figure. In the dim light from that distance, I couldn't even make out if it was a man or a woman.

What the hell is he doing? I wondered. When Binford leaned in and starting kissing the mystery guest, I figured it out pretty quickly. They were still kissing and groping as he pulled what I now assumed was a woman out of the light into the shadow of the woods.

"Hmmmm," I mused, "no wonder he was in such a generous and forgiving mood." I wondered if Elena would be as forgiving.

I moved out of the shadow and into the exterior light. As I turned back toward the house, my eye caught a movement in one of the kitchen windows. Just inside, Elena's profile towered over one of the servers. Their conversation was concluding and as the server moved away Elena turned to look out the window. My eyes went quickly back to the edge of the trees. Nobody.

God, I hoped she hadn't seen him. Maybe it was so bright inside she couldn't see anything but her own reflection.

Then she saw me and waved. Bummer.

Within seconds she was outside next to me.

I tried to get a sense of whether or not she seemed upset. She did seem a bit flustered but I couldn't tell if that was just from the confrontation with the staff.

"What do you think of the fountain?" she asked me, her eyes quickly scanning the edge of the light by the trees. Coincidence?

"I quite like it," I said honestly.

"Rudy hates it," Elena said matter-of-factly.

I tried to sound loosely casual with my next query. "So, how's married life, toots?"

"It's great!" She answered quickly. Maybe she was distracted by something inside and that's why she looked away. I didn't know.

"You guys happy?" I tried again.

Now she looked at me. "Well, yeah. I mean, the first year is hard, everyone tells me that." She paused. It was fascinating how someone so physically commanding could be so timid, and then, "Why? Did Binford say something about us?"

"No, Binford didn't say anything. How many times have I told you, trust your instincts."

She smiled at me. "You always have," and then she sighed, "but it seems like I never do."

Okay, now we were getting somewhere. "What's wrong?" It was best to be direct; I wasn't going to tell her anything, but I'd listen.

"Oh, Cally. It's so different for you, you were always good at everything."

I thought about the few times when I was so addicted to cocaine that I'd stayed up for days on end and had to blow the blood out of my nose so I could snort more coke in. "Oh, not always."

"Yes, really. I mean it. Can I be honest with you?" She looked at me hopefully.

"Shoot," I said, and then winced.

"I've always been jealous of you." Her voice sounded different, deeper, more sincere, as though everything she'd ever said to me before had been through a veil, and I was hearing it clearly for the first time. "I like you, very much, I admire you, but you're so pretty, you're so lucky."

There was my father's face again, vacant and in pain. There was the barrel of the gun and the cold eyes behind it. There was my big, empty house.

"Lucky, true," I muttered and smiled dully.

"Even if your dad hadn't left you his money, you'd be successful, you'd be rich, and men would fall all over themselves to get next to you." She reached out and put her hand on my arm. "You're just one of those people who would be good at whatever they did. You've got it all." The hand left me and waved vaguely in the air.

She sighed and crossed her arms, and her voice sounded even more sincere, a little sad and pained. "It's not like that with me, it never was. I have to work really hard at everything. I'm not complaining, I'm happy, you understand. It's just that, well, I want to do something exceptional." She looked down, way down, at her evening slippers. "And I'm afraid that if I try, I'll find out I can't." She looked at me with a plea in her eyes. "Is it okay that I'm telling you this?"

"Absolutely." I reached out and hugged her. "I'm really honored that you trust me to share that." It sounded a little formal, but I needed to acknowledge her effort.

"I want to talk to you about some ideas I have, since

you're so good at business and making things work. I
know you'd have great advice for me. I mean, look at
me, I'm married and working at my husband's company. I don't know what it is to have anything of my
own. Does that make sense?" She fumbled.

"Successes, you mean," I hinted.

"Yeah, I guess so." She looked out at the lake and
then very quietly, under the sound of the splashing
water, I heard her whisper, "Maybe just my own secret."

Then she looked right back at me and I knew that
she knew something was going on with her husband.
But I didn't think she knew what.

I just nodded again and looked back to where
Binford had disappeared from his own party. "I'd get
one, if I were you," I said.

And she laughed, her eyes twinkling with the
unthinkable thought of misbehaving, of being naughty.

"You can do it. Nothing to it."

As I left her I found myself drawn down the patio
stairs and to the edge of the dark lake, to the quiet solitude. It had become too noisy inside me to hear my own
voice and I needed to ask myself, what do I want now?

I kneeled down on the moist grass and laid my hand
flat against the earth. *Shhhh. Hush now.* After a few
moments I did hear it, I could make it out. The voice
said, *I don't want to be alone anymore.*

When I got home I was surprised to see the unmarked
police car in the drive. I went in through the front door
and found Evan seated in the living room with a coffee
service in front of him. I was pleased Deirdre had been
in to take care of him.

"How was your date?" he asked, unable to keep the

jealousy out of his voice as his eyes appreciatively traveled from the V-neckline of my cocktail dress to my strappy heels, lingering over the leg in between them.

"Brother's birthday," I corrected. "I don't really date."

"No?" He perked up. "I hear it's overrated."

"Did I tell you that?" I asked, dropping on the opposite end of the sofa and slipping off my shoes. "So. Detective, what brings you by?"

"This," he said and pulled out of his pocket a folded piece of paper. On it was my home address and something a little more shocking, the name of the restaurant I had been coming out of the night of the first shooting. Stapled to the back of it was a magazine photo of me at a charity ball.

"We found this in Oswaldo Herado's apartment. Along with roughly forty-five hundred dollars in hundreds."

"Did both brothers live together?" I asked.

"With the rest of the family," he said and went on too quickly for me to dwell on that bombshell "the rest of the family." "This establishes a prior knowledge of the intended victim: you."

"Why?"

"It looks like somebody wanted you dead." He laid the paper flat on the coffee table and smoothed it with his hand. "And they hired the Herados, or at least Oswaldo, to do it. Here's the thing. I've got handwriting samples of both men. They're barely literate. This is written in a sure hand. A little messy maybe but confidant. Do you recognize it?"

"Can I touch it?" I asked.

"Oh yeah, we checked it. It's been handled so much there are no identifiable prints."

I picked it up and looked at it. Bells did not, as they say, ring.

"Nope. Sorry." I handed it back to him.

"We need to establish who would get this money if you were out of the picture." He looked at me directly, and I knew there was no more sloughing it off. "If you don't know, I need you to figure it out."

"Well, let's see. If I'm alive, which I am, it's up to me to determine my heirs. The idea was, I'd have children. But I don't. So, in the event of my death, I guess it would go to my father's closest heirs. His surviving parents, there are none. Brothers and sisters, there are none. Other children, there are no . . ." I hesitated and thought of the claim.

"You're an only child? I thought you said you were at your brother's birthday party."

"And so I was, Detective, brother on my mother's side. He has no blood relation to dad. But in the last few days, someone has come forward claiming to be my father's illegitimate daughter. She has a letter from him, entitling her to a chunk of change."

"Quarters? Or just nickels and dimes?"

I took a second and then decided he needed the whole story. "Twenty million silver dollars."

He whistled through his teeth. And then his brow furrowed in that charming, intelligent way. "Big chunk. This just came up in the last few days?"

"The morning after the break-in," I said, waking up now. "Kind of a coincidence, huh?"

"Baby, there ain't no such thing."

I bolted up to my feet as a thought hit me hard from behind.

"What is it?" he asked rising, too.

"I'm such an imbecile. Come with me." I turned and headed for the stairs. We went up and I crossed to my vanity. I pulled open the top drawer, which was sectioned off into little spaces for jewelry and knickknacks. I rummaged through it. Nothing. I crossed to my underwear drawer, where I kept extra keys to my car and safe-deposit boxes. Nothing. Two more locations brought up nothing.

I gave up and crossed to the bed. Sitting heavily, I turned to Evan, who was watching me with minimum movement, following me with his eyes only.

"It's gone," I said. "I'm almost positive it's gone."

"And what would that be?" he asked.

"The signature stamp. My father's signature stamp. That was what the ink was on the dead guy's hand. I can't believe how stupid I've been. How could I miss that?"

Evan nodded. He didn't look surprised. "And I am to assume that this letter claiming to entitle our young miss to the twenty million was not hand signed but stamped?"

"Oh yes."

"And you didn't think it was important to tell me that, even after I told you there was ink on the guy's hand?" He said it simply but what I heard was, "are you that fucking stupid?"

"I didn't make the connection." I felt ashamed of my mistake, so, naturally, I attacked him, "I'm not the fucking detective, remember?" I was beating myself up for being an idiot just fine all by myself. "I might be an imbecile but at least I'm smart enough to know it, I don't need you pointing it out, too, thank you."

He ignored me, which was smart, because I intended

to go on blaming him for my embarrassment to the bitter end. "Let's find her," he said instead.

With effort, I switched my focus over to her. "Yes, I'd like to meet Ms. Sabrina Valley and hear what she has to say about this claim."

"And I'd like to keep you alive," Evan stated. It shocked the shit out of me. He was telling me that if someone had tried to kill me and had failed, they would most likely try again. I felt cold and a little nauseous.

"Why didn't the brother try to kill me that night?"

"My guess is, he didn't get the chance. Maybe he and his killer, who got away, broke in together with the intention of killing you, but it's possible that finding that stamp made it a different game. In that case, maybe the killer was better served by shooting the brother, making it look like you had fired the shots and he had never even been here."

My head was swimming, "Meaning?" I asked.

"Meaning, that when the killer got the stamp, he could somehow get your money without you being dead." He bit his lower lip lightly, "he didn't need the brother to kill you anymore, but he needed the brother out of the way—or the brother didn't want to hand over the stamp." He looked grim for a moment more, his eyes searching for something in the middle of the room that wasn't there, and then crossed over and sat down next to me on the edge of the bed. His nearness made me feel braver, but I held onto resenting his criticism with all my emotional might. "And you called us. That probably wasn't part of his plan, either."

I looked at him and picked up on the double meaning. "No, that wasn't part of the plan." He smiled and his eyes were focused on me now, his thoughts were back in the present and I wanted him closer than that; my defenses cracked. "Good move though, huh?" I asked, resentfully asking for reassurance, begrudgingly feeling vulnerable to him again.

"Oh yeah." He leaned in and kissed my neck. "See? That alone proves how bright you really are." He kissed me and I lay back, pulling him on top of me, wanting to pull him right up inside me. My fingers worked the zipper of his pants until I got my hand around the delicious thickness inside. *Perfect, yes!*

He pulled his mouth a fraction of an inch away from mine even as he ground his hips against me, pinning my hand, and what was in it, between us. "Is the staff in for the night?" he whispered.

"Yes," I breathed back. "Don't worry about it." I strained up to push my tongue hard into his mouth again and he met me fully. Then he pulled back again with an anguished moan. "Good, I'm glad they're here, you get some sleep." He kissed me once more and sat up.

"What?" I asked, exasperated. "Don't go." I begged and threatened, hoping one of those two tactics would keep him there.

"You think this is easy for me?" His eyes raked my body as though they could feel it. "Shit," he said and ripped my shirt open, his mouth finding my breasts and sucking insistently on first one and then the other, as the palm of his large strong hand pressed against my groin with a steady rhythm that I matched. Then he moved down again, pulling off my pants and raising my legs to let his mouth slide down my skin until he locked his tongue inside me and his hands around my thighs, not letting me move more than thrusting up against his mouth. In seconds I was screaming with release, vaguely conscious of how much I sounded like an animal, in a deeply good way.

When I stopped trembling and had pulled his head away from me by holding his hair in handfuls, I tried to push my way down to him but he held me again and kissed me.

"I can't." There was distinct pain in his voice. He stood up and tried to straighten himself out. The look on his face was concentrated lust. Nonetheless, my annoyance at his ability to resist me returned with compounded interest. "I'll speak to Deirdre on the way out," he said and lingered.

"Fine," I said and climbed under the covers, "you do that." He looked at me, trying to read me as I feigned disinterest.

"Good night." He tested.

"Good night." I smiled at him curtly, trying hard to show that I was trying hard not to show how hurt I was.

He shook his head and laughed ironically. It filled me with indignant righteous rage; how dare he think he could see right through me?

He exited without looking back and I heard him laugh again, softly, to himself.

I sat up and grabbed another pillow and then flopped back onto the bed and growled. Beating my fist into the pillow, I tried to force the feathers, at least, into the shape I wanted them to be. But as the minutes went by and my heart quieted I realized something. I *was* pretty bright, and I'd have to be stupid not to see one thing with glaring clarity.

He was on to me.

16

The next day, I got a call from Hervé. He was beside himself with indignation because he'd been visited by a detective. I told him they probably found out he'd crossed the police line. Then I hung up on the conniving son of a bitch. I wasn't positive he was up to something, but I thought I could smell fear sweat even over the phone.

A short time later, I was in the breakfast room with my coffee and some paperwork when Deirdre entered, closely followed by my favorite gumshoe. Before she had a chance to announce him, I spoke up.

"Deirdre, are you wanted for something?"

"No, ma'am, not to my knowledge."

"Well, you're being tailed by the police," I said, winking at Evan.

"Yes, ma'am. Detective Paley," she finally got out, and then to him, "shall I bring another cup?" She was correct, as always.

"Please," Evan stressed, and he sat down across from me and helped himself to a muffin. He didn't even look tired.

"Well?" I asked.

"Ms. Valley is in town." He raised his eyebrows and took another big bite.

"Where?"

"At one of the finest cheap motels in Malibu." He reached across and took a drink from my cup, a move of familiarity that I liked. "A meager league or two away."

"A 'league?' " I would have laughed but I was having trouble getting a deep breath.

The idea of immediate proximity gave me a kind of relationship vertigo. What if she really was a half sister? On top of everything else, that would be beyond bizarre. And her physical presence in my immediate surroundings made her more than a vague possibility. It made her a threat.

I was aware of Evan watching me. He put down the muffin and leaned toward me so that my automatic reaction was to look up at him.

"How does that make you feel?" he asked, and it sounded like he really cared.

My first response to numb out and pretend I felt nothing other than capable was short-circuited by the knowing look in his eyes. It would have been futile to lie to him. "It makes me feel very insecure."

"Why?"

"Because I don't know who this person is, and if there's a possibility she . . ."—I couldn't say the word "sister,"—"has a claim, it will rock my foundation." I had to stop there.

He stayed quiet for a moment and then he repeated, "Why?"

Now I looked away, to be more alone with my feeling, to try to put it into words. "Because," I started hesitantly, "because my father was the only thing I ever believed was honest in my life. Everyone else betrayed me." The words were so true and painful they burned my throat from my heart to my mouth.

He reached out and pushed my hair behind my ear, letting his fingers stroke my face. "Then, first, we have to find out if it's true or not."

"What if it is?" My voice was choked by the fear of being burned.

"Then you go to the second thing."

"What's that?" I asked, surprised that there was life after that.

"Deal with it, and learn to trust people who deserve to be trusted." His eyes said he meant himself. I thought, that sounds like an awful lot of work.

"What if it's not true?" I asked hopefully.

He smiled at me, "Same thing."

Oh well. My life had gone from predictably stressful to full combat mode in less than a week. I geared up for the unpleasant task before me by jamming myself into automatic expedite mode. "How long would it take us to get there?" I asked.

"Probably not as long as it'll take you to get dressed." His eyes dropped to the front of my silk robe and I felt my nipples harden.

"Why would I want to put my clothes on?" I toyed with him.

"Oh, I don't know, I'd hate to have to arrest you for being naked." He reached a hand over and let his fingers play one at a time over the pearl-sized erections on my chest. "That would be a crime," he said and raised his coveting look from my breasts to my eyes where it stayed until Deidre entered with his coffee. I got up and left the room really slowly, so he could watch.

Then I bolted up the stairs and got dressed really fast, just to prove him wrong.

A couple of leagues took us longer than we expected with the twisty mountainous drive over Malibu Canyon.

The motel on Pacific Coast Highway was not a deluxe model. Built in the strange flat-roofed, slap-it-up-fast style of the fifties, it sat on a hill above the ocean just about where one of the major canyon routes let out onto PCH. We pulled in and parked. I sat in the car while Evan went to inquire which of the fine rooms belonged to my supposed bastard sister.

He came out of the office moments after he'd gone in and motioned for me to join him. In the doorway of the office behind him, I could see the motel manager straining to poke his nose into official police business. Evan ignored him, and I followed suit as we passed him on our way into the motel's courtyard.

The small area was a cement slab with a pool interrupting it. The rooms ran along both sides of the blueish rectangle of water that was sharp with the astringent bite of chlorine. But the far side was open to a scrubby landscape dropping to the sea. We were looking for 6B, but as it turned out, we didn't need to find it.

On the far side of the pool was a nineties version of Marilyn Monroe, dripping wet in a white one-piece swimsuit. She picked up her towel and ran it over her wet blond hair. I watched Evan pause and drink her in. Skinny, she was not. She was carrying about twenty extra pounds by today's magazine standards—and every pound improved her.

Ample-breasted is, I think, the word that might be used, by me anyway. I could see from Evan's wry amusement that he might use another one. She also possessed a stunning face, sexy and innocent. Pretty, definitely very pretty. I poked him in the ribs to snap him back, and he turned to me.

"What?" he asked, and I made a face at him.

We crossed toward her as she spotted us. She held her towel up to pat her cheek dry so that the thin bath sheet fell in a veil-like drape, partially blocking her tight curves. Which made them even more alluring. My supposed half sister watched us advance on her like a frightened rabbit watches a fox.

"Sabrina Valley?" Evan addressed her.

"Who are y'all?" she asked in a voice rich and musical with that innocent Southern drawl that men find so infuriatingly attractive. I hated her.

"Detective Evan Paley."

He whipped out his badge, just like in the movies. Leaning down, she looked at it carefully, childishly ignorant that she was giving him a lovely view of the depth between her breasts.

"Can I help you, Detective? And is this your partner?"

She looked at me for the first time, and I saw a little shock go through her. She knew who I was all right.

Evan noticed it, too. He kept his eyes focused on hers and spoke casually. "No, this is Callaway Wilde. She's here because of an investigation I'm conducting involving her."

"An investigation about what?" She had stiffened a bit at the sound of my name; possibly I had not seemed real to her either until now.

Her pupils had widened in her baby-blue eyes, and her full lips were slightly parted. She looked genuinely scared, and I could just imagine that masculine instinct in Evan raging to protect, protect. Funny how men are so much more inclined to play "big brother" to the sexy ones.

But, of course, I had forgotten whom I was with for a moment. He wasn't buying it. "A murder investigation. May I ask you a few questions?"

"I don't know anything about any murder." She sounded so breathy and sincere. Her mouth quivered, like a taut waterbed with lovers at work.

"Nonetheless, I'd like it if you'd help us." He smiled and gestured to a plastic table and chairs in the shade. "Please."

She turned to the table ahead of us and walked like women used to walk, when they weren't trying to be men. Her body was full and firm, a Sealy Posturepedic body. I'm sure that wasn't lost on Evan, either, but he seemed all business. We sat and she kept glancing at me nervously.

"Do I need a lawyer, or something?" Again that breathy innocence.

"I don't know. Do you?" Evan smiled.

She seemed to relax a little.

"I am mostly curious about your connection to Ms. Wilde. I understand you have certain claims filed against her estate."

She looked surprised and a little scared again. She stole a glance at me shyly once and then couldn't raise her long lashes that high again for a while. "Yes. I wasn't aware that was public knowledge."

"It's not," I said, speaking for the first time. "But I'm not exactly the public, since it's *me* you're suing. I'm going to have to call myself at least an interested party."

Evan caught my eye and I got the idea that I better

let him do the asking, so I sat back and shut up.

"When did you first decide to make this claim?" Evan asked in a friendly tone I recognized as the disarming one.

"I didn't decide to make it. I found it," she said in little excited gasps. She was all kid with a pirate map.

"Could you explain that?" Evan asked in an infinitely patient tone.

"A few days ago, I received a note in the mail with a safe-deposit box key. I went to the bank and found that amazing letter from Mr. Wilde in the box. Along with another one explaining that Mr. Wilde was my father, and he had always wanted me to have that money."

She looked cautiously at me when she said, "father," and then quickly back to Evan. Her lips turned up easily when she finished speaking, as though her mouth was most comfortable sitting in an upright position. Her expression held no enmity for me. She was naturally happy, this one, and now she thought the prize patrol had picked her house on Super Bowl Sunday.

"Well, well." Evan smiled back. "You ever go to Vegas, Ms. Valley?"

"No sir." She looked a little uncertain. "Should I?"

"Absolutely," he said, "and put a hundred bucks down on nine for me when you're there."

She didn't really get it. I guess they don't have roulette where she comes from. But she tried to look pleasant about it.

"And now I think maybe this may be a very pertinent question," Evan said switching to his "pertinent" tone. "Who is your mother?"

Sabrina's eyes twitched a little, and she glanced

down before she answered. "My momma was named Suzanna and she lived with my daddy, Robert Bowden, in Shreveport."

"Lived?" asked Evan.

"They both passed on. My momma died five years back, right before Easter. And my daddy followed her last summer." She choked a bit and her big eyes batted hard to drive away the moisture. But she looked back up and smiled through the tears.

"I thought you said your 'daddy' was Mr. Wilde," Evan said levelly.

"No. Mr. Wilde is my blood father, that's all." She nodded conclusively.

"Are you married, Ms. Valley?"

"No. Why?" She looked at him with intense interest. I thought it a curious question myself, but this was what you call a "line of questioning."

"And was Suzanna your 'blood mamma'?" A little wisp of sarcasm seeped like a vapor into Evan's inquiry.

Sabrina looked down again. "No, but she's my momma. I was adopted, and my parents decided that I should keep my own name."

I got it. Why did she have a different name? Why not Wilde?

Evan waited, and when she didn't answer, he asked again.

"But not your 'blood' father's name. Who is your 'blood' mother?"

"I don't know," she said, and when she raised her eyes again, they were wet with tears.

Pain or fear, I couldn't say, maybe a little of both.

"I think I might want somebody to help me now."

"You mean a lawyer?" Evan asked.

"Yes sir. I don't mean to be disrespectful, but I'm not supposed to be talking to anybody about this. That's what Mr. Underwood says. He's the lawyer who looked over that letter and sent me up here."

"And do you have a lawyer in L.A.?" Evan asked politely, patiently.

"I was referred to one by Mr. Underwood. I'll be meeting with him today. Maybe after I talk to him, I could try to help you more." She was a gently bubbling cast-iron pot of Southern manners.

Evan pulled out the little pad and pencil he carried. "And could I get his or her name please?"

She spoke the name and I was so sure of what it would be that I mouthed it with her, although she added so many syllables I finished before she did.

"His name is Hervé Tesauro."

After that tasty tidbit of information was imparted Evan seemed impatient to wrap up the gathering. So after establishing that Ms. Valley could be reached at the motel indefinitely, we stood and said our good-byes quickly without shaking hands.

"Stranger and stranger," I said in the car on the way back.

"Clearer and clearer," Evan responded. He looked at me for a moment when we stopped at a light. "You okay?"

"Yeah, sure," I said a little coldly. "She's very attractive."

"Is she?" he asked.

"In a fat way," I said bitterly, knowing full well she had a magnificent body.

"Well, nobody who wasn't incredibly sexy could have any share in your gene pool." He put his hand on my thigh and slid it up under my skirt. My eyes rolled back and half closed to slits.

I tried to focus on my jealousy. "She's not my sister. So you do think she's sexy?"

His hand was moving now and, gripping my inner thigh, he slid me easily toward him. The light changed and we started down Pacific Coast Highway.

"She does have a nice body," he said while he was making me all slippery, "and a very pretty face. But really sexy means that and smart." He pulled off onto one of the canyons.

"I'm pretty smart," I said coyly as he found a turnoff and parked.

"You're a fucking genius," he said and laid me back on the front seat. Then he showed me how smart he was with his mouth and his fingers until my body shuddered and I untangled my fingers from his hair. He kissed his way up my body as he pulled my skirt back down and kissed my mouth hard. He tasted good. I was pleased about that.

But I wanted more. "Now it's your turn," I said and put my hand firmly against the zipper of his pants; it was stressed to the breaking point.

He closed his eyes for a minute and let me explore but then he caught my wrist and held my hand away. "Call it an acute case of professionalism, but I've *got* to wait." At least he looked like it pained him to say it; that was comforting.

I returned to the land of pout. "I hope it's not terminal," I said, and I meant it as a warning.

"No, there is a procedure that will cure me, but I have to wait for the tests to come back."

"Well, if it's fatal," I sassed, "I'll be sure to send flowers."

17

So, because the damn case wasn't settled, I arrived home feeling considerably better, but still without that sense of completeness a girl gets from a man that fits. I don't know how he could stand it.

The more I thought about it, the more I started to fret and froth. Thinking about what Ginny had said, I had to admit that his resistance was, maybe, touching a small insecure note in me. I liked to think of myself as *irresistible* and I saw absolutely nothing wrong with that. If he didn't *have* to have me then what was I wasting my time for? Someone else would appreciate me more, be unable to contain himself. *Professionalism my ass.*

For all my frivolous banter about living the lazy life, I was actually extremely busy overseeing my father's corporations. As I headed nervously for the library to get some work done, I reminded myself again that I should really start referring to them as "my" corporations. It wasn't easy going through that door, but I had to get back to my life. The shooting had disrupted every aspect of my life, my sleep, my peace of mind, and my daily routine. Even though it raised a cold sweat to face that room I was determined to do it.

Shaking but determined, I went in. It almost looked like nobody had died there, except for one thing. The carpet had to go. Trying to ignore the images that popped into my brain like gory flash cards, I started in on the pile of papers requiring my review and signature that rose before me on my desk like a massive migraine. Each one had a neatly typed summary attached, written by my very competent assistant, Kelley, who worked mainly out of my office downtown. I signed some documents, made notes in red on others that required changes or review and picked up the phone.

I made a few calls to executives who always cleared their throats as they were picking up the phone before adding just the right note of surprise and delight to hear from me. Most of them did respect me because, as long as things ran smoothly, I let them do their jobs. Otherwise, they wouldn't have their jobs.

A couple of them referred to the items they'd seen in the news about the shootings and made curious inquiries as to my well-being and involvement. I reassured them and told them the same thing the newscasters said, that I had no comment, and went on to the next call.

A few hours later, I sat back in my chair and cracked my neck with a relieved sigh. I wasn't finished, of course, never would be, but at least I was ready to move on to the dozen new chores each call had created. I punched speed dial four and propped my feet up on the desk.

"Hi!" The phone yapped at me. "This is Virginia at Stunts Galore, if you need to get in touch with me immediately call my pager, at . . ."

"Ginny, call me," I said simply and got up to stretch. Seconds later, the phone rang. Struggling actors have those pagers surgically implanted or something.

"Hey," I said, "are you working?"

"No, we wrapped early this morning." She yawned. "How ya doing?"

"Fine, anything exciting?" I asked.

"Medium-speed car chase ending with a jump over a tractor trailer, and about a fifteen-foot fall. So, not really." She waited and I said nothing. "What's up?"

"I must shop and eat." I was all talked out.

"No moonlighting cop?"

"Detective," I corrected. "And that was this morning." She laughed. "Okay, I'll come get you."

She was there in half an hour, I let her drive. I figured if she'd spent her morning jumping a semi, she could get me to a rug dealer on Robertson Boulevard.

After an hour of amusing haggling with the rug dealer, which included me throwing in my Persol sunglasses just to make him laugh, I was the proud owner of a new ocher-tinted Persian floor covering.

Ginny and I walked to where the car was parked at a meter. The sun stung my bare skin, too hot. Ginny beeped the car alarm and I was opening the door when someone called my name.

"Cally!"

I turned in the brightness and saw Elena coming toward me, shopping bags in hand. I felt a little uncomfortable seeing her because I wasn't sure what drama might have unfolded after the party. It wasn't a great time for me to take on someone else's troubles; I felt like I had plenty of my own. But I was concerned about her, especially after our heart-to-heart talk on the patio, so I took a deep breath and reminded myself that it wouldn't hurt me to lend an ear to a friend.

"Hi Elena," I answered. "How you doing?"

"Fine, fine." She turned to Ginny. "It's Virginia, right? Nice to see you."

"Yeah, hi," Ginny said, though I could see no flicker of recognition.

"You remember Elena, my sister-in-law," I said helpfully.

"Of course I do," she said in a dishonest, reproachful tone. "How could I forget?" She smiled, the little snake.

"Well, do you two have time to get a coffee or something?" Elena asked.

"No. But I could use a cold beer. Ginny?"

"Am I going to say no?" She shut the car door again. "There's Chardonnay right there." She pointed at a bar-restaurant across the street. "That okay?"

"Great!" Elena enthused.

We crossed from the hot sidewalk into the cool shade of the bar gratefully and seated ourselves between the potted palms wrapped with tiny white lights and the indoor fountain and ordered. Most of the small talk went pretty smoothly. I noticed Elena went through a couple of white wines like they were lemonades and she was really thirsty. They were making her more and more talkative.

"You know, Cally," she was confiding now, "I just don't understand your brother sometimes. I always liked you."

"Thanks, I like you, too." I passed a quick glance at Ginny, who turned away to keep from laughing. "I guess the insinuation is that he doesn't?"

"It's not his fault." Elena looked up at me, suddenly vehement. "It's your mother's. Now, I don't want to speak against your mom, but sometimes, that woman." I saw her dull brown eyes actually flash a little.

"Don't worry, I have no illusions about my mother."
I smiled.

"The other night, I heard them talking in the other
room, and I'll tell you, it just made my blood boil." She
shook her head and then ordered another wine.

"They think they lost out somehow," I tried to
explain. "I can't get them to be grateful for what they
have."

"But this, it made me mad," she repeated.

I was trying not to bite, but Ginny had no such scru-
ples.

"What did they say?" she asked.

"Well," Elena answered, eager to tell, "they were talking about what would have happened if that boy would
have shot you. They were saying things would be different then."

I have to admit, that seemed a little low, even for
Binford and Rudy. A girl doesn't like to hear that her
family is speculating hopefully about her death.

"What did you say?" I asked, trying to wrap up the
subject.

She looked a little sheepish. "Well, they didn't exactly
know I was listening. I was kind of accidentally walking
by. And well, to tell the truth, I . . . Binford's been acting
strangely lately." She finished with an uncomfortable
glance at Ginny.

I flashed on him making out with the mystery
woman the night of his birthday party. I wasn't sure
that strange was the word for it. Stupid might have been
a better fit.

"Strange how?" asked Ginny.

"I don't know. Real short-tempered with me." She
sighed and then smiled and seemed to remember her-

self. "It's probably just me. I can be a little annoying."

"I don't think so," I said, slipping her a sympathetic look. "I think that he's the one being 'annoying.' "

"I shouldn't talk badly about Binford. If I have a problem I should talk to him, I know that. He's been stressed lately. He's a little upset with his daddy right now." She dropped her voice when she said it, as though it was a no-no to disagree with her husband in any way.

"Binford's angry at Bill?" I asked. "Why?"

"It's because Bill's got such a good heart," she said.

I resisted saying, "and Binford doesn't." She went right on anyway.

"Bill just wants to help everybody. And now it's these gang boys."

When I was a kid, I touched the metal prongs on an electrical cord while I was plugging in the Christmas tree, and it jolted me badly. I had that same sensation now. "What gang boys?" I asked.

"It's this work program. Somebody came to Bill and asked if he would give ex-gang members a job, keep them straight, that kind of thing. Binford was against it, but Bill just can't say no." She sighed. "I think it's wonderful of him, but it's dangerous." She narrowed her eyes and took another drink. "I mean, these boys are criminals!"

"What kind of jobs do they do?" I asked, and took a sip of my Campari and soda. My mouth was kind of dry.

"Easy stuff, box making, loading dock mostly." She snorted a little and missed my hissed breath. "But I have to agree with Binford, I mean, I know these guys have had tough lives and all that, but I just don't trust them." She looked at me, "They've got this look in their eyes, you know?"

I nodded, I knew. "Well, how have they worked out?"

"Two of them have already stopped showing up, two brothers."

Ginny had her head down. I wasn't sure if she had put it together or not.

"And Bill hired them?"

"He insisted! I must say, as upset as Binford was in the beginning, he really tried to make it work. But now he has put his foot down. 'No more', he said."

My head was reeling, and I was grateful when Ginny steered the conversation to other things and monopolized Elena for a while.

I paid the check to stop any more drinks from being ordered, and Ginny and I said good-bye to Elena and decided to drive out to the beach for dinner. I was hoping the drive and a walk on the pier would clear my head, help me make sense of this new information.

Bill! What the hell could he have to do with the shooting and the break-in? Maybe everything Elena had said had a reasonable explanation, but Evan's words just kept ringing in my head.

There's no such thing as a coincidence.

18

We hadn't gone three blocks, when Ginny said casually, "Don't turn around, but I keep seeing the same car behind us."

"What does it look like?" I asked.

"It looks like a red Toyota that somebody just stole."

I adjusted the right mirror. Yep. Nondescript. At least four men in it. All with buzzed heads.

"When did you first see it?"

"I noticed them once after we left the house, but I didn't see them when we got to Robertson."

"Maybe it's a coincidence," I said, meaning there weren't any, of course.

"Let's lose 'em anyway," she suggested, smiling at me as she downshifted into second. I grabbed on to the armrest as she took a sudden right turn while accelerating instead of braking. "Better traction," she explained without taking her glowing eyes off the road. By the time we hit the highway and slowed to a nonincarcerating speed, they were nowhere in sight.

"Okay, I feel better," I said. But I kept the mirror tilted so I could see behind me, and once or twice I spotted a red car way back.

We parked at the long, cheerfully painted pier by Huntington Beach just before sundown. It was that time of day Ginny calls "magic hour." It has something to do with the quality of light on film, I think. Anyway, it's a good name for it. Everybody looks pretty.

We walked slowly along the worn planks, and I updated Ginny on everything that was going on. She was most interested in my progress with Evan and most concerned about the murders. I guess I felt the same. When I gave her a physical description of Sabrina Valley, she just laughed. She loved to laugh, and I loved to hear it.

"It just figures you'd have fucking Marilyn Monroe for a sister," she joked, then added, "I mean, if she really is your sister."

"Which she's not," I said. "If she does have Wilde blood, why wouldn't my father have told me? It wasn't like him not to take responsibility for something that important." That part was bothering me, I had to admit.

"Maybe he didn't know," she offered.

We'd reached the edge of the Pacific Coast, and we stared out in the dwindling light at the curve of the earth toward Hawaii and beyond.

"Then what's with the letter?" I was pissed.

"The letter's a fake."

"How do you know?"

"C'mon." She looked at me and spat it out. "Please, this letter shows up in town the day after the stamp is stolen?" She rolled her eyes. "And the poster girl for La Leche League gets the grand prize a few days later? I don't think so."

"What's La Leche League?" I asked, showcasing my ignorance.

"It's a left-wing support group for lactating women.

They believe that breast-feeding your child until they're twelve will solve all the problems of the world," Ginny said in a monotone rush.

"Oh." I didn't ask how she knew about that. She had a lot of sisters.

"So you don't think she's behind it?" I asked.

"Did she seem that smart to you?" She turned and leaned her butt against the rail.

"I'm smart," I said, mimicking what I'd said to Evan earlier and smiling at the physical memory that swept over my body.

Ginny turned and looked up at me, a smile on her face but in her eyes a warning.

"Well, let's be smart right now," she said. Her voice had become deadly serious. "I want you to turn around, sit up on the top of the railing and just do what I say."

"What? Why?"

"Keep smiling and talking. And do what I say." She turned her attention back down the pier, reassuming a casual, jovial voice. "How you guys doing tonight?"

I followed her gaze and didn't like what I saw: four men, probably the same four buzz-headed boys who had been following us. They had moved in around us, fanned out. They were still ten to fifteen feet away, but they were definitely focused on us. They all wore white tank tops and loose shirts over the tops of their baggy pants. As the shirts fluttered in the sea breeze, I could see the gang tattoos. They weren't pretty.

"Nice night, huh?" Ginny tried again, her voice friendly and conversational. She patted the railing beside her, and I remembered to do what she said. I climbed up on it, sitting facing them. It gave me a tiny bit of vertigo to be perched on the edge of a long, dark fall to cold water. But I knew the psychology. Get your head higher than theirs.

None of them answered. They just exchanged looks, and one of them turned deliberately to watch back down the pier. I saw what he saw: no help for a long way off.

"Can we help you, gentlemen?" Ginny asked, still politely but in a more serious tone.

"Yeah, you can help us," said the smallest, meanest-looking one in the middle. I couldn't look at his eyes. I had seen those eyes before on someone else. They were dead already, so filled with hate and hopelessness. There was no changing that look, no future in it.

"And what can we do for you?" Ginny asked, shifting from a leaning into a standing position, centering her weight as if she expected them to rush her.

"Well, you can get out of the way, if you want. We don't have no argument with you," he said, locking his empty black eyes on me.

"Now see." Ginny's attitude changed, she became challenging. "I never thought you boys needed a reason to fuck with nobody. I didn't think you was that smart." Jesus, she was needling them.

His eyes flicked to her on the word "boys." He didn't like that. He danced a little from one foot to another and looked to the other three, who hissed nastily.

"Shut up, bitch," he mustered.

Ginny laughed. I couldn't fucking believe it, but she did, she belly-laughed, slapping her leg and howling with delight. The men in front of us were totally shocked. I thought she was crazy, too.

"Oh, man, shit. You funny!" She wiped her eyes and straightened up. "Is that the best you can do? 'Shut up, bitch'?" She laughed again, but I noticed her eyes were watching him hard. "Man, you oughta know I like that shit!"

The lookout guy was getting nervous. He turned from his post and hissed, "C'mon, man, do it!"

The number-one guy hesitated only a second more, and then the gun came out. A nasty nine-millimeter. I was hating the NRA right about now. This guy was a poster child for gun control.

"You gonna shoot us?" Ginny asked, a big shit-eating grin on her face.

Big Boy didn't know what to think of her or who to shoot at first. Ginny turned to me and went on as though she thought this was just hysterical. "Get ready girl, we are going down!" She turned back to the punks and raised her arms. "Shoot me, shoot me!"

What happened next happened so fast I didn't sort it out until later. All I knew was that something hard and solid hit me. I heard gunshots at the same time, three quick ones, but we were already falling. Faster and faster, Ginny with her arms around me as we hurtled toward the dark water.

Our heads hit together when we smacked the cold water. We went deep. It seemed like the downward force would never end. But finally the water slowed and held us, and then with a yank from Ginny I started to swim toward what I thought was up. She was ahead of me. I could feel her presence. When my head broke the surface, I gasped for air and the first thing I heard was a hissed, "shhh," from my savior.

Ginny had a firm grasp on the front of my shirt and she was pulling me under the pier. All I could do was try to follow. I knew the men above us would be searching the gray-blue light, trying to find us, trying to get another shot. That thought scared me so badly that I forgot to be afraid of the deep, dark water.

Ginny steered us to one of the huge pylons that support the pier and I reached out my hand to steady myself in the gentle swells; it was slimy and rough at the same time. Barnacles covered with seaweed. I was trying not to breathe too loudly but, between the sound of the surf and the distance we had fallen, I didn't think it mattered much. The back of my neck smarted where it had hit the water.

I turned to Ginny and whispered. "I guess we'll have to swim in and hope they aren't waiting for us."

She was breathing in short gasps and holding tight to the pylon.

"They will be," she said, and I heard the pain in her voice. "Unless someone heard the shots, and they'll probably just think it was firecrackers."

She winced and raised one of her arms out of the water. Even in the dusky darkness under the pier, I could see the hole.

"Ah, Jesus." I was so angry, my throat swelled shut with the emotion of it.

"I can move it. But I need to get out of the water."

I knew if she lost consciousness, it would be a long, hard struggle through the surf to the shore. I didn't even want to think about the implication of blood in the water.

I could see she was wavering, so I swam behind her and put one arm around her waist.

"Okay, just let me support you," I gasped between breaths, trying to keep both our heads above the water. "Here we go."

I started kicking hard, using my spare arm and both

my legs to move as straight back under the pier as I could manage. Within minutes I was exhausted. Ginny was trying to help by kicking, but her good arm was cradling the injured one, and she was whimpering through clenched teeth.

I was sucking in air and getting as much saltwater as anything. I tried to turn my head to see how much farther we had to swim, but I could tell from the pylons that the tide was keeping us from making much progress. Then I heard a hollow wooden thump, the sound a boat makes when it hits a dock.

I was a few feet from one of the giant timbers, so I made my way to it and grabbed onto to it with one arm, keeping hold of Ginny with the other. My legs were shaking with the effort and I just kept repeating the same thing over and over in my head. *You can do it, nothing to it. You can do it, nothing to it.*

But I was starting not to believe it. I looked around for the source of the sound I had heard and in the vague, shadowy darkness, I saw a small wooden boat tied to one of the other supports. And I could make out a man in it. He was peering in our direction, probably wondering what in the hell that was in the water.

"Help!" I tried to get out but a wave slapped my face. "Please," I whispered.

Then I knew—I had to get to that boat. It was twenty yards away, the longest distance I have ever seen.

Pulling myself up for one giant breath, I pushed off hard, pulling Ginny's weight with me. Determined now, I fought my way through the water. No strength left, only adrenaline and dogged motions. *Keep going, do it, kick,* I ordered myself. And then I heard another voice, a voice I hadn't heard for two years and I heard it as clearly as if he spoke into my ear. My father's voice. *You can do it, nothing to it.* It took forever. It was a sea I crossed, an ocean I covered, seemingly endless, but finally, my head bumped against the hard wood of the boat. I reached up for the side, my hand found no solid hold and I slipped down under the water. And then someone grabbed my shirt and I held on to Ginny like she would save me.

The weight of us both being lifted almost capsized the dinghy. I vaguely heard voices and felt someone prying my hand off Ginny as she was lifted in first and then me. We were laid on the floor of the small wooden boat.

A jacket was wrapped around me, then someone was forcing a bottle to my lips and I couldn't smell anything but cheap tequila. It was the most delicious thing I ever drank. In a minute, oxygen and that cactus elixir had revived me and in the dim light that remained I sat up to face my rescuer. He looked exactly like my executioner.

It was a nasty start, but this young man with a buzzed head smiled kindly at me, and even in the fast-approaching darkness I could see that his eyes were still alive. He was wearing a dark green T-shirt, and there were no tattoos on his naked arms. I guessed it was his jacket I was wearing. There was another man in the boat, whose jacket was now covering Ginny. This man was Hispanic also, but older, perhaps the father of the man seated near me.

"Thank you," I said, absolutely overcome by relief. "Thank you. Uh, gracias."

Then I turned quickly to Ginny. She was propped against the little seat, and her eyes were open. It was her turn with the tequila, and she looked like she was enjoying it as much as I had.

The two men were speaking to each other in rapid Spanish. They seemed to be arguing, and the younger one was pointing up to the end of the pier. The father picked up the oars and started to move the boat.

"Oh, shit. I don't speak Spanish, but listen, um, danger, uh, peligro. Hombres . . ." I was at a loss. Now it wasn't just Ginny and I who were in danger, it was these Good Samaritans as well. The younger one looked at me like I was retarded and then cracked a smile.

"Yeah, it's pretty clear you're in danger," he said. Clearly English was his first language. "We heard the gunshots, and your friend here seems to have caught one of them. My dad and I were just discussing the safest place to get you to shore."

"Oh, yeah, thanks," I said. "By the way, I'm Cally and this is my friend Ginny."

Ginny smiled up weakly and waved the fingers of her uninjured hand as though that was all the energy she could muster. "Damn glad to meet you," she whispered.

"I'm Vinny and this is my dad, Roberto."

I nodded to the father, unclear whether he spoke English. He cleared that up for me quickly.

"Charmed, I'm sure," he said with a thick Mexican accent. I liked these guys.

"Look, formal introductions aside, your friend needs a hospital, and it looks like your other acquaintances may be waiting for you on the beach, so I think Santa Monica is our best bet."

"But that'll take an hour to row up there," I protested, glancing nervously into the dark toward the shore.

"Yeah, it would," Vinny agreed. "That's why we'll use the outboard."

He turned and pulled a yank cord. I heard a small but throaty little engine roar to life, and in seconds we were pushing the wind hard against our faces as we approached the carnival-like light of the Santa Monica pier.

We pulled up onto the sand and I jumped out, running for the stairs toward the cop car I saw parked at the top. I yanked the two uniforms, one male, one female, away from their coffee and watchfulness. The woman came with me while her partner called for an ambulance and some patrol cars to try to pick up the boys down the beach.

By the time I got back to the boat, Roberto had taken off his shirt and tied a makeshift bandage. Ginny was still talking, though gritting her teeth from the pain.

"How you holding up?" I asked as lightly as I could.

"Well, you know that old saying about pouring salt on an open wound?" she asked.

"Yeah."

"Well, I've been soaking in it." She smiled, half in jest, half grimace.

"Here's the ambulance. I'll ride with you."

I turned to Vinny and saw the cop questioning him and his father. I crossed over to him and gave him a big hug, then kissed Roberto on his unshaven cheek.

"Officer, these men saved our lives. I want to make sure that they can get in touch with me."

As I recited my phone number to the officer, I took off Vinny's jacket and gave it back to him.

"I want you to call me, I want to do something to thank you."

"It's not necessary," he said with a smile.

"Call me Monday." I started to go and then turned back, "If you don't call me, I'll send somebody to find you." I smiled broadly and climbed into the ambulance.

Ginny pulled the oxygen mask off her face and rasped, "After that first date, we really should send those guys some flowers or something."

I pushed the mask back and took her hand. "Or something," I agreed. I was thinking a nice thirty-foot double-engine fishing boat would suit the bill very nicely.

19

The next few hours saw Ginny in minor surgery and me answering a million questions. I asked that Evan be contacted, and he showed up just as Ginny was being wheeled out of recovery.

"What took you so long?" I asked, relieved at his arrival but vaguely resenting that it was belated.

"You're not the only crime in L.A. you know," he said dryly, but when the uniform had left the waiting room, Even put his arms around me and squeezed tightly.

"I'm okay," I said, tearing up. "I feel like shit about Ginny though."

"The doctor said she's gonna be fine," he soothed. "I heard what she did, she's pretty tough."

"Yeah. She's a stuntwoman. She prides herself on knowing how to take a fall and this time she took me with her. She saved my life."

Evan let me worry a minute before he spoke again. "C'mere and sit down." He led me over to some semi-comfortable armchairs in the waiting area.

"I found something out," I said, focusing again on the cause of my dark fortune. It seemed unreal to me even as I said it. "My stepfather hired alleged ex-gang members to work on his dock, so I probably did see the brother that day."

"Yes, that checked out."

"But what could Bill have to do with it?" I put my head down. "Binford's wife told me that Bill was insistent about hiring them. Jesus, he couldn't be involved in all this, could he?"

"What does he have to gain?" Evan asked levelly.

"I don't think he has anything to gain." I grabbed my head to stop it from flying off.

"How's his business doing?" Evan asked.

"Pretty steady. I haven't seen the numbers for this quarter yet, but I don't have any reason to think they'll change." I knew the bottling plant was a reliable little moneymaker.

"Maybe you should," Evan said.

He was annoying me. What, was I stupid? And what the fuck did Evan know about high finance? He needed to back off. "Look, he wouldn't get my money anyway, and he's . . . no, I just can't believe it."

I stood up quickly as a staff member approached us.

"Callaway Wilde?" he asked in a tired voice.

"Yes sir, that's me," I answered.

"Your friend is going to be just fine. The bullet went into the muscle tissue in her left upper biceps but it missed the bones and major arteries, we've cleaned it well and stitched her up but in fact, she should be able to go home in a couple of days. I'm admitting her to a private room."

"I'd like to cover the cost of putting her on the eighth floor please," I said quickly. Cedars has private rooms, nice. And then they have the eighth floor, with a menu that includes lobsters and space you can actually fit a visitor in. My father and I had been here many times, too many times.

"Fine, you'll have to go down to Admitting and make the arrangements. Do you have any questions?"

"I do, if you don't mind, Doctor," said Evan, and out came the badge. I snuck off to find Admitting while they sat down together on chairs molded of some colorless resin.

Two hours later, I was in the room with a weak but conscious Ginny, who was getting her turn with Evan. I interrupted after a few minutes of fact searching.

"I'm hungry. Anybody else?"

They both turned and looked at me. To my surprise Ginny answered first. "Starved." Turning to Evan she added, "The bitch was gonna take me to dinner. I didn't know it was gonna be hospital food."

"Actually, the food's pretty good here, but I think they've stopped serving." I pretended to look down the hall. "Anyway, I don't see the maître d'. As I recall, Jerry's Deli is across the street."

Evan glanced at his watch. "They deliver until midnight, you've got about twenty minutes."

"Get me a hot brisket sandwich and matzo ball soup. Right away. And don't forget the Dr. Brown's," Ginny reminded. I wasn't sure if she should have the brisket but the broth would be good for her.

"An excellent choice," I said. "Evan?"

"What the hell, I'll take the triple decker sandwich, turkey and brisket with Swiss cheese, coleslaw and Russian dressing on rye."

I stared at him, "Damn, that sounds so good. I usually have basically the same sandwich with a pickle and mustard, but . . ."

"Oh for God's sake," said Ginny rolling her eyes, "call!"

I did, and I took the liberty of ordering a couple of beers for Evan and me. I wasn't sure he would drink his, but I could handle two.

A large Filipino woman in light blue polyester came in with a little tray and asked Ginny how she felt.

"It hurts like a son of a bitch," Ginny said with a big smile.

"Well, I've got just the thing, then," smiled the nurse and intravenously administered a nice, big dose of Demerol.

"So, now, let me tell you both why it took so long for me to get here," Evan said.

"You were picking up a dozen glazed?" asked Ginny, looking more than a little glazed herself.

"Okay, smart-ass. No more donut jokes. I *was* picking something up, though, a couple of bad-ass guys with some ugly homemade tattoos."

That made us sit up. "You got the guys who shot at us?" I asked.

Ginny rolled her head toward me first and then her eyes.

"And actually got Ginny?" I added. She seemed to think that this was an important part of the equation.

"Yeah, probably," he said. "They aren't talking, of course, but they might when I match the gun to this." He pulled a small plastic sample vial out of his jacket pocket and shook it. It made a heavy, rattling sound. Ginny winced again.

I crossed over and took a good look at the bullet. "I always said you had steel biceps."

"It probably would have gone right through a less buff arm than yours," Evan complimented. "We've got a team trying to find any others in the wood of the railing, but my guess is this bullet's buddies are way the hell out in the bottom of the ocean."

"Better them than us," Ginny added, and I couldn't have agreed more.

"True," said Evan, "and as unhappy as I am that you caught one, I, well, I couldn't be more ecstatic that you 'caught one,' if you take my meaning."

"You're welcome," said Ginny. "All I ask is that you fry the son of a bitch."

"In deep fat. Just for you." Evan inclined his head politely.

They actually seemed to be bonding. Strange as that was it was stranger still that it pleased me. I looked from Evan to Ginny and back again. Why was it that little things about him didn't annoy me, the way most men annoyed me after a week or so?

"I'll need you to identify the shooter," he said to me.

"Why not Ginny?" I asked, mortified to have to face those eyes again. But Evan gestured to Ginny, who smiled at us sloppily; the drugs were taking effect. "Ah. Love to," I said.

"It doesn't have to be tonight. We can let him sit until tomorrow. After we eat I'll have to go and ask him a few questions in reference to our conversation earlier in the waiting room," Evan said right on cue, as the delivery guy knocked on the door.

Evan waved me off and paid the man; my money was all wet anyway. I hate it when people are cheap to anyone, but especially someone who's working their ass off for very little money. Evan apparently shared that sentiment because he tipped very well. Maybe he empathized.

The sandwiches were just what the doctor ordered, and I finished mine off. For all her bravado, Ginny only got a few bites down and sat sipping her cream soda as the Demerol took full effect. I took the can out of her hand and pulled up the blanket when her eyes closed. The only response I got was her shifting into a more comfortable position.

"Do you want me to take you home?" Evan asked me quietly.

"No, I'll stay here. Somebody's got to order breakfast." I smiled at him and he put his arms around me.

"Is this going to stop, Evan?" I asked. "I mean, how did I end up in the middle of a gang blood feud?"

"For what it's worth, that part is over." There was a dangerous note in his voice that chilled and reassured me at the same time.

"How do you know?"

"Because I made them understand that if anything happens to you, I will come after them." He hesitated, seeming slightly unsure of how much to say and then he added, "Not as a detective."

He was quiet for a minute. It felt odd to be protected by a part of Evan that was so dark and unpredictable. Safe, in a very scary way. I wondered how often he had crossed the line in his job and how black the side of him was that could do that. And then he said softly, "Now we have to find out who started this."

He kissed me on the top of my head and left quietly. Turning out the lights and moving to the window, I stared out at the hills for a long time wondering why it didn't bother me to know that Evan was capable of murdering someone, why I actually respected it. Finally, in the stillness the voice inside me answered: *If I had lost Ginny, I would gladly have crossed that line into the blackest darkest part of myself, and God help anyone I set out to meet there.*

20

The night before, against Ginny's wishes, I had called her family to let them know what had happened, insisting that she was okay and only needed to sleep, and in the morning they had appeared, parents, sisters, some miscellaneous nieces and nephews and one elderly aunt, en masse.

Ginny's mother, Dorothy, was a formidable woman, very busy running her own business in La Canada. I told her I wanted Ginny to recoup at my house for two reasons, I had the staff for full-time care, and I just needed her. There was a third reason; Ginny loved her family, but they drove her nuts. Dorothy agreed to deliver her to my house as soon as she was released, later that day.

So after an early breakfast I made my getaway. Through a gap in the crowd clustered noisily around her bed, Ginny mouthed the words, "I'm going to kill you," at me as I waved good-bye.

The cab pulled up in front of my home before 8:00 A.M. and I was pleased to see that my car had been delivered courtesy of the LAPD, God bless 'em. I filled Deirdre in to supplement my phone call of the night before and was surprised to find that she had made a big fuss of getting things ready and perfect for Ginny. I'd always thought Deirdre didn't really like Ginny.

Before she left me, she told me that Bill had called, and trying to shake the nasty whispers out of my head, I went to my office and called him.

After a perfunctory exchange of greetings with Nina, Bill came right on the line. "Cally."

"Hello Bill, what can I do for you?" I asked, reassured by the warmth in his voice.

"Well, I thought you might like to play a little golf this afternoon. It's a beautiful day, and if I can find someone to go with me, I'll knock off around lunch."

"Sounds tempting, okay," I said.

"Great, I'll meet you at the club at twelve-thirty."

There was a soft knock on my door.

"Yes?" Deirdre entered, leading with a warning face.

"Ms. Elena to see you, if it's not a bad time." She was holding the door half-closed, thoughtfully giving me an out if I wanted it. I wondered why.

"No, it's not a bad time. Tell her to come in."

Deirdre opened the door the rest of the way and stood aside, eyes glued respectfully on the floor. When Elena passed by her and entered the room, I saw why.

She had obviously been crying, and was still very upset. Deirdre's averted gaze was a kindness, not a slight.

"Elena, what's wrong?" I asked, but I was pretty sure I knew.

"Oh Cally, I tried to ignore it, I thought it would go away, but Binford didn't come home last night. I knew I could come to you, I knew you'd understand. I just can't tell anybody else, but we've been friends for so long." She had her palms pressed together and her thumbs against her mouth, it made her look like she was praying. Maybe she was.

"Oh Elena. Honey, I'm sorry." What the hell do you say? "Come on, let's go sit outside." I crossed past her to the door and opened it to call out to Deirdre. I choked the call back just in time.

My butler was still standing there.

"Herbal tea?" she suggested.

"Please. We'll be at the table in the rose garden. Thanks Deirdre," I said and went back in. "Come on, then." I took Elena's arm and mostly led her outside because she was now crying into her hands. Snatching up the box of tissues on my desk as we swept past, we went out into the reassuring sunshine.

After I placed a tissue in Elena's hand and the full box in front of her, I sat down, waiting for her to compose herself. That didn't happen but she did manage to take in enough air to speak.

"I'm so stupid!" she sobbed.

"No, you're not stupid, he's a son of a bitch," I said smoothly. "Big difference." Unfortunately, Elena wasn't the first woman I'd had this talk with, which is one of the many reasons I don't trust the opposite sex as a rule.

"I can't believe it, we just got married." She shredded the tissue as she spoke and looked up at me. "Did you know anything about this?"

"No." I was semiclean there. "I never see Binford, you know that, but damn, I thought he'd have more staying power than this."

"What am I going to do?" She let her chin land hard on her palm as if to hold her head up.

"You're going to talk to him," I said. "I'm no expert

on successful relationships, as you know, but you've got to talk to him."

"I can't." She cried some more. "What will I say?"

"That you're pissed." I nodded, knowing that she would be soon.

"But I'm not. I'm just so disappointed," she said, deflated.

"Tell him that, that's a good place to start."

"Will it do any good?" She looked at me with the most pathetic eyes. I wished I could help her, but I also wished she would go away and take my fucked-up family with her; not her fault, but all I got from this family was grief. Also, I wasn't good at the girlfriend thing, I knew that, and I wasn't comfortable with anything I didn't excel at, I knew that, too. Frankly, I had no idea what to do.

"I don't know what you think is 'good.'" I tried. I wanted to be a help and a comfort, I really did, but I was so tempted to tell her to run, to be afraid, very afraid of my brother and mother and the dysfunctional relationships they excelled in. I should know. I was trying to cut the apron strings and here Elena was tying herself on. I wanted her to have a nice guy, a clean start. She had always meant well, always been nice to me, to everyone around her, she deserved better.

"I would do anything for him" was all she could muster. "I love him."

"I know you do." I sighed. "Listen, Elena. When my brother married you, I thought, hey, maybe he really is a nice guy. Things have always been so strained and competitive between us that it's been hard for me to tell." I realized as I said it that the same thing was true about my mother, maybe she was nice to everybody but me. "You know how difficult it's been, probably you more than anyone. Hell, Elena, you're right, you've been my friend for a long time, you've seen me through some ugly changes, and you know my family, better than I do." I felt a really warm sense of history with her for a moment.

"Your mother has really messed that up," she said and cried again.

"Let me tell you something about my mother, maybe it'll help you with Binford, I don't know." I paused because she looked up so hopefully that I felt guilty, because I didn't have that much to offer. "Rudy feels wronged by life, and as fucked-up as that is, it feels real to her. You have to remember, and I constantly have to remind myself, that she is in a kind of self-inflicted emotional anguish because she thinks she was cheated. All that paranoia and fear she's created? That's scary to live with." I smiled at Elena but I could tell that she didn't understand. "You have to feel sorry for her, but . . ." This was the big one, the point I needed her to absorb, but I didn't know if she had the self-respect to hear me, "*But, you don't have to subject yourself to it.*"

She blinked twice and her reddened eyes cut away, she didn't get it.

"Elena, I have no advice for you about your marriage, other than this: talk to him. Nothing anyone says will weigh more than what you feel and what you need." I stressed my simple advice to the sticking point. "Don't need this kind of pain, don't choose it."

"You're trying to tell me it's my fault, that I *chose* for this to happen?" She was finding her anger, and it was vaguely directed at me; I should have expected that.

"No, I am *not* saying it's your fault. I'm not even saying that it was your choice to be in this position now, but it *is* your choice to stay there or not. And if you choose to stay there, you may not be wrong. I can't make that judgment, only you can." I knew I had crossed the line and she was shutting down. She hadn't come to absorb my personal living strategies, she had come to hear that everything was all right, that Binford loved her, that it would all work out. So I lightened up.

"Listen Elena, you feel like shit, it sucks I know, and I'm sorry. But you need to talk about it with Binford, shout about it, get the facts. Maybe you're overreacting." Yeah, sure, I thought.

"Maybe I am." She looked hopeful again. "Maybe he just made a little mistake and he's sorry."

"Well, I hope he's sorry," I said, thinking about him kissing the girl at the party. Had Elena seen them after all? "What do you know about this anyway? Has he been seeing someone or what?"

"I'm not sure. He's been distant for a little while. I thought it was just the honeymoon wearing off, you know, but then a few days ago I heard him making a phone call, he was whispering, and when I came in he hung up and acted really strangely. Then at the party, he disappeared for a little while and when he came back, he wouldn't kiss me and he took a shower before we went to bed."

So she hadn't actually seen the woman, just had her suspicions. I wasn't going to say anything. That was more involved than I needed to get. So I decided to go with sarcasm. "Subtle," was all I said.

"I don't know if I can go home and face him," she said, but I could see that she was resigned to it. She had found some strength, and I was glad, she was going to need it.

"Yes you can, you know you can, and the longer you put it off, the longer you're going to worry about it." It was a philosophy of mine, if you had something unpleasant to do, do it immediately, then you wouldn't spend hours or even days worrying about it and still have to do it anyway.

Deirdre arrived with the tea and we were silent while she poured, then she disappeared like a magician's assistant, leaving behind the wisps of steam in our cups.

"This'll help," I said, lifting my cup. "Tea always helps."

Elena lifted the cup and took a sniff of the calming scent. She smiled and her eyes filled with tears again, but this time they were grateful tears, and she smiled through them at me. "You're right," she said. "You're always right."

"No, I'm not. But, thank you." I still felt mystified that she liked and trusted me, it had always been hard for me to accept that someone really did. Not used to it, I guess.

"You're going to be okay." I said. "No matter how this turns out." It sounded dismissive I knew, but there was only so much intimacy I could face at the moment, even with someone I knew as well as Elena. I cared that she was hurting, I truly felt badly for her, but the fact was, I was dealing with a few issues of my own. I was operating at such an intense level of drama and tension in my life that one more crisis was more pressure than I could emotionally bear.

She looked away again and took a sip of her tea, closing her eyes and swallowing slowly. "Thank you for being here for me," she said, and I felt completely inadequate. "But, I just don't know what to do."

I nodded and softened, resigning myself to listening and being a little more open. I knew how to do that, too, sometimes; I knew I needed to do it more often.

"Cally?" her voice sounded weak and broken. "Please, don't say anything about this to anybody."

"Absolutely not. It's not anyone's business but your own."

She didn't say anything more after that. We sat quietly and finished our tea and then she left. I felt sympathetic, but it was her battle, and she would have to rise to fight it, or lose.

Twelve-thirty-five saw me picking a nice wood out of my bag for the long drive off the first tee. I was good at golf, but I hadn't played much since my father died. We had enjoyed playing so much together that it just wasn't the same without him, but it was nice to be out with Bill on a gorgeous day. I realized I missed the game and the outing as well as my dad.

Bill watched the ball land and bounce well down the fairway and nodded sagely, "If you just got out and played more often, you'd be scratch."

"You're up," I said as my phone rang. I could hear someone talking before I got the thing to my ear.

"Tell this woman to leave me alone, I'm not dying!" It was Ginny.

"Oh, hi. You got there. Is Deirdre making you comfortable?" I asked.

"For God's sake, how many times can you fluff a pillow? I just want to take some Vicadon and go to sleep."

"Then go on and do it. I'll be home after I pick out the asshole who shot you from a selection of like-assholes."

"That's right, the lineup. Are you going to be okay with that?" She asked, knowing it wouldn't be easy for me.

"I'm looking forward to it." I lied. The fact was that the thought of seeing those eyes again chilled me, and I was afraid, what if I couldn't do it? What if I wasn't sure? So much depended on me getting this right and I was far from confident.

"You'll be all right." She had more faith in me than I did, that helped. "What are you doing now?" she inquired.

"Golf."

There was a brief crackly silence and then the anticipated tirade. "What was that? Did you say, 'golf'? Let me get this straight—you have my mom drop me off at your house so you can take care of me, I'm lying here wounded and bleeding, most likely dying of gangrene or some such shit, and you're out knocking a ball around, having a good old time."

"It's business. I've left you in excellent hands, speaking of which, what's the deal with Deirdre?" I soothed.

"*She hovers.* It makes me nervous, how do you deal with it?"

"Put her on the phone."

"Yes ma'am?" was perfectly enunciated.

"Deirdre, there seems to be some problem with your level of attention to Ms. Ginny. She would like a pain pill and some quiet time." I switched to a more amused tone. "She seems to be feeling much better."

"Oh yes, her spirit is in no way dimmed or thwarted," she reported. "I will attend to her medication and some water right away." I could hear Deirdre address Ginny as she passed the phone back to her. "Would you care for sparkling water or flat?"

"Tap!" I heard Ginny scream at her and then she spoke to me. "Get your ass back here."

"Yes ma'am," I mimicked Deirdre, and flipping the phone shut, I turned my attention back to Bill.

He shot straight and true. He gets out more often.

I've always suspected it was to get away from Rudy for a few hours.

We climbed into the cart and buzzed down the fairway. Bill commented on what a nice day it was and then paused. I knew something was coming.

"Cally, I have a confession to make," he said, and he sounded a little guilty. Those voices started whispering again.

"Confess away," I said, much more lightly than I felt.

"I asked you out here today to talk a little business." He smiled over at me, and I breathed again. "Fact is, there's another bottling company that's about to go under and they've come to me with an option to buy them out."

"Is it a sound acquisition?" I asked. "Should be pretty easy to do the math."

"Oh, the potential is there. I could bring in several more of our clients' subsidiaries that we can't cover right now. The problem is acquisition capital." He cleared his throat.

"If we can't cover it, that pretty much settles it," I said.

"It's Royal Packaging," he said simply.

We had reached the specks of white in a field of green, and I braked a good bit harder than I meant to. "Royal? Jesus, Bill. That company is three times as big as Signa. We'd have to put everything on the line. And who's going to run it? The parent plant is in Orange County." Buying time, I went around the back and picked out an iron.

"Well, I thought maybe Binford could take over Signa and I'd make the move to Orange County." He came around to face me and put his hand on mine to stop me from drawing out the club. "Cally, I already put in an offer." His expression was relaxed, but there was a bit of sweat on his brow.

"Christ, Bill, didn't you know you'd need my signature on a loan of this size? And what about capital?"

"I offered Signa as the capital." He rushed on before I could react. "It had to be done right away and you were going through your own personal hell, I didn't want to bother you. It would be different if this were your only holding, like it is mine, but even if Signa goes under, you'd be fine." It all came out in a rush. He'd been practicing.

I nodded and looked off down the fairway at the little flag fluttering on the green.

"Rudy put you up to this?" I asked. "She always wanted bigger, more."

It was Bill's turn to stare off, and I was surprised to see great sadness on his face.

"No, Rudy doesn't even know about this. Maybe her ambition for Binford has influenced me some, I don't know. I'd like her to be happy, before . . ."

He broke off and started rummaging through his golf bag as though the perfect club was down in there somewhere, he just couldn't find it.

"Before what?" I wasn't going to let it go at that. Was he finally going to leave her?

Bill found that club, sighed and put his arm around me. "Cally, honey, your mother is sick. She has tumors in the lining of her lungs. She didn't want anybody to know, but it doesn't look too good."

I thought about her crying in the elevator and saying how tired she was, the pinched look on her face the last few times I'd seen her. Still, I couldn't believe it, I couldn't trust her to have an honest need, and I couldn't feel badly for her without suspicion. My emotions where she was concerned were a twisted wreckage; I always had to wait for the smoke and the dust to clear before I could assess the damage.

"C'mon, are you sure this isn't one of her ploys?" I asked irrationally, and before it was out I could see from the look on his face that it wasn't.

"One of the worst things about the illness is that it makes her act funny, paranoid and a little hateful. The pain medication especially, it makes her angrier and forgetful, I think she hates that the most."

"Bill, she's always been like that," I said.

"Not like this, Cally. Your mother has always been a little spiteful, bitter, I know, I'm not blind, but this is different. She was always aware of herself before, now I'm not sure she is, it sort of controls her." He turned me to face him and looked at me.

"Why can't she be treated?" I asked.

"It's complicated. It's a vicious form of cancer and it's metastasized. At this point we're waiting to see where it shows up next."

"Is this going to kill her?" I asked, afraid.

"Yes. Eventually."

I looked down and was surprised at how much emotion came over me. "But nobody knows how long. It could be years," he added.

"How many?" I asked.

"One or two," Bill said softly and then he pulled me into his chest and I cried for a minute.

Whatever else she had become, she was my mom, the person who had held my hand on the beach that day. She'd loved me once, I knew that.

"Thanks for telling me," I said, pulling away, and Bill handed me a clean white handkerchief, which I accepted gratefully.

"Should we go home?" he asked.

I looked around at the trees and the sky and the gentle ripple of the breeze on the lake and thought about how close I'd come to death in the last few days.

"No," I said with determination. "No, let's play. Life's short, Bill. Let's enjoy it."

21

I went straight from the club to the police station for the lineup. I was nervously sitting in the still unfriendly waiting room until Evan came to walk me up. His presence calmed me a little in a thrilling way. The room he led me to was sterile and harsh, any sound you made was hurled back at you by the hard walls and surfaces that comprised it. After we settled ourselves, Evan spoke into a little microphone. A door opened in the side of our theater and out filed six men.

I was expecting it to be hard to remember exactly what the shooter looked like, to be sure, but I could never forget those eyes and it only took a minute. Evan smiled at me proudly when I picked him out without a hint of hesitation. He sat me in his little cubicle and left me for about half an hour. When he rejoined me, he told me what he'd just learned from the kid I identified.

The first shooter on Ventura Boulevard was Oswaldo Herado, a kid who was in and out of the gang for a while. Someone had come to him and offered him the "job" of killing me and making it look like a holdup. All that my latest assailant knew, or would say, about who offered that job to his fellow gang member, was that it was "some Latino guy" who never gave a name, just the money. Five thousand. It didn't seem like much to me, and it turned out to be the price of his life.

The same "Latino guy" had offered me up for revenge to the brother, Luis Herado. My latest assailant had been told that I'd killed both of his buddies. Now it was a matter of gang pride to get me. There was apparently some kind of street etiquette involved. I wondered if there was a little book on it, Emily Capone's rules for surviving in today's brutal society.

Evan told me in that "don't ask" voice that he'd straightened today's selection out on who killed Luis, so I wouldn't be the focus of revenge anymore. But this guy still claimed not to know who the contact was.

"But if it's 'some Latino guy,' then that eliminates Bill," I pointed out.

"He could have used a middleman. Probably would have had to," Evan said thoughtfully. "But we still have to consider that he doesn't really get your money if anything happens to you."

I looked at him for a moment. "Today, he just came out and asked me for some."

Evan looked up with interest. "He needs money?"

"Well, yes, company money," I said a little uncomfortably, "but it's a good investment. Listen, Evan, I just don't think it's him."

Evan regarded me, then nodded in agreement or was just lost in thought, I couldn't tell which. His phone rang.

"Paley." He listened for a moment, and I got the feeling it was something important, but I also stuck up a mental Post-it never to play high-stakes poker across from him. "She's here, I'll let you tell her."

He reached across to me with the phone, and I took it. "Yes?"

Deirdre's crisp, efficient voice came back to me. "Ms. Wilde, I'm glad I found you. We've had a phone call a few minutes ago, I'm afraid I have some bad news for you."

"What is it?" I panicked inside, but my voice rose just a fraction.

"It's Ms. Elena; she's in the hospital. Apparently, an overdose of some kind of pills."

"Is she going to be all right?" I asked as quickly as I could get it out, horrified that I had let her be alone when she was so distressed.

"Your stepfather is the one who called, and he informs us that the doctors are unsure at this point. It seems she is unconscious."

She finished as thoroughly and concisely as was possible. God bless her again.

"She's at Cedars?" I asked.

"Yes ma'am."

I thanked her and handed the phone back to Evan. "Did you hear?"

"Yeah," he said. "Sounds like she tried to kill herself."

"She came to my house this morning, she was upset because she thinks Binford is having an affair, and the other day she definitely drank too much. Maybe this overdose is accidental, you know, too many wines and a couple of sleeping pills?" I looked at him hopefully.

"Well, let's go see what we can find out." He stood up and grabbed his jacket.

That's the thing about a detective, they don't speculate a lot.

After three trips to the police station and one to the hospital in the ambulance with Ginny, I was getting used to tense rides with uncertain conclusions at the end of them, and I was relieved that Evan didn't want to trade guesses about what had happened.

When we arrived at the hospital we met Bill outside Elena's room. He looked tortured. When Evan gently asked him questions he answered in a hushed voice, as though he didn't have the strength to speak full volume. But he was as helpful as possible, supplying the coherent facts. His eyes kept darting up and down the hallway where we stood and whenever anyone passed nearby he stopped speaking and waited for them to pass, ashamed to have a stranger hear this family tragedy. He told us that the housekeeper had found Elena on the floor of her bedroom; an empty bottle of pills with the label ripped off was on the bed stand, along with a half-empty decanter of cognac.

Just as Bill was finished filling us in Binford arrived, and it came out he hadn't been home the night before. Bill had some angry words about that, but it was pretty clear that Binford was already feeling shitty so Bill didn't go too far. Instead he told us that Elena was unconscious, and the next forty-eight hours would be a waiting game. Her stomach had been pumped, but in his opinion, most of the damage had been done.

Bill said this last comment directly to Binford, insinuating that his son was responsible for Elena hurting herself, accidental or otherwise. Evan interrupted.

"Binford," suggested Evan, "why don't you go in and see Elena?" Binford looked at Evan as though he didn't know whether to be grateful or appalled, but he went in anyway, it was all he could do. The look on his face as he pushed open the door was a Polaroid of angst and worry.

"No note?" Evan asked of Bill, after Binford had gone.

"No."

"When did this happen?"

"Don't know when she took the pills. The maid found her around one o'clock," Bill answered. "It would have been last night or this morning."

"It was this morning," I said. "She came to see me around nine-thirty, maybe ten, very upset about whatever it is that's happening with Binford, especially his not coming home last night, she made me promise not to say anything to anyone about it. Jesus, I shouldn't have let her go."

Evan thought about that. "The maid found her? Is the maid there every day?"

"I think so," Bill answered.

"What time does she get there?" Evan asked.

"I don't know, I think around noon." Bill stared at the floor. "Yes. Noon, because I remember Elena saying the same woman worked for her sister in the mornings."

Bill walked heavily over to the bench in the hallway and sat down. "It's my fault," he said, and the tone of his voice was a stone dropping through still water.

"It's not your fault, Bill," I said.

"What could you have done?" asked Evan, abruptly overriding me and watching Bill warily.

I realized he was studying Bill's reactions. Suddenly I was completely disoriented. Evan had taken command, I felt reprimanded and I didn't know how to handle that.

"I could have put a stop to this, a long time ago." Bill stood up suddenly and faced us both. "I have to go. Call me on my cell phone if you hear anything." He turned to go and then stopped and said, with a tinge of fear in his voice, "Anything at all."

I nodded and watched him go. When I turned back, Evan was on his cell phone. I caught the words, "Stay with him." He clicked it closed and turned back to me.

"You're having him followed." I was numb.

"Yes. I want to know where he feels he has to go so urgently." His tone was dismissive, as though I was interrupting his chain of thought.

"You think he had something to do with Elena trying to commit suicide? Are you nuts?" I asked, resenting feeling powerless and left out.

"I don't know yet," Evan said, looking me in the eye. "The one person who seems to be connected to everything that's going on is your stepfather. I am the detective on this case, maybe you need to remember that."

That pissed me off. It surprised me when I found that I was shouting the next words. "He's the only sane one in the whole family!" I was angry with Evan suddenly, as though it would be his fault if Bill wasn't the man I thought he was, if I was that wrong. "You're so goddamned suspicious!"

"Occupational hazard," Evan said calmly and waited to see what I'd do next.

I snapped at him. "It's not a joke, Detective Paley. It's my life."

"I'm well aware of that," he shot back tersely.

The pressure was just getting to be too much for me. "What does that mean? That you're this brilliant detective? That you're trying to save my life? Well, you're not doing a very good job," I said meanly.

"Better than you've been doing."

"Excuse me?" I was boiling. "I've saved my own life several times now. You haven't even found out shit!" I knew I was being unreasonable, I knew it wasn't fair, but I just couldn't stop myself. "You know what, I've got somewhere to go myself. Have me followed if you want."

With that brilliant exit line I spun and started off down the hall. I was just to the door when somebody grabbed my arm roughly and yanked me back inside a darkened storage room. Before I could say anything a hand went over my mouth and another twisted my arm behind my back, holding me firmly. I heard Evan's voice, angry and quick.

"Now you be quiet and listen to me, you little brat. Someone is trying to kill you. Maybe more than one person and I'm not going to let that happen. Just because you've always been so goddamned independent doesn't mean you don't need my help now. And just because you *tell* yourself that you and your money never needed anybody or anything doesn't make it true. Your money has gotten you nothing so far except lonely. You think you're so smooth that I can't see that? Well, after this is over you can be lonely if you want, but *you will not be dead*. I will not allow that." He stopped to breathe with his mouth against my neck and then his eyes found mine. "I couldn't stand that," he whispered.

The honesty in his eyes scared the shit out of me.

And then he slid his hand off my mouth down to hold my jaw, to kiss me hard.

The tears came then, angry, scared, from my deepest,

darkest scarred place. He kissed me anyway, right over them. He picked me up and my legs wrapped around him, trying to pull him into me, to make him part of me. His mouth pushed my head against the wall, his tongue finding mine persistently, painfully in a wonderful way. His hands under my ass pulled me hard against him and I pulled back, drawing his strong chest against me with all the strength and want in my body. His mouth pulled away just a fraction and I could feel his words more than hear them.

"Stay with me," he breathed. I was stunned at the sound of his need. At the force of it, the power that it took for him to reveal that crack in his strength. Here was real courage: showing weakness. Something in my heart reached out and hooked into his. He forced me up against the wall and I found the bravery to admit to myself that the smell of his hair and his skin was all I ever wanted but didn't get for Christmas.

22

As Evan and I drove to Binford and Elena's house to check the scene where she'd been found overdosed, there was an awkward silence in the car. I wasn't able to present a perfect version of myself, to stay cool and removed, and I wasn't sure that was okay. I looked out the window and didn't know what to say.

I felt a gentle warmth on my leg as Evan's hand slid down to envelop my own. I looked across at him and we shared a smile. Big deal, it said, so we're not flawless, what a relief, I like you more this way. I looked out the window again and didn't let go of that strength in his hand until we pulled into the driveway.

"Tell me about Elena Clark," Evan said as he shut off the engine.

"Needy." Was the first thing that came to mind. "I've always been mystified by her behavior toward me. We played on the same basketball team in college for one year and much later I met her again when she was dating my brother, but you would think from the way she acts that she was my best friend since kindergarten." I sighed. "Actually, I *like* her, I don't count her as a close friend only because we don't have that much in common, but I'll say this. She's always been there for me. By that I mean, when everyone else was judging me, she never seemed to. She was, well, consistent."

"So naturally you kept her at a distance?" He looked at me pointedly.

"Okay, so I'm not the easiest person to get next to." I smiled ruefully.

"So what you're saying is, she's in awe of you and wants desperately to be your friend and equal," Evan said simply.

I turned to him. "Oh, well, when you put it that way, I am *such* a bitch."

"No, not at all," he said. "But you are a little hard to get next to, or so you say." He smiled gently at me.

"Yeah, okay, I don't have dozens of close friends," I conceded, "but it's not just that." I wanted to give an accurate account of Elena as well. "She *assumes* a closeness where there isn't one. She pretends a history that never existed."

"Maybe she thinks it existed."

"But it didn't."

"Well, not for you, but maybe what you perceived as a casual social exchange was the most meaningful relationship she had in college, or has now." He said, "That would certainly fit the profile of those who would try to kill themselves. They don't have anyone to confide in or help them out of their depression."

"I am *such* a bitch," I repeated as we pulled into the driveway.

"It also fits that she set it up to be found."

"What?"

"She knew that the housekeeper would be arriving in plenty of time to keep her from dying. That's consistent with an emotional plea for help."

"It's extreme." I nodded, thinking about my drug addiction. "And I can relate to that."

"What about her marriage?" Evan asked as he opened his car door. I opened mine and waited for him to come around before I answered.

"I honestly don't know much about it. Binford seemed very taken with her and I was pleased because before he had always dated girls with cup sizes larger than their IQs."

"I thought IQs were numbers and cup sizes were alphabetical," Evan said evilly.

I rounded my eyes, pushed my cleavage together and said in my breathiest voice, "Oh are they? I always get that confused."

Evan gave me that "you can't fool me" look and then continued. "So she's bright."

"Uh, yes. Relatively. Not a rocket scientist, but she wants to make something of herself, she's just still try-ing to figure out what," I told him.

"No signs of instability or depression before this?"

"Nope, quite the opposite. She always seems very happy and very devoted to Binford."

"What about Binford?"

"Hmm. What about him? I'm afraid I don't know him very well and he doesn't like me all that much," I confided.

"But how was he with her?" Evan asked.

"You mean, was he good to her? Faithful?" I asked.

"Was he?"

"I don't know. Not lately, according to Elena." I took a deep breath, "And, at his party the other night, I saw him sneak off to what was clearly an amorous rendezvous."

"Really?" he asked.

"Yes, really. I don't think Elena saw it, she was in the house, but she definitely suspects something, she told me that much this morning." I turned toward the house. "How could somebody put so much of their self worth in what a man thinks of them that they would try to kill themselves?" I asked.

"Let's not jump to conclusions, shall we?" asked Evan and we started up the front walk.

We had to snake around several police cars and some neighbors trying to find out what was going on.

"Do you ever get used to this?" I asked Evan. "It's a bit tense, as a lifestyle, I mean."

"And yours is relaxed?" He looked at me knowingly and I had to acknowledge the truth of that.

"Yeah, you're right. Safety is highly overrated." Evan met the detective on the scene with a handshake. I was introduced and we went up to the bedroom.

Overall, you wouldn't have known anything had gone wrong in this nice suburban home. Other than the untidy bed, the detectives in dark suits, and the wrappings of emergency medical supplies strewn across the powder-blue carpet, everything looked perfectly normal. The rose motif curtains were half closed, there was a paperback romance novel on the bed stand, and a robe thrown over a floral fabric chaise.

I stood in the doorway looking at the overly pastel bedroom while Evan walked around and asked questions.

"Prints on the decanter?" he asked.

"Hers," the other detective responded.

Evan's head came up at that. "Just hers?"

"Yeah, her private stash, I guess."

Tissues littered the floor next to the bed. Looked to me

like someone had been crying. I said as much and Evan nodded, not paying much attention. He crossed over to a little desk and opened the top drawer. He pulled out a pad and an appointment book. He flipped through it to the date of the day before and leaned down to read it, then he shut it again and placed it back in the drawer.

"Anything?" asked the detective, who sounded a little threatened that Evan might find something he hadn't.

"Not really, but she had appointments for today and the rest of the week."

"So? She wasn't planning on killing herself when she made them, maybe," the detective offered.

"Yeah. Maybe," Evan said and smiled as though that settled it. I didn't think it did.

He looked around a little while longer and then his beeper went off. He stepped out of the room to return the call and his face stiffened as he listened. He shut it off and beckoned to me.

"What is it?" I asked.

"I don't know yet. But listen, Elena had it in her appointment book to visit our favorite lawyer yesterday."

"Hervé? You're kidding," I said, not meaning it.

"We need to find out if she went," he continued.

I checked my watch, seven-fifteen. "We could call the office tommorrow," I suggested, which sounded too simple.

"The meeting wasn't at the office. It just read, 'lunch Hervé.' "

"Oh," I said. "That's going to be a little harder to check."

He smiled ruefully at me and held up a finger. The other detective had gestured to Evan and he crossed over to confer with his co-worker. A casual observer would have thought they were discussing football scores. Evan listened first and then talked while the man standing across from him grew more still and focused. Finally the detective nodded and Evan came back to join me.

"What'd you tell him?" I asked as he whisked me off to the car.

"To run some tests." He knew that wasn't going to satisfy me so he explained that he wanted to know if the cognac was just cognac and where the pills came from. "No label on a prescription, that's a little odd. If you were going to kill yourself, would you care if anyone found out where the pills came from?"

I could only think of one reason. "If I wanted to protect someone."

"Exactly," Evan said.

"Who?" I asked.

"Exactly," Evan said.

He held the door open for me and I slid onto the seat. When he came around and started the car I asked, "What was the phone call you got?"

"It was from the officer tailing Bill."

Afraid of the answer I asked, "What did he tell you?"

"To go to the beach," he said, and put the car in gear.

It didn't take long to drive from Brentwood to the little motel we had visited together once before. I didn't ask any more questions because it was clear that Evan was deep in thought, I respected his intelligence enough to leave him to it. His eyes were bright and every so often he'd tap the steering wheel three times and draw in a breath through his teeth, as though he'd drawn a conclusion, or maybe just thought of a new question. I waited, hoping he'd include me sooner or later, but oddly not uncomfortable with letting him do that in his own time.

When we drove into the parking lot he pulled into a space farthest from the entrance, strange since the lot was mostly empty. I made a move to get out, but he motioned me to stay where I was and pointed up ahead. Standing off to one side, where the scrubby hillside fell away in a gentle slope to the beach, was Sabrina. And she wasn't alone.

She was talking to Bill. Well, she wasn't actually getting to say much, it appeared he was giving her a talking-to. It looked like she was crying and I could see her occasionally trying to interrupt, only to be cut off by what seemed to be an angry onslaught from my stepfather. It sent a chill through me to see them together. What possible reason could they have to even know each other, except one? I hung my head and a few tears, hot and stinging, ran silently down the side of my face.

Evan didn't seem to notice; he'd cracked the window and was trying to hear what they were saying. But the wind was blowing from us toward them and all that could be caught was the tone, impatient and bitter.

After a few moments Bill threw up his arms and walked off toward Pacific Coast Highway. Straining a little, we could see that he had parked his Lexus down the road. Not in the parking lot. Sabrina stood for a moment with her face in her hands, and then she turned and walked into the little coffee shop connected to the motel.

Evan turned to me. "Well, that settles that," he said, and he didn't sound pleased to be right. "He's involved. But how?" He did the triple tap again.

"Okay. Fine," I conceded. "He knows Sabrina. Maybe he put her up to this, he's the one who originally hired the gang kids who tried to kill me. He needs my money to buy a bigger company, but *why*? I mean, he doesn't get my money if anything happens to me!"

"So that's why he needed Sabrina Valley," said Evan.

"Then why try to kill me?"

"Nobody to contest her claim, and if she is your father's daughter, maybe she would get the whole thing." He was thinking out loud.

"And how in the hell does he get Sabrina's money?" I asked.

"Some kind of prearranged deal, I'm not sure." He looked at me.

"It doesn't make any sense!"

"This is not a coincidence, Cally. I'm sorry, but I have to deal with the facts, and so do you." He reached out and took my hand.

I sighed and tried to still my heart. "I know. You're right, I know."

"Let's go find out what that was about," he said.

The coffee shop looked exactly like the hostess who greeted us, well scrubbed, dressed in red and white, a little old-fashioned and run-down but neat and clean enough. Neither was overly friendly.

Sabrina was sitting in a booth turned toward the plate-glass window overlooking the sea, with her elbows on the worn linoleum table and her face in her hands. Her shoulders were shaking softly as she sobbed, a portrait of loveliness and self-pity.

"Ms. Valley?" Evan intruded softly into her sorrow.

She spun around and looked up at us with fear in her eyes.

"No. No more, please. I just want to go home," she said simply, and it was an entirely different girl who faced us now. Gone were the smile and the innocent joyfulness; she looked haunted.

"I'm sorry, I can see this isn't the best time," Evan began, "but I'm afraid I have to ask you a few more questions." He spoke gently to her, respectful of her fragility.

She gulped back a sob and nodded. Spent, she gestured to the seat across from her. We took it quietly.

Evan waited until she blew her nose on the paper napkin and tried to compose herself. Meanwhile, I pretended to study the view that Sabrina had been mooning over. A huge boulder rose up in the middle of the beach, breaking the crescent of the shoreline. It was flat on top and from this distance I could just make out a couple, hugging on top of it, watching the sun set. It looked like a desolate but romantic spot. I made a mental note to have a picnic there, if I lived through this.

Evan began, "First of all, no more what? What is it that is happening to you?" He sounded reassuring, I remembered that, I had wanted to tell him everything.

She looked at him and then at me and then dropped her eyes again. Then she started to speak in that hushed velvet drawl that made her so appealing. "It's just gone crazy, everybody's crazy. I never meant anyone any harm." She looked up into both of our eyes, and damn if I didn't buy it. "You have to believe that."

"What is it we're supposed to believe?" Evan asked, and you just felt you could trust him. I wondered why.

"What I told you. It's the truth. Oh, maybe I didn't tell you everything, and now I can't, you just have to understand that."

"Why can't you?" Evan sidestepped delicately.

"Because I'm afraid." Big, fat teardrops rolled out of her eyes, bluer now with the rims of red.

"Who are you afraid of?" Evan asked. She didn't answer so he went on. "And who will help you if it isn't the police?" I felt that pang of jealousy, but it tempered quickly, he was treating her differently than he had treated me. There was a protective sense about his demeanor but not a sexual one. Like a big brother.

"I didn't do anything wrong," she said quickly.

"I didn't say you did," answered Evan solidly. "What was Bill Clark saying to you?"

Her eyes snapped up to his. "You saw him?"

Evan nodded.

"I, I swear. I don't even know how he knew I was here. But he wanted me to do something." She stopped herself and looked out the window.

Evan waited but she didn't finish. "And you are afraid of him?" I bristled slightly at the thought of Evan protecting Sabrina from Bill. It felt like he was taking her side over mine.

Not the brightest girl, she was trying to be careful of what she said, but it was an obstacle course and she was out of shape. Suddenly, I knew how difficult this was for her. It wasn't her fault, this whole mess, we were both stuck in an ugly web someone else had made to trap us. I resisted saying something comforting and waited to see how she would answer. For the first time, I hoped what she said was the right thing for her own sake, instead of for mine. I wanted her to be okay.

"I'm not afraid of him." She played with her napkin, crumpled it in her hand for a moment, and then spit out, "It's that lawyer. He's a horrible man." The tears came again.

I resisted saying, "I could have told you that."

"Are you referring to Mr. Tesauro?" Evan pushed gently.

"Yes," she mewed.

"What has he done?"

"I can't tell you," she whispered.

"Why not?" Evan insisted.

"Because I'm afraid, because I know he helped someone do something bad. And now he wants money from them. And he wants me to keep trying to get money from you so I can give him some." She looked up at me and her eyes were sorry, pleading.

"Who is he blackmailing?" encouraged Evan, and my thoughts flashed to Bill shouting at Sabrina outside the motel. Flashed to Elena telling me it was Bill who had insisted on hiring the gang members.

"I don't know, he didn't tell me that; I guess I wouldn't know them anyway. He was trying to convince me that he would do something bad to me, he told me that he found those men who tried to kill Ms. Wilde, and he said he could do the same to me." Her face fell into her hands again and she cried harder, fearfully.

"All right, try to calm down," Evan soothed. "We won't let anyone hurt you but you have to tell us what you know. What did Bill Clark want from you?"

"He wanted me to go away. He thinks I'm a bad person, but he doesn't understand." She sniffed. "I'm not bad. It's not my fault Mr. Wilde is my daddy, I didn't even know that before I got that letter, but when I told Mr. Tesauro I didn't want anything more to do with it, he got so mean and he threatened me."

I looked at Evan and he looked at me. What was Bill doing? Was it possible that Elena's suicide attempt had given him a change of heart about using Sabrina to get money, or maybe Hervé was blackmailing him and Sabrina was the one who could expose him?

Whatever he had said to her, she was sobbing again,

and I didn't think she would be much more help for the time being.

Evan spoke as if to a child. "I'm going to have some-one come and move you to another motel, Ms. Valley. When you feel better we can talk more. I'll try to get back to you later tonight. In the meantime, don't leave your room until a uniformed officer comes to escort you. Do you understand?"

She nodded and mumbled an effervescent, "Thank you."

"Wait a minute, Evan," I interrupted. "Can I talk to you for a moment?"

He stood up and walked with me a few feet away without the slightest hesitation.

"Listen, maybe this is crazy, but how would it be if she came to my house?"

"I mean," I continued, "I don't think she's dangerous or anything, and at the very least we could keep an eye on her." I bluffed, slightly embarrassed at my new-found compassion.

"And it's not like you'll have to sleep on the sofa, even with Ginny in 4B," he said dryly.

"I put Ginny in the honeymoon suite," I shot back, not to be outsmart-assed. "Leaving me eight vacant guest rooms and the pool house; I'm guessing Sabrina won't need all of those. So let's ask her. And then what? Tesauro?" I asked.

He raised one eyebrow and then gave me a little smile of approval. I felt a stab of jealousy; of course he was sympathetic to this little sexpot. I'll admit I felt sorry for her, sucked in by Señor Scumbag Esquire, but I also didn't trust her completely, based on her darling blue eyes, and obviously Evan did. Sucker. Typical man. I crossed my arms and turned my back to him.

We crossed over to the table. Sabrina was anxiously watching us.

Evan explained. "Ms. Valley, I'm afraid I can't let you leave town right now and you and I both don't feel very comfortable about leaving you on your own. So, Ms. Wilde has made a very generous offer to let you stay at her home until things get sorted out."

She stared at him and then at me. It was the only time in my life I have literally seen someone's jaw drop. I always thought it was just an expression.

"What? I mean, you would do that?" she stuttered. "For me?"

"Sure." I bit my tongue to stop from saying, "for little ol' you." "I've got lots of room, and nobody will bother you there." I hope, I thought.

"Is it because maybe we're sisters?" She pleaded in a small voice, and the hope in her voice sounded so lonely that it pried that door in my heart back open just a crack.

"No," I said. "It's because we need to solve these crimes and we need you to do it. And because I don't want anything to happen to anyone else." I paused. "To you." That's about as friendly as I could be at the moment to someone laying claim to a big hunk of my money. Oh yeah, and to my father.

She looked out the window again and big tears rolled once more. "Okay," she said finally. "I have nowhere else to go." And I knew that she felt as alone in the world as I did and somehow that sad fact bonded us.

I had avoided Evan's eyes until now and I expected him to be looking at the lovely Sabrina with compassionate protectiveness. I forced myself to look at him. He was watching me, and only me, with frank admiration. I tried to ignore it, to slam the door on him and be safe. But somehow I knew, it wasn't Evan I was afraid of, it was feeling anything at all. He might hurt me, he might fail me. But the voice inside me was calling softly.

Be brave, the voice said, *risk it*.

23

Deirdre didn't even give me the satisfaction of a hesitation when I called to tell her I was bringing her another inmate.

"Deedee, listen, we're going to have a houseguest for an indefinite period. I'll be dropping her off, and let's put her in the green suite, shall we?" I expected a big reaction, no luck.

"I think perhaps the yellow suite would be more suitable this time of year; the garden on the west side of the house is being replanted and the view will be far better to the east," she shot back.

I let the static crackle for a minute. "Deirdre?"

"Yes ma'am?"

"Does anything ever surprise you?"

"Yes ma'am. I am frequently shocked by the appalling lack of taste in American television programming. When can we expect your guest, and will they require anything special?"

I turned to Sabrina, who sat in the back seat looking like a startled deer. "Ms. Valley? Do you want anything special for dinner?"

"Like what?" she asked, completely thrown.

"Like, are you a vegetarian or a carnivore, or do you have a craving for anything? Chocolate cake? Brownies? Fatback?" I asked, not above trying to pack a few pounds on her.

"I like baked chicken. But I'm not real picky."

I turned back in my seat, catching Evan biting his lip to keep from laughing. "Baked chicken, Deirdre, and tell Sophie to leave the skin on it."

"Yes ma'am."

"And whatever else she wants. Make her some cookies or something. Thanks Deirdre, see you in a few." I snapped the phone shut and punched Evan in the ribs down low, where Miss Scarlet couldn't see. He made a sound like the beginning of a laugh and turned it into a cough.

"Ms. Wilde, would you please call me Sabrina? And I don't want to be any trouble. Really, I can just order a pizza or something."

I turned around again and looked her in the eye. "You can do that, too, if you want. But listen to me. First, call me Cally, might as well. Second, I have a chef and several other people who help take care of me; I'm only one person, I'm not very demanding . . ."

Evan coughed again. I pinched his thigh.

". . . and it's boring for them. Right now, actually my best friend, Ginny, is staying with me, she's recuperating from a . . . uh . . ."

"Illness?" Sabrina asked helpfully.

"An accident," I corrected. "She's resting tonight, you'll probably meet her tomorrow. Anytime you want or need something, within reason, just ask for it. The staff will love fawning over you. Especially Joseph," I said under my breath.

"Who's Joseph?" She had heard me.

"The assistant butler. He's . . . well—" I thought about it. The amusing fact was he considered himself quite the smooth ladies man, and I was bringing home a Vargas painting come to life. His reactions would be fun to watch; I wondered how to translate that to her. "Let's just say, he drives a Camaro, and he thinks all the girls will want to go for a ride with him," I concluded.

She seemed to get that. "We got lots of boys with Camaros in Louisiana." She smiled at the joke.

The smile turned to astonishment when we pulled into the driveway of my "house." Well, it's a mansion, really, but I call it home.

As we entered the house, Evan excused himself and went into the library to make some phone calls. The staff lined up to greet Sabrina. As I introduced each person she shook his or her hand and said, "Pleased to meet you." And they responded with a "Thank you, Ms. Valley." And when she looked embarrassed and drawled, "Y'all please call me Sabrina," they tried politely to hide their smiles.

Then I showed her around the house. Ginny was sleeping in one of the suites near my bedroom. I peeked my head in but got no response, I guess the pain medication was effective.

"Feel free to use the pool, there's a sauna in the pool house and a steam shower in every guest room. You can come down to breakfast or punch three on your phone and ask someone to bring you what you'd like. I always like to have my cappuccino as soon as I wake up, but I don't always eat breakfast. If you have any questions about the way things work, just ask Deirdre, that's what I always do." I winked at her and pretended not to notice her awe.

"And this is your room." I gestured as we crossed into the yellow suite. Deirdre had opened the French doors to the little terrace, and below in the garden you could hear the sound of the fountain. The room was not actually yellow but a warm, white tone with strong yellow accents in stripes and solids. It was cheerful. I couldn't remember the last time I'd been in it.

"It's like a picture in a magazine," she breathed, her eyes wide with amazement.

Trancelike, Sabrina crossed the room to the doors overlooking the garden. She'd never seen anything like it, that much was apparent.

"This," she paused and turned to me, "is the guest room?"

Actually, it was one of four guest suites, then there was my master suite and four more guest bedrooms, all with their own fireplaces and decor, and full living quarters for a staff of ten, though I only had six.

"Uh, yes," was, I thought, a sufficient response.

She sat on the overstuffed divan and let her fingers trail over the cream-colored silk. "Wow," she said.

"So, here's the remote, ask Deirdre if you want any movies, there's a pretty good stock of DVDs in a closet downstairs. I have to go."

"Will you be back later?" she asked, like I was her best friend and she'd really miss me.

"Umm." That, I didn't know how to respond to. I'd be back, but I was used to having my own space and schedule and I didn't want to have to entertain her. "I do live here, but I'm not sure how much free time I'll have."

"Oh," she said and she looked lonely again.

"But I'll come say good night when I get in." I started to go then paused at the doorway, "You know, sometimes

I eat in the kitchen with the staff. They're a nice bunch of people. You could do that if you don't want to eat alone."

That seemed to cheer her up.

"They wouldn't mind having me around?" she asked hopefully.

"I think they'll find you very refreshing," I said and bowed slightly to her as I made my escape.

It was a short walk back to the blue guest suite where Deirdre had put Ginny. I cracked the door and crept in. The light in the bathroom was on but Ginny was in bed, it looked like she was still sleeping so I turned to go.

"Where have you been?" she said as she sat up and snapped on the bedside light.

"Oh, let's see, I told you about the golf, right?"

"I'm good up until that. How'd the ID thing go?" she asked.

"Good, actually, I thought it would be hard, but it was easy." I sat on the edge of the bed. "How are you feeling?"

"Oh, you know, it varies from a dull aching throb to a full-blown racking pain."

"Got morphine?" I asked.

"Shit no. They wouldn't give me any. I had to fight for the drugs I got." She shifted her bound arm uncomfortably and grimaced, for my benefit I suspected. "What else?"

So I coughed it up, the whole ugly day so far. She knew how deeply the news about my mother would confuse me so she didn't comment on that but Ginny was horrified about Elena.

"Did she really try to kill herself?"

"We don't know. It could be an accident, or a plea for sympathy according to Evan, because she knew the maid would find her."

"Or somebody could have tried to kill her."

"What for?" I asked but I thought about how angry Bill had been at Binford when we were at the hospital. Why?

"I don't fucking know," she said, and then downshifted. "How's handsome?"

"Downstairs," I answered and was pleased to see her reaction was suitably large. "And somebody else is here, too," I teased before she could say anything.

"Who?"

"Sabrina Valley. You'll get to meet her tomorrow." I stood up. "But right now, you're going back to sleep."

She objected of course, couldn't stand being left out of the action, but the medication had made her groggy and sleepy and she allowed herself to be talked into it.

"Wake me up early," she muttered as I turned out the light.

I caught up with Evan in the front hallway.

"Apparently Mr. Tesauro wasn't at the office all day." I wondered how he found these things out at nine o'clock at night. "I need to make a house call."

"I want to go."

Evan considered the sentiment. "Why?"

"Because, I can help." I was tired of being left out, and getting secondhand information, and I was dying to see the worm squirm.

"Cally, this is an investigation, I need to ask him questions and get his answers."

"And I know what he's said before. I'll know if he's lying, or at least if he's contradicting himself." It sounded good to me.

Evan weighed the possibilities. "It would be interesting to watch his reaction to you being there."

I took it as a done deal. "Should we call first?"

"What?" Handsome winked at me. "And ruin the surprise?"

"What *was* I thinking?" I mused as we swept regally down the front steps and he held the car door open for me. Such a gentleman.

And we went, driving south to Century City, where Hervé lived in a condominium complex off Constellation Drive. The guard at the gate called up and got no answer, but Evan's badge got us the unit number and a parking space. The guard wrote our names down and told us that Hervé hadn't been out since he was on duty.

It was tasteful, the building, very costly. Lawyers make good money, but this was pretty extravagant.

We came around a corner at the end of a long hallway and stopped. Evan knocked and then immediately stepped back against the wall flattening me behind him, his gun seemed to grow out of his hand.

"What?" I asked, annoyed at being smushed against the wall for no apparent reason that I could see. Why the gun?

"Shhhh," he hissed and then showed me. He reached out his free hand and pushed the door. It swung open a few inches. Then he called out, "Mr. Tesauro?" No answer. "It's Detective Paley, I'd like to ask you a few questions, could you come out please?"

We distinctly heard the noise of a door closing but no further sound. Holding one finger to his lips in an entirely unnecessary gesture, Evan pushed the door open farther. "Stay here," he hissed at me and followed his gun in.

I stayed right behind him.

"Mr. Tesauro?" Evan tried again. Silence.

We crossed a short marble entranceway and went into the living room. Cream carpet, big black-and-white art, some rough pine furniture to take the nouveau edge off, not bad. Empty. Evan gestered at me to get the hell out, I shook my head, "no." An open door to the right led into the kitchen. Evan looked in quickly and saw nothing. A short hallway led into the back of the condo. He pointed at me to stay where I was and started toward the bedrooms. I stayed right behind him straining my neck to look around him and see what was ahead of us. Halfway down the hall we both stopped cold.

A doorway led to an office and on the floor of that office was a stain the color of which I knew too well. And in the middle of the stain lay a dead lawyer.

I took a sharp audible breath and Evan again gave me the international gesture for "shut up." He moved around the body and checked for a pulse. I didn't think he thought he'd find one. He didn't. It was hard to see, but it looked like the side of Hervé's head was dented in and matted with blood. Evan walked back to the doorway and looked down the hall again. That's when we heard the sound.

A noise was coming from inside the office's closet. I was still behind Evan, which meant I was totally exposed to the closet's louvered doors. Evan shoved me hard enough to send me sprawling to the floor as he leveled his weapon at the door.

"Police. Okay, come out. Nice and slow."

We heard it again, something like a sob. Evan motioned for me to stay on the floor where he'd knocked me. I rolled my palms up to say "where would I be going," but he was already crossing to the doors, keeping his body between the noise and me. He threw the closet door open and the next thing I heard was my own voice.

"Fiona!! What the hell?" I sputtered.

24

"Come out please and put your hands on top of your head." Evan pulled Fiona out roughly when she didn't respond quickly enough and patted down her body, looking for a weapon I guess. "You know this woman?" he asked me.

"Yes. She was my father's personal secretary. I . . . I . . ." I managed to get out, flashing on my mother's accusation of her being my father's mistress as well, but Rudy made so many outrageous accusations that I barely credited any of them. One thing was for sure, I couldn't make any sense of this. "Fiona, what are you doing here?"

"Wait a minute, just hold on." Evan had produced handcuffs and he snapped them on efficiently as he read Fiona Laasko her rights. I remembered, painfully, how that felt.

"Okay, that concludes the formalities I think. Now, you want to tell us what you're doing here?"

"Evan, she can't have anything to do with this!" I said, still feeling like I'd been hit on the side of the head with a big, frozen fish myself.

"Would you like to tell us what you're doing here, ma'am?" Evan reiterated with one of those "be quiet" looks to me. I shot back a "I already asked that" look.

"I came to talk to . . . him," Fiona said, glancing at "him." She suppressed a wave of obvious revulsion.

"Did he say much?" Evan inquired, unable to resist a touch of that sarcasm.

"He didn't have time to say much, before I killed him." She stood up straight and proud and looked Evan right in the eye.

Evan cocked his head to one side and took a long look down at the crushed skull on the floor and the dryness of the blood. "What did you use to do it?"

Her eyes went to a heavy round glass paperweight on the floor under the table. She pointed as best she could with her hands cuffed behind her back. "That!" she said, and tears started to escape her eyes.

"I assume it's got your prints on it," Evan said steadily.

"No. I, I wiped it off."

"And how did you know the victim?" Evan fired at her.

"He was Mr. Wilde's lawyer. I've known him for years," she said. That was an easy one.

"Why did you kill him?" Pause. That was harder.

"Because, I hate him," she said finally, but not with a great deal of conviction.

"Apparently," Evan said. "Why?"

"He was trying to blackmail me," the answer came in a smaller voice, as her eyes went to the carpet.

I reminded myself to breathe, and Evan and I exchanged glances. Was this who Sabrina was talking about when she said Hervé was blackmailing someone? Could it have been Fiona?

"For what?" Evan tried.

"I won't tell you that," Fiona said and it seemed as good a cover as any.

Evan took her by the arm and motioned with his head for me to leave the room. We sat down in the living room. He made his mandatory mumbled cell phone calls while Fiona and I sat and avoided each other's eyes.

"Let me ask you something else, Ms. . . . ?"

"Laasko," Fiona answered with that particular Finnish lilt.

"Laasko," Evan repeated without the accent. "Why did you stay here so long after you killed him?"

She shifted around and cleared her throat. "What do you mean?"

"He's been dead for hours."

"I suppose I must have blacked out." She was reaching now.

"What did you come here for, Ms. Laasko?" Evan snapped.

"I . . . I told you."

"Don't waste my time, or the lab's. You didn't kill that man, you couldn't have. The top of his skull is crushed. You're not strong enough to inflict that kind of damage, and unless you killed him and then decided to hang around for, oh say, twenty hours, you weren't even here when it happened."

"You don't know that," Fiona blurted obstinately. "I'm not talking anymore. I get to have a lawyer." She turned her face to the wall to cry quietly but with a strangely high percentage of pride.

We asked, he threatened, I pleaded, but nothing we did would make her say anything except, "I want a lawyer."

A soft knock at the door brought the team. Forensics, officers, the whole gang. I'd seen them before. This was three times for me, and that was three times too many. I wondered how the hell people did this for a living.

After he got things underway, Evan came back in to us. A uniformed officer helped Fiona get up, ready to take her to be questioned. She looked terrified.

"Fiona," I said before they disappeared. She turned and looked at me from a faraway place. "Just tell them the truth; you didn't do this."

It took a moment for my plea to sink in. Fiona could see how frightened I was for her and, after a short lapse, she seemed to hear what I had said. She smiled at me and her eyes filled with tears. "Oh Cally." She shook her head. "It's my fault, Cally. Don't be afraid for me." And then she started for the door.

Evan and I watched her go, and I saw his eyes narrow. I asked, "Why would Hervé be blackmailing her?"

"Because she was helping him somehow." Evan responded simply as if that was obvious but unimportant. "But I don't believe he was blackmailing her."

"Why not?"

"Because I don't believe she killed him, so it stands to reason that she didn't have a motive to kill him. She's covering for someone else, so she *invented* a motive."

"Oh," I said, nodding, completely confused. I was remembering how stupid I had felt for not making the connection with the signature stamp earlier and wondering if I should mention the gossip I had heard. Yes, I thought, I should.

"You know, I know this sounds absurd, and frankly embarrassing to me, but my mother, not the world's most reliable source, told me this really insane thing about Fiona and my dad." I was having trouble connecting the thoughts.

"What?" He wasn't paying much attention.

"That they had an affair?" I said it as a question because it didn't make much sense to me.

"Did they?" he asked.

"I seriously doubt it. She also told me once that I was not really related to my father. I had a blood test done over that one."

Evan was thinking. "It's not grounds for blackmail, I mean, nobody cares if a man sleeps with his secretary these days, right?"

"The secretary might."

"Not enough to pay somebody to shut them up, and I don't think she killed him, so it doesn't matter much either way. But thank you for telling me."

"Hey, anytime I can contribute some useless information, I'm here for you." I slapped him between his shoulder blades.

He pretended to sputter. "Thanks, it's good to know I've got you watching my back." Then he took my arm. "Come on, let's go check the guard's guest list," he said.

"You think the killer signed in?" I asked, astonished.

"I don't think whoever it was intended to kill him when they got here," he said grimly.

"Why?" I asked, bewildered at how he could guess these things.

"If you were going to kill someone, would you use a paperweight?" Evan looked at me and pulled me toward the door.

At the guard gate I got another shock. Written in the barely legible scrawl of the guard was the name, Clark, and the time 11:45 P.M.

"Oh sweet Jesus," I moaned, "not Bill."

25

Evan and I didn't speak on the way back to my house; it was late and we were tired. When we pulled into the driveway he and I sat in the car for a minute. I was listening to the sounds of the motor as it slowly cooled and then focused on the sounds of the frogs and the crickets in my garden. Evan pulled me over close to him and held on.

"I guess you'll arrest Bill now, huh?" I said in a small voice.

"It looks that way. But I won't know for sure until we pick him up and get some tests back from the lab."

I nodded, staring straight ahead. "On top of all this I know I need to go see my mother. Oh God."

"That can wait a day or two. Go on in. I've got a lot of work to do. Call my cell phone and let me know if you hear anything about Elena." He turned my face up and kissed my mouth once, soft and insistently, pulling me back so that I could feel again.

It worked. I smiled at him. "We don't know for sure it was him yet, do we?"

"No, we don't."

He walked me up the steps but wouldn't come inside.

The first thing I heard as I entered the house was laughter. Fun, innocent laughter. It was weird, out of place in my mood and appealing to me in my need, and it was coming from the kitchen.

I quickly crossed the marble of the entrance hall and went through the swinging door down the hall and into the brightness of the kitchen. Most of my staff were either seated at the table or milling around the kitchen doing various jobs while Sabrina was actually loading the dishwasher. They all turned and looked at me with that flash of guilt all employees get when they find themselves observed by their boss. Deirdre straightened up first and approached me with a smile.

"Welcome home, ma'am. Can I get you something?"

"I'll take a large glass of claret. Thanks." I looked around the room. "Hi everybody," I threw out. "Hello Sabrina," I said more directly.

Different responses, including a shy smile from my houseguest.

"Would my bad mood spoil your fun if I joined you?" I asked.

"Of course not," Sophie threw over her shoulder from where she stood wiping down the stove. "Would you like some dinner?"

The emptiness inside me was probably at least part hunger. "You know what, Sophie, that sounds great, thank you."

I was grateful that they all seemed to keep their easy mood, but it was hard for me to mix in, so I stayed standing in the doorway, soaking up the casual happy energy and the heavenly lingering scent of baked chicken.

I took the glass of claret off the silver tray and nodded my thanks to Deirdre who leaned casually against the counter. Testing the water, I waded in a couple of feet, stood next to her and asked quietly, "Any news about Elena?"

"Status quo," she said under her breath and smiled sympathetically at my deep sigh.

The rest of the group was talking about some inane movie I'd missed. I sat back and listened and watched their faces. Being with happy people melted some of my anxiety, but in another way it made me feel more left out.

I kept tossing glances at Sabrina. She seemed rapt. Her face glowed, and she frequently threw in comments, which the others built on. It was easy for her to be part of the group. I had never been able to do that, and I admired how natural it seemed to her. Effortless, she really was likable.

The conversation continued around me at the big kitchen table while I ate a huge plate of leftovers. Roast chicken with cornbread stuffing, green beans, macaroni and cheese, kale. I guess they had all decided on a dinner in honor of our Southern guest and though I was stuffed to the lymph nodes, and wouldn't want to eat that way often, it was really good.

When I finally pushed my plate away, I leaned back and looked at their faces. I knew I couldn't put it off anymore. Sabrina's helium mood had to be deflated, popped by me with a nasty five-inch steel pin.

"Sabrina, could you come into the library for a few minutes? I need to talk to you." I tried to smile lightly but I could see the fear flash in her eyes. A lot of bad things had happened to this girl, and I'll bet she'd heard about half of them with an opening sentence like that, or a version of it.

"What is it?" she asked in the hallway.

I opened the library door and we went in. I gave her the bad news right away; there's nothing worse than someone dragging it out with a bunch of dramatic buildups. "It's about Mr. Tesauro," I said as I struck a match and held it to the paper under the kindling. "I'm afraid he's been murdered." The wood was already stacked and the sticks bent the frantic flames as they caught hold. I turned and looked at her.

She was staring at me with absolutely no understanding. Her face was blank.

"Did you hear me?" I asked.

"Yes." She sat down and looked at the logs. "When?"

"Looks like last night," I said and sat down cross-legged on the other end of the sofa facing her. "I know he was your lawyer," I said.

"No. I mean, I guess, but he was bad." She was still looking at the fire.

"You said that before. What did he do?" I asked her.

"He was trying to get your money," she said simply.

"So were you," I said evenly but maybe not warmly.

"He wanted that, too, most of it anyway." She continued to stare at the fire. "I got that letter and I thought it would be wonderful to have that money, maybe buy myself a little shop."

"Or several," I fired a dart at her. Couldn't help it.

"Or something." The dart missed her completely. She paused as if she was finished and then she said, "But when I saw how ugly it made everybody act, I didn't really want it anymore." She turned and looked at me finally. "I didn't know your daddy. I mean, he wasn't really my daddy, he never was there for me, so why would I want what was his? Maybe I did because it seemed like a gift. Mr. Underwood, the lawyer in Shreveport, said I had every right to be angry that he never gave me anything and I was 'entitled' to it. That's the word he used, 'entitled.' But I wasn't angry. I had a daddy, and he was wonderful to me and I loved him. I wasn't angry at all." She smiled, and a big tear rolled down her cheek. "Then somebody else tried to convince me to get it, too." She turned away.

"Who?" But I already suspected that it was a boy. I could imagine the kind of young man Sabrina would be attracted to, a cute, nineteen-year-old gas station attendant with a high school degree and a C average, and I thought about the effect it would have on his small-town mentality to hear that his girlfriend was due to inherit twenty million dollars. "A boyfriend?" I asked.

She nodded and went blank again, like she had just turned herself off. Then she spoke, so quietly I had to lean in to hear her. "He turned out to be a different kind of man than I thought he was."

"They so often do." I tried for levity, but I couldn't help thinking, oh please let Evan be the kind of man I think he is.

"Does your boyfriend know who killed Mr. Tesauro?" she asked me with frank openness.

I snapped my head over to look at her. "What? My boyfriend?" I had no idea it was so obvious. I was sure we'd been discreet. "Are you talking about Detective Paley?"

"Of course," she said and looked at me curiously.

"Who told you he was my boyfriend?" I asked.

"Well, you just sort of stand near him like he is. And you kind of go together." She smiled a little. "And Deirdre asked me how it was going."

"Ah," I said. My discreet staff. But I was oddly pleased with her comment about how we seemed to go together. "No, he doesn't know, but he's got an idea." I tried to backtrack a little. "Tell me about this boyfriend of yours."

She looked up and shook her head.

"Okay, ex-boyfriend, then," I said.

"I met him in Shreveport, he was there on business. He was really sweet, so sweet. Nothing like the boys in Shreveport. He was so much more, well . . . mature. Anyway he came back a few times and we went away together a few weekends. I thought he really loved me, and then when this happened, when I said I didn't want your money, it just . . ." Sabrina stopped and turned to me with pleading, desperate eyes. "Money just makes people act so ugly. You just don't know who they are anymore, or maybe, you find out who they really are." She looked around the expensive room and then smiled apologetically. "I don't mean you, you've been very nice . . ." she fumbled, but I picked up the ball easily. It was a game I'd played many times.

"No, you're right. I know. I've always had money, so I've never known what it is to be desperate for it, so maybe I can't judge someone who does 'ugly' things because they want it. But I can tell you that having money makes it hard to know what someone loves *about* you. I've had bad luck with that, gotten burned a couple of times. So far the men I've chosen to have relationships with were interested in how I looked and how much money I had. In some cases I think it was what I valued most in myself. I'm not sure if the guys messed things up, or me. Probably me." I found myself sharing. It was strange, but it was easy to talk to her.

"Definitely me. At this point I think it's the wall I've built, my excuse."

"For what?" she asked.

"For being hard and cold," I admitted and it was too honest not to be painful.

"Oh, that's just you pretending. You're not really like that," she said as though it was an obvious fact, dismissing as preposterous the notion that I might really be a bitch. My relief at someone, anyone, not perceiving me as some cold ice princess was heartwarming. I could have kissed her.

"What's going to happen now?" Sabrina asked.

"I don't know. I didn't know you had stopped your claim against me," I said, looking at her differently.

"Because I hadn't. I mean, I wanted to, but Mr. Tesauro just told me I couldn't, he got so mean, he threatened me."

"How did he threaten you?" I asked, seeing the ugliness of his crushed head on the floor.

"He said he had hired somebody to kill you, and he could do the same to me." She looked scared.

"You said that before. Was trying to have me killed his idea?" I asked.

"No." She licked her lips and looked down at her hands.

"He hired a killer at somebody's request," I said trying to encourage her to tell what she knew.

"Yes, I think that's what he meant. But he didn't tell me who. I'm sorry." Sabrina shrugged her shoulders a little and suddenly seemed to notice me for the first time in a while. She smiled. "I'm so glad you got them instead. It serves them right." Her blue eyes flashed. "I hope we get to spend a little time together before I have to go back," she said. "But, even though I'd like to get to know you, I really do want to go back." She picked at the sofa fabric, "It hasn't been very nice for me here."

"What will you do about your boyfriend when you get back to Shreveport?" I asked.

She shut down again and looked away. "It's over. I told him I don't want to see him anymore. I was foolin' myself anyway."

"When did you do that?" I asked her, trying to sound girlfriendly.

"Last night."

"You called him?"

"No," she said firmly. "I told him right to his face."

I almost fell over. "He's here?" I asked, shocked. "In L.A.? He came to L.A. with you?"

"Yeah," she said hesitantly. Her eyes darted up to me. She seemed afraid that I would disapprove, or think she was stupid.

I had a weird thought that I needed to banish immediately, "It wasn't Bill, was it?"

"Oh, no!" she said, shocked.

"No, of course not, Bill doesn't travel." I tried to make a joke out of it. "I'm sorry. Of course your boyfriend came to L.A., that's how you knew how badly he'd behaved. I should have guessed." I reached across all that down stuffing and touched her shoulder. "I'm sorry, I know it must hurt. Did you send him home?"

"Yeah. I mean, I don't know where he went and I don't care!" She smiled shyly and a little proudly and then she sighed, an emotionally exhausted release.

"Well, we've had a big day, I guess we better get to bed." I stretched and feigned a yawn.

"No," she pleaded quickly. "Please, can we just stay here for a little while?"

"Sure," I agreed, although I was dying to call Evan and find out what was going on with Fiona, and if he had arrested Bill. "Tell you what. I'll get us some brandy, or maybe you might prefer creme sherry, and I've got to make a couple of calls. You wait here and I'll be right back."

She looked up at me gratefully and settled back into the sofa.

I paged Evan, eager to tell him what Sabrina had said about wanting to drop her claim against me, and got the liquors. When I came back with the two glasses, she was fast asleep. I set down the crystal, covered her with a throw blanket and turned out the lights. Picking up my snifter I looked at Sabrina. Her face was childlike yet strained, like a little girl having a bad dream. She reminded me of someone, not necessarily her eyes or her mouth but something less tangible, an expression. I was trying to think where I might have seen her before or what about her was so familiar when I glanced up onto the mantel at a photograph of my father and myself taken ten years ago. That was it. That was who she reminded me of. Me.

26

An hour later I caught myself watching the phone. It sat there passively and it didn't light up for me, didn't twinkle, didn't perform.

"C'mon, call me back," I vibed Evan.

I grabbed a sweater and went out on my balcony to think. It wasn't much use. I couldn't focus on any one thing, there was no logical trail to my thoughts. Just little wisps and scents of paths that led off, then died away, some vague, some persistently repetitive. Most of the persistent paths were lined with nettles that stung as I tried to follow them.

For instance, how could Bill want to kill me?

That one really hurt. That thought kept coming up and burning no matter how many times I tried to reason it away. I think it hurt most because, while he would never replace my father, he filled that space somehow. He was a decent man who had known and respected my father all his life and it had been Bill's shoulder I cried on at the funeral. He alone seemed to sincerely share my grief. He also knew Rudy and all her shortcomings and all the pain between us.

Being wrong about Bill was one more loss, maybe

one more than I could stand. I found myself thinking about my old cocaine supplier, wondering if I still had his number. A little bit of oblivion sometimes doesn't seem to be the worst thing.

"Detective Paley," Deirdre's voice interrupted my obsessing, and I turned to see her fading away behind him as he stood looking at me.

"I've got to talk to Bill," I said. "This is killing me. I've got to ask him what's going on." I looked at Evan's handsome, intelligent face, and even though I wanted his permission, I knew I would make the trip to talk to Bill whether Evan approved or not.

He sighed. "Well, I happen to know where he is."

"Did you arrest him?" I asked, chilled to think of my warmhearted stepfather in a nasty cell.

"Yes."

"Did he do it?" I asked because I had to.

"We haven't ruled it out, but he seems to have an alibi, and there's no match on the prints yet." He held his arms open and I crossed quickly to him and was encircled. It was nice.

"What the hell is going on?" I said into his chest. "What's happening with Fiona?"

"She still claims to be the killer, and she won't say much else. She's protecting someone, obviously, so we need to try to find out who and why." He lifted my chin and kissed my mouth hard and hungry. I was amazed at how much I wanted him, at how much his touch aroused me even with my life swirling unsteadily around me. He pressed hard against me. I pressed back.

"Can we make love yet?" I asked, breaking the kiss.

"You know the answer to that." He breathed into my hair.

I raised my eyes up to him and let a little exasperated moan escape me. "The inclination is to beg," I whined and looked at him sideways.

He laughed hard. It was the first time I'd really made him laugh like that and I hoped I would learn to do it often. It was a wonderful sound.

"Come on, let's go see if we can shed some light on this situation." He turned and led me out with an arm over my shoulder.

On the way to the precinct I filled him in on what I knew. No change in Elena's condition, most of the Hervé news he took as rote, but Evan was very interested in the boyfriend.

"I'd like to ask him a few questions." He looked at me and then back at the road.

"You think he might have killed Hervé?" I asked, surprised.

"If he blamed Tesauro for Sabrina dumping him, he could have."

"Why would he do that?"

"Because Tesauro let the cat out of the bag about the whole dirty scam, and made her want to nix the claim and everything to do with it, including the boyfriend. This guy has a double motive if he thought it cost him the girl *and* the money. She told you she gave him his walking papers last night?"

"Yes. If she's telling the truth," I said.

"So the timing was right. And where was Ms. Valley last night, I wonder?" Evan shifted in his seat and altered his grip on the wheel.

"You don't think she killed him?" I asked, shocked again.

"No, for the same reasons I don't think your father's

ex-secretary did. It's not really a woman's style. But I've been surprised before." He narrowed his eyes and made that sucking-through-his-teeth sound.

"What did Bill say about talking to Sabrina?" I asked.

"Denied it at first; now he says he was just warning her not to meddle with you. I hate to bring this up, but I did have a thought about why he might be talking to her . . ."

"He's not the boyfriend; I asked her."

He glanced at me again, as though there should be more. It felt like a test.

"How did he know where she was?" I asked; I could see from his face that I'd passed.

"He said Tesauro got in touch with him to see if he knew anything about your father's past, any 'indiscretions' he could testify to if there was a court case. He said Tesauro told him about Sabrina and offered him a cut if he would side with them."

"Scumbag," I said, and felt no respect for the dead.

"Yeah, he sounds like he was eager to end up the way he did." Evan tapped his fingers on the wheel and mused some more. I stared up ahead at the oncoming lights of the other cars and let him think.

"So," he said suddenly, and I realized that I had become the Watson to his Sherlock, "here's what we know. Oswaldo Herado tried to kill you. You killed him. He had been hired by a 'Hispanic man.'"

"Hervé Tesauro?" I suggested.

"Maybe. Possibly. It sounds like it, because he told people that he had hired someone to kill you. Someone broke into your house and stole, we think, a signature stamp. Someone who knew it had to be there. At the same time, Luis Herado, the brother of your would-be assassin is killed by the same intruder who stole the stamp, in your house, with a gun belonging at one point to your father. Someone is trying to make it look like you killed Luis." He paused and said the next sentence in a monotone run-on, "But you've got no motive and we have evidence to the contrary." He resumed his punctuated speech, answering his own questions. "Why? So you'll go to jail. How will that help them? Why not just let the brother kill you?"

"Because they found the stamp and they didn't need to anymore. They can create a postdated will or letter using his signature stamp," I offered tentatively.

"That fits. The gang involvement may be a snowball effect that our mastermind didn't anticipate but had to deal with once it started. The person who stole the stamp didn't need you to be dead for Sabrina's claim to work. But having you in prison would have helped a lot, by getting you out of the way. However, it makes sense that the person who has the stamp is the person who tried to have you killed because it connects the two incidents." Evan was nodding. This was cool. "Next day, you get hit with this claim from the 'sister' for twenty million. The charge is led by none other than your vengeful ex-lawyer, Tesauro. You find out that Bill hired gang members to work for him. You are assaulted by gang members at the pier."

"Ginny is shot," I said pointing my finger and my point at him.

"A detail, which she seems to find important," he said with a glint of fondness for my best friend in his eye.

"Which is understandable," I threw in.

"Absolutely." He smiled, and then his face went cold and hard as his thoughts traveled to something else.

"That shooting seems to be motivated by revenge for the death of fellow gang members," his right hand reached under his jacket to where his gun rested in its holster, the movement looked unconscious, "and I have dealt with that." His voice was distant and black.

I glanced at his eyes. He didn't look back.

Evan seemed to pass out of that darkness as he continued, "Next, Bill tells you he needs a huge amount of cash. Then Bill's daughter-in-law overdoses in what may or may not be a related incident."

"I don't think it is," I opined.

"As I said, may not be related, nonetheless, it sends Bill off, saying he has to go see someone, feeling guilty, it seems. He goes straight to Sabrina Valley, who, if her claim goes through, gets a big lump o' money. She tells us that she's been threatened by that same lawyer whom we find dead."

"Whew. Busy week." My head was spinning to hear the key facts all reduced like headlines on a wet, runover newspaper in the street. All mashed together into a pulpy mess.

"But, there's more. A skeleton in the closet; well, a thin Finnish woman who was your father's closest work associate for many years, who claims to have killed said lawyer. Why? She says because he was blackmailing her. But it seems obvious that she didn't kill him and is only covering for someone. What was she doing there to begin with?"

"Maybe it's something unrelated?" I heard myself repeat.

Evan turned and looked at me. I knew what he was going to say, so we said it together: "There's no such thing as coincidence."

"Do you know what you're going to say to Bill?" Evan asked me.

"Not exactly, I just know I need to talk to him and I need to ask him what he knows about Sabrina." I couldn't say that I needed to see him tell me he wasn't involved, that he didn't do any of this, that I would believe him if he did.

"Well, he obviously knows her," Evan said, like that was only the beginning.

"It's looking bad for Sabrina and Bill, I know." I looked out the window.

Evan whipped out his cell phone and pressed a direct-dial number. I waited.

"Deirdre?" he started when he got an answer. I raised both eyebrows at him. "It's Detective Paley. I need you to let me know if Ms. Wilde's most recent houseguest wants to go anywhere. Call me at the number I gave you. . . . Okay, thanks." He flipped the little phone shut and looked at me.

"You gave Deirdre your cell phone number?" I asked.

"Sure. She likes to know if you'll be home for dinner." He smiled at me.

"I already ate," I replied.

"Too bad, I know a great greasy dive right by the precinct. In fact, there it is." He pointed to a little place that looked more like a triple-X bookshop than a restaurant as he pulled in and parked. It was nearing midnight and the place was packed with cops.

"You never gave *me* your cell phone number," I said, hurt.

"Jealous?"

"No, absolutely not." I crossed my arms and pouted while he parked. "I don't care."

"Secretly, I'm trying to steal Deirdre away," he pretended to confess.

"Go ahead, she's nothing special," I said petulantly. "But apparently you think so." I glowered.

"You are *so* jealous." Evan laughed. I didn't think it was funny at all.

It wasn't funny to find myself facing the precinct again either. I tried to steel myself as we entered the ugly flickering light of the hallway. Acting brave is being brave, I told myself again.

There was paperwork and waiting and finally, a claustrophobic room to wait for Bill. I was shaking and I clamped one hand tightly on top of the other to try to conceal the shudder.

It was a long wait which I spent thinking about my mother's illness and how much more horrible it would be for her if Bill was involved in this mess. I was reflecting on my own unresolved issues with her and wondering what, if anything, I should try to do about them, when the door opened, and I turned to it as slowly as I could force myself to turn.

Bill looked horrible. He hadn't slept, that was clear. He smelled of sweat and fear. His face lit up slightly when he saw me, the way it always did.

"Cally, honey, I didn't do this. You know I didn't do this." He tried to come to me, but Evan sat him down in the seat across a hard, bare table from me and went to lean against the wall.

"What's going on Bill?" I asked.

"I don't know. They think I killed Hervé. I never liked him much, you know that, but I didn't kill him."

"Nobody liked him," I agreed. "The guard wrote your name on the guest list that night."

Bill's eyes widened, and I saw him thinking fast. But he said nothing.

"How do you know Sabrina Valley?"

Bill sighed and slumped back in his chair. "From Hervé. She's just a troublemaker." His voice was angry.

"Is she my sister?" I asked and was surprised to hear myself ask the question. It wasn't a question I had formed first in my mind.

He looked directly at me. "No. I mean, I don't think so. I don't have any reason to think so. In all my dealings with your father, I never knew him to have that kind of a secret. I don't think he was capable of that. He was too straightforward; he was a good man, Cally, you know that."

"Yes, I do. It makes me angry that someone is trying to make me question that."

"Look, Hervé said his father knew about this girl, had made provisions for her, but I didn't believe him. I thought, and I still do, that he was lying, that he was fabricating this whole thing to try to get money." He looked disoriented and his eyes half closed. "I'm so tired I can't think straight."

"We're going to let you go home, Mr. Clark," Evan said, and Bill's head snapped up hopefully. "But don't leave town. We don't have enough evidence to keep you, and your wife swears you were home at the time of Tesauro's murder. It's possible someone could have used your name to gain entry to Mr. Tesauro's complex."

"Thank you." Bill was genuinely sincere, and I could tell that Evan had treated him well and fairly.

"I'm sure if you know anything you'll tell Detective Paley," I said, feeling a measure of hope that I could believe my stepfather.

"Cally, please, you've got to believe me. Listen." He licked his lips and leaned forward, his eyes were pleading, but there was something in them, something he was holding back. "I would never, *could* never do anything to hurt you. Or anyone I love." He sat back again and looked up at Evan. I noticed he wouldn't look at me again.

"Good-bye Bill. I'll talk to you later," I said.

He nodded, spent. Evan opened the door for him and had some words with an officer. I sat alone until Evan came back in and closed the door.

"Did he do it?" I asked. And then without waiting for an answer, I went on: "I mean, even if he did set Sabrina up and had some kind of deal worked out. Even if he set Hervé up to look guilty and killed him, why would he want to kill me?" I opened my hands, palms up and stared at the wall as if the answer would appear there. "I mean, he doesn't get a penny of my money."

"Unless Sabrina's claim held, then she'd get it all, less Hervé's standard cut of a third, and he'd get a percentage, too," Evan said softly.

I brought my hands to my face and pressed hard against my eyes.

"Yes, there is that." I stood up slowly, scalded by the thought of the possible connection between them. I was trying to push away the thought of one other reason that Bill might go to that extreme; my mother's obsession with money, but I couldn't bring myself to tell Evan about that embarrassingly painful part of my life, not tonight. "How about that greasy dive? I could use some watery, burnt coffee," I said instead.

"Good choice." Evan motioned to the door, and I forced my body to a brittle upright stance, fighting against the pulling need to lean on Evan, to bend against him and let myself be comforted. He had to maintain his professional indifference to me in this place and I knew that if I bent and he pushed me back I would break. I didn't have enough trust in myself to give him any. Desperately I wanted to try it, to give in to being vulnerable and I found myself thinking of my inability to take that risk as a weakness instead of a strength. *Pretending to be tough isn't bravery*, I thought, reeling, *it's fear, I'm afraid*.

The realization immobilized me. Somehow we had arrived in the reception area of the precinct and I stopped and put my hand against the glass door to hold myself up. I couldn't move, or look at Evan but I needed him to reach for me, to help me, to read my mind. *Tell him*, my brain screamed. *He can't help you if he doesn't know!* But I was terrified that he would see my weakness.

"Callaway, are you all right?" Evan was beside me, his voice concerned but steady.

I struggled with myself, with my fear. "I'm fine," I forced myself to say because I had always said that. I could feel him watching me, weighing me. Every cell in my body wanted to fall against his shoulder and cry, let it out, show how I really felt. *You should be able to handle it by yourself*, said an evil voice inside of me. Evan's hand came around the small of my back and he started to pull me toward him. *Don't be so fucking weak*, the voice continued, angry and hurt now.

"Cally," Evan began.

Straightening up, I took two steps forward, still without looking at him. "I'm fine." I repeated and kept walking. *I don't need anybody*, the voice said but I could feel my heart crystallize and start to crack.

Evan fell in behind me and assumed my formality. "Forget the coffee. I'll drive you home."

27

I didn't sleep very well, but I slept late. Evan had told me when he dropped me off the night before that he'd be by in the early evening to talk to Sabrina. When he got up, I presumed.

Lying in bed I thought about the distance I had placed between myself and Evan and my heart sank.

Deirdre floated in with the elixir of life, my cappuccino. I drank it while I got dressed, wondering what I would do today and dreading what I knew I must.

Mother. It was hard enough to see Rudy without knowing she was dying. Now that I did, I felt a sense of panic and of failure. That I needed to make peace, have a relationship with her before it was too late, fix everything. Hopelessness accompanied me out of the house.

Unable to fight the overwhelming sense of sadness about so many years spent fighting instead of loving, I drove to her house and rang the bell. The housekeeper answered and told me that Rudy was taking a nap. I overrode her objections and climbed the stairs, quickly crossing the landing into my mother's bedroom. She was in bed, with the TV picture showing a talk show, but the sound was off. Prescription bottles and medications littered the bedside table. Rudy's hair was a mess, and she wore no makeup to cover the wan, yellow tone of her skin and dark circles under her eyes. She looked like shit.

I paused for a moment and she didn't seem to be aware of me. She just stared out the window without interest.

"Hey, Mom," I called out softly but cheerfully and crossed into the room. "Sleeping kind of late aren't you?" I smiled and sat on the divan across from the bed.

She did not want to see me, that much was clear. Her hand flew unconsciously to her mussed hair and after a frightened glance at me, she turned and pretended to be busy with the paper on the sheets beside her.

"I think I'm entitled to relax in my own home," she snapped, but without her usual pepper. "You didn't call."

"I think I'm entitled to see my mother without an appointment," I countered. She grated on me, sick or not.

"Why don't you go downstairs and get some coffee. I'll be right down." She was still trying to keep her face turned away from me.

"Rudy, I don't care if you have all your makeup on. Can we please just talk?" I begged from a raw place.

"About what?" she asked, sitting back against the pillows.

"You heard about Hervé?" I asked.

"Yes." Her mouth tightened. "I did. I also heard that my husband has been arrested." She glared at me as though that might have been my fault.

"Someone's been trying to kill me," I said, "and it

hasn't been the most delightful of experiences. Detective Paley thinks the same person behind my attacks may have killed Hervé because he knew something."

"Don't be ridiculous, who would want to kill you?" my mother spat out.

"But I'm okay, don't get too worked up, Mom. Thanks for your concern," I responded.

"You never needed any," she said and looked away.

That stung. Somehow she always could find a way to hurt me. I peeled off the offending statement and put it aside. I'd learned to do that.

"Listen to me." I summoned my reserves of patience. "I had a thought. I don't think Bill would ever try to kill me, period. I can't and don't believe that he would be behind that. And, except for one thing I would never think he would plot to steal my money. But I do have this one nagging doubt."

She snorted a half laugh. "What is that?"

"You," I said.

She stared at me with fear in her eyes.

"He might have done it for you," I voiced the thought I'd had the night before, "so that he could give you and Binford what you always wanted, what you've always made him feel incapable of giving, what you've driven him crazy for. Money, my money." I watched her, removed for the moment to the position of an objective observer.

She stared at me, and then she laughed. It was a long, deep, bitter laugh that ended in a fit of coughing. After she'd spit some phlegm into a tissue, she searched through the pile of pills on her bed stand. She located a bottle and struggled with the childproof cap for a second before pouring three capsules in her hand and down her throat. Then she looked right at me. "I'm dying. Of course you know that; dear, sweet Bill would have considered it his duty to tell you."

"Yes, he told me."

"Weakling," she muttered.

"Why do you hold him in such contempt?" I asked, standing, amazed that I was defending him but moved by her spite to do so.

"Because he let your father walk all over him his whole life, that's why!" She couldn't raise her voice for fear of another racking cough, but the intensity of her voice cranked up. "Because he could never give Binford what you waltzed off with, what you never earned."

"And you did, is that what you think? You earned it?" I asked. "You know what, I wish you had the money and I didn't, because then you might know it won't make you happy. Nothing will make you happy. You're bitter and you're mean." I was close to tears; this was not what I had come to say. She'd drawn me in again.

"You have no idea," she said and lay back, closing her eyes. "Get out. You turned away from me years ago, you never needed me, all you wanted was your precious father. Well, he's dead. Get out."

"That's not true! You made me choose between you and Dad. I never wanted to do that. I was nine years old, for God's sake!" I could hear the childish hysteria in my own voice. "If I had chosen you, I never would have seen him again. You would have made sure of that. He let me see you whenever I wanted. And by then you had Binford, and it was like I didn't exist."

"You want to know who tried to kill you?" Rudy asked, opening her eyes and nailing me with a cold, rheumy stare.

"Yes," I said, but inside I was screaming "no!"

"Me." Her mouth twisted into a distorted expression of pain and hate. "I did," she said.

I reeled, took two steps back, hit the front of the sofa with my legs and sank onto it. I could vaguely hear Bill's words on the golf course, telling me that the medication made her crazy, paranoid.

"I hired Hervé to try to kill you, to stop you from killing my son." She wheezed a little and tried to clear the mucus from her throat.

"What? I never tried to kill Binford. He's my brother!" I gasped.

"You always hated him, you were always jealous of him, he was the boy, the rightful heir, you knew you'd have to kill him someday." She was raving.

"Rudy, stop it. You don't know what you're saying. It's the medicine, you're talking crazy." I tried to soothe her—and myself.

"I did it, you hear me?" She swung her legs out of the bed and stood up. As she did, she started coughing again and had to brace herself against the headboard.

"Rudy, please," I pleaded. "You know this isn't true, it can't be." But my mind was reeling; it all made sense. Bill would try to protect her if she was behind the murder attempts. He would have tried to protect me from Sabrina, even more so out of guilt. I had seen my mother at Hervé's office.

"Get out!" Rudy screamed. "Go get your police friend and throw me in jail for the last miserable months of my life, I don't care!" She sat back on the bed, and I ran.

I ran into the hall and right into the housekeeper, muttering apologies. I ran down the stairs and got into my car. Revving the engine, I pulled out onto the street fast, too fast. I took the quiet Westwood suburb like a teenager in a stolen car, and it wasn't until I hit the main road that I made myself slow down, pay attention, think.

I let a fraction of my anguish out in a strangled cry. My mother! My own mother! Could it be true? My heart flopped up and down, suffocating like a fish on cement. Flip, smack, flip, whap. It had to be the medication; it had to be the illness. Bill had warned me.

"Evan," I said out loud. "I've got to talk to Evan." Pulling over into a corner park, I cut the engine. Then, after sitting in shock for a moment, I reached for my cell phone with vibrating hands. I dialed Evan's pager and waited for it to connect, entered my cell number and hit the end button. Leaning my forehead against the wheel and clutching it so tightly it hurt, I tried to anchor myself to something. The phone rang and I leaped for it.

"Evan?" I gasped.

"Cally? What is it?" He sounded like I'd woken him from a deep sleep, but his raspy voice was filled with concern. Speaking his name had betrayed all my fear. All the fear I had been afraid to show him.

"Evan, I've got to see you. I went to see my mom and she said that . . ." The tears started to come and I couldn't stop them. I was angry with myself for crying like a child, but it felt so good to release them, "She said that she did it. She was behind it, I don't know if it's true, but . . ."

"Cally, listen to me. Are you in danger?" He was fully awake now.

"No, I don't think so, but I don't know."

"Where are you?"

"I'm in Westwood, on Wilshire Boulevard near Beverly Glen."

He sighed. "Okay, you're right around the corner, why don't you come here. Or do you want me to come get you?"

"No, I can drive, I'm okay," I said. I wasn't that much of a baby.

I drove up to the address he'd given me and stopped, looked at the house, the gates, the landscaping, and checked the number again. It was nice. Way too nice for a detective. Trying to sort it out, I shook my head. He must live in the guest house or something.

I pulled into the driveway and reached out to buzz the phone, but the gate swung open and looking up, I saw a video camera. Nice setup. The huge wooden gate swung open silently, and I drove in.

Evan was standing on the front steps wearing a sweatshirt and jeans. I pulled around the circular drive and got out right in front of him.

He seemed unsure of how to respond to me and I felt myself fighting to present a strong front, but when he put his arms tentatively around me I couldn't resist and I caved in against him. He countered by enveloping me in an embrace that was everything I hoped it would be.

"Who lives here?" I asked, as he led me into the gorgeous living room, large enough to hold two fireplaces and several seating areas. The walls were a deep masculine green and the floor highly polished cherry hardwood, I could tell at a glance that the art was authentic and expensive.

"Right now, I do," he said with a little laugh and he

seemed to enjoy my confusion. "I'll explain later. Come on. Here." He poured me a shot of something golden brown from a cut-crystal decanter. I drank it back. Smoky, expensive, single malt scotch. He poured another, but I just held onto it. "Come on, sit down," he said gently.

We sat on a chocolate-brown leather sofa.

"Okay." I took a deep breath. The scotch was working its way through my body, but I was still shaky. I told him what my mother had said and then what Bill had told me about the drugs and the illness. Evan watched me and listened, and I could see him processing everything. When I finally finished talking I took a sip of the scotch, but it seemed too strong now and I set down the glass.

"I'm sorry about your mother." He put his hand out and brushed my cheek.

Pity; I hated that. "It is what it is," I said, not wanting to go into that closet full of monsters. He didn't have any idea how horrible it really was, losing a mother, twice.

"That's got to be really hard for you."

Shifting out of his reach by leaning for my glass, I shut that down. "It's okay, I've handled worse." I dismissed the intimacy and took a drink. The scotch was bitter and burning now, but I forced myself to swallow without gagging or making a face.

He was watching me warily. I could actually see the second that he decided not to press me to explain my feelings about her.

"Who killed Tesauro?" he said almost to himself, changing tack.

"She didn't say that," I said. "I didn't think of that." I felt vaguely relieved.

"She could have hired someone," he mused. "I think there are two people who know more than they are saying." Evan got up and took my hand. "And we need to talk to both of them. I'll get dressed." He didn't let go of me though. He pulled me upstairs and to my amazement into the master suite. My perplexity about why he was occupying that room was buried under the avalanche of everything else that had happened.

"Are you house-sitting?" I asked him.

He smiled again. "Good guess. You ought to be a detective."

I smiled a little, pleased that I had made some sense of something.

He let go of my hand as we crossed into the room and pulled off his sweatshirt. "Have a seat," he said. I was closest to the unmade bed, so I sat there. Except for a bedside lamp, the room was dark. Evan crossed to the blackout curtains and drew them back, filling the handsome room with the bright light of the day.

The sunlight also fell on his handsome body as he undressed. My, my, it was about time. He mused out loud again as he peeled off the shirt and then the jeans.

"First we need to talk to Fiona Laasko. She's still in jail, and she knows something, I'm sure of it. We'll need to see her reaction when we tell her someone else is confessing to a related crime. I think it should be very interesting." I was only half listening to him because I was much more interested in something else, the tone of his body. He looked very strong but not pumped up or overly muscular. Just perfect. It was hard to concentrate on anything else. I'd only seen him fully dressed before and this was much better than I'd imagined. And that was already good. He didn't seem to notice my infatuated distraction until he stopped in front of the bathroom door.

"What?" he said, looking at my face.

"I've never seen you naked." I smiled.

He raised a finger of one hand and hooked the thumb of the other in the band of his boxers. "And you still won't." He walked into the bathroom and I heard the shower start.

The boxers flew out and landed on the carpet. "Goddamned tease," I muttered.

28

We were halfway to the jail when Evan picked up the thread I had cut at his house.

"I really am sorry about your mother."

"It's not important right now."

"Why don't you let me decide what I think is important, okay?" He was speaking softly but there was a note in his voice that would not be ignored or dismissed. "When I tell you that I'm sorry I'm not bullshitting you. It also doesn't mean that I pity you in any way. It would help a lot if you could just accept that for what it is."

"Well, that's what I'm here for, to help you," I said bitterly and didn't even know what I meant, just a nasty knee-jerk response.

He breathed deeply in and out once and then he was still. I sat there furious with myself. Was it so hard to share that I had a crappy relationship with my mother? It wasn't my fault that Rudy had treated me the way she did. *Make him understand, don't be so afraid. Show yourself.* I couldn't speak for a moment but finally, somehow, I found the courage to say what I was feeling.

"Listen, I'm sorry. I know I suck at this, I'll try to explain." I took a deep breath. "Rudy, my mom, she is always saying things that aren't true. Like, about Fiona and my dad," I laughed nervously. "The morning after the first shooting, she tried to tell me my dad had an affair with *her* after she was married to Bill, and . . ."

"Let me guess," Evan commiserated, "Binford was his son."

"Yes," I laughed again, sadly this time and then sobered; it was too awful to be funny. In the last few days I had heard that my mother was dying, been shot at twice, and almost drowned, but this, sharing a hurtful truth, was by far the scariest thing of all. I braced myself, actually hung on to the armrest and tightened the muscles in my chest, forcing myself to leap into the flaming hoop. "All these years I've just sloughed off her lies and bitterness. But it's been terrible. Like running my hand over rough wood and pretending not to notice the splinters. Even when they get infected and fester. Having a mother like Rudy has made me, I don't know, embarrassed and ashamed." I turned to the window to hide the tears that surprised my eyes. The warmth of Evan's fingers brushed my cheek again and this time, without looking back, I pressed against them.

"I'm sorry," he said softly.

"It's okay," I intoned from habit, once again.

Evan's fingers found my chin and turned my face to him. We were stopped at a light and he made me look in his eyes. "No." He said, "It's not okay. It hurts to have a mother that doesn't love you the way you need, and I'm sorry."

I looked at Evan and something warm flowed through me, a wonderful sense of triumph over myself. And something else, surrender. "Thank you," I said and meant it. "I wish you could have met my father."

Evan was respectfully quiet and then he said softly, "I would have liked him, I'm sure." He took my hand again and squeezed. Then he pulled into the parking lot of a public library.

"You need to pick up a good mystery?" I asked.

"I need to do some research. You want to come in?" he asked.

"No thanks, I'll sit here for a minute."

He went into the library and I did exactly what I said I was going to do. I just sat there and let my mind wander over the bigger picture. Everything that was happening to me wasn't all bad; it was time to clean the mud out of my life, I'd been putting it off and living in muck for so long that I'd gotten used to it. No matter what else happened, I would shed a thick layer of bullshit from my life, I needed to choose what to replace it with, and that made me think of Ginny. I gave her a quick call to check in, but I cut it short, telling her I'd be home in a couple of hours, when I saw Evan come out of the library.

"What did you find out?" I asked.

"Something good." His eyes twinkled.

I twisted my mouth sideways. "So this is it then, the beginning of the end. You're keeping secrets from me." I crossed my arms and pretended to pout.

"I'm a man of mystery," he said and winked. "Chicks dig it. Besides, you could have come in."

" 'Chicks dig it'?" I asked, laughing.

He looked at me and deadpanned, "You mean they don't?"

I spent the ride to the precinct trying to find out what he knew; I was unsuccessful.

Inside the station, the small visiting area consisted of a few tables and chairs. When they brought Fiona in, she looked exhausted. She was in an orange poly-jumpsuit courtesy of the county, and her short, white-blond hair was stuck to her head. Her defiance was gone; one night in prison had clearly sapped her fortitude.

"Ms. Laasko, we need to ask you some more questions," Evan began. And from the sigh that escaped her, it was obvious how many answers she'd given since we saw her last.

"I'm tired. Can't you just leave me alone?" Fiona asked, but I could see that even this short ordeal had weakened her commitment to claim responsibility for a crime she didn't commit.

"No. I can't. There's a killer out there free, and I have trouble sleeping when it's my case." Evan looked at me and I blinked back innocently, though I read his message loud and clear.

"I can't help you," Fiona looked down at her hands.

"Are you aware of a Sabrina Valley, a woman who has made a large claim against Ms. Wilde's estate?"

I was still looking at Evan, and he leaned in as he asked the question, completely focused on her subconscious responses.

She froze for an instant and then looked up at him deliberately. "No. I am not."

"No? You knew the deceased, you said he was blackmailing you, what was it he knew about you?" She didn't answer, so he went on. "You know that she has a letter from your former employer, Mr. Wilde, stating that she was his daughter and upon his death she was entitled to twelve million dollars."

I glanced up at Evan. He knew the real amount. Why was he misstating it? But then I knew. Fiona looked suspicious and opened her mouth to speak and then shut it.

"You also know that you are one of the only people in a position to help forge that letter. Because you had access to Mr. Wilde's signature stamp."

"I never did such a thing. I don't know anything about a Miss, what did you say, Valley?" Fiona regained some of her former strength.

"Who's behind Mr. Tesauro hiring someone to try to kill Ms. Wilde?" Evan continued.

Fiona looked confused. "I don't know anything about that. I was shocked when I heard it." She turned and looked at me.

I spoke up now. "You told me, the day I came to your apartment that I couldn't trust anyone. Did you mean you?"

It took her a second to answer, and when she did it was reluctantly, "Yes. And Hervé."

"What about the signature stamp. Did you still have that?" Evan was succinct.

"No. No. I gave that back when we closed the office." Fiona thought for a moment and then she said, "I assume Hervé inherited one from his father's office."

Evan didn't glance my way, but we were both thinking the same thing. Hervé hadn't inherited the stamp; he had stolen it.

"What language do they speak in Finland, Ms. Laasko, Finnish?" Evan asked casually, but he was still watching her like a cat.

"Of course." She was out of patience.

"Laasko, Laasko, that's an interesting name. What does it mean?" Evan asked and crossed his arms, his face set. "I mean in English, of course," he mocked.

Fiona had frozen stiff. She didn't answer at first and then recovered slightly and said, "It is just a name, it doesn't mean anything." But she didn't meet Evan's intense gaze, and she certainly didn't look at me.

Evan's voice softened and he uncrossed his arms. "I know who you're protecting Ms. Laasko, but I'm not sure it's necessary."

I was lost. I looked from Fiona to Evan and back to Fiona. Tears started to stream down her face, but she remained defiant.

"Laasko means 'valley' in Finnish, doesn't it?" asked Evan softly.

"That doesn't prove anything," Fiona said through clenched teeth.

"No, but a quick test will." He sat down in a chair across from Fiona and laid it out. More for my benefit than hers I suspected. I was in a state of startled paralysis.

"About twenty years ago you took a leave of absence for 'medical reasons.' Was that a pregnancy?" Evan paused. "Are you not in fact, Sabrina Valley's biological mother?"

Fiona broke, and it all came rushing out. "She didn't have anything to do with it. She didn't even know who her mother and father were!" She tried to stand to plead, but Evan put his hand on her shoulder to restrain her, to try to keep her calm. "It was me!" Fiona shouted. "I'm the one who planned the letter with Hervé, and he tried to blackmail me, that's why I had to kill him!" She finally looked at me and I was sure that the muscles in my face had petrified. "Cally. I'm sorry."

"She didn't know you were her mother?" Evan asked.

"No. Now, she does. She didn't when she was younger. She just knew that I was a friend of the family; but when her mother, Suzanna, died and then Robert got sick, he knew that Sabrina would be alone, so he asked if it would be alright to tell her. But he didn't tell her who her father was. He didn't actually know."

"Was it Daddy?" I asked from a strangely distant place. "Was he the father?"

Fiona never took her eyes from mine. "Yes."

I nodded, strangely tranquil. Since the night I had seen the resemblance in the photograph I had only been waiting for proof to let myself believe it.

"Did he know he had another daughter?" Evan asked, and everything I trusted rode on the answer.

"No," Fiona answered. "He didn't know." She took a shallow breath, then a deeper one and let it out. "He would have been good to her, I knew that. He was a good man, but the pregnancy was an accident; we had a relationship for a while, yes, but we both knew it wasn't anything permanent. We were attracted to each other and enjoyed each other's company, but we were never in love. I wanted my child to be part of a family, raised by parents that loved each other, not a rich man's bastard."

That snapped me back. Daddy's little bastard. "How did you hide it from him?" I asked dully.

Fiona went on. "Before the pregnancy, your father knew I'd been having some stress-related stomach problems, nothing serious, so when I found out I was pregnant, I told him I had developed ulcers and my doctor wanted me to get away to rest for a while. I had a friend from college in Louisiana. She had told me that she and her husband couldn't have children of their own and they were very sad. So, I . . . I let them adopt my baby girl." Fiona paused and smiled, as though the memory was fond, bittersweet, but all for the best.

"And the claim letter?" Evan got us back on the track.

"A forgery, obviously. Hervé wanted a percentage, and

he had always known about Sabrina. Years ago, when I worked closely with his father, I knew Hervé and we were friends, of a sort. When I left on my leave of absence he came to see me, saw that I was pregnant and badgered me to tell him who the father was. I needed to talk to somebody and I made the worst decision of my life telling him." She sighed. "It was a huge mistake."

Evan took a deep a breath. "Ms. Laasko. I am not going to hold you for murder."

Fiona put her hands up to her face and burst into relieved tears. "Oh, thank God! Oh thank you! I don't know if I could have lived through this, but I kept thinking it was my fault, I got her involved in all this by letting Hervé know about her, and by never telling Frank about her. She would have been financially set if I had, but I knew when Robert died she would have nothing and it was my fault."

"However," Evan said before she could gush too much gratitude, "there is the matter of forgery and fraud." He stopped and seemed to consider.

"When I heard what Hervé was planning, I tried to talk him out of it, but he threatened me and I guess, on some level, I thought it would make up for her losing her parents." Her whole body curled forward as she made the confession.

"That makes you an accessory to blackmail, although I do think that there are extenuating circumstances involved," Evan allowed.

"I didn't know what else to do," Fiona said quietly, and it was the truth.

"You could have come to us, and maybe three people wouldn't be dead right now," Evan said harshly. He was being lenient, but he wasn't going to maple-frost it.

Fiona nodded. She wasn't going to deny the truth in what he said or let herself off easily from the weight of the consequences.

"So, in light of this new information, I'll have a talk with the D.A. I imagine if you can make bail, you should be free to go until a trial date." He stood up again.

"Thank you so much," Fiona said to him earnestly.

"I'm doing my job. It would have been a lot easier if you had told me the truth in the beginning," Evan retorted. He was tired, out of patience.

As we hit the door, I turned back to Fiona and said, "I told you so." And smiled.

She smiled back. And although I was sad that one of the few people I thought I could count on had betrayed me, I was also somehow relieved to feel that she hadn't really ever meant to.

"I can't believe it," I said to Evan as we headed back to the car. "I've got a sister."

"You might not get to keep her for very long," Evan looked at me meaningfully.

"But you said it wasn't necessary for Fiona to protect her," I reiterated.

"I know." He opened the door for me.

"How can you be sure?" I asked.

"The fact is, I'm not. I needed Fiona to retract that confession and trust me. But it sounds like Sabrina has some serious explaining to do."

"What about Rudy?" I asked tremulously.

"She's not going anywhere. We'll get to her."

"If she doesn't get to us, first," I said, trying for humor.

"There's always that," Evan said, and I couldn't tell if he was kidding or not.

29

On the way home, I called in to check my messages. Various business calls, Ginny cursing me for not being home, and a call from Dana Scheiner.

"Jesus," I muttered as I listened to her quick, succinct call. "It's not enough to try to stay alive, you've got to go on planning for when you die," I said to Evan and punched in Dana's number.

"Dana Scheiner?" he asked me, and I felt his connection to her in one of those jealous bones in my body I would never admit to having. I decided to ask him how well he knew the svelte attorney.

"Yes," I answered him with an uninterested smile, and then I spoke into the phone, "yes, hello, uh, Ms. Scheiner, please." I listened. "Callaway Wilde." While I waited, I addressed my driver, "Thanks for recommending her, she seems very sharp."

He nodded and looked amused, which just fanned the fire.

"She's very attractive, too," I added, watching.

"Mmmm," he hummed his agreement.

"Do you just know her professionally?" I asked, and his amusement turned to a laugh.

"You mean like my 'professional' relationship with you?" He laughed again. I found myself burning at the thought of him being intimate with her, with anyone; what's the point of thinking I was special if he just moves from one to the next? Apparently I was deluding myself.

In an attempt to be reasonable, I thought of Joe and two other men I'd had as lovers in the last year; it didn't help.

Thankfully, Dana came on the line before I could depress myself further.

"Callaway, hello. I've finished going over your father's will, and everything looks ironclad. Smart man, your father. As far as Sabrina Valley's claim goes . . ."

I cut her off right there. "It doesn't go. It's a forgery. We've got a confession on that."

"Oh?" She paused for the first time since I'd met her, and I heard papers rustling as she shifted gears. "Okay then, you'll still need to give some thought to the details of your will, who will inherit from you and how much. It can be individuals, or charitable organizations or any combination."

That got me, I'd been so busy being the heir I'd forgotten I'd need to name one. "Well, I suppose it will be my children if I ever have any."

"Okay, there are a lot of ways to break that down, which we can discuss the next time I see you, but think about who you'd like to name until you have kids." She wanted me to be as prepared as she would be at that next meeting.

A thought hit me. "Dana, let me ask you something. If I died now, would Sabrina be entitled to my money as my father's heir, illegitimate or not?"

"*Is* she your father's heir?" Dana asked without the slightest bit of personal interest.

"Possibly." I paused. "Probably."

"Well, you have to understand that at this point, your father's relations and his desires are null and void. The money is no longer his, it's yours," she said. "I can't believe your former lawyer didn't make that clear. You may have grounds for getting him disbarred."

"Maybe, but I don't think I'll pursue that."

"Why not?"

"Oh, call it beating a dead horse." I winced as I said it.

"It's up to you." She dismissed that topic and moved on. "So as long as you understand what I'm telling you—there is no probate, there is no valid claim against your father's will. It has been fully executed."

"Meaning, what?" I asked, stymied.

"Meaning, it's your money, all of it. If you died now, without a will, his relatives are out of the running, but yours are not."

"My relatives? But I don't have any children."

"I know. So your estate would be split in equal parts, after taxes and debts, by surviving siblings and parents. I understand you do have those?" she reminded me.

"Yes, well, my mother," I said with a chill, "and a brother, but he's not any relation to my father."

"But he's *your* sibling. It doesn't matter if he was related to your father."

"Oh." I was starting to shake again. "And what about Sabrina Valley?"

"If she can prove she's legally a blood relative, she could definitely contest the will, acknowledged sister or not." Dana waited only a second, and since I didn't fill that time, she moved on. "Okay, so give me a call when you want to meet, and we'll set it up right away for you. Good news about the claim, huh? Bye."

"Good-bye." I listened to her click off, and then I shut the power off on my phone.

"What?" Evan asked when I didn't volunteer anything.

"Now I'm really confused," was all I could offer.

For a few minutes I holed up inside my head and Evan didn't intrude. When I'd sorted it out alone as best I could, I shared the info with him.

"I see," he said when I finished relating the half of the conversation he hadn't been privy to. "Who stands to profit from your permanent absence? Rudy, Bill because he's married to Rudy and would share her cut or inherit it when she died," he let that hang a minute while we both wondered how long he'd known she was dying, then he completed the list, "Binford, and maybe Sabrina." We fell silent again while I considered the benefits of being an orphan. "Hervé was connected to all of them, but he's out of the running," he finally added. "So who needed to get him out of the race?"

By now we were pulling into the driveway, and it was dusk. Most of the windows of my house were dark, and the shadowy graying light was the perfect accessory for the mood I was wearing.

By the time we got to the door, Deirdre had switched on the lights in the entrance foyer and vanquished a bit of the gloom.

"Any word about Elena?" I asked her without much hope, everyone had my cell phone number and I hadn't heard anything.

"Unfortunately, no." She inclined her head somberly.

The news didn't improve my mood either; poor Elena. "That means no change, I guess."

"Apparently not." Evan frowned. "Good evening Deirdre."

"Detective." She nodded to him. "It's a pleasure to have you back, again." Her eyes flicked to me on her last word. I pretended not to notice. We dispatched her for a glass of wine now and a light dinner later, and I went to find Ginny. Evan did the disappearing act into the library for phone calls trick.

Deirdre had told me I'd find Ginny in the media room and she was right, of course. Ginny was curled up on one of the sofas with a tray next to her covered with snacks, a pot of tea and accoutrement, her pain medication, bottled water and a handheld computer game.

She turned to the door when I came in. "Hi there. How you doing?" I asked as I flopped down next to her and let my body relax in stages. "Pain?"

"No thanks, I've got plenty." She picked up a remote control and switched off the movie she'd been watching, something foreign with subtitles. "Okay, spill it. What's been going on?"

"Jesus, I don't even know where to start." I reached back and lifted my hair, gathering it into a thick ponytail and then twisted it into a knot on top of my head, work mode. "It's been a painful day for me, too."

With her good arm Ginny reached out and snatched her medication from the tray. "Vicadon?"

"Thanks, I'm trying to quit," I half joked.

"They're not really much fun, fortunately," she said; neither of us addicts had ever been much for pills.

"Let's see, how long have you been conscious?" I asked.

"Since you sicced my family on me at the hospital at an ungodly hour yesterday morning."

"Your mommy loves you, now be good." She took the point. "Okay, let's see, I'll just give you the highlights, but not necessarily in order of importance. Sabrina dropped her claim against me, I found out she really is my sister, Evan arrested Bill for murdering Hervé, and I had a major breakthrough in my personal bullshit."

She blinked twice but seemed to be waiting politely. Finally she said, "Is that all? I thought maybe you'd have something interesting to tell me after I've been shut in all day."

"I'll try harder tomorrow," I said.

"Well, it'll have to do; start with the breakthrough."

"Okay. It's big," I warned. I felt silly about it so it was easier to joke. "I shared something painful about myself with Evan."

"You did not!" She semikidded, "Stop it. You opened up? To a man? No way."

"I did."

"Did it hurt?" she teased.

"As a matter of fact, yes," I said seriously.

"Good for you." She smiled warmly at me; only she could understand how momentous this silly little thing was for me. "I'm proud of you." She really was, it looked like she might cry.

"Thanks, me too." I shifted quickly into telling her about the other events of the day. She couldn't accept that Bill was behind anything and refused to consider the possibility.

"It can't be him," she insisted. "I'm sorry, he's the only one who's not related to you."

"But he could still get my money, through Rudy."

"I don't mean that, I mean he's not blood, he didn't inherit this insanity gene the rest of the family was born with."

"Oh, right. Well, that makes me feel much better," I said. "Bitch," I added.

"You only got a little bit of it, half a helix or something, I don't know how that DNA shit works, but your mom is emotionally dysfunctional on a cellular level and your brother has been so influenced by her that I'm pretty sure his core is as twisted as a Slinky, too."

"Oh, I didn't mention my mom."

She picked up on the morbid note in my voice and settled down. "What?" she asked, very concerned.

So I told her. About the illness and the confession and she sighed and raged quietly and even cried for me. It helped so much. But even with Ginny I needed to shift the focus off my pain after a short time. I was working on it, but my tolerance for intimacy was very low.

"But, moving on," I said, "What do you think of Sabrina?"

"She's very pretty." I was surprised at that answer.

"She seems nice, maybe not the brightest, but nice, don't you think?" I prodded.

"She's very pretty." Ginny nodded definitively.

"Not the worldliest, I agree, a bit Lil' Abner . . ."

"She's very pretty." Ginny's eyes were laughing and her head was still bobbing.

I started nodding in sync with her, "Yes," I said as though hypnotized, "she's very pretty. Why are we saying this over and over?" I intoned.

"Because if she tries to make me comfortable one

more time, I'm going to kill her," Ginny said in the same cadence.

I laughed. "You might have to get used to it," I said without realizing the hugeness of the comment.

Ginny noticed it. "Really?"

I fumbled, "Well, I mean, now that I know she's my sister, I'll have to get her something for Christmas, right?"

"Really?" Ginny was smiling at me.

"Oh, leave me alone." I muttered, getting up. "I've got to go find her anyway."

"Really?" She said it one too many times; I flicked her on the head with my middle finger as I passed her.

"I'll see you later," I said, and I could hear her laughing as I headed back toward the library.

As I was crossing through the entrance hall again, I found myself disappointed that Sabrina hadn't appeared.

Opening the door to the library I mentioned this to Evan, kind of. "I'm surprised Sabrina didn't bound down to meet us, panting and yapping," I said, a little cruelly perhaps, but I would have liked to have her be happy I was home, an unfamiliar desire.

"Bit puppyish, is she?" he asked.

I faked a grimace. "I feel like I should put newspaper out when I leave her alone."

"Well, that's what the staff is for," Evan quipped, and gestured to the fireplace. "May I?"

"Please." I looked around. The room seemed dreary even with the illumination from the lamps I'd lit. Outside, there was a misty marine layer that sat on your bones. "Maybe she doesn't much want to talk to you," I said seriously.

"That could very well be. How's your bodyguard?"

"Oh God, don't let Ginny hear you call her that," I warned. "You'll never hear the end of it."

He laughed, "I think I can handle it."

"She's doing fine. Sabrina is driving her nuts already." I smiled wryly, two more opposite personalities were hard to imagine.

Deirdre returned with an excellent Chilean cabernet and two glasses. Just the thing.

"Deirdre, where's our other houseguest?" I asked.

"The last I saw her, she was headed up to her room to change into her swimsuit. That was approximately a half hour ago," she answered.

"She was going for a swim now?" I asked, surprised, gesturing to the rapidly chilling evening.

"I'm not sure if it was swimming or the sauna, but it would be the fourth such venture out for her today," Deirdre said without a hint of judgment.

"She thinks she's at Disneyland, doesn't she?" I asked, amused. I was honestly pleased to be providing her a playground. It was great to share it with someone who was enthusiastic about it.

"Ms. Valley seems to be enjoying the amenities to their fullest." Deirdre allowed herself a smile. "The young lady has kept us all very busy today."

"Thank you Deirdre, I hope it hasn't been too much trouble."

"Not at all, she is refreshingly appreciative." Deirdre inclined her head slightly and shimmered out. I looked after her.

"Did she just insult me?" I asked with mock indignation.

"I think she zinged you a little." Evan nodded, sipping his wine. "And I think she'll probably get away with it," he added lightly.

"Of course she will, she's irreplaceable, but I just want you to know I know she did it." I took my glass and sat down righteously in the overstuffed armchair.

"I do think we should speak to Ms. Valley. I'll go out and ask her to come in," Evan said, pretending it was an imposition.

I leaped back up. "Oh, would you mind? I'm sure if she's naked in the sauna with beads of glistening sweat dripping down her body, you'll be kind enough to hand her a robe, if you can find one. Thank you so much but, no, I think I'll go. You just sit your butt down."

Evan smiled. I think it amused him that I was jealous, and it pleased me that he didn't care if I went instead of him. I crossed toward the doors.

"Thank you," Evan said from behind me.

I turned, "For what?"

"The visual," he answered and before I could feel the debilitating sting of jealousy he continued, "but you don't mind if I make it your naked body glistening with sweat, do you?"

I smiled, very pleased. "Not at all." I gestured generously, "It's your fantasy, go crazy."

"Oh, I am," he said and gave me that look that liquefied me. I had to attack him or turn away.

I opened the French doors and started off across the lawn to the path through the hedge that led to the pool. The mist was disconcerting and chilly. I crossed my arms as best I could while taking care not to spill a drop from my wineglass.

The wind was picking up a little and the cypress trees

bent their Dr. Seuss heads with the weight of it. A movement by the pool house drew my eye and I heard a splash.

"Jesus," I mumbled under my breath, "she is swimming. Freak." I shivered a little and picked up my step. The mist was veiling my view slightly, and I distinctly heard a noise away from the pool, by the pool house. Could Sabrina have company?

"Sabrina?" I called out just as I heard another sound.

Now there was no mistaking it. Someone was definitely by the pool house. Heavy footfalls in gravel sounded as they ran away from the pool area, crashing through the shrubbery, scuffling as they climbed over the stone wall.

I froze as I listened and then, very afraid of what I might see, I moved forward quickly, covering the last twenty feet of path in a purposeful stride.

Sabrina was floating facedown in the pool, her hair spread out around her. As I started to run across the slate around the pool, I was vaguely conscious of the sound of my wineglass smashing where I had thrown it. One more stride and then I was in the air briefly before I cut into the cold water. Two strokes and I was on her. I yanked her head up out of the water and as I was paddling for the side, I started yelling bloody murder, while simultaneously praying that wasn't what it was.

"Evan! Deirdre! Anybody!" I screamed with all the breath I could spare. Still supporting her weight, I climbed out onto the side of the pool, and wrapping my arms under hers I squatted and half pulled, half dragged her limp body from the water. She was wearing a heavy terry-cloth bathrobe, and wet, it must have added forty pounds to her deadweight. Summoning all my strength, I heaved. When I got her out and laid on her back I quickly checked for breathing and couldn't find any signs of life.

I rolled her on her stomach and shoved hard on the center of her lower back. As I suspected, water came rushing out of her mouth. Again, I pushed. More water. I flipped her back over and started giving her mouth-to-mouth as best I could remember from the class I took in college. In a moment I was aware of Evan beside me. He was checking for a pulse, and when he found none he started CPR. I stayed on the mouth-to-mouth and he did the heart pumps; he told me what to do and I did it. Five pumps, two breaths.

Now I could feel the staff gathering around us. Someone appeared with blankets, Deirdre was on the pool phone, calling 911. Ginny was kneeling behind me, taking over the verbal count so that Evan could focus on his job. Everyone was trying to find some way to help, and when they'd done what they could, they stood around us anxiously.

We kept it up. Breath, breath, five pumps, breath, breath. It seemed like forever. It felt like she was dead.

Then she coughed. A rheumy, liquid cough, and we rolled her quickly on her side as she started to vomit, bringing up the water, gasping to clear her lungs. Not conscious, not completely, but breathing, heart beating, living.

Then I noticed the blood. Deirdre had turned on the outside lights and my hands were smeared with it. Evan checked and there was a nasty lump with a gash in it on the back of Sabrina's head. Joseph handed us a rolled-up towel and we placed it against the wound, pressing gently. Sabrina moaned, clearly suffering.

I looked up at Evan. Sabrina seemed to be out of imminent danger for the moment. "Evan, I didn't see who it was, but they went over the wall, over there." I gestured with a quick tilt of my head because one hand was supporting Sabrina's forehead and the other was holding the towel on her cut.

He nodded and rose. His gun and his cell phone came out of nowhere and he was calling for a patrol car before he even passed through the shrubbery.

Deirdre called out. "Joseph, get a flashlight." And Joseph grabbed one quickly out of the pool house. He followed Evan into the greenery, and, I assume, handed the flashlight over because he was back in a minute.

"He said not to touch anything unless we have to," Joseph told us. We all heard the siren of the ambulance, and Deirdre picked up the phone to buzz open the gate as Joseph headed off to let them in and show them the way.

The paramedics, one male, one female, were quick yet unhurried. They had her on a backboard tied down with an oxygen mask on her face before I could finish telling them what little I knew. After a quick glance at the gash, they bandaged her head, but they seemed much more concerned about her breathing and whether they should "assist it." I wasn't sure what that meant, but after she spit up some more water, which involved rolling her, backboard and all, onto her side again, they seemed to decide against it.

They were lifting Sabrina onto the stretcher when Evan came back and identified himself to them.

I told him quickly what I had seen and the timing as I remembered it.

"Are you riding with us, Detective?" the female half

of the paramedic team asked as they started to roll across the lawn.

"No, I'll stay here and wait for the patrol car, I'll check in at the hospital within the hour."

"I'll ride with her." There wasn't any mental debate for me over that one. I couldn't imagine waking up in a hospital ER with no one I knew around me. I wanted to be there for her. Carmine came out of the house with a bundle of dry clothes for me and I took them gratefully, figuring I'd change in the ambulance. "I don't want her to be alone," I said simply.

"Neither do I," Evan agreed, "but I'm sending an officer to be with her as well. I'll have them meet you at the emergency entrance of the hospital." He pulled my arm and we walked away from the others. "Listen," he said to me intensely, "someone might not be too happy that they didn't finish this, and I don't want you alone, either."

"I'll stay with her."

"Cally." He stopped me. "Whoever did this is a vicious, dangerous person. Do you understand?"

"Of course I do. If I didn't before, I just dragged an understanding out of the deep end of my pool," I said, a little annoyed. "Why would someone want to kill Sabrina?"

"I don't know yet."

"Hopefully she'll be able to tell us who it was," I said, relieved as the thought occurred to me.

"I doubt that very much," Evan said grimly.

"Don't you think she'll be all right?" I asked, my fear for her hitting suddenly. I'd been too damn busy up to now to think ahead.

"I hope so, but there's the possibility she won't be.

Even if she is, I don't think she saw a thing," Evan said decisively.

"Too dark?" I didn't think so.

"Cally, where was she hit?"

"Right here," I answered, putting my right hand on the back of my head. "You saw it." And then I saw it, too. "Whoever it was hit her from behind."

"She never saw it coming, or you would have heard something. She would have called out while you were coming across the lawn. You heard the splash, right?"

"Right."

The ambulance driver appeared in the break in the cypress trees lining the driveway. "We're ready to go."

"I'm coming," I called and started off after them.

"Cally!" Evan tried to stop me, but I kept right on going.

"I know! I'll be careful!" I threw over my shoulder and he said nothing more. But I was afraid—and with good reason.

30

The magazines in the ER lounge hadn't been very current or interesting the last time I'd been here, with Ginny. Being bored, coupled with the fact that I was more tightly wound than an atomic clock, put me in a nasty mindset. Answering all the questions on the paperwork had taken a good, long time. I had called home and asked Deirdre to look in Sabrina's purse. She had medical insurance, so I relayed all the information. I had hesitated at the line that asked if I was any relation to the patient. I had left it blank, pretending I'd missed it. I sat in the stark waiting room and looked up every time someone approached the desk.

Finally, an attractive but overworked intern with gray, tired eyes wearing rumpled greens came to see me. She was looking down at the form I had filled out.

"Ms. Wilde?" she asked.

"Yes, I'm Callaway Wilde." I stood up and came to meet her.

Her eyes went back down to the clipboard. "Now, are you a family member?"

"No," I said hesitantly, and then I took a deep breath and a second cold plunge that evening. "Yes."

"Meaning?" The look she directed at me was dubious.

"Meaning I just found out she's my sister; at least, I think she is. It's a long story." I shook my head and didn't apologize. It wasn't real clear to me, either. "What it comes down to is, I'm all she's got." It affected me deeply to say it. I could relate.

"Well, it's early yet, she did regain consciousness for a few seconds, but that was a nasty crack to her head and we are really going to have to keep an eye on her. I've given her a painkiller so she can sleep. We're going to send her upstairs when she stabilizes."

"When can she go home?" I asked, wondering where the hell home was.

"I'm not sure yet. She needs to stay at least a couple of days until we're certain her lungs are cleared and that there are no long-term effects from the wound on her head and the oxygen deprivation." The doctor looked like she was through with me.

"What kind of long-term effects?" I asked, not through with her.

She took an impatient breath. "Amnesia, blindness, brain damage, to name a few."

"Don't sugar-coat it, give it to me straight," I said sarcastically.

"Look," the doctor said, and I got that this was probably near the end of her twenty-four-hour shift, and it had been a busy one. "I'm not saying any of those things will happen, but when she came around she wasn't able to say her name. We're just going to have to be patient."

"Can I see her?" I asked.

"Sure, she's in four," she said and opened the door to the ER proper, letting me pass through.

I found Room 4 and opened the door cautiously.

They had shut off the lights so she could sleep. I crossed over to the form draped in sheets and a blanket. She was hooked up to a plethora of tubes and instruments. It was odd but I liked her better like this. Less threatening, I suppose. It was impossible to be jealous or resentful of her in this incubatory state. Mostly, I was sorry for her.

"Sabrina?" I whispered.

Her eyelids fluttered a little, but they didn't open. I put my hand on the one of hers that didn't have an IV in it and squeezed a little to let her know someone was there. I don't think she noticed.

"It's me, Cally, I'm here." I let go of her hand, it felt so cold, and I stood there not knowing what to do next. The hum of the technology around us did little to fill the emptiness. I felt a similar buzzing inside myself. Why was I feeling afraid? Did I not want to lose her? I didn't even know her. She had crash-landed into my life and I hadn't even had time to get used to the idea. How was I supposed to feel in this bizarre scenario? I decided it was okay if I didn't know yet.

"Okay," I sighed, "now what?" It didn't feel right to just go back to the waiting room. I didn't know if she could hear me or not, but I needed to say something. Maybe it would help me sort things out.

"Bummer, huh?" I said, testing the sound of my own voice and how it felt to speak out loud to someone who might as well be in another building. It seemed as good a start as any.

"This whole thing's a mess," I continued. "I guess this pretty much takes the culpability off you, anyway." I looked down at her babyish face. Even unconscious I felt I'd better clarify. "Culpability means blame or guilt, by the way." I paused again. "So things are looking up. Sure, there's some maniac out there trying to kill us. At worst, it's a professional hit man, or someone whose motives we don't know shit about, and at best it's my own mother."

I laughed a little at the insanity of it. What else could I do?

"At least you're not related to her." I paused and shifted around uncomfortably. "And that's a good thing because Ginny says she's got the wrong ingredients in her cellular soup, or something like that," I added. She wasn't responding. "Of course, you've got Fiona, but she doesn't really count, does she?" I gazed down at Sabrina and something occurred to me. "In a way, we both have mothers we don't know very well. Not much help. And we both have a half sister we don't know at all. Not much of a family, huh?"

I shuffled my feet some more and glanced around the room.

"Why don't I shut up and let you rest," I said, mostly to myself. I was watching her naive face and it hit me how different she was from me; trusting, so capable of love and excitement and vulnerability, and I wanted her to live, to show me how to do that. We were vastly different people but our needs weren't so far apart. We both needed someone and if it was true she liked me, maybe I could learn to care about her, too.

"I won't let anything happen to you. I don't know what will happen next, or how this will turn out, but I won't desert you." I knew that I really meant it.

I was starting to feel really silly. "Now get better, damn it," I said as gently as I could. "I'll see you upstairs when you wake up." I stopped myself from adding, "if you wake up."

Evan was in the waiting room with a female police officer he introduced as Officer Ellsworth.

"She's in four," I said as soon as the handshaking was over. She nodded and didn't wait for anyone to open the door for her.

"Did you find anything?" I asked.

"Footprints, maybe some hair, though it could be your gardener's. We'll have to compare. It was snagged on a branch."

"I hope it ripped out a huge chunk," I said. "Look, they gave her a sedative so she's going to sleep for a while. I think I'll go home and grab some stuff, and then I'll come back and stay with her."

"Is that all the doctors told you?" Evan asked.

"No, they were much more discouraging. They didn't strictly rule out death, but I think they are hopeful that could still be one of the possibilities."

"It's their job to prepare you, to be realistic," Evan sided.

"I know." I tried to let go of my cynicism, but I was deeply attached to it, as it was the only thing that was keeping me standing upright. "Can you drive me home to get my car?"

"First of all, you are going to get some sleep at home, you can come back here in the morning," Evan ordered. "But, I think there's someone we need to speak to tonight," he said, and my heart skipped so many beats that I could easily have been in need of emergency services myself. I knew he was talking about my mother, and I knew how painful it would be.

We walked out onto the curb and started for the parking lot. I saw a man coming toward me, slumped forward in movement and submission, and I recognized the somber demeanor of my half brother.

"Binford!" I called out through the vast concrete parking garage. His head snapped up. Clearly, he hadn't expected to see anyone he knew. He looked toward me and leaned forward, squinting. Then, almost hesitantly, he started to move to us. I'm sure I wasn't the first person he wanted to see.

"Hi, how you holding up?" I asked lamely.

"Cally," he said hoarsely. "What are you doing here?"

"Wishing I was here less. How's Elena?"

He broke his introspective gaze and seemed to notice Evan. "Detective." He nodded, and then turned back to me. "Haven't you just been to see her?"

"Elena?" I felt guilty that we hadn't, so much had been happening, and I was distracted by the need to confront Rudy. "No, actually, we came in with someone else."

His face blanched, and he swayed a minute.

"Who?" he whispered, afraid.

"Not Mom," I said quickly, sorry I hadn't thought of that before. He was so much closer to her than I was. "It was a houseguest of mine; she had an accident in my pool."

"What happened?" His color didn't improve much.

"We don't know yet," Evan answered for me, and I was grateful that he took the lead. "We'll let you know. How is your wife?"

"She's, uh, the same. I don't really know." He was drained. His mother was dying, his father was a murder suspect, and his wife was basically comatose. I felt for him. His hands ran roughly through his unkempt hair. "This isn't right. Everything's gone wrong," he said.

Personally, I thought that was understating the situation.

It certainly didn't seem like the time to go into it. I looked up at Evan and the slight negative incline of his head was perceptible only to me.

"We have to go. I'll be back in the morning, and I'll go see Elena then. Let me know if anything changes." I put one hand on Binford's shoulder and felt him tense. On an impulse that felt strange to me, I hugged him. It seemed wrong that it was so unfamiliar, that hugging him was like hugging the solid trunk of an oak tree. For the second that I pressed him to me, I was aware of real hope that from all of this evil might come one drop of good. That Binford would relax and hug me back, accept my love. I was angry that he didn't, that I needed the connection more than he did.

He pulled away first, and I let him. We said our good-byes, and he walked off in a half trance of worry and distraction, hurrying into the hospital.

I watched him go and my heart felt like a stone.

"What kind of a family do I have?" I asked quietly.

"Well," Evan started gently, "I wouldn't really describe it as traditional." He put his arm around me.

"Would you describe it as fucked-up?" I said and tried to sound only mildly bitter. "I would." I looked up at him and I could see that he sensed all my pain but he surprised me again, there was no pity in his gaze. "I can't fix it." I dissolved as I admitted that horrible deficiency to myself; secretly I had always thought that one day, I could.

"Sometimes," he said with a very sad smile, "we have to build a new one. We keep trying to get what we need from people who can't give it, but it doesn't mean we can't get our needs met somewhere else."

I thought of Sabrina, lying in that bed, of Ginny

always ready to listen and understand without judging, and I sensed Evan waiting for my response.

I wanted to argue, to be angry, to insist that I was doomed to my loneliness, to hang on to that. But instead I heard myself say, "You're right." And it was the second bravest thing I ever said.

31

We drove in silence to Brentwood. I glanced at my watch, nine o'clock. I presumed Rudy and Bill would both be up. Evan noted my nervousness.

"I want you to remember something when we're in there," he said sternly.

"I know. You're the detective," I said, wishing he would've done this one alone.

"Yes, but that's not what I want to say." He took my hand, entwining his fingers in mine. "I am with you, you are not alone." He looked at me, forbidding me to forget his support through the next ordeal.

The housekeeper let us in again with a look at me that she would normally direct at a particularly rancid piece of garbage. She actually wrinkled her nose. God knows what she had been told or had deduced. I was tempted to explain my side of the story, but I knew whatever I said wouldn't matter.

Bill was in the bedroom, speaking hushed and urgently on the phone. He turned away when he saw us and wrapped the call up quickly. Rudy lay on her side, thin and asleep. She did not look good.

"How is she?" I asked my stepfather.

"Resting, thank God." He glanced at Evan nervously and then gestured us out into the hall, his mouth seemed dry. "Look, I'm not sure what she said when you were here last, but I told you, this disease and this medicine are making her say crazy things. She doesn't even know what she's saying half the time." He ran his tongue over his lips to moisten them.

"I'll need to speak to her doctor." Evan pulled out his notepad. "Also, if you could give me the names of the medications she's taking, that would be very helpful."

"Of course, I'll write it all down for you," Bill said quickly. "Cally, your mother doesn't want to hurt you, you know that, don't you?"

"I don't know what to think, Bill. Much less what to know."

"I need to speak to you about the Royal acquisition." He was very nervous.

"This isn't the time," I said.

"It has to be the time!" he snapped, and then caught himself. "Look, if I can't come up with the payment, I'll lose Signa."

I didn't look at Evan, but I was conscious of him shifting his weight from one foot to the other and back again.

"You mean *we'll* lose Signa," I said a little coldly.

"It's all I've got," Bill said, no apologies. I must say, I saw his point.

"Why, Bill? You've always been happy with Signa; it's a very successful company you can be proud of. Why are you suddenly so intent on becoming a conglomeration?" I really needed to know.

"Because your mother is dying and it's all she ever wanted and I let her down!" Bill's voice was full of his frustrated tears, and he turned away from us.

That shut me up. I was stunned by the depth of his feeling for Rudy. She had always been so conniving with me that it was hard for me to understand how she could inspire that kind of devotion in someone else.

"Bill?" My mother's voice came from the bedroom. "Bill, are you all right?"

Bill turned back, wiping his tears away quickly, and walked past us into the room.

"It's okay, honey. I'm just talking with some people." I heard him move across the room. "How are you feeling?"

"Pretty shitty," came Rudy's reply with a nasty cough. "Thanks for sitting with me. What a depressing bore I must be, and I look like hell."

"You look beautiful to me," Bill reassured her, and even from the hallway, I believed him.

"You always were a fool," my mother said with such surprising tenderness that it was a compliment. "Who was here?"

There was a pause, and then Bill answered. "It's Cally and Detective Paley. Now lie back, Rudy, they just want to talk to you."

"I don't want to talk to them." Rudy raised her voice as much as she could and it sounded as though she was speaking through a wet rag. "I don't want to talk to you, Cally. Go away."

"Rudy," Bill's voice was loving but stern. "She's your daughter and you will speak to her."

It was quiet again. Evan put his hand on my arm but he couldn't reach me.

"Come in Callaway," Bill invited.

My body seemed to be made of stone, but I moved forward. Evan came in behind me.

I didn't know what to say. Evan read her her rights.

Rudy laughed as best she could. "Am I under arrest?"

"Not yet, but anything you say can be used against you, I want you to be aware of that."

"She must be a good fuck, my daughter."

I was shocked, I couldn't speak. Neither could Bill. Evan didn't miss a beat. "I wouldn't know," he said smoothly.

Rudy turned her head and put her glasses on to regard him as a schoolmarm would a lying student. But he neither broke nor wavered. Finally, she turned away from him with a sigh.

"Yes, I think you might do." Rudy took her glasses off in a way that made them seem very heavy. "If you don't fall in love with her money, that is."

"Are you concerned about your daughter's welfare?" Evan asked.

"I tried to kill her, but if she's going to live, she might as well be happy." Rudy waved an imperial hand. "She wins, I lose. Leave me to my ungraceful exit."

"Rudy, stop it," I interrupted, unable to take any more. "Did you really try to kill me?"

"Yes. I did. I hired those boys who were working for Bill, I promised them money. They were more than willing; it's boring making boxes, I'm sure."

"How much did you promise them?" Evan asked.

"I don't remember. Not much, a couple thousand."

"Did you pay them?" Evan pursued.

"I didn't have to, did I?" Rudy snapped, "They failed."

Bill cut in, pained, "Rudy. You did no such thing!"

"Bill, what difference does it make? She thinks I hate her so much, let her have some justification. Let her live in peace." She turned to me. "Callaway. My daughter. I lost you a long time ago, you belong to your father, maybe you always did and that's what made me so angry. I've been a terrible mother, I know. I tried to make it up to Binford, but . . ." She paused, but she never looked away. "But that doesn't count. It isn't easy for me to say this, but I'm sorry."

At this point Evan interjected. "Mrs. Clark, I need to get a statement from you, and more important, I need information about an attempted murder earlier this evening."

"Another one?" Rudy's once-grand sense of humor stood hunched in the shadow of her twisted smile.

"Yes." Evan smiled, too. "Are you aware of a young woman named Sabrina Valley?"

"No."

"So you did not have someone try to kill her?" Evan said matter-of-factly.

"Just a minute," Bill squeezed in, "nobody tried to have anybody killed."

"Yes, I'm afraid they did, sir. Ms. Wilde twice and Ms. Sabrina Valley once, that we know of. It is also possible that your daughter-in-law Elena's overdose was not a suicide attempt." Evan let that hang as he walked around to the foot of the bed so that he could look at Rudy—and vice versa—without her having to strain her neck. "And that same someone, we presume," he continued, "was successful in killing Hervé Tesauro."

"Not necessarily," said Rudy, her eyes sparking to life, "Anybody could have killed Hervé, everybody wanted to. He was a jerk."

"So I gather," Evan allowed. "Still, it seems more than just a coincidence."

I was watching Bill's face when Evan brought up Sabrina Valley's name, and he had blanched a bit.

"I take it whoever tried to kill this Sabrina person wasn't very good at it?" Rudy asked, amusing herself still.

"What makes you say that?" Evan wanted to know.

"You said 'attempted.' "

"True. But she is in the hospital. Being watched over by one of our finest, by the way." Evan smiled again, albeit grimly.

"Who is she?" Rudy asked. I looked at Bill, and he looked at me. Evan turned his eyes to mine, and what I read there was that it was my call.

I blew out an exasperated breath. "She's my half . . . sister."

Rudy looked at me blankly.

"Fiona's daughter," I added a little resentfully.

Rudy started to laugh. It was a deep, sonorous, raggedy laugh, it was beautiful and painful to hear and I'm sure much more painful for her. "Perfect," Rudy spit out as she started to cough. "Perfect." She was hacking now and she couldn't breathe. The laugh was gone, replaced by a caustic, terminal cough.

Bill rushed to her side. She was gesturing for the pills as tears streamed down her face. Bill was bulldozing through the multitude of brown plastic bottles until he found the one he was looking for, knocking the others on the floor.

Evan came around and leaned Rudy forward, supporting her chest on his arm. Bill got a glass of water and the pill and somehow, between attacks, Rudy got it down. In a few moments, during which I felt utterly useless, she began to calm.

Evan laid her back on the pillows Bill had stacked up and then he started to pick the prescription bottles up off the ground. I saw him glancing at the labels. Always the curious one.

When Rudy's breathing was restored to a nasty, scraping labor, she turned to me. I was still helpless.

She tried to speak and started to cough again. Bill begged her not to try, but she persisted and so I moved closer to her so she could speak softly.

"Try to forgive me," she said barely audibly. I was the only one who heard the words. It almost killed me.

"Rudy," I stopped myself, this might be the last time I spoke to her, it had to be now. "Mom," I started again, "there is nothing to forgive."

"Yes, you know there is." She tried to smile at me, and that smile was deeper and wiser than any I had ever received. And then she closed her eyes and turned her head away, fighting not to cough.

Evan pulled my sleeve. I lifted my concrete feet and turned to the door.

Evan spoke to Bill, who was leaning, concerned, over his wife, "Get me that list of medications when you can."

Bill looked up and nodded. Then he followed us to the door and down the hall to the landing. "Listen Detective, you can't take anything that she says seriously, she would never . . ."

"I don't," Evan cut him off, "not for the same reasons as you, but it wasn't her."

Bill's worried but intact face contorted into a mask of pain. He sobbed once, and then with a few breaths he calmed his twisted features back to a semblance of the Bill I knew. He put his arms around me. Not to give me comfort but because he needed it for himself.

And I cried, too. I felt the pain and I didn't stop myself. And I knew that it was alright, that neither Evan nor Bill would think less of me for it. I cried from that place that is more alone than the stars are far. To know such depth of feeling is a rare thing.

At least, I hope it is.

32

The morning was gray. The remnants of last night's mist hung over the dawn the same way I had draped a blanket over my shoulders as I sat and drank coffee on my terrace. I just wanted to be left alone for a while, to wallow in my loss and confusion.

As the sunshine eased the condensation in the air, the cobwebs in my head lifted slightly, too. My mother wasn't dead yet. I had some reason to believe she hadn't really tried to kill me—Evan had actually found the payment money in Oswaldo's effects and she had said she never paid them—and for the first time in years, she had actually made an overture of, if not affection, than acceptance. Things could have been worse.

I sighed large and long and then stood up and stretched my arms, cracking my neck bones and pushing the tension out from my spine to my fingertips.

It was time to fulfill my promise of the night before to Sabrina, to be there when she woke up. But first I had a phone call to make.

I called my financial adviser and told him to okay the loan for Signa to purchase Royal. I tried, unconvincingly, to tell myself it was strictly a sound business move. I knew it was a last gesture to my dying mother; there was nothing else I could give her.

I packed an overnight bag, just in case, and got in my car to drive myself to Cedars. There was a black and white in my driveway, and the officer inside studied me intently but I forced a smile and a small wave as I pulled out into the street. On the way to the hospital, I called to get the room number and check on Sabrina's condition—no change.

When I got there I went straight up to the third floor. Down the corridor I could see Sabrina's room, number three-twelve, across from the nurses' station. A chair was by the door, for the police officer, I assumed. Except, it was empty.

As I drew near, a nurse appeared from another hallway, her head bent over a chart. She sat at the unoccupied station and I addressed her across the counter.

"Excuse me."

She looked up, harried but polite. "Yes?"

"Is there a police officer watching that room?"

"Yes, he's been here all morning. He went to the rest room and asked me to watch the door for him." She smiled at me.

"But you weren't here," I said, pointedly.

"I was called to a patient's room," she got defensive immediately.

"I see." I didn't really. "How is Ms. Valley?"

"Your name?" the nurse asked, reaching for another chart.

"Callaway Wilde."

She flipped through the chart. "ID?" she asked, very professional now.

I already had it out.

She perused it and then answered, "There's been no change. She's had good reflex response but no consciousness."

"Thank you. I'll go in and see her."

"Fine."

"If you could let the officer know I'm here when he comes back?" I asked, not wanting to surprise him.

I crossed hesitantly to the swinging metal door. There was a small rectangular window and glancing through the shatterproof diamond pattern I saw Sabrina's legs, but a man leaning over her obscured the rest of her body from my view. I could only see his back but he was in a perfect position to have his hands on her throat.

I spun back to the nurse and shouted, "Get the police officer! Now!"

Her face snapped up, alarmed at my intensity and she started to move, but if I was right about what I saw, I didn't have time to wait for anyone. I barreled into the room and grabbed at the shoulder of the stooping man, yanked back hard, and received a shove in return that sent me spinning across the room. My head smacked against the wall, stunning me, but what I saw was twice as hard as the wall.

It was Binford. And his face was wet with tears. He turned back to Sabrina, and my cartwheeling brain was trying hard to focus, to land right side up.

"Binford, no!" I cried out, "don't hurt her!"

Even the shock of realizing that he must have been her attacker was nothing compared to his rage.

"I would never hurt her!" He shouted at me through clenched teeth.

He turned back to Sabrina and knelt beside the bed,

taking her hand in his as though it was an injured baby sparrow. I straightened up warily and assuming a defensive stance, I got between him and the door. Forcing my voice to be calm, I began to speak to him as I would to a frightened but dangerous German shepherd.

"It's okay Binford, nobody's going to hurt her, or you." The door opened forcefully behind me, and I only avoided getting clocked again by leaping sideways. The last two weeks of my life had whittled my reflexes to a sharp point.

The officer was taking in the scenario with a practiced eye. Behind him, the curious face of the nurse showed through the door.

"Everything all right?" he asked, taking in the situation quickly with a sweeping visual inspection.

"Yes, Officer," I said so that Binford would hear me, but I shook my head "no." My eyes went to his badge. Gifford. He had the wary, competent demeanor of an experienced officer. I felt completely confident in him and decided to take my cues accordingly.

Officer Gifford put a hand on his gun hilt but didn't draw the weapon. He began to circle slowly around until he was across from Binford, his eyes now targeting my brother's hands.

"Sir," the officer spoke calmly and with great authority, "I need you to stand up please and place your hands on your head."

Binford didn't respond for a long few seconds; it seemed as though he hadn't heard. Both his hands still cradled one of Sabrina's.

"Sir, I'm going to need you to do what I say." Gifford remained motionless. "Stand up, slowly, and place your hands on your head."

Binford turned his head and looked at the officer, but he still didn't raise his hands.

"Please don't make me leave, I won't do anything wrong."

"Stand up, sir."

Binford started to beg. "I can't leave her, I love her, don't make me leave. What if something happens to her?" He broke down and started to sob, clutching at Sabrina's hand.

The officer glanced to me questioningly but only for a fraction of a second. He was alertly intent on Binford. He pulled his gun out of the holster and held it in both his hands but he kept it pointing toward the floor.

"He's my half brother, Officer, Binford Clark. I don't know what he's doing here. I didn't know he knew this girl, but he's been under a great deal of stress."

At those words, Binford's emotional response turned abruptly. He laughed—but there was no amusement in it. "Stress?" he howled. "Yeah, you could say that. I've been under some 'stress.'"

"Let's all stay calm, sir," Gifford intoned in a soothing way. There was quiet for a moment. Neither man loosened his grip, one on a gun, the other a hand.

"Binford?" I stayed very calm. "You weren't trying to hurt Sabrina, were you?"

He spun toward me. Now he was furious. "No! Damn you, you ruin everything. I would never hurt her. I love her, I thought . . ." He broke off again, confused.

"Hands on your head," demanded the policeman, but he kept his voice placating.

"I thought . . ." Binford looked confused and he stood slowly now, keeping his eyes on Sabrina. "It doesn't matter what I thought, not now, it only matters that she's okay." He backed to the foot of the bed and covered his face with his hands.

Officer Gifford stepped in quickly and put handcuffs on Binford.

"Okay, let's go somewhere quiet." Officer Gifford said, "I'm sure Detective Paley would like a word with you."

"I'm sure he would," Binford hissed, and he turned his eyes to me, eyes filled with hate. "It's all your fault." He spat at me, "If she dies, so help me God, I'll kill you."

33

When Evan returned my page I filled him in. It was all falling together. The name on the guest register had been Clark. But not Bill Clark, Binford Clark. Evan said he had considered that as a possibility but because all the other connections seemed to point to Bill, he had followed that lead. But Binford would have had an in to the ex-gang dockworkers as well. It made sense that if Bill knew about Binford's affair with Sabrina, he would have had words with her after Elena had tried to kill herself. That's why he felt it was his fault, because he hadn't tried to stop Binford's affair before. Binford knew Hervé through business and could have found out about Sabrina from him, could have gone to see her; he was head of sales and traveled often. And if he knew what Hervé wasn't telling me, that he was in line for my money, my half brother could have wanted to kill me to get it all for himself. If he had enlisted Hervé's help for that, and Hervé had tried to blackmail him with that info later, Binford would have had reason to kill the lawyer. It made sense that both Rudy and Bill would have tried to protect Binford if they knew or even suspected what he was up to.

Binford, however, had a different story. Yes, he had been involved with Hervé in finding out about Sabrina and helping to forge the letter which, he was adamant on this point, she knew nothing about. But he had not planned on falling in love with her.

That's where the similarities in our deductions and his explanations ended. He refused to admit that he had anything to do with trying to kill me, or Hervé. He pouted and raged and was as insistent as anyone I've ever seen. When Evan asked him outright if he had tried to overdose Elena, he looked legitimately shocked. He would have divorced Elena, he said, but he would never have tried to kill her. He said he felt terrible that she had found out about Sabrina, and that the knowledge had made her so desperate.

But the worst thing for him had been Sabrina's reaction to Elena's suicide attempt. When Bill had told her about the overdose and made her feel responsible, she had wanted nothing more to do with Binford, or the money. She had turned away from him. He was sick about it. He loved her, needed her. He would do anything to get her back.

All this came out in the first hour or so, after which Evan had Binford taken to the station to be booked for forgery and questioned further.

After Evan left, I checked on Sabrina to make sure she was alright and still sleeping, and then I had to go home where I could cry in private.

I tried to hide my raw eyes and voice from Deirdre when I came in and she kindly looked away when I told her I was going to the cabana and wanted to be left alone for a couple of hours. After a good ten-minute jag of sobbing, I quieted down and Ginny appeared to sit beside me, sent to comfort me by my butler, no doubt, who always anticipated my needs.

Ginny didn't ask or touch, or even speak; she just sat in the chair next to me and watched the light on the water, and waited. When I could, I told her what had happened and she sighed and shook her head.

"Sibling rivalry," was all she said. After that we sat silently for a long time until we spotted Evan coming along the walk. Ginny turned to me, "You want me to stay?" she asked.

"No, thank you, I need to talk to Evan."

"Got it." She stood up, "I'm here," she said, and passed Evan on the path with a hello and a touch of their hands; it looked like they were on the same tag team.

"Well?" I asked when he reached me.

"I don't have enough on him to make the arrest for murder or attempted murder," Evan said as he sank into the deck chair. "He's got a loose alibi for the time frame of Hervé's murder, we're checking it out, and the hair on the branch turned out to be your gardener's."

"Which means?"

"No material evidence yet at the scene of the crime. We've got him for sure on two things, fraud and adultery." Evan grimaced. "Which doesn't go far toward easing our troubled minds."

"It's got to be him."

"I know. I've contacted the guard at Tesauro's condominium to come in for a lineup. If he can ID him, I've got the beginning of a case."

"What about the gang members?" I asked, incredulous.

Evan looked at me sympathetically. "I assume it was

Hervé who did the contacting there, or some other go-between who we haven't come across yet. And if it *was* Binford, the two men he would have dealt with aren't talking."

Meaning they were dead, of course. I leaned back, deflated. This police stuff was complicated.

"I just want to know if it was him. Part of me can't believe it." I looked at Evan and I'm sure the pain in my face belied the nonchalant tone of my voice. "Do you think Rudy knew?"

Evan took my hand and stroked the top of it. "At some point, she must have; she went to such effort to protect him. It's possible she was just guessing, or she could have figured it out for herself."

That didn't make me feel much better. I knew that my mother was responsible for instilling the idea in Binford that I had robbed both of them, denied them their fortune. It was something that started long ago.

Deirdre came onto the patio and coughed politely. Evan released my hand, and I used it to shade my eyes from the sun behind her.

"Yes, Deedee?"

"The doctor phoned from the hospital and asked that you return his call at this number." She handed over a neatly written note.

"Thanks. Did he say what it was about?" I asked.

"No, ma'am, just requested that you return his call. Would you like anything?"

"I'd love some iced tea please, Deirdre," Evan said, as though ordering from a butler were the most natural thing in the world. He was learning. I liked that.

"Sounds great," I agreed. "How about a pitcher and two tall glasses?"

Evan stopped just in front of me and put his hands on my shoulders.

"I'm saying . . . he thought it was you."

Of course. How stupid of me; that's why Evan had warned me that night that whoever attacked Sabrina was vicious, that's why he'd had a police officer parked in my driveway ever since.

I swayed a little and walked stiffly back to the chair. It could easily have been me. And nobody would have heard a thing.

"Jesus Christ. I've got a guardian angel working overtime, don't I?"

"At least one," Evan replied, and he sounded like he was referring to himself. I flashed on my dad, looking out for me, remembered hearing his voice encourage me when I was in the water with Ginny.

"So it was Binford," I said, tired and strangely relieved.

"We need to find out. Let's go see Ms. Valley first, and then we'll go to the precinct for the lineup. That will tell us something." Evan offered his hand to help me up out of my funk and exhaustion.

The next hurdles were to see Sabrina and get through the lineup to identify Binford. I could have jumped those easily if it hadn't been for the marathon I had already run. Emotionally, my body had started burning off muscle and climbing one more rung of one more ladder seemed to be beyond my endurance and strength.

Looking from Evan's hand up to his face I said, "I don't know if I can."

He came down beside me and I put my head on his shoulder. "You can."

"How do you know that?"

"Because you're the bravest person I ever met."

I had to laugh at that. "Why? Because I shot some-body?" I asked.

"No," he said and took my face in both his hands, "because you showed me what you were most afraid of."

I smiled at him, he was right, that was much harder than pulling a trigger. I stood up. "You're right, I can do it." I offered him my hand and said simply, "Let's go."

34

How are you feeling?" I said, leaning over Sabrina. It always seemed like a stupid question when someone was lying in a hospital bed. Obviously, they weren't feeling too fucking great.

"My head hurts," she drawled. "And I feel real tired." She took my hand that was near hers, and it surprised me. I tried to make it look like I had meant to take hers, but I don't think she cared.

"I'm just so glad you're here," she said and started to cry.

"Shhhh. It's okay, I know you're scared, but I think it's all going to be okay now."

Evan waited a moment for her to sniffle and try to smile at us, and then he spoke. "Ms. Valley, if you can remember anything about the night you were attacked."

"Was I attacked? Is that what happened?" Her eyes were as wide as they were blue.

"Yes," I said. "Someone hit you on the head from behind while you were standing by the pool. Did you see anything, or anyone?" I asked.

She squinted and started to shake her head "no," but obviously it pained her too much to do so. She said it instead. "No. I remember being outside. I was just standing there looking at the water, thinking, and then, I woke up here."

"I'm sorry I wasn't here when you woke up," I said and I meant it. "I tried to be, but there's been a lot of other things going on."

"Who would want to hurt me?" Sabrina asked Evan.

"We're not sure, but we think it's possible whoever it was mistook you for Ms. Wilde." I could sense Evan giving out his information in measured doses so that she could absorb it, process it.

"Do you know who?" she asked, and this time, both her gaze and her question were directed at me.

But Evan cleared his throat to keep me from answering. I looked to him. He pulled up two chairs to the bedside, motioning me to one and he took the other.

"Here's where it gets a little difficult, I'm afraid," Evan said gently. "There may be something you can tell us that will help us." He smiled at her and then he added, "No holding back anymore, okay?"

She looked at me and I watched her weigh the danger I was in with what she'd been through. Finally, she nodded. "Okay." I felt her grip tighten on my hand.

"We have reason to believe that the person who did this is Binford Clark."

He was interrupted by a sharp intake of breath; if I hadn't expected it I would have thought she'd been pierced by a sharp pain.

"He's the man you were seeing, isn't he?" Evan asked gently.

Sabrina blinked back guilty tears. "Yes," escaped her in that strange, mewing voice she had when she was afraid.

"When did you first meet him?" Evan prompted.

"I don't recall exactly, over a year ago." She turned to me. "It's like I told you, he was in town on business, and we met. He was very charming."

"Did you know he was married?" I asked.

Her eyes couldn't hold mine, so they flicked around the room, trying to find a point of interest on which to rest. "Not right away, but when he did tell me, he said it was over. He said they were separated and he wanted to get a divorce from her."

"At what point did he learn about the letter from Mr. Wilde?" Evan asked.

"Oh, right away, he's the first person I called, of course. He gave me all kinds of advice; he's the one who told me to get a lawyer. He recommended Mr. Underwood, and Mr. Underwood recommended Mr. Tesauro." She seemed to see the light of the connection as she said it, and it made her squint.

"Were you aware that Mr. Clark is Ms. Wilde's half brother?" Evan tested.

A jolt went through her body so powerful that she tried to sit up.

"What?" she cried and looked from me to him. "What are you saying?" She looked so alarmed and confused that at first I misread her panic.

"No, don't worry, Sabrina. He's not related to you," I soothed.

It was apparent from the look on her face that that thought hadn't even occurred to her and it did now. "Oh my sainted aunt," she moaned, and leaned back rolling her eyes up and around, searching for relief. "You mean he was, is, her brother? I don't understand. So he knew about her all along, or what?"

"What do you want to know?" Evan offered kindly, unsure where to begin.

"He was so horrible when I said I didn't want that money anymore. I mean, he acted like he had a personal interest in it. I thought it was just that he wanted me to be rich, so he could have some of it, that he was just greedy, but . . . it was something more, wasn't it?" She was trying so hard to get the wheels of her brain on the track.

"Yes, it was something more," Evan agreed. "He did have an investment in it. It was his idea, and he'd worked hard on that idea for a long time. At least that year, maybe more. A lot of work was going down the drain."

She brought her hands to her face. "I knew that money meant too much to him, but I thought, I really thought . . ." She stopped and bit her lip hard to keep it from quivering.

It was my turn to speak. "He did."

Evan stayed silent, so I went on.

"He did love you." I sighed, thinking of him crying and cradling her hand; I thought he had loved her, in an obsessed way. I squeezed her hand now, I didn't want her to feel like she had just been used.

"Listen to me Sabrina." I waited until she focused on my eyes and found some strength there. "We found him here, in this room, very distraught. I think he really did fall in love with you, and it wasn't part of the plan. And it was clear that he's very concerned about what would happen to you."

"Well, that's comforting," she said, as bitterly as her soft voice would allow, and I smiled sincerely at the first glimmer I'd had that she was capable of sarcasm, and a sense of humor.

I actually laughed. "There's hope for you yet," I said, and though Evan understood completely, Sabrina herself looked mystified by the comment.

"The important thing now," Evan interrupted, getting back on that track thing, "is whether you can remember anything that will help us."

"Help you what?" she asked.

"Put him in jail," I said. "He's tried to kill me several times and maybe his wife, and we presume he did kill Hervé Tesauro."

At the mention of wife, I saw her flinch, but when I mentioned Hervé's murder, she searched our faces intently.

"But why?" she asked. "Why would he want to kill you or Mr. Tesauro?"

I took a deep breath. I had to remember how long it had taken us to sort this out. I leaped in. "It's a long story, but because I have no will, if I died, he and my mother would get the money that my father left to me. As to why he would want to kill Hervé, we're not sure, but we think because he was threatening you, or he was too involved and Binford wanted him out of the way."

"Why would he want to kill his wife?" she asked, afraid.

Evan looked at me and I let him field that one. "We don't know yet if he did try to kill her or if she tried to kill herself or if it was accidental." He left it there, but Sabrina took up the thread.

"But anyway you look at it, it's probably because of me, isn't it?" She turned away from us and stared out at the smoggy sky. "That's why I told him I couldn't ever see him again. I thought she tried to kill herself over me. I couldn't live with that." She had a sudden thought. "Is she okay, his wife?" Sabrina seemed genuinely concerned. It was touching.

I started to answer and then stopped myself and looked at Evan. It was clear we had things to do, visiting Elena for one.

"She was the same, last time we heard anything, which was from Binford yesterday morning, so I'm not sure how reliable that info was." I stood up. "I think we should go check on her, and then we'll let you know."

"Okay," Sabrina said dubiously. I'm not sure if she was afraid of what she'd hear or afraid of being alone.

"Don't worry," I reassured, "we'll be right back, and you're safe now, Binford's in custody."

"I'm not afraid of him," she said and smiled, giving a poor impression of bravery. "I guess I just need to do some thinking about where I go from here. All of a sudden I feel like I need a plan." Her eyes teared up and the mock courage evaporated. "And I really don't have one."

Evan stepped in now, bless him, since I didn't have a clue what to say. "Your plan is to rest and not worry about anything. When your body and your mind are healthy again, I'm sure you'll have lots of ideas. It's no good trying to fly when you're waiting for your feathers to grow back."

We both smiled at her and she seemed relieved to have permission to just lie back and rest again. She really was such a child.

We went out into the hall and I shot Evan a look. "My, my, aren't you full of that down-home wisdom."

"Hey, I've been in the South," he said. "Once." He added in response to my raised brow, "I had a connecting flight through Atlanta."

Elena was in another wing, and it took us a minute to remember where it was and another ten to find it. When we got to the room, Evan glanced through the glass and tensed visibly.

He pushed the door open quickly and we both walked into a room and stared at the empty bed. The sheets were stripped, the tray was clean, and Elena was gone.

Evan spun back past me and charged the nurse's stand.

"Excuse me," he said, flashing the symbol of his authority. "Has the patient in that room been transferred?"

My heart was in my mouth. All I could think was that the transfer had been to the morgue.

The nurse was infuriatingly slow, but I guess getting their information right at a time like this was crucial; they hated getting sued as much as anybody. She dug out the clipboard and rustled through some papers.

"No, sir. She was released," she finally let go.

"Released?" I sputtered. "But she was unconscious yesterday."

The nurse looked through the papers again. "No, she's been conscious for two days and doing so well that the doctor decided to release her this morning." She fluttered the papers some more and then looked up at us, totally disinterested in the shock on our faces.

Evan looked to me. "Well, that's good news," he said. I had to admit, it was good news.

"But why didn't anyone tell us before now?" I wanted to know. "Binford said she was the same yesterday."

Evan took my arm and led me away from the now

curious woman at the desk. "Obviously, Binford didn't want us to know when he ran into us yesterday." Evan froze. He released my arm and cleared the distance we'd walked back to the nurses' station in two strides.

"Could I see that chart please?" he asked the nurse.

"Are you family?"

Evan rolled his eyes. "Yes, I'm the family detective."

She didn't seem to approve of his sarcasm, but she handed the chart over. Evan flipped to the last page.

"Shit," he muttered. Then handing it back to the nurse, he amended his manners. "Thank you, so much."

He strode back to me and pulled me along with his momentum.

"What?" I asked.

"Guess who signed her out?"

I paled. "Binford, of course." I tried to calm myself. "But he saw us coming in, he knew that he hadn't killed me the night before, that the jig was up, even if he did try to overdose Elena so he could be with Sabrina, and we don't know that for sure, he has no reason to try to kill Elena now!"

Evan held the elevator door open as I passed through and punched the ground floor button swiftly. "That's one possible theory, it's a little incomplete, but it's very rational. *You* are thinking very sanely." His eyes made their point so hard that they seemed to hold me in place against the side of the elevator.

"And he's acting insanely," I followed.

"He's out of his ever-loving mind," Evan said.

35

I tried to call Elena and Binford's house several times on the drive over but the machine kept picking up. We whipped into the driveway, well aware that if anything had happened, we were probably far too late.

Evan rang the bell but there was no response. He walked quickly around the house, trying windows and doors while I waited out front in case someone came. He found nothing unlatched and I was still alone in front of a locked wooden door when he returned.

"Okay then," Evan smiled thinly. "Time for a little breaking and entering."

He picked up a nice-sized rock lining the walkway and smashed out a pane of glass in a panel next to the door. Then he reached in and unlocked the door.

"Voilà," he announced, and did the gentlemanly thing by going in ahead of me.

"Mrs. Clark?" he called out. The silence was booming. Evan and I went quickly through the downstairs. Nothing.

Everything was clean, orderly, neat. The living room was uninviting, especially now, the den falsely cozy looking, the kitchen sterile despite too many Americana craftsy touches.

We went up the back stairs, by the kitchen. Evan drew his gun as we passed down the hall, lined with color eight-by-ten portraits, giving each room a cursory once-over. The master bedroom was at the end of the hall. I was nervous, but I can't say I expected to find much. I mean, if I were going to kill someone, I certainly wouldn't put them in my bed.

The door was opened slightly and Evan called out again, softer, "Mrs. Clark?" He pushed the door open, and we started to go in.

"Okay, just hold it right there," came Elena's voice. She came into view as the door continued to swing wide. She was holding a small gun and pointing it at us.

Evan sighed and put his gun hand down quickly so as not to frighten her out of the single wit she seemed to have left.

"It's all right, Mrs. Clark. I'm Detective Paley, and you know . . ."

"Callaway!" Elena looked so shocked to see me sneaking into her house behind a man with a gun that I had to stop myself from laughing. I would have been terrified, too.

"Elena. I'm so sorry. We smashed out a window to get in because we thought you might be hurt, or . . ." I broke off. I didn't want to say "dead."

"But . . . what . . . I don't understand what you're doing here. I was asleep and I heard the window break. I didn't know who it was, and I've been so afraid," she mumbled, sinking down on her bed and letting the gun rest on the covers.

"I'm sorry," I apologized. "We called several times and you didn't answer," I explained.

"I shut off the ringers. I needed to rest. I haven't . . .

slept very well the last couple of nights," she said, still looking disoriented.

Evan and I approached her, and he took her gun and placed it on a table across the room.

"We are very glad to see you up and around," he said. "Now, do you feel up to answering some questions?"

Her eyes darted up at him like a trapped hare. "I don't know about that," she ventured.

"Elena, we're trying to figure out what's been going on," I said soothingly. Hoping she would see that we would understand if she had tried to kill herself, or even if Binford had been behind it. "We know some of the story."

"You do?" She still looked scared.

"Yes," Evan assured her. "Up to a point. We know that your husband was having an affair with Sabrina Valley and that you were very upset about that."

"Is that her name?" Elena looked at him. "Yes, I was very upset."

"Do you know anything else about your husband's activities?" Evan asked, probably wondering as I was, how much this poor woman could take right now.

"He tried to kill me," came in a tiny voice.

"How did he do that?" Evan asked in that passionless way that made it possible to speak about the unspeakable.

"He gave me those pills. I don't remember all of it, but I had something to drink and I was very groggy and he kept giving me more pills, telling me I needed them, that they would help. I remember thinking this is too much, too many, but I was so out of it and I wanted to think that he was taking care of me. Then I don't remember any more." She lay back down on the bed.

Evan crossed closer to her and looked at her directly.

"He's in custody now, for another crime. You're safe. I'll need you to make an official statement when you feel up to it. Could you do that?"

Elena had sat back up, and her pupils were huge with fear. "What other crime?" she asked.

"Maybe it would be better if we went over all this later," Evan suggested.

"He's my husband! Tell me, what other crime?" she cried emphatically.

I was surprised. Hadn't she just said he tried to kill her, and now she seemed to be protective of him? Evan, however, took it all in stride. I guess there would be many conflicting emotions in Elena right now, conflict I'd witnessed many times before.

"I'm afraid I can't tell you everything yet, not until I have a little more evidence, but he did admit to forgery."

Elena dropped her head into her hands. I thought she was just sitting there, until I noticed her shoulders shaking.

"Damn her. Damn her and damn him," she sobbed. "He was trying to help her for a long time, wasn't he?" She looked up at Evan and he nodded slowly. It was important that he didn't lie to her.

"Is there someone who can come and stay with you?" Evan asked. "I don't want you to be alone. I don't think it's a good idea."

Elena wiped her face angrily and shook herself a little. "No. I don't think that's a good idea, either. That's the whole problem." She laughed a crazy, sad laugh. Then she said, "The housekeeper should be back anytime now. I sent her out to do some errands and shopping to keep her from running that damn vacuum cleaner while I was trying to sleep."

"Elena," I said, "you need a friend to be with you now. How about your sister? I'll call her."

She nodded, resigned. "Okay, her number's on the desk. I was hoping to keep her nosy nose out of this, but I guess I can't."

I found her sister's number and called. Her sister was home and said she'd come right over, after asking for news a little too enthusiastically. I understood why Elena was reluctant. The last thing you want at a time like this is to have to explain everything to someone who's going to enjoy and probably repeat it. While I was on the phone the housekeeper came bustling in downstairs with groceries. I went to meet her to explain the broken window and make sure she would stay in the house. She was planning on staying over, so Evan and I felt reassured about leaving.

Before we did, though, Evan had a couple of last questions.

"Mrs. Clark, are you aware of where the pills your husband gave you came from?"

"Yes," she answered, "he said he got a prescription. He sometimes has trouble sleeping."

"I see. And you had an appointment in your book with Hervé Tesauro. Was he your lawyer also?"

She looked uncomfortable. "Not exactly."

"Meaning?" Evan pursued.

"Meaning, I called him to ask his advice about a good divorce attorney. We met and he gave me some names." She didn't look proud. I guess to many women, divorce equals failure.

Evan looked at the door to the bathroom in the bedroom. "May I use the rest room?" he asked politely.

"There's one in the entry hall downstairs."

"That's okay, this one will be fine." He was already crossing into the bath off the bedroom.

"It's probably a mess," Elena cautioned.

"No problem." He smiled.

We waited uncomfortably. When he came out he turned back to her at the door to the hall. "Thank you. I'll be in touch with you soon," he said.

I gave her an awkward hug. She seemed too preoccupied to return it.

We were outside before we spoke again.

"Interesting," Evan mused, and I took the bait.

"What is?"

"I checked his medicine cabinet; I found several prescriptions for Binford Clark, two antibiotics, expired, and one for diarrhea."

"But we found the bottle beside her."

"With the label ripped off. Why would he do that if he was trying to make it look like a suicide? It would have been more convincing if she would have taken her husband's pills."

"So he got the pills just for her. I wonder where from?" I didn't expect an answer. I did, however, get one.

"From your mother," Evan said simply. "They matched one of her prescriptions. But, I have to wonder," he rubbed his tired eyes and took a deep breath, "if Elena was angry enough at Binford it is possible that she took the pills herself to make him feel guilty or even to blame him."

"Why would she do that?"

He shook his head, "Oh, you'd be surprised. She could have done it to get back at him. Listen, she took the pills, or Binford fed them to her, in the morning when they both knew full well that the housekeeper was coming in a few hours. Binford's other plans, like Sabrina's fake claim, were well thought out, so it doesn't follow that he would be that stupid about something this major."

He was right; I was surprised. "So she took too many pills on purpose? I mean, of course she did, but she took them to accuse him of trying to kill her? Isn't that awful risky?"

"So is murder. Anyway, I don't know yet that she did do that," he massaged his face again, "but in this case, I can't rule anything out."

Jesus Christ, I thought, will this never end?

"After the lineup I have to get some sleep," Evan said, and he did indeed look more than a little REM-wave deprived. "Where do you want to go?"

"With you," I said and got the warning but wishful smile I was expecting. "But I guess I'll have to settle for sleeping on the chair in Sabrina's hospital room."

Evan's hand met my own halfway and he pulled it to his lips. The smooth pressure that met my fingertips promised so much more than sex. It thrilled and scared me.

Our eyes followed our hands and met midway.

"It's almost over," he said with a mellifluousness I wouldn't have thought possible in a voice so masculine. I wanted him so badly it was to the point of aching need.

But I nodded and wondered *how* it would end. If my death didn't provide the grand finale, would the curtain close with my mother and brother in jail? Were they behind this whole nightmare?

Anyway I looked at the situation, the sooner it was resolved the better.

36

The guard from Hervé's condominium complex was old, and the thickness of his glasses indicated a myopic tendency surpassed only by the legally blind. Evan had sent a plainclothes officer to pick him up and bring him to the precinct for the lineup. Evan had not met the guard before, and I could tell from the quick tightening of his mouth that the guard's coke-bottle bifocals didn't bode well.

"Shit, he's a defense lawyer's dream," was all I could get out of him. He took a file from a uniform and scanned it quickly.

"Mr. Todd, thank you so much for coming in." Evan extended his hand and I was grateful that the man was able to locate and shake it.

"Anything I can do. Mr. Tesauro was A-OK by me." Mr. Todd nodded his head slowly and felt he should add something. "Always gave me a nice tip at Christmas and a bottle of wine, too." He smiled at me, no doubt remembering warmly the stupor he'd achieved with a cheap bottle of Zinfindel. "Not everybody remembered." He was still nodding. "But he did. And I'm sorry to see him go."

Him and the wine, no doubt, I thought, but I smiled back sympathetically, thinking how ironic it was that someone who barely knew him thought of Hervé as a nice guy.

"You told me on the phone that you felt confident you could positively identify the individual who visited Mr. Tesauro that night. Do you still feel that way?" Evan asked.

"Oh, yeah. Got a photographic memory. I couldn't tell you right off, but if I see 'em, I'll remember." He started nodding again, and I wanted to reach out and hold his head still.

"You do see a lot of people coming past your gate. That's a large complex," Evan added.

"True. It's a big job." The bobbing continued.

"Well, then, let's go in. Shall we?" Evan gestured to a door. "There'll be several individuals, take your time, get a good look at them all before you make any decisions."

When the six men filed into the small room, I noticed Binford right away. He looked confused and beaten down mentally. I also recognized one of the uniformed officers, now in civilian clothing. They all turned toward us and stood awkwardly, shifting their weight, trying not to look at the mirror before them.

Both Evan and I turned to Mr. Todd, who was regarding the men in silent disinterest. Then he smacked his lips a little and took off his glasses. He slowly started to polish them.

We waited.

He put them back on and leaned back against the table that sat unevenly on the floor of our little hiding place. He crossed his arms and looked down at his watch, then back up at the men on view.

"Uhm, Mr. Todd? Take your time, but do you recognize any of these individuals?"

Mr. Todd looked around at Evan. He looked back at the six men. He looked back at Evan.

"Is this a joke?" he asked slowly.

Evan bristled a little at that. "No sir. It is certainly not a joke. We are talking about a murder case. Am I to understand that you do not recognize any of these men here?"

"Oh, no, I recognize somebody." He smiled and then he pointed to the sandy-haired police officer standing under the number two. "That man there."

Evan sighed and rubbed his eyes, but Mr. Todd wasn't finished.

"That's the young police officer who came to ask me questions at my house." He peered intently at the man, leaning forward a little. "Yes, that's him alright, Officer Handleman, I think he said. I remember the name because I had a cousin married a Handleman, spelled the same and everything."

Evan smiled in spite of himself. "Mr. Todd, do you not see the man who visited Hervé Tesauro the night he was murdered in this group?"

"Nope."

"Thank you." Evan started to turn away.

"Wasn't a man."

Evan froze and turned back to the elderly watchman.

"Wasn't a what?" he asked incredulously.

"Mr. Tesauro's visitor, it wasn't a man." He smiled at us. "You never asked me if it was, you just kept saying, individual, so I thought you knew." He started nodding again. "Thought maybe it was one of those sex discrimination laws or something, you couldn't say the sex of the accused." His eyes glinted. He was obviously enjoying being in on official police business.

"A woman?" Evan's voice was as confused as my brain. He walked to the microphone and spoke curtly. "Thank you, that's all."

He stood and watched the men file out with unseeing eyes. Then he turned to Mr. Todd, and said, "There was a woman who came the next day, she was on the guest register. An attractive woman, early forties, short blonde . . ."

"Wasn't working in the day. I got off around two, went out for a beer with some buddies, and well, I'm not as young and spry as I used to be. Used to party, party, party. But now, well sir, I went home and slept pretty much all day." Then he smiled and started the infernal nodding again. "I know the lady you mean though, she came sometimes, nice looking."

"But the name on the register said 'Clark.' " Evan was trying to thread a needle to sew the pieces together.

"That's right. Clark. Ms. Came a lot. Seemed harmless enough." He straightened up and stretched.

"Rudy?" I asked, shaken again.

Evan silenced me with a gesture, and I was glad to oblige.

"Mr. Todd," Evan continued patiently, "could you describe Ms. Clark?"

"Average," he said. "Brown hair, not pretty, not ugly, not fat or skinny, kinda' medium. All around average."

"Was there anything that stood out or was unusual about her?" Evan queried.

Mr. Todd had been staring off into space, seeing the person he was describing. He looked right at us now. "She was real tall."

Evan opened his file and took out a photo.

"Is she in this photograph?" he asked. I looked over his shoulder and saw Binford and the rest of my family with a couple of friends I didn't know.

"Sure," he said, the head bobbing incessantly. "That's her, right there." He pointed an accusing finger.

I felt my way blindly from the room. Closing the door behind me I stumbled to the nearest chair and sat down hard. "Jesus Christ," I muttered, "Elena."

37

But she was in the hospital!" I almost screamed at Evan. We were in the car, traveling fast back toward the very edifice I had just mentioned.

"The maid found her the morning after Hervé was killed," was all Evan would say.

"But, how could she have attacked Sabrina? Elena was just released today!"

"We'll see. We know she has a motive to try to kill her."

Feeling as though I'd been through an earthquake, I sat, deceptively quiet, and tried to straighten the images I had of each person that had been knocked askew by the tremors. Bill, my mother, my brother Binford. My father, for God's sake, had a daughter he didn't even know about. Sabrina, the stranger who had come after my money, was now my half sister and seemed to be the only decent human in the bunch. And now Elena, always seemingly so fond of me, looked to be the most malignant of all. One fucked-up portrait gallery.

"It makes some sense though," said Evan. "Ties up some loose ends. You said that Elena was the one who told you about the gang members. She was trying to incriminate someone beside herself."

"She told us that when we had a drink with her, but she said it was Bill who hired them, and that Binford was against it."

"Her feelings for Binford would be easily confused, sometimes she would want to protect him, sometimes she would want him to be blamed," he offered. "That's actually very common when a spouse has been betrayed." Evan thought for a moment while I reflected that I felt that ambiguity about my mother. "The gun we found at your house the night of the second shooting, the one that belonged to your father, she could easily have gotten that from Binford."

"No. It was a man I saw at my house, that much I'm sure of." I was positive.

"Stocky, dark."

I nodded.

"Possibly Hervé?" Evan looked at me deliberately.

I gasped. Of course. The stooping movements, the body language. It had to have been him.

"But why would Elena be involved with Hervé?" I demanded. "He came there to find the signature stamp, to help Sabrina. Elena wouldn't have wanted anything to do with that!"

"And that is exactly why it makes so much sense. Hervé had his own agenda, everybody did. Elena had Hervé hire someone to try to kill you, at the same time Hervé was working the Sabrina/Binford/fake claim angle which she knew nothing about. The first attempt on your life," Evan reasoned as he took my hand and squeezed so hard it hurt, "did not work out the way they planned it. So they planned a second one in your home. But in the meantime, while they were there, Hervé got his hands on the stamp and double-crossed Elena by killing your would-be murderer and trying to make it look like you did it to get you in trouble or out of the way."

"And she found out about Sabrina, his involvement, and killed him," I finished for him when he paused for breath.

"Exactly. And our security guard, Mr. Todd, said she came often. So it stands to reason that she was planning something with Hervé Tesauro for quite some time. He was the go-between for the gang members."

We had arrived at Cedars once again. Evan parked the car and we hurried upstairs.

The same nurse was seated at the counter. She did not look amused.

"Hello again," Evan rolled on in one breath. "I need to know who was on duty last night."

"That would be me." She smiled a challenge, batting her lashes. Evan looked at her nametag.

"Ms. Jerdin, is it?" he ventured.

"Yes." She was blatantly patient.

"Were you aware if Ms. Clark was in her room all evening?"

She cocked her head to one side and lowered her chin, looking up at him with sarcastic eyes. "To the best of my knowledge. But I do have other patients, Detective . . . ?"

"Paley. Detective Paley." He didn't offer a hand or any other formalities. "How often do you check on the patients?"

"It varies, at least once an hour."

"And she was in her room, or her bed, every hour on the hour?" Evan stressed, making it clear how important it was that she get this right.

His question gave her pause; I could see that. "Well,

technically, yes," she answered, "but I had some new patients admitted last night and I had to spend some time assisting a doctor in another room. So it's possible. . . ." She stopped and her brow furrowed.

"What?" Evan's voice was growing more urgent.

"I do remember going in about 7:00 P.M. for the after-dinner round, and she wasn't in her bed." She pulled out a chart as she spoke. "I just assumed she was in the rest room, the door was closed but the light was on. I normally would have gone back in to check in a few minutes but . . ." She flipped around on her interminable chart and found what she was looking for. "But that was when I went to assist the doctor. I didn't get back to the rounds until shortly before nine."

"Was she there then?" Evan persisted.

"Yes, sleeping," the nurse concluded.

"Was there no one else to check in on her during that time?"

"There are other nurses on the floor and even at the station, but they would have only answered a call or gone in to give medication."

Evan leaned over the counter. "Was Ms. Clark receiving medication?"

The nurse checked again. Then her head came up and she answered assuredly, "No."

Evan took my arm and we started away from the nurses' station as he tossed a thank-you over his shoulder. Then we both had the same thought and our eyes met.

Sabrina.

Her room was jarringly empty. So was the hall outside her room. Evan had released the police watch when Binford had been taken into custody. In hindsight, it no longer seemed a wise decision. The nurse on her floor told us that a woman had come to visit Sabrina. The woman had assured the nurse they were going to take a walk around the halls.

That had been more than two hours ago.

We took off out of the hospital like bulls out of the gate, but when we hit the car we were forced to stop and think.

"Where? Where would she take her?" I asked, trying to get control of my swelling fear and focus.

Evan's cell phone rang and he spoke curtly into it, "Paley . . . yes . . . damn it." He hung up without a good-bye; he was tapping the steering wheel, thinking.

"She wants her dead because of Binford. She'll want Binford to see. She'll want to pick somewhere that was special to the two of them." He was speaking quickly to try to keep up with his deductive reasoning.

"But where? The only place I ever saw them together was in the woods by Bill's house, but I don't think Elena knew about that." I was sifting through any information I could remember, and nothing was clicking.

"I wonder if she knew about the beach motel," Evan said, looking at me.

"Why would she take her all the way there?" I asked.

Evan started the car and pulled out his cell phone. "Because she knows Binford will come looking for Sabrina, and because that's most likely where they met when she came to town."

"Binford's in jail. He's not looking for anybody."

"That call I just got?" He glanced across at me with anger in his eyes. "Your mother made his bail. He walked this afternoon."

38

We drove fast. Scary fast. I tightened my seat belt more than once. I called everywhere we could think of, but nobody had seen either Elena or Binford, including the clerk at the motel. Evan had an officer go to the room. It was empty.

Still it was the only idea we had, so we drove. And as we drove, the sky darkened, clouding over, and then it started to rain.

We pulled into the driveway of the motel and Evan got out to meet the officer in the patrol car. I could see from ten paces there was no news. I got out and wandered to the edge of the motel to look around, trying to think and clear my head.

The scrubby hillside rolled away under my feet, down to the beach as it reached the bottom. I couldn't see far in the dimness and here at the shore the rain was more of a heavy mist. I strained my eyes, searching the darkness. I looked off down the edge of PCH for someone or something.

Think, I told myself. Don't panic. Think. When we came here last Sabrina was in the café, but that was far too public a place. She was staring out the window with those moon-eyes. She was crying and looking at that couple way off who were watching the sunset sitting on that . . .

"Rock," I said out loud. That romantic little outcrop on the edge of the world.

That's when I heard it, just a catch of a sound on the breeze. Someone shouting or crying, I couldn't tell which. It came from the beach in the darkness before me, mingled in the insistent rolling of the surf.

"Evan!" I called, and when he reached me we both started down the embankment and struggled on through the deep sand.

Entering the almost total misty darkness once we left the faint ring of light from the motel, we stopped to listen again.

Nothing. Rolling waves, wind, nothing in the middle.

Then a voice. A fractured piece of pleading.

We started off again to the right, keeping the sound of the waves a few yards to our left. Soon we came to the faint shape of the rock I had seen through the café window, and now we could hear voices clearly.

My eyes were adjusting to the dimness and my ears were so alert that the words when they came were sharp and painful.

It was Binford. He was begging. I couldn't catch every word, but I could hear the desperation, the attempted pathetic apology, the placating phrases. My guess? It wasn't working.

Evan's firm grip stopped me from moving forward. We had come up against several large boulders, and I started to try to find a way to climb over them. I could now make out Evan's silhouette, which shook its head "no." Instead he pulled me toward the beach side, and we slowly made our way around the out-cropping.

We found a break in the rock and moved cautiously forward, toward the voice. Above us, the darker clouds gave way to the bright moon and an unsteady light shone on the three figures in front of us.

Sabrina was there, prone on the sand. Her face was turned upward and her eyes were closed; I couldn't tell if she was dead or alive. I hoped it was her life Binford was still begging for and not his own.

Elena was just a couple of feet to Sabrina's left. She was pointing her gun at Binford, whose back was to us. Evan stopped me and we froze, watching.

"Elena, listen to me," Binford was pleading.

"Shut up. *Shut up.* I listened to you before, you said it was over. I've done everything for us, it was all in place. We could have had everything your perfect sister had. She was always too good for both of us, too perfect and pretty to associate with me, too rich to care about you. We could have had it all! You know that."

"I know, but it didn't work out. And that's okay." Binford was desperate, searching. "Now we can all go home, we can be all right again. But if you kill her, you'll go to jail. Please, Elena, I don't want to lose you."

Elena laughed. It was a laugh filled with nothing. She just plain didn't care.

"Binford, please, spare me. Why do you think I invited you here?" She gestured with the gun. "To listen to you justify your heinous behavior? You are more stupid than I thought." He started to move toward her and she pointed the gun directly at his head.

"Go ahead. It all works for me. This is really very

simple. A rejected lover kills the woman who jilted him and then in pain and remorse, he kills himself." She laughed again, this time with a chilling sound of amusement. "What I love the most is that this is the second time you'll be trying to kill her. Oh, it's just priceless that you almost drowned her before."

"It was a mistake! I was trying to kill Callaway, for you!" Binford was furious, now. I was shocked. "I knew how much you wanted us to have it all and if Callaway died I would have inherited all her money, *for us!* I knew how hard you'd worked for it. I wanted you to have it, I did it for you!"

"You did it for her, don't lie to me, not now," Elena said and gestured to the heap on the ground. Sabrina still hadn't moved. "Anyway, it's too late. Callaway can keep her money, she can win again, and again and again, I don't care anymore, I hope she rots in hell." She raised the gun level with Binford's head again. "And maybe you'll see her there."

And then the thick dark clouds moved in again, blocking out any available light.

What I did next, I did without thinking, so I have little or no memory of the order of it. I think that Evan came out from behind the rock with his gun and shouted something. Binford lunged at Elena, a gun went off and I ran forward toward Sabrina. Throwing myself to the ground next to her, I pushed her away from the other struggling figures.

The next thing I was aware of was that one of the figures broke away and ran the short distance toward the water. I could hear the steps and the breathing of the other two still scuffling near me. I heard the gun go off again, but I had lost all sense of direction and distance in the wind and the dark. I didn't know where the shot came from, or where it went.

I put my fingers on Sabrina's throat to check for a pulse and when I did, I heard a small voice and felt the vibration of it in my fingertips.

"Callaway?" came the drawling disbelieving question. "Is that you?"

I smiled and choked back the surprising relief that overwhelmed me.

"Yes," I answered. "I'm here. It's going to be all right."

But I knew it wasn't yet. There was just enough illumination for me to see now that it was the two men scuffling on the sand. So it was Elena who had run. I was trying like hell to distinguish which one was Evan so I could help, when one of them broke away and tried to run. Obviously that was Binford.

I was standing now; Sabrina was between the running figure and me. I tried to move toward him, but the sand and the girl hampered me, I felt like I was in slow motion.

As Binford tried to run past us, Sabrina's hand shot out and grabbed his ankle firm and hard. He pitched forward and after he landed, he lay still. I wouldn't have thought a girl as voluptuous as Sabrina could move that fast, much less think that fast. I was impressed. I helped her up and said as much.

"Way to go, baby!" I enthused. "You got him."

"Well, somebody had to," she said angrily. "He was not gonna get away with this." Her voice dropped. "Not this time."

Evan was breathing hard as he pulled Binford's hands behind his back and put handcuffs on him. Rolling him over, Evan ran his hands over Binford's face and head.

"He's got a nasty lump on his forehead," he announced, trying hard to catch his breath. "He'll be out for a few. Now where's his better half got to?"

"Out there." I pointed to the dark surf, and as I did the moon broke through for a brief moment, and what we saw was sad and horribly final.

39

I didn't know a gun would fire if it was wet," I said into the silence of my library, interrupting only the crackle of the fire.

"Me neither," answered Sabrina.

"I could have told you that," Ginny said morosely.

" 'Course, I know a lot of stuff now I didn't know a couple a weeks ago," Sabrina added and took a sip of her drink, brandy now. "I wish I hadn't seen her."

Elena's first shot had gone wide, but her second had hit its mark, and when we pulled her from the surf, there was nothing we could do for her.

I wanted to distract Sabrina. Thank her, too, in my own way. "That was pretty quick work, stopping Binford like that."

She looked up at me, surprised. "He tried to kill you, and almost killed me trying to do it. It just made me so mad that he might get away."

"Good for you." Ginny beamed at the innocent as though she was her personal prodigy.

"It's strange, though," I mused, "I mean, it was Elena trying to kill me from the beginning. Elena who killed Hervé, she even overdosed herself so she could blame it on Binford. My mom thought it *was* Binford behind everything so she confessed to the murder attempts. But why *would* Binford want to try to kill me by the pool so late in the game?"

"I don't know." Sabrina's eyes filled with tears as she raised her glass to her plush mouth.

"I can tell you that," said my favorite male voice from the doorway. I looked up to see Evan standing in front of Deirdre. He was taking off his coat. He made to throw it on the nearest chair, but it was intercepted in midair by Deirdre, who whisked it off silently to hang it where its wetness wouldn't leave a mark.

He came straight to me and gratefully accepted my glass as I offered it to him. He sat next to me in the big armchair and took a chest-warming drink.

"It was his last attempt. He thought if he killed Callaway and inherited her money then Sabrina would stay with him, and then he would expose Elena as the one behind it all, blame Callaway's death on her."

"But Elena wasn't in her hospital room that night," I said.

"I know, but a witness at the hospital saw her sitting outside. Apparently Binford called and told her to come out and meet him, then he never showed. He needed her not to have an alibi." He looked at me and added, "I told you he thought things out thoroughly."

I shook my aching head. "Is he insane?"

Evan shook his head. "No, just greedy and desperate. Even sane people will do insane things for love." He looked at Sabrina kindly. "Or money," he finished, looking at me.

"Or both," I put in.

Sabrina put her drink down and dropped her head

into her hands. She started to cry. "I made such a mess out of everything, didn't I? I just fell for every single stupid lie."

I crossed to her and put my hand on her shoulder.

"That's enough of that," I said sternly. When her tear-stained face turned up to me in surprise and fear at my disapproval, I smiled.

"Are you through blaming yourself? Did you try to kill me, or plan any of this?" I asked directly.

"Well, no," she sputtered.

"Is it your fault Fiona never told you who you were, or got you embroiled in all this?"

Sabrina turned her big eyes to Ginny, "What does 'embroiled' mean?"

Ginny patted her leg, "Kind of like, sautéed against your will."

Sabrina looked understandably flummoxed. "But she never meant to hurt me, or you either Cally, I don't think."

I hadn't had time to reflect on that much but I did now. "I don't think so either, Sabrina; hopefully we can both forgive her and let her get on with her life after this whole thing is over. I don't wish anything bad on her." Sabrina seemed relieved. "But are you responsible for her behavior, or Hervé's, or Binford's for that matter?" I asked her.

"No."

"Then it's time for you to buck up and stop acting like such a victim. If you're gonna stay with me and be my . . ." I hesitated and felt my throat clamp down on the word, a label I wasn't sure I was ready to plaster on somebody but I forced it out ". . . sister, you're just gonna have to learn to kick some ass." I looked away and reached for my glass from the amused Evan. I took a deliberate sip. "I'm sure Ginny will back me up on this."

"I do," said Ginny as though she was reciting wedding vows.

"Ginny could hold an ass-kicking seminar," Evan suggested.

"And you can be my demonstration volunteer!" Ginny said to him.

Sabrina was speechless for a moment. "You, you want me to stay here with you?" she stuttered.

"Well, where the hell else are you gonna go?" I smiled at her again and looked over at a framed picture of my father and myself on my desk. "Besides I think, no, I *know*, that my father . . . our father, would have wanted you to have every opportunity, and he would certainly have wanted us to know each other." I looked to her, then back to the photo again and for the first time since my father's death it didn't make me hurt, it made me smile. *I love you Daddy.* And it felt good to have had him, to know that he was there somewhere in my past holding up a light so that now, when I looked back, I didn't see only darkness.

She followed my gaze to the photo of a father and daughter who had loved each other so much.

"Do you think he would have liked me?" she asked.

"No," I answered. "He would have loved you, as much as he loved me." I held out my hand. "Deal?"

She swept my hand away and leaped to her feet, enveloping me in her warm, fleshy hug. It was a few moments before I could disentangle myself.

"Now, I'm not giving you half my money, you understand," I continued, to be perfectly clear. "But I think that when you decide what you'd like to do with your-self, go to college, or set up a little business, I'm all for it. I'll help you get started. I'll help you get a plan."

She squealed and jumped on me again. I was very pleased to make her happy, though I wasn't exactly sure how long my back could take her enthusiasm.

"Can I have a boutique, too?" Ginny asked. I shot a look at her over Sabrina's shoulder. "Nepotism, I knew it, I'll just take my bullet and go."

"What the hell would you do with a boutique?" I asked her, "You want to sit there all day and be polite to people?"

"Okay . . . no," she said. "No boutique."

"How about a cruise down the Nile?" I dangled, knowing Ginny couldn't refuse an exotic vacation. She stood up and started for the door. "Where are you going?" I asked.

"I gotta pack."

"The Nile?" Sabrina asked. "You mean like, Egypt?"

"Ever been there?" Ginny asked her.

"Gosh no, I've never been outside the United States."

"All right. You can go, too." Ginny invited her along, and I had to admit to myself that it might be great to have a little sister. It might be just what I needed. Maybe I didn't need to be so alone.

That made me think about family.

"I feel horrible for Bill," I said to Evan, still over Sabrina's shoulder. "I already left a message for my accountant to approve the money he wanted for the merger so at least he can give Rudy what she wanted. But to lose Binford and Elena like this."

Evan nodded and Sabrina released me. "He's not los-ing Binford; Binford's just going away for a little while.

And I have a feeling that he's gaining a daughter." Evan smiled at me and then his eyes cut to Sabrina. "Or two."

"You think he'll forgive me?" Sabrina asked.

"Yes, I do," I told her. "And you know what you can do?" I asked her.

"What?" She was wide-eyed.

"Well, since you are no longer a guest in this house, you can run into the kitchen and ask Sophie to make us something to eat. It just hit me how hungry I am." And I realized, eyeing the handsome detective, that I was.

"Excellent plan," Evan said and rescued my drink before Sabrina attacked me again.

When Ginny finally dragged her out, the room was less celebratory and far more highly charged. Evan came and stood behind me. Anticipation crackled in the air like high-tension power lines sizzling in a drizzling rain.

"Any questions?" he asked.

I was afraid to ask it. What would it be like, after all my waiting? What if it wasn't as good as I had built it up to be? What if, even now, he said "no"?

"Is this investigation over?"

He crossed to the door of the library and closed it, turning the heavy key that rested in the lock with a resounding click. Then he crossed back to me and put one finger into the brandy. Pulling it dripping from the crystal, he touched the finger to my lips and then setting the glass on the mantel he started to lick it off, slowly, deliberately, and with ravenous hunger.

He pulled back long enough to look into my eyes and answer my question. "Case closed."

The next thing I felt was his hand under my shirt, supporting the weight of my breast, as the other hand worked quickly to pull the shirt over my head. It only took a moment for me to relieve him of his jacket and shirt, the gun making a loud thud as it hit the floor still in the shoulder harness.

I slowed down; after all my eagerness, I was wary, even a little afraid. He was deliberately slow and soft, savoring, and sating, both of us. He seemed to be taking his time with each movement, as though he had thought about it, anticipated it, fantasized about it, and there was no hint of feared disappointment in him. When we were finally stripped of any interference, I tried to drop to my knees in front of him but he held me up, damn well determined to continue with his plan. With his eyes in mine, we pressed our skin together for the first time and any hesitation was lost, the overwhelming heat of him pulsed through me, and I forgot my nervousness and my fear, forgot everything but him. He wrapped his arms around me and I surrendered to him as he lifted me off the floor and met and exceeded my expectations. His need and his desire matched my own so magnificently that I never wanted to stop. We built to a heat that would melt metal. Orgasming together with an abandon I had never allowed myself before. When reason returned, feeling somewhat self-conscious, I opened my eyes and focused, and found him looking at me adoringly. He kissed me again for blushing. We fell onto the sofa and laughed together for a long, wonderful time.

I was lying with my head on his chest when there was a knock at the door and Sabrina called out.

"Hey, y'all, pasta's ready!"

"Leave them alone!" Ginny's voice came from farther back; amplified by the marble of the entrance hall it sounded like a divine order. "I told you to get away from that door!"

"We'll be right out," I called toward the door without making any move to rise. "Meet you in the kitchen." We listened to Sabrina giggle and then to Ginny's reprimand fade away as they crossed back toward the kitchen.

"Do I have to take you by the ear? Because I will, don't make me watch you. . . ." Was all we could make out.

"Little sisters can be such a pest," I sighed.

"Wait till she wants to borrow your clothes," Evan answered and put his nose against my neck.

"You sound like you know something about it," I asked, shocked that I had never thought to ask before.

"Oh yeah, little sister and a little brother. But it was always Marianne who wanted to borrow my shirts. I used to catch her sneaking them out of my room."

"Oh my God." I smiled. "You're a brother, probably a son." I experienced a moment of panic. "You're not a dad, are you?"

"No, not yet."

"But you've got a family. Please tell me they're nothing like mine."

"Nope, normal." Evan nibbled against my chin.

A little fear crept in. A middle-class family, my wealth. Who would want my money? How much did he?

"So whose house were you sitting?" I asked, hopeful of a rich relative.

He pulled back and looked at me. He regarded me with a stark curious look. "You really don't know?"

"Should I?" I asked, trying to remember if there were any clues.

He smiled and took my hand. Tracing the outline of my fingers, he didn't look in my eyes, but he never let go of me.

"Do you think I want to be with you for your money?" His voice was vulnerable to hurt or accusation.

"No. I never thought that," I lied passionately.

Now he looked at me.

I tried to explain. "Okay, don't take it personally. I never thought you weren't honestly attracted to me, I've just never been with someone who could separate the two."

"They couldn't? Or you couldn't?" he asked, rolling on top of me and pinning both my hands back by my head.

I hesitated, thrown.

"Tell me the truth," he said, "or I'll be forced to torture you."

"Both, I guess," I admitted reluctantly.

"Yeah, I always felt the same way." His mouth was an inch from mine. "Good thing we're both loaded, huh?"

I laughed. He was so sweet to make a joke of it.

"What's so funny?" He bit my lower lip softly.

"You're loaded all right," I answered, pressing my hips against his and laughed again.

"I am," he said simply and kissed me really hard. I liked it.

"What do you make a year?" I challenged. "We might as well get it out now."

"Promise you'll sleep with me anyway?" he asked and grasped my wrists more tightly when I tried to move my arms.

"Sure, I'm not a snob." I smiled. "I believe in equal sexual opportunities regardless of race, religion, or income. Besides, it's too late to say 'no,' " I added coyly, praying he didn't ask me next. He probably made in thousands what I made in millions. Most men find that emasculating.

"Last year I cleared just about eighteen million." His eyes looked away like he was trying to remember something. "Of course, that's not including the sale of the casino in St. Thomas, but I'm calling that rollover money, because it will be reinvested in a new hotel construction project as soon as the deal is finalized."

"Eighteen thousand is more like it." I started to laugh but he cocked an eye at me. He looked so serious that I almost believed him. "They pay detectives a lot more than I thought," I concluded.

"No, they don't. My siblings and I inherited a shitload of money from my grandfather, and my brother and my sister are very good at, and very into, taking care of it. I'm not. So they appreciate my staying out of it and they send me checks. Of course, I do have to show up for board meetings every once in a while, which is a pain in the ass, but worth it. I've got a special closet for those suits." He smiled at me again. "It was my house you came to. I have another one in Montana, I think you'll like that one. And we also own a villa in Provence if you prefer France."

"No, I like Montana," I said, not sure how much of a fool I would look like if I laughed again and he wasn't kidding.

"I'm not kidding," he said and I felt him pressing down on me, his need growing again.

"Neither am I. It's a pretty state." I raised my head and tried to kiss him. He pulled back, just out of my reach.

"I'm rich," he clarified. "Not as rich as you, but you'll never have to buy lunch again. I'm a detective because that's what I always wanted to be. Loaded or broke, I would be a detective. If I didn't have any money, I would want to be with you." He stressed his point with a physical action that I received gratefully.

"But . . ." I started.

"Shut up," he breathed, watching my eyes and moving with me slowly. "And I would still want you if you didn't have a goddamn penny."

I surrendered and melted into him. Of course, we are who we are because of everything we've been through in life. Everything we have. Money, too. Apparently, we'd both been through a great deal.

Now, just maybe, I had found someone to go through everything with. I knew it wouldn't be easy, that this was just the beginning of facing all my fears and resistance, to opening up and being with someone, learning how to love, and most frightening of all, learning to be loved. It was daunting, exhilarating, and scary. Everyone had always thought of me as the girl who had it all, everyone but me. I was the only one who knew my life was filled with excuses and barricades and defenses.

Evan and I rolled until I was on top of him; he wrapped his arms around me, pulling my face down to his until we were six inches apart. As he moved I felt every bit of his body and I couldn't hide from the pure honesty in his eyes. "This is it, you are the one," he whispered intensely, and for the first time in my life, I heard the voice inside me say something it had never uttered, never felt.

Yes, I do have it all.